IN BRUNO'S SHADOW

GUERNICA WORLD EDITIONS 56

TONY ARDIZZONE

IN BRUNO'S SHADOW

TORONTO—CHICAGO—BUFFALO—LANCASTER (U.K.)
2023

Guernica Editions Founder: Antonio D'Alfonso

Michael Mirolla, general editor
Ben Ghan, editor
Interior and cover design: Errol F. Richardson
Cover artwork: Flammarion engraving (excerpt)

Guernica Editions Inc.
287 Templemead Drive, Hamilton (ON), Canada L8W 2W4
2250 Military Road, Tonawanda, N.Y. 14150-6000 U.S.A.
www.guernicaeditions.com

Distributors:
Independent Publishers Group (IPG)
600 North Pulaski Road, Chicago IL 60624
University of Toronto Press Distribution (UTP)
5201 Dufferin Street, Toronto (ON), Canada M3H 5T8
Gazelle Book Services, White Cross Mills
High Town, Lancaster LA1 4XS U.K.

First edition.

Legal Deposit—First Quarter
Library of Congress Catalog Card Number: 2022940214
Library and Archives Canada Cataloguing in Publication
Title: In Bruno's shadow / Tony Ardizzone.
Names: Ardizzone, Tony, author.
Series: Guernica world editions ; 56.
Description: Series statement: Guernica world editions ; 56.
Identifiers: Canadiana (print) 20220263868 | Canadiana (ebook) 20220263914 |
ISBN 9781771837774 (softcover) | ISBN 9781771837781 (EPUB)
Classification: LCC PS3551.R395 I5 2022 | DDC 813/.54—dc23

For Diane,
Nick, and Anna

Anđela

Međugorje, April 1983

Twenty years before Dubravka came to live in Campo de' Fiori in Rome, in the attic room of a pensione that looked down upon Giordano Bruno's statue, she was unaware that the older woman who clutched her sleeve and asked if she might accompany her up the rock-strewn path leading to the cross on top of Mount Križevac was an angel. To Dubravka, the woman – dressed casually in a dark unbuttoned sweater over a blouse the rich color of carved ivory, and a sky-blue skirt patterned faintly with flowers – seemed like just another hopeful pilgrim who'd made her way from her homeland to the ground where two years earlier the Lady had appeared to a group of local children, and where, word had it, was still appearing and performing miracles.

The spirit adjusted the purse hanging from her arm and smiled. She'd traveled to Međugorje to get a vial of holy water for her brother's dying wife. Međugorje was a place of daily miracles and blessings. The small town in southwestern Bosnia and Herzegovina was teeming, clotted with jagged rows of vans and cars and countless tour buses parked alongside makeshift wooden stands and carts from which vendors sold souvenirs. Thick crowds milled about the stone plaza fronting Saint James, the town's church, its twin towers standing tall, like a pair of guards, each topped by a pyramidal roof and cross. Pilgrims faced the church and prayed, arms outstretched like a crucified Jesus. Others knelt and bowed their heads as they worked the beads of their rosaries. The crowds stepping down from their tour buses clustered in circles as they consulted their paper maps, then asked if anyone had seen the visionaries who, it was said, made their way each day to the site of the Lady's first appearance, where they'd kneel and pray. Many who made the journey to Međugorje were eager to join them, with the hope they might receive a vision too. On the grassy fields outside the church, rows of priests ready to hear confessions sat patiently on metal folding chairs beside signs displaying which languages they spoke and understood.

The spirit continued to hold onto Dubravka's arm as they walked. The talk in town, she informed Dubravka, was that earlier that week one of the visionaries, a girl who hardly knew a word of Italian, lifted her eyes after a conversation with the Lady and was able to speak the language fluently. The visionary was Marija, the sixteen-year-old girl who'd joined the others on the second day of the apparitions on Mount Crnica. The name *Marija* pained Dubravka the moment the spirit said it, though Dubravka fought to hide any feelings on her face.

Dubravka was eighteen. Modest, with clear eyes the color of Turkish coffee, full lips, nearly black hair in need of both combing and cutting. She was thin, gangly, still dressed as she had while living and working in Mostar – long gray skirt, simple long-sleeved blouse, black headscarf. She wore no makeup, and by the way she wrapped her scarf around her hair she was sometimes mistaken for a Muslim or a nun. Perhaps this was what had attracted the older woman to her, Dubravka thought, as she struggled to quell the emotions the mention of Marija's name had aroused within her.

It happened on the holy girl's birthday, the woman was saying. I was able to talk to her myself. She was speaking with a group of pilgrims just outside her house at the foot of Apparition Hill, more than happy to greet everyone. The girl's pronunciation of Italian words was nearly perfect. Now she's just like me, the woman said proudly, able to speak and understand both Croatian and Italian. The woman's name was Anđela.

Anđela's face was soft and round, her dark eyes steady, cheekbones lightly brushed with peach-colored blush. She resembled any of Dubravka's aunts back in Dubrovnik, a woman who'd put on weight as she aged, whose eyes revealed that she'd seen more of life than anyone should have, and if you pressed her she would be willing to share some of it with you. Hovering about her was a wispy smell, something sweet, like church incense. A smell that invited the nose to want to take a step closer. Dubravka took a step closer. The woman's Croatian was slightly accented, sprinkled with Italian, and as the pair continued their walk with the others up the hill she told Dubravka that though her family was truly Croatian she'd actually been born in Italy, in Molise, in Campobasso, and now she lived with her brother in

Rome. It was a long story, she said, her free hand waving in the air. A clear sign that later on she was hoping to tell it.

The pair were climbing the rough terrain of Mount Križevac with a group of the faithful that included two men – brothers, Dubravka guessed – who walked with considerable care, doing their best not to slip. The men carried their mother between them in a wooden wheelchair, her twisted legs covered with bandages, a few stray ends of which flapped freely in the breeze. The shorter brother clutched the wheels, the taller the chair's back. The taller brother wore black suspenders to hold up his brown pants. As the group ascended the hill everyone recited the Hail Mary in their native languages, the front half saying the prayer's first part, the back half the second.

Set at intervals along the path were the Stations of the Cross. Each was depicted on a large bronze slab in bas-relief. The images portrayed the central events on the day of Christ's crucifixion, beginning with his condemnation by Pontius Pilate, ending with his body being taken down from the cross and entombed. Pilgrims making the climb paused at each station to say more prayers, reflect, catch their breath, sip from canteens, light cigarettes.

It was at the sixth station, where the woman from Jerusalem known as Veronica breaks from the crowd to wipe Christ's bloody face, when Anđela leaned toward the slab beneath which both she and Dubravka were kneeling and began coughing vehemently into her handkerchief. The rosary beads entwined in the woman's fingers swung back and forth as she coughed. Here, she said, take this, handing Dubravka the rosary. The woman was coughing up blood, Dubravka could see. For a moment Dubravka thought she could smell the blood, and then without thinking her mind slid from thoughts about herself and her unsure life and her bitterness toward Marija and all of the possibilities that Marija had stolen from her into a fierce, intensely focused prayer about the woman and her failing health.

At the time Dubravka felt lost, adrift, without goal or direction. Other than her daily prayers and the sense that Father Josip had instilled in her that she was something special in the world, someone who in the realm of things perhaps even mattered, rather than the disgraceful, traitorous slut her father had judged her to be, spawn of her traitorous slut of a mother, may her name never be given voice, her sole solace was drink. At the time Dubravka drank a little each day, normally in the evenings, at least when she was working in Mostar. It was easy to drink late at night after work in Mostar. It was what was expected, what was done. But now that she was on the road, not really sure where she was going other than she was certain she wasn't going back to what she'd left, she faced all of the empty hours that needed filling. All of the doubts. The resentments. Already that day she'd sweetened her morning coffee. As Anđela coughed into her handkerchief, Dubravka felt something surge from her chest, then pour out of her – erupting, uncontrolled – toward the woman she'd only just met, and the miracle took form.

IT HAD SOMETHING to do with focus, Dubravka later reasoned. Concentration. As if thought was like sunlight, normally scattered, diffuse, yet within her there was some sort of magnifying glass able to condense the light into a single beam and make it stronger, more intense, and then direct it wherever she wanted, like a child crouched over a dry leaf in a sun-lit field, adjusting the glass in her hand until the leaf began to smoke and flame. She knew that on sunny days in Dubrovnik boys sometimes knelt on Saint Blaise's front steps catching ants with the narrowed beams from their magnifying glasses. They made a game of it, frying the ants' segmented bodies into crispy bits, joking that they were powerful demons come to take the ants' souls and transport the creatures into Hell.

It also had something to do with the Earth itself, Dubravka concluded. With the Earth's many tremors and frequent quakes. That day in Međugorje there had been a series of tremors. She'd learned about them that night in the town's bar.

Having grown up in Dubrovnik, Dubravka knew there was a long, tragic history of earthquakes in the region, in both Croatia as well as Italy. She'd borrowed books from Father Josip and read up about it. With his help explaining the words she didn't understand, she learned that while the actual ground we live and walk on appears to both eye and foot as solid, dependable, something only a fool wouldn't trust, in truth the Earth is constantly under tension, and at any moment it might explode. The ground is made up of gigantic plates of rock perpetually in motion, grinding against everything they touch. Rather than be stable, anchored down, firmly set in place, as one might reasonably suspect, the plates float on the Earth's mantle and move about each day, roughly at the rate fingernails grow.

Father Josip said it was like everything else that God made. Darkness and light. Demons and angels. Sin and virtue. Opposing forces struggling with and against one another. And in this battle the constantly grinding Earth always eventually shifts and shakes, and one plate slides beneath another, and the force the clash generates rips the ground above.

After Anđela stopped coughing she gasped for several seconds, doing her best to catch her breath. Can I get you something, Dubravka asked. The woman shook her head, then reached into her purse and told Dubravka she wanted to give her a card. The card listed her brother's name – Giorgio – and the address of the pensione their family owned in Rome. Here, Anđela said as she calmed her breathing, allow me to write a note on the back. Show this to Giorgio in Campo de' Fiori when you meet him. Anđela reached again into her purse for a pen and dropped her bloody handkerchief to the ground.

Dubravka watched the cloth catch in the air and open as the scattered bits and blots of blood the woman had coughed onto it reassembled before Dubravka's eyes into the form of a cross.

Dubravka blinked. Certainly, she thought, what she thought she'd just seen was a trick. She slipped the rosary into her pocket and picked the cloth up from the ground and held it open as Anđela scribbled on the back of the business card. Yes, there in the center of the cloth was a cross made of blood, still wet, glistening in the afternoon light.

Međugorje's sun was known for its many tricks. It was said that at times the sun danced in the sky or spun over the mountain like a pinwheel. For several moments Dubravka gazed up at the sky. A cloudless blue. From the weeds and brush lining the path came the high-pitched rasp and call of insects.

The others around them were talking now, standing, eager to move on. A woman knotting her long scarf, speaking in French, was already starting another round of Hail Marys. A man with one patched eye glanced up the hill and pawed the ground restlessly with his foot, like a horse. Anđela gave Dubravka the business card and drew in a slow breath as the two brothers stood, wiping dust from the knees of their trousers. They patted their mother's shoulders and decided that on the hike up to the next station one son would carry the woman in his arms, the other would hoist her wooden chair upon his back.

Dubravka remained kneeling, staring at the cross on the handkerchief, then at the image of Veronica kneeling before Christ on the slab, holding up her headscarf, which bore the image of Christ's face. Dubravka looked back at the handkerchief. She recognized a similarity between the cloth and the slab, a repetition of sorts, like a pair of lines set one after the other in a poem. Like a rhyme – two words mirroring the other's sound – a sameness with a difference.

The miracle of the handkerchief took place on the day that Dubravka had arrived in Međugorje, after her two years of living and working in Mostar, where she'd hoped to find Marija and Stanislav. This was after Dubravka's less than pleasant life with her father in Croatia and her years of work in the kitchen of Zagorac's, Marija's father's small restaurant on Ulica Od Puča in Dubrovnik's Old City. Her month in Međugorje was before Dubravka entered the cloistered convent tucked on the side of Sveti Jure, the Biokovo mountain range's highest peak, where for twenty years the young woman labored as a kitchen sister, preparing food and caring for the wants and needs of the more affluent choir nuns, before Dubravka made the decision to leave the convent's walls and re-enter the world and cross the wide sea to Italy, retracing the path taken generations before by Anđela and Giorgio's family, landing in Termoli in Molise and then going inland to Campobasso, where their family had taken refuge decades before, then crossing Italy's mountains and rolling green hillsides to find Giorgio in Rome's Centro Storico, in Campo de' Fiori, in the shadow of the monument erected in honor of the defiant Giordano Bruno.

San Paolo fuori le Mura

Rome, 12 August 2004

Twenty-one years later, the unconscious rush of compassion and prayer still wasn't something Dubravka could understand. She'd come to assume it had been a one-time thing. Though she occasionally tried, she couldn't simply squint her heart and cause the feeling to pour out of her, like some magical gift given a character in a movie or a comic book. The focused rush in Međugorje seemed to have occurred all by itself, for reasons Dubravka decided were related to her perception of another's need. Someone's silent cry, so quiet it was perhaps not even heard by the crier themself. And in turn the cry had awakened within Dubravka a sort of empathetic response, similar to someone saying that their heart goes out to you, though with Dubravka it was the energy of thought, a fierce surge of transformative prayer.

Now in Rome, a year to the day after she'd first knocked on Giorgio's door, the surge would return, and with the exception this afternoon of the actor Agostino, whom Dubravka knew by his work on Rome's squares, it would be triggered by strangers. Seven altogether, beginning on the morning after Christmas and lasting for just over three months. A man's face rushing past hers on the crowded Piazza Navona. A young woman by the Largo di Torre Argentina bus stop crossing the street to the Area Sacra to gaze down at the feral cats. A tall blonde in a leather jacket wanting to talk about movies as she slid a twenty-euro bill into Dubravka's charity box. A Roman faux centurion considering the differences between two staircases. A man in grief who needed to be shown how to fold a long-sleeved shirt. A woman kneeling in an adjacent pew in church reciting the rosary. A shy guest at Giorgio's pensione.

Each a pilgrim, having come to Rome hoping to satisfy a specific need. Their eyes locking with Dubravka's for a moment. Sometimes a word or two were exchanged. After Dubravka watched the pope's televised funeral procession wind its slow way through Rome's streets, the ability would vanish and Dubravka would settle into the woman she believed she was born to be and be glad of it.

During Dubravka's years in the convent she never once felt it. Likely, she thought, it was because the convent was absolutely humming with prayer. All of the kitchen sisters silently praying, the choir sisters singing. Or at least that was the appearance everyone in the convent gave. She knew the convent's air was also tempered with occasional sadness and boredom and resignation.

There were those in her convent who believed that the world would literally come to an end if it were not for their daily prayers. They knew that outside the convent walls the world was an unimaginably sinful place, profoundly immoral, beset with demons in every disguise, intent at each moment on inventing new forms through which to express evil and draw others beneath sin's tempting veil and into its glamorous grasp. The sisters believed that if it were not for their prayers the planet itself would cease to exist, peppered by descending bombs, the sky grayed by mushroom clouds bursting on every horizon, the ground swallowed by angry seas, the Earth itself rising up and breaking apart, surmounting gravity, thrusting skyward and flying off in chunks into the emptiness of space.

MIRACLE. SUCH A big word. So powerful. Though dismissible, Dubravka knew, particularly to those who found science the answer to everything. But a miracle wasn't so much when you really began to consider it, Dubravka thought. After all, a miracle is only a change, a sort of transformation that can't be explained by logic or scientific law. A sudden yet still sensible difference. Water turning into wine. A miracle wasn't water changing into an artichoke. Blind eyes sprouting fava beans. No, it was blind eyes filling with sight. An expanding tumor abruptly shrinking. A person stone-cold dead one moment, the next warming and gasping for air. There was even an old story about Dubravka herself, told and retold by her father and his friends as they drank copious amounts of slivovitz, that when Dubravka was a child she'd died one evening and then the next morning came back to life. This was on the night of her mother's departure. The night her mother made the soup. Or the night of her mother's abandonment, depending on who was telling the story.

The miracle of the handkerchief involved an echo, a doubling of one thing with another. One woman's veil, another's hanky, with blood forming an image as the constant between the pair. Each day as Dubravka had made her way from Međugorje to the convent in the Biokovo mountains, she spread Anđela's handkerchief open and prayed before its cross of blood. Once the convent admitted her, the handkerchief was taken from her along with the rest of her belongings. The Mother Superior did allow her to keep Anđela's rosary, but only after Dubravka protested that if they took it as well she'd immediately leave.

Unknown to Dubravka, Anđela's handkerchief was picked up by one of the choir sisters, who admired the cloth's quality after seeing it lying in a box of items waiting to be burned. By then the cross of blood had scattered itself back into brownish blots and smudges. The handkerchief was then given to one of the kitchen sisters, who was told by the choir sister to scrub and bleach it until the cloth was clean.

TWENTY-ONE YEARS later came the bright summer afternoon when Dubravka was crossing the Piazza Bocca della Verità outside Santa Maria in Cosmedin, where she paused as she often did to admire the church's elegant Romanesque bell tower and where she noticed the street performer, Agostino. She was on her way further south, to the vintage market run by the Community of Sant'Egidio, which cared for the poor and homeless and the city's increasing numbers of new immigrants, and where she volunteered. Agostino was dressed strangely, formally, like a banker or politician, in a stiff dark suit. In one hand he held a rubber mask that he repeatedly struck against his thigh, as though he were flogging his leg in mounting frustration, as he argued with one of his comrades, Gennaro, the group's other leader, the one with the big nose and wavy hair. Gennaro was similarly dressed in a dark business suit. The rest of the troupe stood around the Temple of Hercules Victor in long black robes, their faces made up to resemble skulls. A few were positioning the cardboard props that were meant to resemble a bed and several blood-splashed oil cans tattooed with euro and dollar signs.

Dubravka understood the group was preparing to present their daily performance piece. That was Agostino's work. He was something people called a performance artist. Agostino thrashed the mask across his thigh again and then again. Nearly everyone in the square could overhear his argument with Gennaro if they wanted.

Around them knots of tourists pushed their way into the church, not to visit the church itself but instead to stick their hand into the gaping mouth of the immense sewer cap, the Bocca della Verità, the Mouth of Truth, on display in the portico. The idea was that if you were a liar the marble disk would bite your hand off. Word had it that since the Middle Ages the drain cap was a test for the fidelity of wives, and that once one wise Roman woman who was asked by her rich, elderly husband to place her hand into the creature's mouth arranged for her young lover to rush up to her just before the test and embrace and kiss her. She would slap him, call him a maniac, push him away. Then, while her hand lay inside the cap, she'd testify that the only men who'd ever touched and kissed her were her husband and, of course, the crazy fellow who'd just assaulted her outside on the square. A good story for a pensione's part-time housekeeper to be able to share.

As Dubravka passed the Temple of Hercules Victor, she heard Agostino tell Gennaro and the others that he'd given the matter considerable thought and from that moment on he was done, finished, that he was leaving them, that he needed to invent for himself something new. Something not seen before. A fresh work of public art. Dubravka knew nearly all of the performers, at least by sight if not name, because they all routinely worked Rome's squares, as she did, after she completed her morning duties at the pensione. Dubravka could often be seen passing out flyers for this or that urgent cause or collecting donations for various human rights concerns. Though the street performers claimed they didn't have leaders, Dubravka knew that even though they were rivals Gennaro and Agostino were the ones everyone looked up to. They were the group's alpha males, the young men who held and bore authority with ease, as if power were a cloak wrapped around their shoulders, as if it had been given them at birth.

Watching Agostino toss the mask to the ground and turn away from his friends, Dubravka began to feel much the same way she had felt with Anđela that afternoon in Međugorje. Her mind was just finishing another Hail Mary when the words of the prayer stopped and the feeling came.

The feeling began with a woozy sense of dizziness. The light in the piazza grew clear and sharp. Santa Maria in Cosmedin's bell tower swayed suddenly in the wind. The marble columns of the Temple of Hercules Victor turned rosy for a moment as the sounds of the tourists clamoring by the church's doorway fell away. Then Dubravka's eyes met Agostino's as he turned toward her, and for a moment – a few seconds, five, maybe ten – time stopped.

AT THAT MOMENT something within Agostino – his frustration or spirit or soul – felt soothed, calmed, as if he'd swallowed a drug. He felt a sudden tide of warmth wash over his forehead, and he was certain he should nod to the Croatian nun who was steadying herself – both arms out – after appearing as if she were about to faint. He somehow knew he should walk past her wordlessly and continue down the road alongside the Tiber.

Agostino walked past the Ponte Sublicio and then over the Ponte Testaccio and then back again over the Ponte della Scienza, not knowing where he was going, only knowing that his body knew where it was headed. He crisscrossed the bridges spanning the river like a child scribbling a maze on a map. After nearly an hour he found himself in Ostiense and the triangular Parco Schuster. Ahead of him stood the imposing basilica of San Paolo fuori le Mura. What he'd do there, he didn't know. All he felt was that he should go inside, that the church held something important for him if he looked closely enough.

Saint Paul's Outside the Walls wasn't a church Agostino often visited, though it was one of Rome's four main papal basilicas, known primarily for its magnificent triumphal arch as well as its circling round of papal friezes set above the scores of granite columns in its immense nave. Beginning with the apostle Peter and now ending with John Paul II, the likeness of each pope was displayed in a line of bright mosaics beneath the church's clerestory windows. The papal medallions alternated with scenes from Saint Paul's life. Beyond John Paul II there were only a handful of empty spaces for the popes yet to be named.

Were there seven vacant circles? Eight? Agostino considered it would be bad luck to count them. It was said that when all of the spaces were filled the world would come to an end. The last pope whose portrait joined the others would witness the end of time and all of God's creation as we know it. As Agostino stared up at the mosaics, he considered that given John Paul II's waning health the world's final days would soon be one step closer.

Whenever Agostino visited a church he crossed himself, said a prayer for his mother, then sought out his favorite works of art, which nearly always were the church's paintings. When Agostino was younger he'd been a painter, or at least he had tried to paint, tried hard, done his best, though soon enough others whose opinions he respected and valued convinced him that his work was only fair, derivative, and therefore ultimately and finally a failure. His work was void of that sacred element – that special combination of stroke and genius – that caught and held the viewer's eye and made it memorable.

Agostino knelt in the basilica's vast nave, staring up at John Paul II's mosaic, and then his mind turned to thoughts about the saint himself, Saint Paul. Agostino was familiar with the saint's story. Born in Turkey in the city of Tarsus, the Jewish Saul was a Pharisee who devoted his early life to hunting down and imprisoning Christians. It was said that Saul participated in the stoning of Stephen, Christianity's first martyr. One day while on the road to Damascus, a powerful light from above knocked Saul off his horse and left him lying on the ground. A voice from above called out. Saul, why do you persecute me? Saul lay on the ground. Blind. Transformed.

Why had he come to this church where the holy saint was entombed? Agostino wondered. He stood and looked down at his arms and legs, clad in the business suit Gennaro had chosen for him the day they'd visited the tailor, when Agostino initially agreed to play the part of Silvio Berlusconi in Gennaro's performance piece.

Agostino considered Saint Paul's transition. In the church of Santa Maria del Popolo, there hung a painting depicting the moment of Paul's change – Caravaggio's *The Conversion on the Way to Damascus*. Agostino loosened his tie as he walked across the nave toward the main altar, beneath which the saint was entombed. As Agostino neared the tomb, he did his best to remember Caravaggio's painting. Wasn't the dominant figure in the composition a horse, a truly mighty beast, dun coat splashed with white, body fiercely muscled, one front hoof raised, towering over Saul's prone body? The Pharisee's cape was spread out on the ground beneath his body, his helmet and sword fallen to the side, his thin legs spread, his arms and hands raised to the sky. Agostino stopped where he stood, took off his jacket, and raised his arms and hands to the sky.

He felt like falling to the floor, and so, because he was a performer, he surrendered to the impulse. Without fully realizing what he was doing, and in spite of the others around him in the church who turned toward him now and stared at him curiously, Agostino dropped his jacket on the basilica's floor and then fell backwards down onto it as he raised his arms, shut his eyes, splayed open his legs, opened wide both his hands. Yes, Agostino thought. Yes! It was at that moment, as he physically re-created the figure portrayed in Caravaggio's painting of the saint's conversion, that Agostino understood why he'd come to San Paolo fuori le Mura and what he as an artist must now do.

OVER THE FOLLOWING months, Agostino set to work.

He researched Caravaggio's life and examined his paintings in Rome's churches and museums. Agostino studied the stories, considered the rumors. With his savings he purchased an antique sword, and with his girlfriend Valentina's help he practiced his swordplay before the mirrors lining the back wall of the garage in Trastevere where the couple lived. He blew the dust off the boxes of his old paints, purchased fresh rolls of canvas, wood for frames, a quartet of lanterns and several mirrors to reflect the lantern's light, precisely as the master was said to have done. Agostino would literally live the part, he vowed. Although his sword was slightly anachronistic with the character he'd portray – with the man he would attempt to embody and become – Agostino hoped Caravaggio himself, if he could somehow see him, would not entirely disapprove.

Agostino was confident he had the background for the project. He'd studied commedia dell'arte in Venice and stage combat in Florence and street theater here in Rome. The rest of the guerilla troupe Agostino had belonged to were committed to continuing to perform Gennaro's anti-war piece, the one that Agostino had walked away from. The piece featured George W. Bush and Silvio Berlusconi lying in a mock bed, cuddling beneath a blanket on which was written *Guerra in Iraq!* Standing beside the pair would be the placard drawings of oil barrels dripping with blood. The rest of the troupe, faces painted to resemble skulls, would walk in circles in their black hooded robes. To punctuate the message a few would carry scythes, and all but the pair playing Bush and Berlusconi would offer the passing crowds a leaflet detailing the war's casualties and cost and extent of Italy's involvement.

No subtlety, Agostino had told the group as they stood by the Temple of Hercules Victor on the Piazza Bocca della Verità. Forgive me, Agostino had added, I don't mean to be the one to throw stones, but shouldn't art strive to become true? Agostino disliked being so obvious, so simple, so transparent. He was coming to think of himself as a prankster, more of a provocateur than a mere agent of a singular message. He understood that Gennaro's Iraq scenario was popular because people liked seeing something they easily understood. Most nodded their heads, then walked away, unaffected, not giving the tableau further thought. Tourists often asked the actors with scythes to pose beside them for photographs. They rewarded the troupe with coins collected by the younger members in straw baskets. Most of the crowd dropped the leaflets – glanced at but hardly read – on the ground where they swirled in the wind like autumn leaves before being picked up by the youngest members of the troupe and, if not crumpled, passed out again.

But now, thanks to a distant uncle's death and generous will, for at least a few months in the coming year Agostino had no pressing need for money. Let the others paint their faces and wear the Bush and Berlusconi masks, he thought. If they believed that was art, well, so be it!

Of course Agostino's plan was impractical, but wasn't all art impractical? His years of trying to learn to paint were certainly impractical. But impracticality was why art was art, he believed. And wasn't the true purpose of art the idea that the artist needed to present to the audience something new, something surprising, unexpected? Agostino didn't believe in the imperative to explain or justify his work. If he was the only person on this madly spinning ball of water and dust who understood what he was doing, well, that alone would have to suffice.

It was enough, Agostino believed, for the artist to present an image, be it a portrait or an action or the words of a text, that didn't immediately reveal its intentions. A true image conveyed an emotion expressed precisely in form. A true image needed to be dynamic, forceful, recognizable. A vortex of fused ideas endowed with zest. For years Agostino had tried to create that on canvas. He knew that someday, in some way, he would succeed. As for now, he'd do his best to create it in living, breathing life.

He would make his debut as Caravaggio on the Piazza Navona on the day after Christmas.

Sveti Vlaho

Dubrovnik, February 1977

E ven as a child, she felt safest inside a church.

    Of course when Dubravka was an adult she'd say it was because of the presence of the Almighty, but as a child she liked churches mainly because whenever she was inside one she felt protected. She felt comforted by churches' thickly mortared walls topped by lovely arched ceilings propped up by mighty stone columns. Even if the church walls were made to crumble by an earthquake or an enemy's falling bombs, she knew there was a good chance the columns would remain standing. And if they didn't and she was crushed by the pillars' mighty blocks and all of the air in her lungs was squeezed out until they were flat as paper sacks, and all of her blood was spilled onto the floor like rakija from one of her father's tipped-over bottles, at least then she'd be with God.

    Churches were also decorated with countless fascinating details – side altars and little niches and stations, statues of angels and saints, things you could look at a hundred times and still see something new, something you hadn't really noticed before. Details that made her feel proud for having seen them, that tickled the smart girl within her, that evoked an even stronger sense of calm reassurance as well as delight.

    Dubravka liked the way her footfalls echoed on the stone floor of Saint Blaise as she walked up its center aisle. She liked the feel of the backs of the church's wooden pews as she brushed her fingertips against them. She liked looking up at the imposing columns flanking the main aisle, then seeing the altar and its tall wall of gold and silver decorated with white angels, in the center of which stood the golden statue of the saint. She liked the deep scent of incense and the softer smell of melting candle wax that always lingered in the air. Sometimes she would blur her eyes and make the lights in the chandeliers hanging from Saint Blaise's ceiling fuzz and turn into rays, like something extraordinary shooting out from a spaceship in a science-fiction movie.

Even though she was only twelve, she'd seen science-fiction movies, noisy films full of panic and screaming, goldfish-eyed aliens that swooped down like bad angels eager to destroy all life on Earth. But Saint Blaise's ceiling lights weren't from a bad spaceship. No, she thought, they were the lights of something kind and friendly, a smooth-haired messenger sent by God, sent down to the terrible war-mad planet to hover over its many soldiers and armies and bring peace and harmony. Or sometimes Dubravka would forget about movies and make the lights turn into the rays of loving grace emanating down from the hands of the Blessed Virgin, as she'd seen on the holy cards Father Josip sometimes gave her. She'd look up at the blurred lights and hold her hands down at her sides, pretending she was the Lady, pretending each of her hands was shooting out golden beams of grace.

Most of all Dubravka liked looking at the soft red glow of the sanctuary lamp. In every church she visited, the lamp was positioned to the right of the main altar, sometimes fixed to a stone column, other times dangling from the chancel arch inside a trio of chains. A simple candle set in a red glass container, kept burning day and night. Day after day, night after night, week after week, eternally. Dubravka knew the light signified the presence of Christ, Christ in the form of the Blessed Sacrament, locked securely in a gold chalice inside the tabernacle on the altar.

Dubravka thought she would very much like to be given the job of replacing the candle within the lamp whenever it came close to burning out. She imagined she'd need a very tall ladder. She'd be careful climbing the rungs of the ladder. She'd hold on with both hands. Under her care she'd make sure the lamp's flame would never flicker and go out.

DUBRAVKA ALREADY KNEW the world outside the church was filled with danger. Only four years before, the city had been struck by a massive earthquake that killed over a hundred people and damaged over a thousand of Dubrovnik's buildings. Still, the Church of Saint Saviour, wedged between the Franciscan Monastery and the Pile Gate at the other end of the Stradun, the city's ancient limestone-paved main street, hadn't been destroyed. The church had been built back in the 1500s in gratitude by the survivors of an earlier earthquake. The humble church survived yet another quake a century later, one that killed half of Dubrovnik's population and leveled much of the city, reducing the town's lovely tile-roofed houses and shops into rubble.

All of this Dubravka learned from her father. He told her that many believed the church had failed them, failed them twice before, and now three times. A clear lesson about religion's utter uselessness. Religion was phony, a waste of effort and time. Something for old women and weak men with weaker brains. But Dubravka sensed that the three quakes' destruction would have been far worse had Saint Saviour never been built.

Churches calmed her. Her mother said that from birth Dubravka had been a nervous, fretful, anxious child – or were those her father's words, spoken again and again, after her mother disappeared? Her unhappy father, perpetually finding fault in her, often confusing her with her mother, calling her names not fit for the mangiest dog, seated at the wooden table in the kitchen drinking glass after glass of slivovitz while the child did her best to amuse herself playing at his feet on the floor.

The father would show her his bruised knuckles. He was a man who enjoyed telling others his opinion, and who seldom backed down from a fight. Before facing an opponent he'd have another drink and then spit into his hands. Sometimes after nights of fighting his knuckles looked torn, like the insides of ripe plums. Fermented plums were the secret to a good bottle of slivovitz, one of the several types of rakija – distilled fruit brandy – the man enjoyed, and which he purchased at the open-air market in Dubrovnik's Gundulić Square. Homemade. The higher the proof, the better. From travarica to biska to loza, the man drank them all.

Here, he'd say, opening and then clenching his fists, give my hands a spit. He'd offer his hands to the child, pretending there was someone in the room to fight. Dubravka would do her best to work up some spit, but it was never enough. Is that all you've got? her father would ask. Believe me, you'll need more than that if you want to get by in this world.

Had Dubravka invented her memories of her mother? She had one memory of the woman leaning down over her while she was lying in bed, giving both her cheeks and her forehead a soft kiss, then slowly brushing her fingertips over her eyelids as if to insure they were closed. Dubravka had another memory of her mother standing at the foot of her bed, her hands covering her face, weeping. She had a memory of the father behind her, gesturing to the door, shouting words the child failed to understand. Now her father didn't keep even a single picture of the woman in the house. Her name was never to be mentioned.

Dubravka played on the floor with her wooden blocks, stacking them to make a roofless house, whispering conversations among the imaginary builders. All of the builders were women since it was said that it was Dubrovnik's women who'd carved and carried the stones that made up the walls and pillars of the Church of Saint Saviour. One of the women would be Dubravka's mother. This would be back in the old days. Of course Dubravka's mother wouldn't be alive then, but this was make-believe.

After the women built the church Dubravka made with her wooden blocks, the girl would spit into her hands and give the rug a tiny shake, then another, a few moments later a third. These would be the early tremors. Dubravka knew that if you paid attention you'd feel the early tremors. They would give the women warning, time to gather their children and run outside, away from the tumbling walls. Then after everyone was safely outside, Dubravka would shake the rug again and again, stronger and stronger, until the blocks began to shift and slide and the walls the women built began to fall.

Here, her father would say, offering the child sitting among her tumble of wooden blocks a glass. Drink. His hand would toast the air. Živjeli, he'd say. May you live.

Živjeli, Dubravka would answer.

She knew it was necessary to make a toast when drinking. Paint thinner, her father called it. Petrol. Lighter fluid. A drink to take the hair off a bear.

The child always accepted the glass from her father. She knew that after she endured its burn the liquor would calm her. Make her feel less nervous. Less frightened. She'd toast her father, his shoes, the fallen walls of her church, the women who'd carved and carried the heavy stones. Then, rather than sip the drink as she was instructed, she'd tilt back her head and toss off the shot in a single gulp.

The slivovitz would sear her mouth and numb her tongue, then scrape its rough way down her throat and begin warming her in a sweet and gentle embrace.

DUBRAVKA FEARED NOT only earthquakes but also the world's many enemies. If she were to believe her father and benefit from his wisdom, she was to assume everyone she encountered in life was an enemy. That is, at least until they proved themselves repeatedly and undeniably to be a friend. And even then she was to distrust them, to look for the hidden knife all of them carried, while to their face she should pretend she was their dearest comrade.

All one had to do was look at Dubrovnik to see that it was a fortress. Its double line of massive walls circled the Old City like a fist. The city's walls were reinforced by several towers, fortresses, casemates, and bastions that not even the devastating earthquake of 1667 could destroy. Many who lived in Dubrovnik gave credit to the city's protector and patron, Saint Blaise. Today, the third of February, was his feast day.

Everyone in Dubrovnik knew a version of the saint's story. Though he was born in the fourth century, six hundred years later Saint Blaise appeared late one night in a church to a parish priest named Stojko. Some say he appeared to Stojko in a dream. In either event the Armenian bishop warned Stojko of an impending attack on the city the following morning by the Venetians – Dubrovnik's jealous trade rivals – whose fleet of ships, apparently sailing up the Adriatic on their way home, had dropped anchor just outside the harbor. Stojko wisely woke the city's council, who alerted the city's troops, who securely shut the city's gates and armed the walls and saw that, yes, indeed, the Venetian ships whose lying captains claimed they were pausing for a day or two only to take on fresh water and supplies were readying a surprise invasion. Forewarned, the city and its inhabitants were saved.

Dubravka's father didn't much believe in dreams or entering churches and preferred the version in which, after having drinks with friends, Stojko was stumbling home drunk when he saw standing in the shadows near the Stradun an old bearded man, a bishop by all appearances, holding in one hand his bronze crosier, a fancy mitre topping his head. The stranger identified himself as Saint Blaise – *Sveti*

Vlaho in Croatian – and told Stojko of the Venetians' plans. So now you can see how good it was for all of us that Stojko was out that night drinking!

Sometimes when Dubravka's father came home drunk late at night and the child woke up, alone in the tiny house, frightened, her father would stroke her cheek and laugh and tell her there was nothing to fear, that he was only outside talking to Sveti Vlaho.

The city was so grateful to the old bishop that a church was built in his honor, and over the next thousand-plus years Dubrovnik held a holy festival on Saint Blaise's feast day. The celebrations began on the previous day, Candlemas, a day commemorating the Blessed Virgin. Special Masses would be said. Doves would be set free into the air. At dawn the following morning, every church in Dubrovnik would sound its bells. Musketeers dressed in red berets and capes would fire their ancient guns. Mass would be said outside the city's cathedral, the site of the saint's warning. Then everyone – beginning with a long line of bishops somberly carrying sacred reliquaries, followed by city officials and the musketeers and Dubrovnik's priests and nuns, along with musicians and townspeople bearing banners and flags, children in white who'd just made their First Holy Communion, and pilgrims from all over the world who'd simply traveled to Dubrovnik – would march in procession up the length of the Stradun to the steps of the Church of Saint Blaise.

Dubravka didn't like the musketeers and their smoking pistols, and she always thought the parade down the Stradun was far too long and crowded. The girl wasn't fond of the bishops dressed in their red finery, acting as if they were the most important people there. She also wasn't sure about the holy relics, which looked to her like pretend metal arms and hands – parts of a robot, studded with filigree inlays and jewels – inside of which were supposed to be actual parts of the saint. After the Romans killed Saint Blaise, Dubravka wondered, how did someone know to grab up bits of his body? Where were the bits taken? How were they preserved? Or were these supposed to be miracles, body parts that somehow didn't decay and stink? No, the girl thought. She knew about meat and how quickly it rotted. These relics were false, phony things. Symbols. Harmless maybe, but not worth standing in line to kiss or touch. What young Dubravka did like was the ceremony that followed the ringing of the church bells and the firing of the muskets and the Mass and the parade – the blessing of the throats inside the church.

BLAISE HAD BEEN a bishop as well as a physician, known to cure both humans and animals. As he was being led by the Romans to his death, a woman rushed toward him, her dying son in her arms. The child was choking on a fish bone. Blaise raised a shackled hand in blessing, and the child coughed out the bone and was saved. That story Dubravka could believe. There was another story about a woman who gave Blaise two candles so that he might be able to read the Bible in his dark prison cell. She gave him the candles to thank him for bringing her pig, who'd been attacked by a wolf, back to life. Dubravka had trouble imagining that tale. It didn't seem sensible. More than once the girl had gazed up at slaughtered pigs hanging head-down from giant hooks in the butcher's cold meat-storage room, where her uncle, Marija's father, often purchased sides of meat. Once the animal's steaming guts had been spilled out onto the floor, there seemed no way to put the creature back together again. Miraculously coughing out a stuck fish bone was much more believable.

The child recognized that the pig story was told to connect Blaise with the two candles. In church the priests held a pair of long candles, blessed the previous day on Candlemas, their flat ends softened and plaited together into a knot, then bound with a red ribbon, like a girl might tie the braids of her hair. The ribbon was red because Saint Blaise had been a martyr. The red was meant to symbolize his blood. The braided end of the candles formed a handle that spread open into a large V, like the blades of scissors. The priests would gently place the candles around the necks of the children, who stood in line waiting to kneel at the altar rail and be blessed. Then their throats would never swallow fish bones.

Through the intercession of Saint Blaise, bishop and martyr, holy patron of our city, the priests would recite, may God deliver you from every disease of the throat and from every other illness.

DUBRAVKA LOVED BEING blessed. She always lingered at the altar rail, slowly crossing herself, glancing up at the warm red glow of the sanctuary lamp, before she stood and returned to her horrible and lonely ordinary life. As her life outside church rushed back and filled her mind, it would take her a moment or two to check her sadness. First she'd feel disappointment over losing the sense of joy, then recognize what the loss she felt was about.

Today she walked back to her pew and knelt and looked up at the alcove over the altar and the two white angels holding up the gold-plated statue of Saint Blaise. She thanked the kind saint for protecting her from danger. The saint's eyes stared out at the church and its congregation, one hand raised in blessing, the other holding a miniature version of the walled city of Dubrovnik, symbolizing his continued protection of it.

As she stared at the miniature version of Dubrovnik, she realized that in the tiny Dubrovnik in the saint's arm was another even tinier Church of Saint Blaise. The girl then had a daring idea, to stand and do her best to blend into line again, this time on the church's opposite side, where a different priest was blessing throats. The thin one, who was always kind to her, who sometimes gave her holy cards. The one with the bad leg. Father Josip. Dubravka sensed that even if he noticed she was in line a second time he wouldn't refuse her. Why not ask to be blessed again? she thought. What would it hurt?

After all, there were scores of statues of Saint Blaise positioned all throughout the city. His image was set in the stone walls of nearly every important building in Dubrovnik. Most of the Saint Blaise statues faced the sea – holy protection against invaders. Invaders came from the sea. The sky as well if one considered science-fiction movies and their stories about aliens in their whirling flying saucers that could hover overhead and shoot down deadly rays. Dubravka thought some statues of Saint Blaise should be pointed up at the sky too. And Saint Blaise statues should also be placed face-down on the Stradun, as protection against the Earth itself and its unpredictable habit of trembling and quaking. Her favorite Saint Blaise figure was the very smallest one, barely two bricks tall, set in a niche in a wall by the Old City Harbor.

As Dubravka grew older the statue of Saint Blaise would often remind her of the Infant Jesus of Prague, who raised one hand in blessing and in the other held a miniature globe, symbolizing the Earth.

On top of the Earth held by the Child there was a golden cross. Still later Dubravka would see the statue of Saint Blaise as similar to both the Hand of Fatima and the Hand of Miriam, often more simply called the Hamsa.

But for now the child stared gratefully at the statue of the old bishop as she neared the altar rail for a second time, imagining she could see the Church of Saint Blaise at the far end of the Stradun in the miniature version of Dubrovnik the golden figure of the saint held in his hand. She very much liked the idea that a saint held her city in his hand. She imagined that meant Saint Blaise held her too. She imagined that if her eyes were powerful enough she could look through the doors of the miniature church and be able to see herself there, in line, gazing up at the altar, now nearing the altar rail and Father Josip, exactly as she was now, about to receive a second blessing.

Dubravka brought a hand up to her throat and softly stroked it, pleased that at least for now, at least for today, she would be protected.

By the Fountain of the Four Rivers

Rome, 26 December 2004

Beside her narrow bed, in the wide attic room in Giorgio's pensione where she prepared breakfasts, Dubravka could look down upon the vendors setting up their stalls that each day crammed the Campo de' Fiori, and in the square's center see the statue of Giordano Bruno, the genius philosopher, mathematician, cosmologist, who was imprisoned, tortured, and ultimately hung upside down and burned to death by the Church for his beliefs. Having worked all her life in kitchens, beside hot ovens and open flames, Dubravka can only begin to imagine the utter horrors of such a death. The excruciating pain. So bright and sharp and stinging. So insistent and demanding of the entirety of your attention.

She felt a strong kinship with Bruno because she also has her own ideas and beliefs. Like Bruno, of course, she was Roman Catholic. Like Bruno, ordained a Dominican friar, Dubravka had taken the vows. Like Bruno she was fond of making good use of her mind and questioning assumptions, and like Bruno she frequently arrived at her own conclusions. She did her best to think ideas out to their logical ends. After all, she thought, wasn't that why God gave people the ability to reason? Bruno's imposing statue defiantly faced the Vatican and served, to anyone familiar with his story, as a reminder that faith and the institution of the Church were sometimes two radically different things.

And so now on this chilly December morning, as Dubravka rose from bed and thanked the Almighty for the blessing and challenge of a new day, she turned on the radio as was her habit, then dropped to her knees and gazed out her windows at the vendors opening the canvas awnings that stretched over their stalls. She tried to take in the full meaning of what she was hearing – the day's tragic report of an earthquake and tsunami in South Asia.

"Dear Lord," Dubravka prayed, "have mercy and compassion." Then she checked herself, realizing that once again she was being impudent, that even after her many years in the convent she still needed to learn how best to pray. Who was she to ask of God something so obvious, as if the thought of compassion and mercy hadn't occurred to the Almighty? As if God wasn't always – in each instant of time – exercising both mercy and compassion along with immeasurable love. Dubravka believed that if God were to look away for even a fraction of a second the world would be overwhelmed by demons, and the leaping flames that had licked and consumed Bruno's body would be like the most gentle kiss.

Then, in the next half-second, she reconsidered her thoughts, the idea that to God something might or might not occur. This was how Dubravka's mind worked, advancing a thought and then going back over it, retracing it, teasing out its strands like a girl trying to comb her tangled hair. How simpleminded of her, she realized, to think that the tense of any verb might apply to God since for God time has no meaning. Since God knows everything in every moment. Since for God there are no ends or middles or beginnings. Dubravka knew she needed to remember this. Dubravka wanted to be able to understand God.

No narrative, she thought. The only reason God gave us the concept of time and narrative – beginnings, middles, ends – was so that we might learn that our actions have consequences. So that we might understand the lessons causality has to teach. If God has any sense of time at all, she considered, it would be a single moment in which everything that has ever occurred, was occurring, and ever will occur was happening simultaneously. That meant she was always living in Dubrovnik, always searching the streets of Mostar, always working in the convent, always kneeling beside her bed here in Rome.

She lowered the radio's volume. The news of that morning's earthquake and tsunami was far too devastating for her mind to absorb. She decided she should set her thoughts of it aside until after she went downstairs and completed the day's work.

At least for now, Dubravka knew her task was to care for Rome's visitors. To work for Giorgio, who'd taken her in, to offer his guests their breakfasts, bake their daily bread and pour their morning teas and coffees, answer their countless questions, supply them with directions to wherever they were planning to go that day, as well as to pray that they might find what they came to Rome searching for. Regardless of what they would tell her, how they'd traveled to Rome to visit this or that museum, to walk along the ancient ruins in the Forum, tour the Colosseum, sit on the Spanish Steps, dine at this or that famous restaurant, she believed each visitor to Rome was a pilgrim in search of something, and the key to their search was spiritual.

She turned off the radio and glanced again out the windows, where she saw a trio of workers walking past the statue, more than likely toward the Advent fair beginning its day on the Piazza Navona. The radio squatted on a wooden table beside Dubravka's bed, next to a glass of water she'd drawn last evening from the kitchen tap. Her nightly routine. Before bringing the water up to her room, she'd squeezed half a lemon into it. The lemon's juice and pulp hovered on the bottom of the glass like a cloud. Dubravka crossed herself again, swirled the liquid in the glass, drank. Then she spilled into her cat's bowl a scoop of kibble from a tin she kept atop her bookshelf.

The cat's name was Anđelina, Croatian for *Little Angel*. Born in the attic room on a bed of freshly washed towels, the creature ate with the fastidiousness of an English queen.

Dubravka gathered her things and walked downstairs to the closet that held one of the pensione's sinks and toilets. She moved quietly so she wouldn't wake the guests. Dubravka washed as she'd learned to wash while living in Mostar, when she made her morning prayers at a nearby mosque, beginning with her right hand and forearm, washing each three times, then her left hand and forearm, again three times. Then she washed her mouth, nose, face, head, and stepped out of her slippers and splashed a bit of water on her feet. Yes, she decided as she walked back up the staircase to her room, after she dressed and finished her work in the kitchen, she'd follow the laborers and go to the Advent fair at the Piazza Navona.

She remembered that there she was certain to see Agostino, who told her not to acknowledge him even with the slightest smile or nod since beginning this morning he would be embarking upon his new performance piece. Don't even look my way, he said. Ignore me. Pretend I am to you a stranger, since from the twenty-sixth forward I will not be myself.

She'd fashion a new sign for her box and begin with the holiday crowds by the Fountain of the Four Rivers. Later she'd walk about the Centro Storico. In the coming weeks she'd take her box elsewhere around the city. Dubravka would make sure her sign was seen, at the very least offering everyone who passed her a reminder of the need for compassionate and merciful aid for the victims of this latest tragedy.

AMID THE CROWDS milling about the Piazza Navona's Fountain of the Four Rivers and the living statues and mimes, the gaunt Santa puffing on a Marlboro as he paced beside his sleigh, the young Chiara tapping her foot as she worked the pearl buttons and yawning bellows of her organetto, the sleek-haired Ying Yue painting a tourist's name above a stand of bamboo behind which peeked a playful panda, the gray-haired Marcel in the saffron Sgt. Pepper jacket slipping his hand into a costumed glove and moon-walking his fingers across a table to the music pulsing from his boombox, the ivory horses on the antique German carousel rocking merrily forth and back as the platform upon which they were pinned spun around and around, and the scores of Advent fair food, souvenir, and gaming stalls flanking the square – amid all of this, Agostino drew in a deep breath and brandished his sword.

Today was the start, the debut, the first act in the series of tableaus that would comprise his latest performance piece. Agostino held out his sword, enjoying its heft and balance, the easy way his hand could grip the leather-wrapped wooden handle, rub the perfectly positioned thumb rest, nestle inside the comforting, protective web of twisted wire that came down just past his wrist. It was as if the sword had been made just for him, was a natural extension of his arm. The sword was a double-edged schiavona, basket-hilted with a polished brass cat's head pommel and embedded iron quillons. How mighty it felt to swing it! Agostino smiled with pleasure as he inscribed zeroes and eights in the air. How splendid it was to slash the air! His aim was intended to provoke, to upset, to unbalance.

He'd chopped his dark hair so that it fell in curls across his brow, and grew a mustache and dark soul patch. He wore skin-tight leggings and a chocolate-colored vest over a blouse with striped puffy sleeves, and to nearly everyone pausing to take notice of him he seemed to be only another costumed character on the square, yet another performer in the circus-like festa that was the Piazza Navona during the weeks of

Advent and the twelve days leading to the Epiphany. Another seeker of money, another willing subject for a souvenir photograph. Yet if those in the crowd looked more closely, they'd see that on the sampietrini before him there was no open cap or cup, no petition for their coins. If they observed him with greater care they'd see that he was something else, a visual representation, a true street artist, presenting himself as a historical figure – a rogue, a genius, likely also a murderer.

Becoming surly was the most challenging part of his performance. By nature Agostino was amiable, though in an argument about aesthetics his tongue could be sharp as his blade. Now, as a tourist wearing a fanny pack offered him money, Agostino threatened the man with his sword. As another tossed a coin onto the cobblestones at his feet, Agostino sneered and two-stepped away. After nearly an hour on the square he stood still, silent, thinking himself a living, breathing symbol. A sort of time traveler. Yes, he thought, he was the reincarnation of a man from another time, and at that moment he tapped into what he'd studied and opened his mouth and began to speak, unloosing a free-flowing rant.

Part Italian, part English, Agostino told the passing crowds that genuine artists didn't uphold the ideals of beauty and truth by becoming bootlickers, that the saints shouldn't be portrayed as idealized images clad in immaculate robes, standing on pristine clouds, stripped bare of life's grime and grit. No, he told those who paused to stand around and stare at him, the very saints who had walked this wretched Earth were made of flesh and blood, muscle and sweat – people with lined faces, dirty hands, broken fingernails, unwashed feet. People wandering Rome's streets and alleyways. People even now, today, at this very second of time, making their way through this very square. True art was physical, he announced as his free hand slapped his leather vest. Its generative sources were ever-present in the natural world. He swung his sword ecstatically in the air, as the great master Merisi was reputed to have done on this piazza four centuries before. His feather tumbled forward from his cap. As Agostino felt himself channeling Merisi, his dark eyes lifted toward the chimneys and spires outlined against the sky.

Recognize me, brothers and sisters, he shouted to the Italians, for I am of your very soul! Here – and now his words included all the others standing before him – open wide your senses and allow my image to lodge itself like a splinter in the creases of your brain.

Do you understand? he cried. Yes? Yes? You're not comprehending a thing I'm saying, Agostino told a group who'd paused to gesture at him and laugh as if he were a clown. You might as well be the horses on that carousel. Going round and round in circles, thinking you're getting somewhere. Your heads, Agostino told them, they are made of wood. Your hearts, plastic toys from China. You're a herd of harnessed donkeys, standing ankle-deep in the muck of your own waste, gnawing the dried branches of dead trees. And still you laugh? How ignorant! You come here to Rome, why? To stuff your mouths with our food? To pose for a photograph before our ruins? To wander about our hundreds of churches, the histories of which you don't even try to understand? To go to Saint Peter's Square and gaze at the pope's apartment windows during the last days before he dies?

Agostino's words were like ladders, and with each phrase he could feel himself climb higher, working his way upward, rung by rung, toward some point of clarity. At this moment, as his face reddened and the cords in his neck surged visibly, he felt himself connecting with the true, native spirit of the master Michelangelo Merisi, born 29 September 1571 in the Lombardy hill town of Caravaggio, the town from which he took his name. Agostino felt his soul begin to merge with Michelangelo Merisi da Caravaggio's. Or was it Caravaggio's soul merging with his? Whatever, Agostino thought, Caravaggio's mix of genius and violence coupled with his rejection of the conventions of his time would make anyone trying to channel him swell with pride. Yes, on this first day as Agostino swaggered about the Piazza Navona, sword in hand, dressed like the brash young figure reaching for his weapon in Caravaggio's *The Calling of Saint Matthew*, Agostino believed he was becoming Caravaggio.

You flock here to Rome to experience something truly Roman, Agostino shouted as he slashed his double-edged schiavona through the air. What on Earth could be more true and Roman than to offer you my image, give you the flash of my blade, the wine-tainted perfume of my breath, a momentary glimpse into the depths of my mind and soul?

BEHIND THE PERFORMANCE artist, whom she was careful not to recognize, Dubravka sought donations for tsunami relief. She wore a loose gray dress, black stockings and flat shoes, a tattered cloth coat and azure scarf, and held at chest level a worn wooden collection box, the kind churches often anchored near tiers of votive candles. *S.O.S*, the sign on the collection box read. *Tragedia Sud-Est Asiatico!*

Her eyes were soft and dark. Her raven hair was pinned back modestly. She wore no makeup. Her lips bore only a trace of balm. She said nothing to those she passed, allowing the sign on her box, its clear and obvious plea, to speak for itself. If one looked closely one could see her whispering her favorite prayer, Thomas á Kempis's A Prayer for the Grace of Devotion – *Oh Lord, my God, you are all my good, and who am I that I should dare to speak to you? I am your poorest and meanest servant* – as she walked slowly among the growing Christmas season crowds gathered around the great fountain.

The sun was high and bright, the late December day so clear and crisp that nearly everyone other than Dubravka and Agostino and the North American couple from Boston was smiling. Throughout the piazza there was the sound of water, splashing, surging, rushing, popping, hissing – a tumbling and shifting kaleidoscope of sound so pervasive that after a while the ear took the sounds for granted and no longer heard them.

THE COUPLE FROM Boston, Ben and Elena, moved past it all, past the booth selling lottery tickets and the candy and torrone and ciambelle stands, past the carnival game stalls and the merry-go-round topped by a leaping horse, past the towering Babbo Natale in his red cloak teetering about the square on his obvious pair of stilts, past the curiously feral-eyed performer with the sword. Forced by the crowds to walk single file, Ben and Elena were doing churches before deciding on a place for lunch. "Rome is the city of a thousand churches," Ben read that morning in his guidebook, "and each offers the visitor a unique story." Though he and Elena felt they were ordinary, with nothing in particular that distinguished either of them, their pale complexions and North American features made them stand out in the crowd – a pair of dull, well-fed birds among a flock of sharp-beaked, wiser, darker ones.

Elena did her best to rise to the standards around her, wearing her finest clothes – a loose copper-colored skirt that fell just below her knees and a silk cream blouse beneath a cardigan sweater and umber coat – and even tying her scarf like the Romans did, to the one side, with the ends pulled fashionably through a loop. Her body was lush, full-figured. She was amazed that nearly all of the Roman women on the street appeared as if they were wearing their best clothing. Their easy sense of style and fashion intimidated her. They were perfectly dressed and coifed, moving through the streets with nonchalance, as if oblivious to everything around them.

Ben remained faithful to his Ivy League days, the version of self he'd crafted and refined during his years at the university, a blend of the casual and the elegant. He'd taken private speech lessons to moderate his Boston North End accent. Tall and relatively thin, with the physique of a tennis player, he wore Top-Sider loafers and designer khakis, classic poplin shirts and cashmere sweaters shipped from Turnbull & Asser in London. His life was money, the trading and transfer of equities and stocks. Like many of his generation, he'd made and lost a fortune during the rise and collapse of the dot-coms. Funny money, he forced himself to think. Theoretical figures on a computer screen. The lost fortune was real and not real, though bile still burned his throat whenever he thought about it.

The woman in the tattered coat and sky-blue scarf offered her collection box to Ben as he hurried past, and for a moment their eyes met and his gaze lingered on the softness of her mouth, the fullness of her lips, then swept back to her dark eyes, deep and wide as a foreign sea. He was unaware that at that moment the woman staring back at him felt an undeniably dizzy and immensely powerful surge of prayer.

S.O.S., he read. *Tragedia Sud-Est Asiatico!* Yes, he realized. Somewhere in Asia earlier that morning there had been an earthquake and tsunami. He'd heard something about it before he and Elena had left their hotel. The announcer's voice had read the names of affected countries – Indonesia, Malaysia, Thailand, Myanmar, India, Bangladesh, Sri Lanka, Somalia, Kenya. The list seemed nearly endless. But instead of reaching for his wallet or his pocketful of change – Ben wasn't used to how many coins a person received in change while traveling in a country that used the euro – he reached for Elena's hand. He pulled Elena past a boy in a knit cap hawking a bouquet of helium-filled balloons – Pikachu, Spiderman, Pink Panther, Winnie the Pooh, Nemo – and toward a row of Advent fair stalls, several offering plaster figurines for presepi – Nativity scenes – others with figures of La Befana, each witch-like doll with a long crooked nose and pointed chin speckled with warts, her stick arms holding a straw broom. Some Befanas were small as a thumb, some nearly as large as newborns, with battery-powered eyes that flashed fiery red while a sound-activated mechanism inside them triggered a raucous laugh, a squawk that in turn activated the doll next to it, which caused the dolls beside it to screech, and so on and so on, each doll affecting the next like tumbling rows of dominoes, their shrieks mounting in intensity as the couple passed.

Ben pulled Elena past a woman spinning cylinders of pink cotton candy – Zucchero Filato, Bianco & Fragola – and a toothless man roasting marroni on a grill. The chestnuts' split shells glistened like yellow cat's-eye marbles, the kind Ben had played with as a child. He pulled Elena toward the roped-off tables and chairs of a restaurant and then finally onto a patch of open sidewalk, where their path was clear.

Behind them, a man ate a panino beside a stall offering porchetta di Ariccia. "La porca, la porca! C'avemo la porchetta, gente!" the stall's vendor cried. The pretty organetto player who sat beside the fountain swung her wild black hair from side to side as she skipped her way through a tarantella. At the edge of the crowd surrounding the musician, an Italian boy wearing an AC Milan scarf stood behind his North American girlfriend, his arms coiled around her chest like two pythons. The girl wore a black baseball cap – the San Francisco Giants, Ben recognized. A white-faced mime in a red beret imitated a tourist talking on her cell phone, trailing her step by step, holding one hand up to his ear, nodding whenever the unaware woman nodded. Nearby sat an artist displaying mildly recognizable charcoal sketches of Marcello Mastroianni, Robert DeNiro, Marilyn Monroe. With his dirty plastic boot, Santa crushed the butt of his cigarette on the ground and posed for a photograph with a reluctant child, her parents cooing like pigeons in an attempt to make the frightened girl stop crying. The puppeteer from Palermo pulled skirted fishnet gloves onto the first two fingers of each hand and danced the can-can, kicking his fingers higher and higher with each step. The living statues – Levitating Swami, Passed-Out Drunk in the Bronze Suit, Tutankhamun, Statue of Liberty, Clown in the Tuxedo with Top Hat and Flower – remained unmoving as a vendor from Senegal, his complexion the soft color of rain-splashed teak, sprayed the air with arcs of rainbow-flecked soap bubbles popping from the mouth of a plastic gun.

In the Fontana dei Quattro Fiumi – the Fountain of the Four Rivers – the Danube straddled a large rock, arms raised in tribute to the coat of arms of Pope Innocent X, the rich Pamphili whose ego and wealth had commissioned the sculpture, essentially a quartet of stone arches decorated with platforms on which sat each river god. The Ganges stared out blankly at the passing crowds, holding between his legs a mighty oar. The Rio de la Plata lifted his right hand against the sky while the Nile, whose source at the time was unknown, covered his head, hiding his face. Around them were various animals and plants common to each river's region. A wary lion, emerging from a cave in the fountain's depths, as if about to leap. Opposite the lion, a clearly nervous horse. Sea dragons writhing on the fountain's floor, tails waving, mouths gaping. A tall, majestic palm, fronds brushed back as if from a strong wind. Pear cactus clinging to a wall of rock. Fruits. Flowers. The papal crown and crossed keys. In the center towered a Roman-made version of an Egyptian obelisk, topped by the Pamphili dove holding an olive branch in its beak. All of it designed to boast that the Roman Catholic Church and its pope ruled over the entirety of the known world.

Beneath their canvas awning, scores of Befana dolls hanging from hooks looped with elastic cords screeched to one another like a jungle of wild birds. A portly attendant clapped his hands and poked and prodded the witches with a stick to keep them laughing. Above his stall hung a wide, red-lettered banner.

AUGURI A TUTTO IL MONDO

And all the while the waters in the great fountain cascaded and splashed, rushed and swirled, leaping and seething in the center of the busy square.

San Luigi dei Francesi

Rome, 26 December 2004

"She's an old woman the Three Wise Men asked to join them," Ben explained. He and Elena were walking from the Piazza Navona toward the next church on their itinerary. "She was sweeping the ground outside her house when the Wise Men passed by. They called out and asked her to join them. She said no, she was too busy. But later, after she heard that the Son of God had been born and she'd missed her chance to see him, she rushed from her house still holding her broom and, not knowing who the newborn king was, gave gifts to every child she could find."

"So she's like Santa Claus," Elena said.

Ben nodded. "Santa Claus on Twelfth Night. The eve of the Epiphany, where she gets her name. Bringing fruits and nuts and candies to the good children, coal to the bad." They neared the rushing traffic on Corso del Rinascimento, which they crossed with care. Vespas and motorini buzzed like waves of angry hornets in and around cars and trucks as the wary pedestrians inched their way across the crosswalk. "Did you see the lumps of black sugar some of those stalls were selling? Carbone dolce, for the bad children."

"But there are no bad children," Elena said.

"We should get some," Ben said.

"I prefer ours to be good, thank you."

"I mean lumps of black sugar."

They walked into a shadowed alleyway, their footfalls on the sampietrini echoing between the high walls. "But it doesn't really make sense, does it?" Elena said after a while, after she decided once again not to tell Ben her news, after she realized he was referring to the candy. She'd tell him later when they were alone, maybe in their hotel room after lunch or that evening over dinner. Yes, she decided, she'd let him order a bottle of wine and refuse a glass, and of course he'd ask her why she wasn't drinking. At first she'd say nothing, then get him to guess. Elena very much wanted to be sure this time since a year and a half ago she'd miscarried. She tapped her fingers against the side of her skirt, counting. Yes, eighteen months. There was something about announcing the news that would make this pregnancy more real and therefore more vulnerable.

She remembered a saying her Southern Italian father had taught her about talk and silence, that the hen's unseen eggs were never stolen. It made perfect sense. It was why people in Italy's South enclosed their houses and everything they treasured behind a maze of walls. Perception invited envy and theft. Perception opened the door to loss. Though Elena knew it wasn't feasible, part of her wanted to wait before telling anyone, even Ben, until after the child was born.

She fingered the edge of her scarf. "But didn't the Wise Men come from the East?"

"From the East? Right. Of course."

"I may not be a wiz at geography but Italy's west of Bethlehem."

Ben said nothing for several steps. "Probably the Befana's pre-Christian. Some remnant of a pagan god or festival. You know, something mixed in with everything else."

"With that patched dress and hooked nose, she's like a character out of a fairy tale."

"The witch in *Hansel and Gretel*."

"I like her broom. The idea of it, this time of year. Sweeping away the old, starting out fresh and new."

"Well," Ben said, turning toward her and smiling, "I think that's part of it, and that's why we took this time off, why we're here."

"We three kings of Orient are," Elena sang. "Casper, Melchior, and Balthazar."

"I thought it was Gaspar."

"Casper," Elena said and laughed. "The kids in school used to joke that one of the Three Wise Men was Casper the Friendly Ghost. And the gifts they brought the Christ Child were gold, Frankenstein, and myrrh."

AT THE CHURCH'S open doorway, past the pair of carabinieri outside the Palazzo Madama casually cradling their submachine guns, an elderly Romani woman sat hunched on the steps. She wore a striped, plum-colored dress, bright green sweater, a ragged shawl. In her lap lay a straw basket that held a few coins and a strand of oval beads, a broken length of rosary that resembled roasted coffee beans. Head down, she offered all who passed a holy card, and if they dropped a coin into her basket she added her blessing. As the two North Americans hurried past she stared at their shoes, reciting her plea – For the love of God give to me – as if it were a single word.

The couple walked past her, slowing only to pull open the church's inner door. Once inside they stood silently, allowing their eyes time to adjust to the relative darkness. Motes of dust drifted softly down the shafts of light filtered through the church's clerestory windows. Flames from lit votive candles fluttered in their glass jars. The church smelled faintly sweet, a mix of incense and melting wax, and beneath that lay another smell, something darker, deeper. As Elena crossed herself with holy water from the stone font, she tried to identify it. Wood, she thought. Exceptionally old, routinely polished wood. Since this second pregnancy began, she was particularly sensitive to odors. Her hand lingered on the font's curled lip – half of an open scallop shell – that protruded like a pout.

They were far from alone, Elena realized. Whispers spiked with sibilants pierced the church's silence – the scrape scrape scrape of a metal rake's tines against a sidewalk. Yes, a good dozen or more people were gathered wherever Ben was now heading, his head buried in his guidebook. Elena watched him hurry away.

The height of the church's square marble columns, their arches filigreed with gold design, lifted Elena's focus toward the tall, broad clerestory windows and the rich honeycombed ceiling, which pulled her eyes down the length of the barrel-vaulted nave toward the altar and its magnificent fresco – *The Assumption of the Virgin* – then back and further up into the splendid open bowl of the sanctuary's dome. The cupola was brilliant white, coffered in gold hexagons inside of which were splashes of gilded stars and rosettes. Elena found the designs enchanting. Imposing marble figures in high relief climbed their way upward and into the dome. The church was simply stunning, opulent, giving the eye an overall impression of impeccable order, undeniable stability and strength, sunlight softened by the richest browns and golds.

Elena felt that the church had the calm self-assurance of something precisely fashioned. It was exactly the kind of church Ben would like – dignified, clean, resplendent in the late morning light, in perfect proportion with itself – a church in which little appeared overdone, the sort of well-appointed church that might remind one of wealth and comfort, of money, of its own sense of self-worth.

She walked down the center aisle, stepping as gently as she could, placing her weight on the balls of her feet so that the high heels of the new black boots she'd purchased on tony Via del Babuino wouldn't resound quite so loudly. She couldn't understand how Roman women could bear walking each day in high heels, particularly on central Rome's uneven cobblestones. Sampietrini, they called it. Their ankles and legs must be made of iron. She'd change her shoes after lunch at their hotel. Yes, and that evening she'd cover her empty wine glass with the flat of her hand and make Ben guess. Elena genuflected, crossed herself, knelt in a pew, bowed her head, and prayed. "Hail Mary, full of grace."

She didn't know how Ben would react. The issue wasn't that they didn't want children – they did, and of course they'd tried before. Nonetheless, after the miscarriage Ben seemed almost relieved, telling her that losing the child might have been for the best, that perhaps it simply hadn't been the right time. According to Ben there was a right time and a wrong time for everything. It was how he made his living. It was how he lived his life. Elena lifted her eyes from her folded hands and glanced around the church for her husband, who stood among the noisy tourists clustered near the chapel on her far left.

BEN STOOD AMONG the others gathered before the chapel, straining to see the Caravaggios, for which San Luigi dei Francesi, the national church of France, was best known. Covering the three walls behind the squat marble altar rail marking the Contarelli Chapel were three early paintings by Caravaggio depicting central moments in Saint Matthew's life – the apostle's calling, his later inspiration by an angel, the tumult of his ultimate martyrdom and death. A coin box to the right controlled the chapel's lights.

The bright color of Matthew's robe drew Ben's eye to the center painting, *The Inspiration of Saint Matthew*. It pictures the saint standing at a table, pen in hand as he writes in a book, staring up at an angel wrapped in a swirl of white linen hovering over his shoulder. The angel, a curly-haired young boy, counts out something on his fingers. Matthew appears alarmed, listening intently, doing his best to record what he's being told. His tunic and robe, soft yellow and orange, fall to the floor past his bent knee, which rests on a stool that totters off a stone ledge toward the viewer. The effect, Ben noticed, is one of rapt attention coupled with action. The whirlpool of the angel's robe sweeps the eye first up and then back down toward the balding head and beard of the saint. Obedience, Ben concluded, looking again at Matthew's face, now noticing the thin gold halo circling his head.

The Martyrdom of Saint Matthew depicts a horror. A full dozen figures, each in motion, their bodies lit as if the source of light emanates from the painting's center, surround the fallen saint, wearing an alb and chasuble, lying on the floor. He rests on one elbow and raises a hand against a muscular, nearly naked man who has grabbed Matthew's raised wrist and with his other hand readies the sword that's about to kill him. Above Matthew hovers an angel, this one with feathered wings, lying on a cloud. The angel stretches its hand down to give Matthew a palm branch, symbol of the victory of martyrs. The palm branch hangs an inch or two above Matthew's raised hand.

It's like a still from an action movie, Ben thought as he studied the painting. A frozen moment, with the others gathered there framing the central action as they recoil from the violence that is just about to occur. Ben noticed that behind Matthew and his murderer were a pair of steps and the front of an altar – Ben concluded it was an altar since the painting showed part of a Maltese cross – and as a result Matthew's death was taking place inside a church. Ben saw that a single lit candle stood on the altar. As his eye traced the line down from the candle's soft flame to the stalk of the angel's palm branch and Matthew's raised hand, Ben realized that Matthew wasn't raising his hand to ward off the attack but rather to grasp what the angel was offering him, the martyr's palm.

Most of the others pausing by the chapel's altar rail to gaze at the paintings spent only a few minutes there, as if the Caravaggios were boxes to check off on a list. Seen that, done that. Ben realized he was being judgmental. Still, he felt that assessment and judgment were key elements of his job. He also knew he was deliberately saving what he was certain would be the best for last – that only now that he'd studied the other two paintings could he look at the one considered the true classic, the undeniable masterpiece, the Caravaggio on the Contarelli Chapel's left wall, *The Calling of Saint Matthew.*

The Calling shows a room where the customs collector Matthew, then known as Levi, sits with four others as Christ and Peter enter and point across the table to a bearded man, calling him to follow them. Two other men – one with eyeglasses, the other beardless – stare down at the table counting the coins before them, oblivious to all else. Another pair – youths in striped shirts and feathered caps – stare at Peter and Christ. The youth beside the bearded man draws himself back, eyes wide, as if curious or amazed. He rests one arm casually on the bearded man's shoulder. The other young man, armed with a sword dangling at one side, leans forward, one hand on the back of his stool, preparing to rise, his other hand inches away from his sword's hilt, at the ready to fight. Sunlight streams from the doorway behind Christ, who is identified only by the thinnest of halos. He extends his right arm, his hand gesturing toward the group, as the bearded man in the center seems to pull back, his right hand pointing to his chest as if asking, Who, me? The effect is a moment of shock – fear coupled with surprise. Peter's hand also beckons to the group, so the composition seems to be a conversation among a trio of gesturing hands.

The lights illuminating the chapel and its three paintings shut off with a loud click. Ben reached into his trouser pocket and drew out a fifty-cent coin and dropped it into the light box. He felt this gave him the right to stand closer to the paintings.

He recalled how his guidebook mentioned that *The Calling* contained intentional anachronism. While the five men sitting at the table were dressed as Caravaggio and his contemporaries in the late sixteenth century dressed, Jesus and Peter were clad in clothes appropriate to their time. The idea here was perhaps that Matthew's calling wasn't a fixed moment set in the past but that Christ could call on someone in any era, at any time.

40

Both Ben's guidebook and the displays in the church discussing the paintings identified the bearded man with his hand to his chest as Levi, but Ben tried viewing *The Calling* with a skeptical eye. His years as an analyst taught him not to automatically accept what everyone else believed was true. If anything, their tacit agreement should invite him to consider the alternatives.

Since Levi was a customs man, a tax collector, he had to be one of the three older figures, so that dismissed the two startled boys. Ben knew that Caravaggio was bold, brash, frequently controversial in his selection of common people from Rome's alleys and streets as models. It was said that he deliberately chose a well-known Roman prostitute to pose as the Virgin standing with the Christ Child in a doorway. *The Madonna of Loreto*, which hung in Sant'Agostino. He and Elena planned on seeing it later that afternoon. Ben also knew that Caravaggio painted nearly nude, laughing young boys for wealthy cardinals who favored laughing young nude boys. Caravaggio's paintings were often considered overly realistic and therefore vulgar, as he was. One of the pilgrims depicted in *The Madonna of Loreto* had scandalously filthy feet. Several times Caravaggio was said to have thrown stones at Roman guards. He wrote satirical poems about a rival, and famously threw a plate of artichokes at a waiter after the man refused to tell him whether the carciofi had been cooked in oil or butter. Caravaggio was often involved in drunken brawls and fistfights, and on the Piazza Navona, the very square he and Elena had crossed earlier that morning, he was routinely apprehended for threatening passersby with his sword. After Caravaggio killed, possibly unintentionally, an opponent over a game of racquets, the pope sentenced him to death. Caravaggio fled south to Naples, then Malta and Sicily. Hoping for a pardon, he sailed back north with three new paintings he trusted would buy his freedom, but before reaching Rome he died of fever.

What if Levi was the bespectacled man to the bearded fellow's right, or the dark-haired fellow in the painting's bottom left corner, the one keeping his head down while his hands counted the money lying before him on the table? What if Matthew was one of the two ignoring Christ? Maybe the bearded pointer was simply someone else, another customs man, say, or someone who'd come to Levi's quarters to pay his taxes. After all, Ben noted, the heads of all three men were in the painting's light. What if Caravaggio was purposefully being ambiguous, suggesting that at the moment of calling one never really knows?

No, Ben decided after a while, the idea was too modern, too ironic, even for an artist as unconventional as Caravaggio. Still, the reading made the painting even richer since there certainly must have been times when Christ called someone and was ignored. Would that make Christ persistent? Ben wondered. Would Christ call a second time? A third? Ben shook his head. No, the displays in the church and the guidebooks were likely accurate. The well-dressed bearded man pointing to his own chest was Matthew, caught precisely in the moment of his recognition and fear.

Elena came up behind Ben then and wrapped her arms around his waist. "Startled, isn't he?" she said in a whisper, gesturing toward the bearded pointer.

She saw exactly what she was supposed to see, Ben thought.

"He's the picture of amazement," Elena continued.

"He knows his goose is cooked," Ben said. "It's the end of the world as he knows it."

"'And I feel fine,'" Elena responded, then softly hummed a few bars of the R.E.M. song. She poked her husband's ribs. "Listen to us, quoting rock lyrics in a Roman church. We'll be excommunicated."

Ben laughed. "I won't tell the pope if you don't."

"Come on," Elena said, "let's get something to eat. I'm starving."

As they walked down the side aisle neither glanced back at the sacristy's doorway, which displayed above its top rail a winged skull carved of white marble in bas-relief. On their way out of the church, Elena dropped several euros into the basket of the old woman, who stared at the hem of Elena's copper skirt as she offered the rich foreigner and the man who hurried past her blessing.

"OF COURSE I'D go along with it," Elena was saying. They were sitting across from each other in a booth in a swank wine bar on the Piazza di Pasquino, sharing a platter of antipasto. "Wouldn't you? I mean, you'd have no choice."

"You'd divorce me?" Ben said, laughing, feigning disbelief.

"This isn't an issue of divorcing or not divorcing someone," Elena said. "If Jesus himself appeared to me? If he asked me to follow him?" She shook her head. "Something like that, Ben, it would absolutely change a person's life."

"You'd cut your hair, make vows of poverty and chastity, enter a convent?"

"Sure, or at least I'd like to think I would. I'd do it in a heartbeat. And I'd vow obedience as well if that's what God asked me to do."

"No you wouldn't."

"Yes I would. If God asked. Without a second thought."

Ben drew in a breath. "No, you just like to think you would." He was serious now. "People like to think that in any given situation they'll do the right thing, take the path that's moral, but in reality people end up doing what they've always done." He shook his head. "If you want to know what someone will do tomorrow all you have to do is look at what they're doing today. Past behavior is among the best predictors. People don't just snap their fingers, do a one-eighty, transform their way of life."

"Honey, we're talking about a visitation from God."

After their initial jokes – the first thing Elena would do was put disinfectant on Christ's wounds, while Ben would offer Jesus a single malt and sit him down to talk stock options – they grew serious. "OK," Ben said and sighed, "so let's just say for the sake of discussion that such things are possible. After all, here we are, two very lapsed Roman Catholics in the most Roman Catholic city in the world." He nodded, as if to be certain she followed him. "No offense, Elena, but both you and I and just about every other person in the world would run away from God as fast as our legs could carry us. We'd deny him and do whatever we could to get back to our normal way of life."

"Speak for yourself, Ben. I know it's not hip, but I'm a lot less lapsed than you think." Elena paused. "I know what's in my heart."

The wine bar was a busy place, with a long aisle separating its double rows of booths and varnished tables. Above each table at head's height a black netting was strung on which patrons were meant to place their bags and coats. Everywhere above the nets were shelves stacked with bottles of wine, standing in rows that brushed the bar's tall ceiling. Ben had ordered a glass of Barbaresco, a Nebbiolo grape variety that he suspected would pair well with a bowl of pizzoccheri. Elena said it was too early for wine and drank mineral water. She'd ordered pasta with a Sicilian sauce.

"I don't want to have to apologize for my family's religion," Elena told Ben after a while. "And I don't think I believe you. You're just saying you'd be unaffected."

"Thank you, no," Ben said, "but when it comes to visitations from deities I'll take a pass." He sipped his Barbaresco. "Life's complicated enough."

"You wouldn't be in the least bit curious?"

"No."

"Seriously, you wouldn't be overcome with awe? You wouldn't even listen to what the vision had to say?"

"Remember back in grammar school," Ben said, "when we were taught about those apparitions from the Virgin? You know – Lourdes, Guadalupe, Fátima? Mary suddenly popping up in front of a gang of poor kids? Most of my class envied the kids because that's what the nuns expected of us, that we'd welcome the visions, but I didn't. Not a single bit. I knew I'd be so scared I'd be the first to turn and run."

"No, you wouldn't," Elena said. She thought of the French girl from Lourdes, Marie Bernadette Soubirous, who obediently washed her hands and face with dirt after being asked to do so by the Blessed Virgin. She thought of the shepherd children in Fátima, Portugal, to whom Mary revealed three secrets before the sun in the sky swirled and danced. "No, Ben," Elena insisted. "I know you. I know your heart. If something like that happened to you, just the sight of Mary's cloak would melt your soul."

"Talk about melting your soul. For the love of God, try a bite of this pizzoccheri."

Elena reached across the table with her spoon and sampled some of the pizzoccheri, a Northern dish made of buttered noodles, potatoes, and melted cheese. "I always envied the visionaries," she said after she smiled and then reached across the table for another spoonful. "In church sometimes I'd squeeze my eyes shut and try to imagine what they'd seen. The glowing apparition of a beautiful woman, standing there before me. Imagine it for a moment. The divine revealing itself."

"This wine – you should order a glass – it's superb." Ben paused after Elena waved the offer away. "I don't know why you're not drinking."

"Once in school," Elena said, "the nun – I think her name was Sister Felicia, yes, Sister Mary Felicia, she was new, in her first or second year of teaching – anyway, she gave each of us a little blue composition booklet and asked us to write down what we'd do if the Virgin Mary appeared to us."

"I hope you were honest and said you'd wet your pants."

"I wrote that I'd do whatever was asked of me. I'd change my life. Regardless of what anyone else thought." Elena hesitated, then laughed and slowly shook her head. "When my mother would ask me to do something around the house, I sometimes made believe I was carrying out a task assigned to me by Mary herself. You know, something simple, everyday, like drying the supper dishes or dusting the living room or vacuuming. The nuns suggested we do that. Cultivate joy from obedience and servitude. So I'd do whatever my mother asked me to do as carefully and perfectly as I could, with happiness in my heart, all the while pretending I'd be rewarded later with a sign. With a miracle."

"Miracles," Ben said and smiled. "After this past October, that's certainly something I've come to believe in." His glass of Barbaresco was empty. Thinking of his favorite team, the Boston Red Sox, he was in a good mood now. "Ortiz's walk-off homer in game four. Now that was a miracle if there ever was one."

"Ben," Elena said.

"Of course Mueller's single in the ninth to drive in Roberts and tie the game has to count as one too." He wagged his head. "Talk about overcoming the curse of the Bambino!"

"You don't ever really pray anymore, do you?"

"I sure do. But mainly when the winning run's on second or third base."

"Ben, that's not what we're talking about."

"Down three games to none," Ben continued, "their backs to the wall, three outs away from elimination. And my boys come back with a victory! How can you think about it and not be thrilled?" He gestured to a passing waiter for another glass of wine. "Ortiz's RBI single in the bottom of the fourteenth the following day. Schilling pitching game six in Yankee Stadium with a sock soaked with blood, earning the win and forcing an improbable game seven. Hang paintings of those moments in a chapel and I'll happily kneel and bow my head in adoration."

Elena stopped listening as Ben continued down the list of plays that won both the American League Championship and the World Series for his beloved Red Sox. Instead she watched as a waiter paused at a cabinet against the wall in the center of the wine bar and swung open a low drawer hinged at its bottom and then bent and cut a section off a loaf of bread. The compartment he swung open was full of fat loaves of bread. The waiter's arm sawed up and down, like a carpenter's. He cut half of the loaf nearly all the way through, into thick slices that fanned open like the pages of a book, leaving the half loaf in one piece, the crust on the opposite side intact. Then he dropped the remaining bread back into the bin and carried the cut bread in a basket to a table where a man in a dark suit with a round bald spot on the back of his head – a monk, perhaps, or a priest – sat with a few friends.

Canadians, Elena guessed, by the laughing couple wearing matching red sweaters sporting maple leaves. The suited man turned sideways and for a moment Ellen saw his Roman collar. He sat next to an older woman who looked Italian. Yes, likely a Canadian church group, here in Rome for the holidays, the four now passing around the basket, breaking bread together, as the priest bowed his head and the others followed his lead and crossed themselves. Then a slim, lovely woman – Asian – rushed in through the doorway. "Lucy," the four Canadians cried out. "Our lost, wayward lamb Lucy. Lucy, we're so glad you could join us."

If Christ or the Blessed Virgin ever revealed themselves to her, Elena thought as she sipped her glass of mineral water, she'd try her best not to be frightened. She'd do all that was asked of her and afterward try not to feel proud. Of course she understood Ben's point, that most people would resist. They'd deny what was happening and do whatever they could to cling to the life they were used to. The daily grind of ordinary life was hard enough, she thought, without being assigned new things to do.

Still, Elena knew, the Virgin would never appear to someone like her. She was too comfortable, too affluent. Compared with the rest of the world, she and Ben possessed riches beyond imagination. If God ever made himself evident to her, it would be to remind her that before she could enter the kingdom of Heaven she'd have to pass through the eye of a needle. Elena remembered Sister Felicia explaining that there was a gate outside the walled city of Jerusalem known as the Eye of the Needle. It was so narrow and squat that in order for a camel to pass through it at night, when the city's gates were locked, the beast had to be stripped of everything it carried and work its way through the tiny passageway on its knees. That was the true meaning of what the apostle Matthew meant in the Gospels. They were to think of that gate, Sister Felicia said. They were to imagine a camel with its clumsy hump emptied of all of its belongings, trying to crawl through a narrow gap on its knees.

No, Elena decided, as laughter from the Canadian's table washed over her booth, the Virgin Mary would choose some poor woman in South America or India or Korea. Or like now, Croatia, or was it Bosnia and Herzegovina. Medugorje. She'd appear in some place torn apart by war. As for Christ, maybe he'd walk through the doorway of a billionaire at a board meeting on Wall Street or Hong Kong or the headquarters of a Swiss bank, or else he'd choose a humble farmer somewhere in the Southern Hemisphere tilling the drought-cracked soil of a field with a wooden hoe. Christ wouldn't pick a stocks trader from Boston and his librarian wife, who on the weekends did her best to sell real estate, and who wasn't above suggesting to her clients that they bury a statue of Saint Joseph upside down, face staring out at the street, near the *For Sale* sign in their front yard.

Elena remembered the rest of what she'd written in her blue composition booklet. That after doing whatever tasks the Virgin asked of her, she'd enter a convent, maybe even a cloistered convent, somewhere miles away from everything else. Somewhere far away from cities, someplace surrounded by trees, enclosed by mountains, towering rock walls, a place of perpetual silence, a convent where she would work and pray, where the only sounds would be the shuffling of feet and the soft clang of lids and pots in the kitchen and occasional ringing bells and the nightly song of prayers.

Her pasta – gemelli – was fresh and perfectly al dente. She knew that in Italian the word *gemelli* meant *twins*, and for a moment Elena wondered if she might be carrying twins. She reached down her hand and touched her abdomen. A hint of anchovy in the Sicilian sauce lent the dish a luscious depth. She could eat what she wanted, at least for a little while, she realized. She smiled. The developing child or children within her gave her appetite sudden license. Elena picked up her fork and ate freely as Ben continued happily talking about his world champions Boston Red Sox.

THEY PAUSED IN the piazza outside the restaurant to look at the talking statue of Pasquino, for which the square was named. The statue stood against a wall closed in by a row of parked motorcycles and Fiats. A pair of cats – one a gray tabby, the other black with white mittens and locket – perched imperiously on top of the hood of one of the cars.

As the story went, in the 1500s the statue stood outside the shop of an opinionated barber named Pasquino, who dared not voice his views about the government lest he be arrested. Regardless, he wrote out his opinions about Roman politics in satirical verse, then at night when no one was looking hung his rhymed lines on the statue. Soon his satires became known as *pasquinades*. Then, under the cover of darkness, other Romans snuck into the square to hang their penned criticisms of Church and state on the statue too. After the pope ordered soldiers to stand guard over the statue, seizing anyone who dared to place even the slightest scrap of paper on it, other statues around the city began talking too.

The talking statue itself was a formless mass – an armless torso with a stump of a right leg and a nearly featureless head. At the statue's base lay a bouquet of decaying red roses, the edges of each petal curled and black. Taped to the statue were dozens of verses in Italian and English, most of them criticisms of George W. Bush and the escalating war in Iraq. One wrote the "s" in Bush's name in the shape of a swastika. There were countless complaints against Prime Minister Berlusconi. A few sad farewells in English from people who lived in Rome and now through twists in their lives were forced to leave. On fresh squares of paper were poems in Italian about the South-Asian tsunami.

"Tragedia Sud-Est Asiatico," Elena said aloud, pointing to one of the verses. The images she and Ben had seen on television in their hotel room that morning were so painful that she had to shut the set off. Certainly, Elena thought, if Christ and the Virgin Mary were still making apparitions they'd walk among these suffering souls, soothing them, lending them comfort and strength. They'd appear to the families whose houses were swept away, the parents whose children were trampled in the widening panic to escape the rushing waters, the mothers who felt the terrible sea rip their infants from their grasps and swallow them up in the muddy, raging waters. If the presence of the divine still manifested itself in the world, Elena thought, no doubt it was working overtime today in South-East Asia, where it was reported that hundreds of thousands had been killed.

She felt a moment of bitterness. She knew that God was incapable of causing evil, but what would it have taken God to have prevented the sky-high waves from striking the coasts of the many countries affected? The twitch of an eye? The least flick of a wrist? Wasn't it contradictory to praise the Almighty and thank him for a beautiful day, then somehow absolve him of all responsibility for a natural catastrophe?

No, she thought, in response to her own doubts. Just as the nuns instructed, it was both useless and vain to try to understand the mind of God. God's ways were strange and mysterious. As Hamlet told Horatio, there were more things in Heaven and Earth than were dreamt of in their philosophies. Our attempts to understand God's ways were as futile as an ant trying to lift a mountain, and certainly as feeble as taping a verse of protest on a nearly formless piece of stone.

THE CRAMPING BEGAN on the walk back to the hotel, and by the time they reached their room Elena said she needed to lie down. She lay on the bed tightly, curled like a child's fist. For a while she slept, or at least it seemed so to Ben, who filed their lunch receipt with their other expenses and tallied their expenditures in a small ledger. Then he punched their personal code into their hotel room safe and counted their remaining euros. The safe issued a soft beep as he pressed each number of the code. Ben used a number no one else might know, the street address of his parents' brownstone in Boston. He wondered how the dollar stood in relation to the euro. Then Elena awoke and went to the bathroom.

"I'm bleeding," she said a moment later. Her lower lip quivered as she leaned in the bathroom doorway. She trembled, then began to cry.

The ambulance rushed them through the weave of narrow streets. It made that scary two-tone siren sound, *NEE-eu, NEE-eu, NEE-eu,* that always reminded Ben of chase scenes in French and Italian movies. The sound made everything seem less than real, as if all that was now happening were somehow underwater or occurring to someone else. Ben held Elena's hand and could feel himself beginning to shut down. He could sense parts of himself detaching. The detached parts wanted to stand somewhere else and remain safely unaffected. He noticed how the plane trees overhanging the sidewalk edging the Tiber's banks formed a symmetrical arch as their branches dipped down toward the river. He wondered if plane trees and sycamores were two different types of trees or the same species of tree but with different names. He stared at the graffiti painted on the riverbank's walls. On the rocks in the rushing river stood a trio of cormorants, two of them sunning themselves, their dark black wings stretched outward, like Halloween bats.

They were taken to the Fatebenefratelli Hospital on Tiber Island. A pair of orderlies in green scrubs flicked their cigarettes into the bushes before easing Elena's gurney down from the ambulance. The electric doors of the hospital opened, and in a moment the gurney was whisked away. Ben was required to wait in line to see a woman seated before a computer monitor, then attend to the paperwork. He had trouble understanding what was expected of him. Several times someone was called over to translate. Finally he was pointed toward a room and instructed to wait.

THE HOSPITAL WAS a busy place, more like a train station than a hospital, Ben thought, sections neatly partitioned, nearly everything marked by signs. Ben paced the room in which he was told to wait. It was crowded, with plastic chairs spaced unevenly against the walls. The air held the mixed smells of antiseptic and pine floor cleaner. Several people dozed in the chairs. In one chair an elderly woman dangled the glistening glass beads of a rosary. The only decoration on the walls was a dark wooden cross.

"It will be hours," a man waiting there told Ben. He spoke in English. "Hours and hours before they return, and then what they will tell you is that they know nothing."

Ben nodded, not really understanding.

"Then they will tell you to wait. Then it will be hours once again."

Again Ben nodded.

"I have been here since last night," the man said. He opened both hands and raised them to waist level, then gave Ben a broad shrug. "You might as well go outside. Visit the coffee bar by San Bartolomeo, only a few minutes away. Coffee will keep you awake. You are from America?"

Ben nodded a third time.

"Well, maybe with someone from America it will be more quicker. Maybe not. But in any case the waiting" – again he shrugged – "it will be hours before they return."

Their trip was supposed to have been a celebration, a new beginning, something that would refresh and invigorate their lives. Ben remembered that when Elena had suggested they go somewhere over the holidays he was in a foul mood, watching the Red Sox lose their third game in a row to the Yankees. It was precisely because of Ben's hatred for the Yankees that he made Elena a proposition. Sure, he said, I'll gladly talk about a trip if the Sox come back and win on Sunday. After their surprising victory that Sunday, Elena reminded him about what he'd said. Laughing, playing along, Ben proposed a more complex deal. Let my boys win again tomorrow and we can drive somewhere north. And if they come back later in the week and win again? Elena said. You mean if my Sox win the championship? Ben asked. The words were nearly too delicious to come out of his mouth. Then we'll fly somewhere, Ben said. And if they go on to win the World Series? Elena said. No, Ben thought, that was far too much to think about, let alone ask for. If they win the World Series, Ben promised, we can go anywhere in the world you want.

Rome, Elena said without hesitation.

Deal, Ben said.

They shook hands, then laughed and kissed. Now, Ben thought, he'd trade the thrill of each of his team's victories for Elena's wellbeing.

HE WAS BEGINNING to feel nauseous, tight-chested, as if he couldn't breathe, so he decided to walk outside, if only for a moment of fresh air. Confused by the hospital's halls, Ben walked out through the building's front entrance. He didn't know the island was shaped like a ship, that travertine had been added to the island's banks so that they resembled a ship's bow and stern. It was late afternoon. A steady wind blew at him from the north. On both sides of the river, lights sparkled brightly, then melted and blurred as if they were splattered stars. Ben wiped away his tears. He drew in a deep breath to steel himself. He told himself to calm down, that he wouldn't know anything until there was something to know.

Rome was busy celebrating the twelve days of Christmas. Traffic on both sides of the river rumbled by, occasionally slowing to a stop, then speeding away again. There was the *NEE-eu, NEE-eu, NEE-eu* of another ambulance. The impressive square dome of the great synagogue, the Tempio Maggiore, rose majestically over the line of trees. Elena had said she wanted to visit it. Of course, they could go there tomorrow, he decided. Will she be up for it? he wondered. A pair of gulls broke suddenly, taking wing from beneath a line of overhanging plane trees on the far bank.

The currents in the Tiber were impressively swift, and the river itself was filthy, the color of churning mud. All Ben could hear now was the sound of the furious, rushing river. A fisherman stood to one side, his line taut in the fast-moving waters. On the bare branches of the bushes and trees lining the banks hung the torn remnants of hundreds of white plastic bags, the kind given to customers in shops. There were so many bags caught in the branches that the trees appeared covered with lint or decorated for the holidays. In the fierce wind the bags whipped and crackled. The fisherman nodded as he held with both hands the long pole connected to the plumb straightness of his steady line.

A flock of starlings rose in the sky, then swirled into a tight black knot and spread out like a cloud again. Ben walked with his back to the wind, toward the church and the twin bridges linking the island to Rome and Trastevere. He could barely hear the starlings now over the roar of the rushing river. The birds swarmed thickly, their murmuration expanding and contracting, fluidly taking shape, presenting as a single dark mass, then separating into two, then blending again into a rolling, pulsing darkness spread high in the sky. More noisy birds filled the branches of the trees on the Trastevere side of the bridge.

Crossing the bridge from Rome on his way to Trastevere was the performer with the striped shirt, feathered cap, and fancy sword Ben had seen on the Piazza Navona. He was walking alongside a pair of monks or priests in black hooded robes. One of the monks carried a walking stick that, as Ben neared the three men, he saw was actually a scythe. Ben then noticed that there was something wrong with both monks. The wind blew their dark hoods back over their heads and Ben could see their painted faces – their white cheeks, foreheads and chins, their blackened noses and lips and eye sockets. The twin skulls gazed at Ben for a moment and then the group paused to form a circle, in which one cupped his hands and lit a cigarette as the other skull said something, and all three performers laughed.

JUST BEYOND WHERE the group stood was a four-sided spire and a church, San Bartolomeo all'Isola. Ben knew he should probably return to the waiting room, but the iron gates of the church stood open, inviting. Ben guessed he had another few moments of time.

Arched windows to the right of the nave let in a fading light. Ben gazed up at the ceiling but the light was too dim to make out any details. He was drawn to the main altar, where protruding from the center of the third of its seven steps was an ancient carved white marble wellhead. Ben wasn't aware of Tiber Island's long history of healing the sick. He didn't know that the Church of San Bartolomeo all'Isola was built on the site of the temple of Aesculapius, the Greek god of medicine and cures, and that the wellhead was equally old and its waters were believed to be miraculous. On the step beside the wellhead lay a small oval of shining water pooled in a shallow depression on the stone.

Ben hesitated, his memory triggered by the detail. He recalled an incident from his boyhood in North Boston, back when his faith was active. Barely thirteen, an altar boy dressed in a black cassock and white surplice, assigned to serve the early 6:45 Saturday morning Mass, he stood at the altar lighting the candles beside the tabernacle. He used the parish candlelighter, a long wooden pole fit with a wax wick and extinguishing brass bell. As he lit the two candles he sensed – unmistakably – someone standing suddenly behind him. He knew that the only other person in the church was the priest, smoking his usual pre-Mass cigarette in the sacristy as he donned his vestments.

Ben was afraid. He imagined that if the presence were the devil he could make the sign of the Cross and perhaps banish the demon back to Hell. This was after *The Exorcist* and its many imitators had made the rounds. Ben had seen them all. He both loved and hated the films. They frightened him to the core. Yes, he thought in a moment of Hollywood bravado, he could whirl around and strike the demon with the candlelighter. And if in retaliation Satan struck him dead, well, just imagine the rich rewards in Heaven that awaited an altar boy slain by Satan on the steps of his North End parish church!

Then in the next half moment the part of Ben's mind that turned ideas around and questioned things imagined that the presence might not be a demon. Perhaps the presence was a saint or angel or, even worse, Christ himself. Just a few weeks before, a traveling missionary priest had visited his classroom to talk about the concept of vocations.

Not vacations with an "a" the priest had told the class. Vocations with an "o." He had all of the children shout out a loud "o." It was an exciting break from the nun's usual lessons to shout in class along with a foreign missionary.

Callings, the man said. That's what vocations are. Callings. A summons, an invitation to service. The priest had the rugged jaw of a hockey player, hair so thick and wavy you'd think he'd stolen it from a girl, a voice so deep and confident it made you want to do nearly anything it asked of you. The priest mimed knocking on a door. Pretend that I'm our Lord, Jesus Christ, and I'm standing out on your stoop. *I've chosen you*, I say when you answer my knocks. Then I ask you a question, the most important question you'll ever be asked by anyone in your life. Are you ready to hear that question?

Yes! the children shouted.

The missionary smiled, then mimed knocking on the door again. His voice fell to a whisper. He paused for dramatic effect, and with one hand brushed back his marvelous hair. *Will you give up everything you have to follow me?*

The class sat motionless, silent.

That means giving up all of your belongings, the priest said in a soft, even voice. All of your toys. Your baseball bat and glove. Your Barbie dolls and all of their pretty clothing. Your favorite clothes too.

By now the children were stunned. A few were already nodding in agreement.

Or say you're simply standing somewhere and you feel someone behind you, and then you feel the slightest tap on your shoulder. The missionary had the children touch the shoulder of the child who sat in front of them. Don't turn around, the priest said. Pretend for a moment that what you feel is the hand of Christ himself, and he taps your shoulder with the same hand through which the sharpest of spikes was driven as he was crucified for the forgiveness of your sins. That same bleeding hand now touches your shoulder, and as you turn you hear him ask, Are you ready to give up everything and follow me?

As Ben stood staring at the ancient wellhead on the altar steps of San Bartolomeo, he remembered how the idea that he was about to be asked to follow Christ and have to give up everything in his life had terrified him so greatly that a hot line of urine burned its way down his leg. Ben remembered looking down at the floor, watching the urine puddle around his shoes. He had to squeeze the candlelighter beneath his arm and draw his wet cassock up to his knees as if it were a skirt and scurry back to the sacristy and confess to the priest what he'd done. By then he was in tears and could hardly speak.

The priest stubbed out his cigarette and led Ben to a bathroom in the rectory, where he told the boy to change his clothes and wash himself. A spare roll of toilet paper sat atop the toilet's tank inside a knitted cozy on which was a row of bright green shamrocks. For some reason the shamrocks – symbol of the Holy Trinity, one God with three divine persons, or faces, distinct yet equal, eternal and consubstantial – made Ben cry even more. The priest gave Ben underwear and a pair of Bermuda shorts so big they bunched at his waist. He had the boy run back to the servers' room for a fresh cassock. When Ben returned, the priest was kneeling before the tabernacle, wiping the pool of urine from the floor.

IN HER BED in the ward of the hospital, Elena struggled to open her eyes. She lay on her back, confused, trying to locate herself. For several moments she was convinced she was a girl in her parents' house and that she'd done something terribly wrong.

She could hear a man and a woman talking, distantly, as if they were in a nearby room. Their voices suggested both alarm and concern. Regardless of what they were saying, Elena knew that what they were talking about was her fault. Something horrible had happened, and she was to blame.

That was why she liked libraries, because no one was allowed to speak or argue in a library. For a moment she felt how enjoyable it was to sit at one of the library's long wooden tables, writing in her blue composition booklet. How she always felt at ease strolling among the library's silent, ordered rows of books. How the spine of each book stood tall and straight on its shelf, proudly displaying its title along with its call number. How all of the numbers were in order, organized in tidy rows. How the shelved books enclosed and comforted her, like the walls of a fortress, like the arms of a dear friend. How the sweet, mildly nutty, slightly dusty smell of books was to her a dark, soothing perfume.

Why couldn't she understand her parents? Were they upset because she was in a library? They were talking so insistently now that Elena knew it was crucial that she make sense of what they were saying. Her thoughts were like soap bubbles hanging before her in the air. No sooner would she reach for one than it would pop. Then another bubble would form, and a lazy moment would pass – or was it a matter of minutes, several minutes, longer, an hour or more. Had she fallen back to sleep? Was she drifting in and out of sleep? She shouldn't be sleeping, she thought, alarmed now, particularly if she was in her school's library. She should be working or studying!

Someone was touching her shoulder now – the school nurse? – and Elena realized that the voices she thought were her parents' were actually those of a man and a woman on television. Elena forced her eyes to focus on the television monitor angled down toward her bed from the corner of the hospital room in which she lay. She looked up at a nurse who smiled down on her, then gave her shoulder a soft squeeze before walking away. Gradually Elena understood that two Roman newscasters were reporting the latest developments concerning that morning's earthquake and tsunami in South Asia. Images of the furious waters played over and over again behind the newscasters' heads on a wide grid of segmented screens.

Then the memory of who and where she was rushed back, and Elena's eyes welled with tears. She moved her right arm to make the sign of the Cross, and as she did so she felt the pain of something fierce and stinging – the sharp needle of an intravenous line connecting her to an IV drip – taped securely to the back of her hand.

And though Elena would continue to blame herself, to go over each and every thing she'd done and hadn't done during the weeks she was pregnant, the doctors would insist that it wasn't her fault, that the fetus simply wasn't viable. Something about chromosomes, either too many or not enough. How the fetus could never have developed normally no matter what the woman did. How this was not uncommon among first trimester miscarriages.

WHEN BEN RETURNED to the room where he'd been told to wait, the Italian who'd spoken to him earlier was no longer there. The old woman with the rosary was gone too. In their place was a family, one with several children, swinging their legs on the plastic chairs. One child lay on the floor with a box of crayons and a coloring book. Another played with a green dinosaur and a small figure of the Befana. The child made the dinosaur – a Tyrannosaurus rex – leap up and try to bite the Befana as she flew back and forth over the creature's head. Then the Befana dove down sharply and gave the dinosaur's snout a smack with her broom before the beast pushed her down to the floor and ate her.

Finally a doctor in scrubs walked in with a nun in a blue habit. The nun wore a veil and tunic that were dark blue, the color of a late evening sky. In English the doctor explained to Ben that Elena had actively miscarried.

"That can't be right," Ben said, "She's not – "

Likely they would need to perform additional procedures, and certainly she would need to stay in the hospital for a few more days. They would know more later that night or the following morning.

He could see her in a few hours, the doctor said, but not now. As for now she needed rest. As for now they had given her something so that she'd sleep.

The white bandeau, coif, and guimpe the nun wore beneath her blue veil seemed unnaturally bright. Hanging below the guimpe atop her dark tunic was a large cross, nearly the size of a man's hand. The cross was the color of bone. Ben stared at the large, bone-colored cross.

The nun's eyes met Ben's as she said something to him in Italian. She extended her arm toward him, pointing, the index finger of her hand outstretched like Christ's, like in the painting. Ben didn't understand what she was saying but he could see that the hand was signaling to him, and then he understood that she wanted him to come with her, to follow her, so that she might lead him to a place where he could pray.

Lepinja

Dubrovnik, February 1981

You know he comes around to see you, Marija said. You, the girl repeated, extending her arm and pointing a finger. Wake up and face your life. He's not hanging around the back door, smelling of fish, waiting for me.

Marija and Dubravka were baking bread in Zagorac's kitchen, Marija's father's restaurant on Ulica Od Puča in Dubrovnik's Old City. Just a few blocks off the Stradun, during the height of tourist season Zagorac's dozen or so tables were usually full. The restaurant specialized in the skinless sausage ćevapčići. Minced pork, beef, and sometimes lamb mixed with garlic, onions, paprika, and other spices, the small kebab was grilled and served with lemon wedges, a splash of sour cream, and ajvar, a sauce made of eggplant and red peppers, along with lepinja, a fluffy flatbread Dubravka and her cousin were responsible for making. An old radio set high up on the kitchen cupboards, out of reach, played while the girls worked, set night and day to a station offering instrumental music from across Europe and Western Asia. This afternoon's program featured classic Italian songs from Napoli. "O Sole Mio." "Santa Lucia." "Finiculi, Finiculà."

But that makes no sense, Dubravka said. This boy, we hardly know each other. Why in the world would he want to talk to me?

Stupid, Marija said. You know nothing. Less than nothing.

The times I've walked past him, Dubravka said, he nodded to me and smiled, but I thought he was waiting for you.

No, Marija said. She seemed annoyed. You are so completely dumb.

Me, dumb? Tell me, how can you be so sure?

How do you think? Marija said. I opened my mouth. I asked him.

You talked to him? Dubravka said. That was bold.

Marija laughed. Bold? You really don't know anything, do you? Talking to the boy was nothing. I only asked him a simple question.

Truth was, Marija knew full well he was no boy. The young man she spoke to was at least nineteen, if not in his early twenties. His name was Stanislav, a fish seller whose family was from Mostar in Bosnia and Herzegovina. He was quite proud of himself and his ability to work on the sea, both by spearfishing off Lokrum Island in the Adriatic's clear waters – he caught white sea bass, dorado, drum, a few snapper, using a trident spear – and assisting his father on their boat bringing in the nets and sorting the day's catch. The father allowed the son to pocket the money he made from the restaurants that purchased the fish he speared. As a result Stanislav felt himself both powerful and rich. When he was on land he walked about with his head tilted slightly, chin down, gazing out at the town and whoever passed by him with a dark, brooding, challenging demeanor, like someone both looking for and ready for a fight. He was tanned, keenly muscled from swimming and diving, with dark eyes and short hair clipped nearly to his scalp. When he was in Dubrovnik he lived with his father near the Serbian Orthodox Church of the Holy Annunciation. When in Mostar, he stayed with a pair of widowed aunts.

Dubravka laughed since the conversation made her nervous and at the same time excited and a bit frightened. She was sixteen and a more plain version of her cousin. The girls would joke that if they were photographs Marija would be in full color, Kodachrome, while Dubravka would be in old-fashioned sepia or simply black and white. Maybe a bit blurred, a bit washed out, Marija would add, stepping back and framing Dubravka with her thumbs and first fingers, like a photographer setting up a shot. Your features, she'd tell her cousin, they seem a bit out of focus. If you were bread I'd pop you back in the oven. I'd also do something about your flat chest. Sometimes Dubravka studied herself in a mirror. She felt her arms were too long. Her nose, a bit too wide. She wanted shorter, more dainty arms, as well as a thinner nose, like the arms and noses on the women who graced the shiny covers of magazines.

The two girls were roughly the same size and often borrowed each other's clothes, though Marija was more compact and much more shapely. They were often mistaken for the other until the viewer got close. Marija was two years older, nearly eighteen, with smooth olive skin and luxuriant long black hair. Full lips. Dark brown eyes that pierced whatever they looked at, like sharpened arrows. She wore blouses that revealed a bit of cleavage and was more than pleased with her body, its absolute and undeniable youth. She swore she'd never end up like her mother or her mother's six sisters, miserable dumplings in housedresses and babushkas. Overcooked apples smothered in thick layers of dough. At least Dubravka's mother had the good sense to get away while she was still young.

Marija was certain that someday she'd get away, at least across the sea to Italy if not up to Hungary or Austria or perhaps even over to Switzerland and France. She didn't yet know how she'd accomplish it, but she was certain someday she'd get her chance. Maybe some rich young foreign tourist would see her on the Stradun and smile, then follow her to her father's restaurant. He'd be the son of a millionaire and have his own helicopter. Late one starry night they'd fly away together into the sky.

Marija was bright, clever. So clever she was able to hide a few bottles of slivovitz in the kitchen's cupboards behind stacks of pots and pans no one ever used or looked into. A drink or two — sometimes more — helped break up the boredom of daily work.

I tell you, Marija told her younger cousin, he's out there waiting for you. I'm serious. He swore to me on his mother's grave he just wants to talk. Marija laughed. So talk to him. I dare you. Just don't believe a word he says.

Why don't you talk to him? Dubravka said.

Marija laughed again. Didn't you hear me before? I already did. It got me nowhere. Trust me, she told Dubravka, I'm more than familiar with his type. He thinks he's the real shit, like all the boys from Bosnia. But at the same time don't be stupid about it. He's not like the others from around here. Marija paused. Besides, we both know that you're old enough now for a boyfriend. And who knows — she gave out yet another laugh — maybe this one could be your chance to escape.

ESCAPE, DUBRAVKA THOUGHT. She very much liked the idea of escape, and already she felt she needed to make plans. What they would be she didn't know yet, but she knew that without a plan one risked wandering about in circles. Dubravka confided her thoughts to her confessor, Father Josip, her favorite priest at Saint Blaise.

Father Josip was a thin man, rumpled, with a bad leg and waddling limp, fond of hand-rolled cigarettes and travarica, a grape brandy infused with a variety of herbs. Ever since Dubravka could remember he had always been kind to her, sometimes calling her *dear* or *little chicken* or *my child*. Sometimes with the hand that passed out Holy Communion he stroked her shoulder or touched her arm. Recently he'd paused by the pew where Dubravka was kneeling to ask why she was spending so much time in church while the other girls her age were out on the Stradun or walking along the city's harbor, doing the things girls her age normally did. If you stay in here too long, he joked, you'll have nothing new to tell me when you're inside the box. He gestured toward one of the church's confessionals.

Dubravka didn't know how to answer. She enjoyed praying. She enjoyed reciting the words of prayers with what she thought of as her mind's whisper, a quiet voice that only she and God could hear. She'd go over each phrase slowly, dwelling on its meaning. When she recited the Hail Mary and came to the phrase *Blessed art thou among women*, admiration for the Blessed Virgin would swell in Dubravka's heart, filling her warmly with joy. She felt pride in being female. She was grateful to the Almighty for having created the Virgin Mary without sin, as God did his son, and she was grateful that the Catholic Church acknowledged this. She believed that Mary, a first-century BCE Jewish woman from Nazareth – a nothing little scrap of a town in Galilee – was the closest any human being ever came to being God. Of course, that wasn't counting Christ, but the comparison was hardly fair since Christ was both God as well as God's son. Mary of Nazareth was fully human.

Other parts of her prayers tripped her. The Our Father had the phrase *Lead us not into temptation*. Dubravka had no understanding why God would ever do that, or why we were asked to waste our breath imploring him not to do so. Was this some sort of dare or test? Wouldn't tempting us with sin be against God's nature? Wasn't temptation the work of God's enemy, Satan?

Dubravka tried explaining her fascination with prayer to Father Josip as they walked from the church's nave to the rectory, where they sat on faded upholstered armchairs in a room that sorely lacked fresh air and open windows. Sunlight angled down from the barely open windows onto a worn Anatolian carpet. Bits of dust streaming down from the windows sparkled in the still air. Dubravka politely declined something to drink and tried to explain that if she could do anything with her life she'd like to devote it to thought and prayer.

No boyfriends? Father Josip asked. He was sipping a glass of travarica. Shreds of tobacco from his cigarette clung to his lower lip. Ash spotted the front of his cassock, which appeared in need of a good washing.

Dubravka blushed and shook her head no. She liked Father Josip, especially because she was familiar with the story of how his bad leg came to be injured. When Father Josip was a boy, he was out hiking one day in the woods and saved the family's farm dog from an attack by a wolf. He sacrificed both his ankle and lower calf in the process.

No boyfriends, the priest repeated, as if it now were fact.

At a back window there was a sudden tap tap tap, something doing its best to get out. From where Dubravka was sitting she was certain it was a hummingbird.

Moljci, Father Josip said as he made his way toward the window to open it further. Moths. They fly in at night, attracted by the light. He gestured toward the clear glass globe encasing the light bulb dangling from the ceiling. They think it's the moon. He hobbled back to his chair, then asked Dubravka if she thought she had a calling for a religious life.

No, Dubravka answered again. She didn't think she wanted to become a nun. She didn't want to make priests their dinner and wash their laundry.

HE COULD BE your way out, Marija repeated. The fish-seller. Stanislav. She mouthed the boy's name slowly, as if it were a dare. There was an element of teasing – or was it jealousy? – in her voice. Dubravka couldn't tell. He told me he has family up in Bosnia, Marija continued. And he has plans to return. I'd leave in two seconds flat if I had the chance.

But you know that he's a Serb, Dubravka said. Now that the lepinja had made its first and second rises, she was dividing the mound of dough into equal portions. Later she'd need to roll each portion into a ball and flatten it in preparation for its third rise. Dubravka liked that about lepinja. It was a bread that required three times to rest and rise.

So what? Marija said. What about our brotherhood and unity?

Of course, Dubravka said. But if my father ever found out I was talking to someone Orthodox he'd slap me from here to Split.

Dubravka knew her father hated Serbs. He believed Serbs couldn't be trusted. They schemed to take over all they saw and would lay claim to anything they could get their hands on. They were an unclean race, he'd say, in league with Russia and Mongolia. All three make use of the Cyrillic alphabet, her father would point out. Serbs also had a different religion. The hypocrisy of this, Dubravka thought each time she was forced to listen to her father's ravings, from a man who went to church only on holidays, and even then hardly paid attention and normally ended up falling asleep.

Plus, all Serbs were communists, he'd tell Dubravka in a whisper no one else but the pair could hear. They'd murdered hundreds of thousands of Croat soldiers and ordinary citizens – men, women, even little children – who took refuge in Bleiburg, in Austria, just after the war ended. After the Croats surrendered, the British promised them protection. But then the bullshit Brits handed them over to the Partisans, who herded the Croats into fields where machine gunners were lying in wait in the nearby weeds. They stripped the Croats of all they had and then mowed them down as if they were playing a shooting game in an arcade. They followed this up with the križni put, the death march. Those still alive were forced to march. They were given no food, not even a drop of water to drink. The path from Austria down through Slovenia, Dubravka's father told her, is littered with hundreds of unmarked mass graves.

My father is just as bad, Marija told Dubravka. She opened a cupboard and moved several pots, then drew out one of her hidden bottles taken from behind the restaurant's bar. If I had an Orthodox boyfriend, he'd crucify me. Marija dropped her head and stuck out her tongue, spreading her arms wide as if hanging on a cross. Crown my head with thorns, she said, looking back up. Stab my side. You can look for me in three days but God knows I'll stink like last week's garbage. Then Marija laughed and poured out two glasses and handed one to Dubravka. Živjeli! she cried.

Živjeli, Dubravka said as she sipped from her glass.

From the times we talked, Marija said after a while, he seemed really nice.

The bread was now in the oven. Dubravka handed Marija her empty glass, which Marija refilled. You know, Marija said, in a way I envy you.

You can't be serious, Dubravka said.

Sure. I am serious. She paused. You're the chosen one.

No, Dubravka said. You must be wrong.

Yes, Marija said. I was so bold I asked him outright if he was here for me or for you. I wouldn't be talking to you now if he'd have given me a different answer.

Another Neapolitan folk song played from the radio. "Mare Verde." The girls drank and laughed and held hands as Marija began talking about Dubrovnik's available boys, detailing their virtues and many flaws, as the forgotten lepinja in the oven began to burn.

THEY MET AT the Old City Harbor. Early evening, three days after their first few conversations outside Zagorac's back door. You're sure you want to see me, not my cousin, Dubravka had asked. Stanislav nodded. Their eyes met, then looked away, then met again. Yes, he said, I'm certain. I don't know why you even ask. It's insulting. I mean no insult, Dubravka said. You intrigue me, Stanislav answered. You're not like all the others.

Dubravka told her father there was a special Mass and subsequent event at Saint Blaise, and so she'd be home late. She'd pinned back her hair with matching barrettes and wore a simple pink dress and off-white sweater – her favorite, the one with small plastic buttons that resembled hearts. Stanislav had on a clean T-shirt, sneakers, and jeans. His black nylon racing windbreaker, the special kind with the cool vertical red stripe, hung open, unzipped. He'd showered and, by the small cut on his chin, shaved. Best, he didn't smell of fish.

I'm happy you came, he said when Dubravka approached.

At first Stanislav seemed not to have much to say other than to display to Dubravka his familiarity with the harbor. He pointed out fishing boats and told Dubravka their names as well as a few details about their owners. He listed what fish the boats usually brought in. He gestured toward Lokrum Island and said that was where he liked to dive. He pointed at the harbor's breakwater and told Dubravka what she already knew, that in ancient times a huge chain had been attached to it to prevent invading ships from entering. He nodded to locals repairing their nets, who waved a hand as they called out to him. Overhead, gulls squealed as they soared through the evening sky.

Next month, he said, I'd like to take you to Mostar. Just for the day, or maybe you can tell your father you're with your cousin and we can stay overnight. He winked. He asked Dubravka if she'd ever crossed the Stari Most, Mostar's Old Bridge, then explained that on the second-to-last day of July all of the sixteen-year-old boys in Mostar would jump from the bridge into the Neretva River below, leaping from a height of over twenty-seven meters, and the jump would change the boys into men.

You need to be really brave to do it, Stanislav said. So far he'd made the jump six times, the first when he was thirteen. I was terrified, he said, but then I simply stepped forward and closed my eyes. I mean, I knew I could die, but I'll die someday anyway, right? When I came back up from the water I remember hearing the crowd. They were cheering my name. If a boy doesn't make the jump, Stanislav added, he'll be shamed for the rest of his life. His life will be a failure. He'll never get a job or marry. People have been jumping from the Old Bridge for over four hundred years.

He told Dubravka about one jumper who twisted his torso as he fell and broke his back and now has to live in a wheelchair. Each year on the day of the jumps he comes in his chair to watch, Stanislav said. His brothers wheel him. A handful of others who jumped died from heart attacks, he said, likely from the sudden shock of the cold water. Some died from falling into the water the wrong way. The water can be as hard as stone. It can break your neck. Stanislav made a quick snapping motion with his hands and explained how the bravest jumpers would thrust themselves from the bridge and spread out their arms so that they resembled wings. Swallows, he said. The best divers soar like swallows. The best jumpers fly from the edge of the Old Bridge like birds. Now each year when he made the jump, he spread out his arms so that he would soar like a bird.

For a while the pair walked in silence, and then Stanislav reached sideways and his fingertips stroked Dubravka's hand. She decided not to pull her hand away. They took a few more steps and then Stanislav held Dubravka's hand.

THEN HIS VOICE softened and he talked about his work, taking fish from the Neretva and the lakes nearest Mostar as well as the sea here in Dubrovnik. Dubravka was so taken with him that she forgot to worry about being seen. He would be here only for another few weeks, he told her, to help his father bring in the nets, though he could stay longer if he liked since his true preference was diving and spearfishing. He was teaching himself to hold his breath in the water for increasing lengths of time. That's why you'll never see me with a cigarette, he said. He knew divers who smoked cigarettes. They ruin themselves, he said. I may have my vices, my many vices – his eyes sparkled as he looked into Dubravka's eyes and laughed – but smoking cigarettes isn't one of them.

They walked out along the breakwater toward the Porporela, the lighthouse on the breakwater's tip. The sun was setting – a brilliant orange orb – over the Old City. They paused to watch the sunset, to share it, standing close to each other in the evening breeze. Dubravka worried that her palms were sweating. They were still holding hands.

You should know that when I dive, I can hold my breath only for so long, he told Dubravka. During those moments I must decide what to go after. He shook his head and smiled as if what he had to say meant something more. There are some fish I have no problem catching. I see it at once. Easy prey, you know, the fish I always come across, the common ones. When I was younger I was happy to spear them, happy with what I could always catch and bring up into the air, but then there are others –

The ones that hide, Dubravka said. She tried to imagine what it would be like to dive, to search for fish among the rocks and weeds in the water.

Yes, Stanislav said, exactly. The ones who keep themselves scarce. The ones I need to wait for nearly every day even to get close to.

She understood then that they were no longer talking about spearfishing. So you think of me as a fish? Dubravka said after a beat.

No, Stanislav said. I think of you as a young woman. He stroked his chin, touching the cut he'd made while shaving. The first time I saw you I was refilling my water bottle at the small fountain in the square. You were climbing the stairs about to enter that church. Sveti Vlaho. There was something about you – he shook his head slightly and smiled – I can't really explain it. I could hardly look away. It drew me toward you, and so I waited by the fountain until you came back out. And then I followed you and discovered where you worked, then where you lived.

I don't know that I like being followed, Dubravka said.

Believe me, Stanislav said, I meant no harm.

And so now the spearfisher wishes to spear me. Her face flushed with embarrassment.

Stanislav lowered his eyes and ignored her words. With the back of his hand he stroked her hair and then her cheek. Then he leaned toward Dubravka and kissed her. She offered him her cheek. He held her then. Then Dubravka offered him her mouth and they shared another kiss. Then they kissed again.

They talked for a while longer and then Stanislav suggested they agree upon a plan, which Dubravka took as a sign since she believed in plans. Stanislav knew of a place near the harbor where they could meet. There were several small huts – sheds, really, standing in ragged rows – where the local fishermen stored their gear. He'd borrow someone's key, he said. Look for the net shed with the lock that snaps open easily. In case anybody else walks by, I'll make the lock appear as if it's closed. In two nights, Stanislav suggested, since the moon was waning. In two nights there will be no moon, and no one will know. No one will see you, or me, in the darkness.

As they walked back to the Old City Stanislav put back on his brooding face. He wore it like a mask, Dubravka realized. It was like the city's walls, put up to protect himself. The girl hurried home, and the next day she related everything to Marija, breathless, as the pair snuck into Zagorac's kitchen and Marija brought out another of her hidden bottles of slivovitz to share.

Playing on the radio up high on the cupboards was a program of Croatian folk music, a song featuring a tamburitza orchestra, the notes of their stringed instruments quivering in the air and then tumbling, like a waterfall of broken glass.

Santa Maria Maddalena

Rome, December 2004 / January 2005

Alongside the tram terminus from Trastevere and the famous Teatro Argentina and the busy taxi stand and bus stop at Largo di Torre Argentina lies an Area Sacra several meters below street level. Like many other sites in Rome, after the old houses and shops slouched against one another were torn down, what lay beneath street level insisted it was far more interesting than what had been designed to be built above. The remains of four Roman Republican temples were discovered. The site was then partially excavated. Iron railings were erected along the adjoining sidewalks, restricting entry but allowing passersby to gaze down at the ruins. Wild grasses sprouted alongside the uncovered temple steps and columns and the large chunks of travertine that from above suggested wooden toy blocks knocked over by a child on a rug, and in time the Area Sacra di Largo Argentina became a sanctuary for feral cats.

Lucy knew these details about Rome's cats, having offered the topic as a possible assignment to the older children in the Montessori school in Vancouver where she taught. Now, as she stood with her Canadian church group, who exited the #64 bus and gathered in front of the big bookstore on Corso Vittorio Emanuele II before heading up a side street to see the Pantheon, she agreed to meet Father Dan and a few others for lunch once again at the wine bar near the Piazza di Pasquino, where they'd met the day before. Then she asked if anyone wanted to join her to look at the cats, knowing full well that no one did.

As the others walked away, Lucy noticed a woman wearing a tattered cloth coat and an azure scarf standing by the busy taxi stand. The woman held out a box – *S.O.S. Tragedia Sud-Est Asiatico!* Lucy smiled and gave the woman several euros. Her soft dark eyes held Lucy's eyes so kindly that Lucy found herself nodding and smiling and then for some reason thanking her. As Lucy broke from the woman's gaze, she felt somehow changed.

Lucy liked the ease of traveling with the church group, but once everyone arrived at their destination she preferred going her own way.

She was slight, black-haired, fashionably slim. The morning sun was strong though the air was brisk, cold, even for late December. Her church group planned to be in Rome for two weeks after departing from Vancouver and catching a connecting flight in Amsterdam. Father Dan had arranged things, and if all went as scheduled the group would be taking side trips to Orvieto, Siena, Florence, Assisi, Naples, and Pompeii. They'd return to British Columbia on the sixth of January. By then Griffin would have finalized the details of his divorce, and she would have had her Italian holiday.

People hurried down the sidewalk edging the Area Sacra – businessmen in long dark coats, stylishly dressed Roman women, their faces unreadable, mouths a slight frown, high heels clicking resolutely as they walked. An elderly man in a gray sweater and pants, wearing a houndstooth newsboy cap pulled down nearly over his eyes, strolled by, carrying a shiny red box of panettone by its string. A nun walked past with a girl in a checked skirt and zipped hoodie. Likely a novitiate. The girl wore several different colored elasticos – scrunchies – on her right wrist as bracelets. The nun's habit was the color of freshly poured tar. Then an ambulance split the traffic as it sped fiercely down the street, its siren blaring *NEE-eu, NEE-eu, NEE-eu*. Out of habit Lucy bowed her head and made the sign of the Cross.

A group of university students leaned against the railing, pointing at the umbrella pines lining the area, then down at the ruins and the cats. Lucy saw them then, on the ground below, creeping out from their hiding places. Some sauntered about, tails raised. Others sunned themselves on the stones. Lucy counted seventeen cats, then quit as more emerged. One handsome black cat had a perfectly white-tipped tail, like an artist's brush dipped in paint. The sun felt warm on Lucy's face, and she realized she was smiling. She felt an affinity with the cats because in her own way she, too, was a sort of stray, abandoned after her birth in South Korea and taken in by a Catholic orphanage, where she lived until she was nearly three. Then Lucy noticed the posted notice.

The notice was written in both Italian and English, stapled to a section of plywood posted on a large marble block. It showed a picture of a long-haired calico named Feronia. Apparently the cats in the Area Sacra were each given names, and apparently Feronia had been captured or stolen on Christmas morning by two men said to be homeless. The men had been seen snaring Feronia with a noose attached to a pole. There was a phone number to report any eyewitness information.

The students lit cigarettes and joked about the sign. One boy sang out the cat's name, *Fer-o-ni-a*, hand curled by the side of his mouth, like someone beckoning a distant lover. Then a second boy cried out, "Hey, I just thought of this. What do you call a kidnapped cat?" The students blew their cigarette smoke into the air and laughed in anticipation of the punchline. "A catnap."

Standing downwind of their cigarette smoke, Lucy laughed despite herself. As the smoke drifted toward her she raised her head hopefully toward it, sniffing the air like a dog. Then she frowned and grew sad and appeared as if she were going to cry as she stared again at the photo of the sweet-faced kidnapped cat.

IT BEGAN INNOCENTLY enough several months ago at the Butchart Gardens outside of Victoria. Or at least that was when and where Lucy first noticed it.

She'd just spent a blissful half hour in the park's Japanese Garden. Another outing planned by Father Dan. The garden was complete with arched bridges, stone lanterns, small waterfalls, and a reflecting pond – an ideal setting for an early morning stroll down its serene paths that wound their way between low lying annuals, gracefully sculpted trees, and lush red maples with leaves as fine as the best Irish lace. In Victoria there was an exquisite Irish lace store Lucy thought she would have to visit. Maybe she'd pick up something there for Griffin. So far they'd been careful with gifts, concerned about material evidence, but after the holidays, well, what would it matter? She'd get Griffin something small but perfect. Or better yet, she thought, she'd wait until she was in Rome and buy something for him there.

The garden's silence invited her thoughts to form and drift. They were pierced only by the haunting hollow thump of the boar scarer, a length of bamboo suspended between two poles, the lighter end open and cut on the bias, positioned beneath a trickle of water that caused the tube to fill and fall downward to empty, then rise up as its heavier end knocked sharply against a rock. A path led to the Rose

Garden, where some of her parish group already gathered. Lucy saw the Mackenzies walking with Father Dan and Mrs. Fiorello.

Lucy entered, amused by both the flowers and their names. Stretching their open petals toward the sun were Elizabeth Taylor, Dolly Parton, Betty Boop, Ingrid Bergman, Michelangelo, Julia Child, Othello.

"Some are designed for the eye, for their beauty," a man in a linen jacket remarked to his partner. "Others for the nose." He took notice of Lucy and nodded politely, then bent at the waist and positioned his nose over a rose named Honey Perfume. "Marvelous," he said, nodding. "Sweet and mildly spicy," the second man observed, as if the pair were discussing wine. The first man sniffed the flower again and smiled.

After they moved on, Lucy bent and with her first and second fingers gently lifted the soft, apricot-yellow petals of Honey Perfume up to her nose and smelled nothing.

Then she tried others – Mikado, Fragrant Dream, Love Potion, Abracadabra, Tahitian Sunset, Crimson Bouquet, Prairie Joy – and still all she could smell was nothing. Certainly these roses couldn't have been grown only for the eye. She would relate the incident to Griffin, and he'd laugh and assure her she was mistaken.

Still, she knew that while the others were mewing about the delicious, delicate odors wafting through the magnificent garden, her ineffectual nose couldn't smell a thing.

THE TECHNICAL NAME for her condition was anosmia, and little was known about it. Even worse, according to the doctors, there was no known cure.

Have you fallen and hit your head? the doctors asked, or have you recently had a sinus infection? Some months ago I had a bad cold, Lucy answered. And did you take antibiotics? Only what was prescribed, Lucy said. And you're quite certain you haven't had any sort of head injury? Something you might be overlooking? Maybe you don't remember having nightmares and having fallen out of bed? It's not at all uncommon for people who have night terrors to have episodes of sleepwalking during which they sometimes injure themselves. Sometimes they forget that they've fallen. Lucy said no. Or perhaps someone or something struck you on the head, the doctors said. Accidentally, perhaps. Your husband or a boyfriend. You needn't be afraid to tell us if your boyfriend or husband hits you.

I'm not married, Lucy answered. Though soon, after the holidays, if all went as planned, she and Griffin would be engaged. Griffin insisted they wait until after Christmas, when he'd talk with his wife. He could hardly break the news to her before then. Of course Lucy understood why – he had to let the year run out. After all, he owed his wife at least that. He'd call Lucy in Rome as soon as he and his wife had their conversation.

The doctors scheduled Lucy for an MRI, which came up clean. They referred her to a specialist, who pushed Lucy back into a special chair and probed her nose this way and that, then blasted her sinuses with a bitter, burning spray. The spray made Lucy's shut eyes see a sudden white sparkle, as if Celebration of Light fireworks were exploding in her brain. Then a nurse entered the room and shot Lucy's arm full of corticosteroids. Come back in a couple of weeks, the specialist told her. If this doesn't do the trick, we'll try the shot again.

LUCY DIDN'T LIKE the idea of taking steroids. They'd make her fat. "I'd rather not smell a thing than be fat," she told Griffin the day after she saw the specialist. She sat at the edge of her bed in her apartment, picking up her blouse from the floor where Griffin had tossed it. Her arm was still sore from the shot. Griffin was in the bathroom, toweling off after his shower.

"You can't mean that," he called.

"I do," Lucy said and stood, slipping on her blouse but leaving it unbuttoned over the pink brassiere and matching panties she'd purchased in Victoria in a shop just down the block from the Irish lace store. She was keen on rationalizations like *less is more* and *more than a handful is a waste* and a *moment on the lips, a lifetime on the hips*. Her diet revolved around the principle of denial. Lucy tasted things and always left a little something on her plate. When food was pressed upon her, she responded by saying she'd have just a bite, and meant it literally. She often held food in her mouth, not swallowing. As a young girl whenever her adopted mother admonished her slow eating habits by telling her to think of all the starving children overseas, how they'd be grateful for just one bite of the food she wasn't putting into her mouth, Lucy's response was that they were more than welcome to it.

If anything, the thought of hungry children made Lucy want to eat even less. She had no real memories of her years in the orphanage. She'd look at old online photos of children in Korean orphanages, study the children's faces and clothing, make note of their bad haircuts. Why should she stuff herself when other kids in the world were starving? She could still very easily be one of them. When Lucy attended Mass, she would pray that all the food she didn't eat could miraculously be given to the world's hungry children. Since her adopted family enrolled her in Roman Catholic school, she attended Mass each weekday morning. Even now as an adult Lucy could walk away from a plate of food imagining that if she ignored it the food might somehow make its way across the ocean and into the mouths of hungry children.

She sauntered across the room toward Griffin, conscious of how fetching she must appear in her open blouse and matching bra and panties. "Besides," she said, "if I was fat I doubt you'd love me half as much."

Griffin laughed and said what he was supposed to say. "Luce, oh Luce, you silly little goose, I'd love you even more since then there'd be more of you to love."

She didn't like to shower immediately after sex. She preferred allowing the odors of the man and the sex they shared to linger on her body, like a cape one might wear on a cool summer night. Lucy was never one to mask her body with perfumes, though she did use lotions and oil, shampoos and conditioners, each of which had its own particular odor. She never used anything with too noticeable a scent, though she liked smells, had come to take them for granted. Now the jars and bottles on her vanity had only texture and color. After the trip to Butchart Gardens she opened every one, held each one up to her worthless nose. Food carried no smell, and along with it little or no flavor. The expensive wines Griffin brought with him when he visited her apartment offered no bouquet. It was like being trapped inside a sealed box surrounded by an impenetrable bubble.

There could be a fire behind her, and unless she saw its smoke or heard its crackle or felt its heat she wouldn't even know it was there. The specialist cautioned her about fires, suggesting that if the cortisone shots didn't work each room of her apartment should be equipped with a smoke alarm. He cautioned her about leftover food and said that from now on she needed to date foods stored in her refrigerator since she wouldn't be able to detect if and when things went bad. Evidently, he implied, there was an actual history of anosmiacs who were burned in house fires or fell ill with food poisoning. The specialist also suggested that she replace her gas oven with an electric one since she'd be unable to detect the odor of gas in the event of a leak. Anosmiacs were also known to gas themselves, he said.

"You mean by accident rather than on purpose," Lucy said.

The doctor failed to understand her joke.

"It's laughable, really," Lucy told Griffin.

"What?" Griffin said. "I'm sorry, love, I wasn't listening." Griffin was fit, muscular, a regular at his club's racquetball court. He stood in the bathroom admiring himself in the mirror, which had steamed up but on which he'd cleared a porthole the size of a dinner plate so he could see himself as he dressed. He turned his body this way, that way. He was nearly hairless, like a marble statue. Two white towels lay bunched at his feet like clouds.

"That I should have this condition," Lucy said. "All because of a measly sinus infection." She paused. She wanted Griffin to stop looking at himself and take her into his arms and assure her that in a few weeks, or at the outside a few months, she'd be back to her old self again. She wanted Griffin to remind her that after he talked with his wife the two of them would be able to actually be together. Most of all she wanted to be able to smell him again. She remembered that he smelled of leather and cedar and sometimes when he came to her after being at the gym he smelled ever so slightly of sweat – manly sweat, something light and reasonably crisp and clean, like the fresh needles of young pine.

"Well, perhaps I should look into getting a smelling-nose dog."

He didn't get her joke.

"You know, a seeing-eye dog," she began to explain, then stopped. The joke wasn't funny. She didn't even know why she was making jokes.

Her situation wasn't funny. She wasn't herself, or at least she didn't feel like herself. She felt like a knock-off, an imitation. And now, standing in her bedroom in her open blouse, she felt as if she could cry.

"You'll be just fine," he said, giving her a wink, as he stepped over the towels that lay on the floor. He turned to the mirror again and combed his hair.

"And do you know what's ironic?" Lucy said after a while, as Griffin walked into the bedroom and began dressing. "That my name is Lucy. Lucy's the patron saint of the blind."

In school the nuns had each child research the story behind their name. Catholics named their children after saints, each of whom had a story, and the best stories – the most exciting and marvelously colorful – were those of the martyrs, the ones who'd refused to betray their faith. The men normally endured unimaginable torture and suffering. The women were usually lusted after by pagans before they were killed. Lucy knew that children adored stories and that every religion was grounded in them. Like gems in the finest lapidarian's shop, each story – each life of a saint – was cut and polished by the ages into a narrative that lay clearly on the edge of credibility. Each story straddled the incredible field of faith.

Lucia of Syracuse was a young virgin who'd lived in fourth-century Sicily. At an early age she vowed to dedicate her life to Christ. Her mother insisted that she marry and arranged a wedding to a suitor who was a pagan. After Lucia refused, the pagan denounced her as a Christian. When the governor's men came to her house, intending to take her to a brothel where she'd be raped before she'd be killed, since it was against Roman law to execute virgins, Lucia became as immovable as a mountain. The men were unable to drag her away even after bringing in a team of oxen. Bundles of wood doused with oil were piled around her feet and set afire, but the wood refused to burn.

On the holy cards the nuns gave the children, Saint Lucy was depicted holding a plate on which rested her twin eyeballs. According to legend, prior to the arrival of the governor's men the pagan suitor tried to convince Lucy to marry him by flattering her looks, telling her that, above all, she had beautiful eyes. The girl then left the room and plucked her eyes out of her head and placed them on a golden platter.

"Here," Lucy told her suitor when she returned to the room, "if you desire my eyes so much you may have them."

"Not to worry," Griffin said. "Just do what the doctors say and in time you'll be bright as a new penny." He knotted his tie and carefully adjusted its length, bent and tied the laces on his shoes, then kissed her sweetly on the cheek as he looked at his watch and then at the door. "Trust me. The doctors know what they're doing."

SHE MET GRIFFIN at a parent-teacher conference at the Montessori school where she worked. Griffin's son, a bouncy boy named Bradley, fond of dinosaurs and whispered conversations with whatever objects lay near his table, had difficulty keeping to himself and concentrating during the times when the children were supposed to work independently. Not interfering with the learning process of others was one of the school's central rules. Lucy was used to talking with mothers about issues such as these, but seldom with dads alone. She was surprised when only Griffin met with her one evening in her classroom.

They sat on tiny chairs and talked openly about Bradley. After a while Griffin looked into her eyes and admitted that there were problems at home, serious problems between himself and Bradley's mother. Griffin wore a crisp gray suit and had clear blue eyes and white, straight teeth and exceptionally clean, manicured hands. As the conference ended he let one of his hands rest for a moment on the back of her hand, as his eyes met with hers and he thanked her for her time and attention. She agreed to meet with him the following week to further discuss the situation. Griffin stood and smiled and, with the same hand that had just brushed against hers, gestured at the classroom and their absurd little chairs and suggested that their next meeting be at a coffee shop downtown. As Griffin pushed in his chair without making a sound, it seemed only reasonable for Lucy to agree.

The coffee shop was down the block from a popular Gastown pub, which was a short walk to Lucy's apartment building. Lucy resolved the situation with Bradley by having him sit close to her, giving him a small slice of power, and making him a set of classification cards – pictures of different dinosaurs and labels corresponding to the parts of their bodies as well as their names. She urged him to move about slowly in the classroom, like his favorite herbivore, the Brontosaurus, and suggested that when some of the younger children were napping his dinosaurs might benefit from some down time too. Let them rest, Lucy told him, then during recess you can rub the sleep from their eyes and make them romp and roar. Out on the playground during recess, Bradley growled like a gleeful Tyrannosaurus rex. Soon some of the other students became interested in dinosaurs and asked Bradley for help learning their names.

Griffin's delight over the improvements in his son's situation was charming. The pair walked down the block from the coffee shop to the pub and then to Lucy's apartment, where it was not too many steps from the sofa and chair in the living room to Lucy's bedroom.

AND NOW AS the devastating news of the Boxing Day South-Asian tsunami worked its way around the world, Lucy found herself sitting in her Roman hotel's breakfast room reading about the tragedy in *The International Herald Tribune*. She broke a still-warm cornetto in half, took a modest bite, and then sipped a cappuccino. The cappuccino had the creamy texture of boiled milk and the flat, dark taste of coffee but no aroma. Lucy had always liked coffee at least as much for its odor as its taste.

In her purse was an unopened vial of pills, some anti-fungal medication, given her by the doctors. They came up with a new approach each time she saw them. After a while she realized they really didn't know what to do, that they were throwing random theories and new prescriptions at her like blind men playing ring toss.

She let the vial remain in her purse, untouched, and stared at the photos of the tsunami's wreckage and its victims in the newspaper. She'd read that the rupture in the plate lying on the ocean floor that shifted and thrust itself upward off Sumatra was longer than California's coastline and that the immense underwater earthquake had lasted a full ten minutes. Over a quarter of a million people – people whose Asian faces resembled hers – were either missing or killed. The death toll was likely to reach beyond three hundred thousand. Up in her room she'd watched the images on TV, one horror flickering after the next. Tables and lawn chairs rushing across the surface of a hotel's swimming pool, as the pool itself was swallowed up and the people near it did their best to leap out of the water's way. A woman clinging to her child with one arm as with her other arm she held fast to a palm tree. Automobiles and trucks tumbling as if they were toys tossed by a giant down a street suddenly overwhelmed by a surging flood of debris. The grieving face of a woman, her hands squeezing the side of her head, screaming as she ran toward the camera. The dark, churning waters, rushing forward behind her, higher and now still higher, toppling both the woman and the camera back. A half-moment of perfectly blue sky.

It wasn't quite real to her. Nor was it quite real that she was now in Italy. It was as if only part of her were here. How different Rome's air must smell compared to the air of the Pacific Northwest! she thought. She took another sip of her disappointing cappuccino. She comforted herself with the thought that soon – today or at the latest tomorrow – she'd hear from Griffin, now that Christmas day had come and passed.

Approaching her table were the Mackenzies, Ned and Iris, wearing – as was their habit – matching sweaters. Today's theme was snowmen. "May we join you?" Iris asked. She carried a small white teapot, the wet tags of two tea bags clinging to its side.

"Tragic, isn't it," Iris said as she sat, indicating with a nod Lucy's open newspaper. She tsk-tsked and wagged her head. Ned carried their plates of food, a bit of everything the hotel offered. Breads and meats and cheeses in triangular foil wrappers, cherry tomatoes and hard-boiled eggs, cartons of yogurt and hard dry cookies and neat pre-cut slices of cake.

"Wonderful morning," Ned said. "I've been outside, and the morning air – " He paused as he set both plates down on the table. "Did the waiter bring you that cappuccino?" His head whirled about, in search of a waiter.

"Sleep well last night, dear?" Iris asked.

Lucy answered yes, though in truth she hadn't slept well at all. It seemed that no sooner would she fall asleep than she'd waken. On overnight trips with the church group she insisted on a single.

"We slept like rocks," Iris said. "Ned was sound asleep before his head hit the pillow. Though, I must admit, the mattress was hardly thicker than my winter coat."

"I can feel my appetite returning," Ned said, "now that we're adjusting to the local time." His fingers waved in the air, like a pianist playing a silent tune, and drew the attention of one of the waiters as he gestured toward Lucy's cappuccino.

"Oh," Iris laughed, "I don't think his appetite ever leaves him." Ned laughed along with her, slapping the gleeful snowman bulging on the front of his sweater.

"And what have you planned for today, dear?" Iris asked. "Father Dan's looking for a church where he can say Mass."

"Well," Ned said, chuckling, "as far as looking for churches, he's certainly come to the right place."

"It's all been arranged," Mrs. Fiorello said, who nudged a vacant chair back from the table with her foot as she approached. She set two big bowls – stewed prunes and cold cereal with milk – alongside Lucy's newspaper. "A church in Monti, near the Colosseum."

"How did you sleep, dear?" Iris asked.

"Come ho dormito?" Mrs. Fiorello said with a smile. "Come una pupa."

"I see your Italian is returning," Ned said. He nodded thanks to the waiter for the cappuccino, then reached across the table for the sugar packets and, like a dog with a favorite toy, shook several furiously back and forth in his hand.

"At home it tends to hide, but here" – Mrs. Fiorello's hand gestured in the air, a flower opening its petals or the water spouting in a fountain – "sono felice."

"We slept like rocks," Iris said again, popping a wedge of cheese and a small cherry tomato into her mouth. "Ned was snoring up a tornado before his head hit the pillow."

Soon the rest of the group joined the others in the breakfast room. Lucy sat politely, listening to their conversations. There were times she despised them. They were certainly good people, but at times they were tedious, pedestrian – the price one paid for company.

In the photos in the newspaper, a woman whose child had been torn from her arms by the floodwaters stared numbly at the ground. A boy stood weeping beside the slumped, dead figure of his mother, her shoulders round and glistening in the inappropriate sunshine.

There was a photograph of a shoreline where victims of the tsunami lay in a slurry of mud and debris. Another picture of bodies in a pile of rubble, limp arms and legs dangling from a stew of ruin, jutting out from between jagged planks of wood and pieces of twisted, shorn metal roofing. A boy pulling the hand of his younger sister as they scuttled over what looked like a river surging with wooden boards and broken sections of walls. In the foreground of another picture of the dead, as if placed there purposefully by the photographer, was a child's plastic doll. Beside it, a second doll's disembodied head. One photo depicted a makeshift morgue and its near-endless rows of corpses, each wrapped tightly in white like a mummy.

On Lucy's plate lay her cornetto, a single bite taken from one of its torn halves.

LUCY WASN'T EXACTLY sure when the thought of praying for a miracle came to her. Was it after she met the woman with the tattered coat soliciting funds for the tsunami victims? Walking now up Via dei Cestari, a narrow lane of shops offering items specifically made for the clergy – sparkling silver chalices, gold ciboriums and monstrances, imposing crucifixes and life-sized statues of the Holy Family and saints – Lucy considered the nature of prayer as she dropped her still unopened vial of anti-fungal pills into a trash can.

She decided prayer was more or less simple petition, hopeful energy unleashed into the air. Something like the notes and poems taped on the formless statues that dotted Rome's squares, or the persistent knock of Butchart Gardens' boar scarer. Yes, she thought as she passed a vendor with thick dreadlocks and a crocheted rastacap, his spread blanket offering an array of fake designer handbags, prayer was very much like the repetitive knock of a length of bamboo repeatedly falling against stone. Lucy realized that if she could have any prayer granted it would be that she could smell again.

She knew it was a foolish wish, selfish and sentimental. She knew that if she were a better person she would pray for world peace or an end to hunger and poverty and the abuse of the world's women and children. She should pray for the orphans of Korea. She should pray for solace for each victim of the tsunami. Nonetheless, she yearned to feel complete, and now each day as she went about trying to live her life her dead nose reminded her that she was incomplete. At times the feeling was so overwhelming that she slipped into a funk, a deep depressive hole in which she was tempted to sit and sulk, paralyzed and numb.

As for praying for a miracle, a cure, well, wasn't that consistent with the history of Rome? Several of its churches were built on sites where the miraculous had happened. And wasn't it possible for the miraculous stories suggested by the iconography of each church to continue to occur? All you needed was faith, she thought. Faith and perseverance, and perhaps a bit of luck. She felt that part of the trick lay in finding the proper shrine, the right saint to intercede on one's behalf.

Back in school the nuns had taught that each saint in Heaven was the advocate of a specific cause, the guardian of some particular aspect of life. It would be as if each of you were assigned a specific task concerning the maintenance of this classroom, the nuns said. Ask the child with the thumbtacks, whose charge is organizing the bulletin board, to sweep the floor, and for lack of a broom the floor will go unswept. The nuns told stories about people who petitioned the wrong saints, how a woman wishing to sell her house prayed not to Saint Joseph but to Saint Anthony, patron of lost things, and as a result the woman kept finding things she'd misplaced while her house remained on the market. It was then that Lucy noticed a Madonnella – a Little Madonna – one of central Rome's five hundred or more public Marian shrines.

The shrine hung from the corner of a building and depicted the Blessed Virgin in a blue veil, eyes raised to the heavens. Over the image was a golden crown, and under it the words *Ave Maria* etched on a curved banner. Beneath the shrine was Gammarelli's, personal tailor of popes since 1798. Lucy entered the shop and bought a pair of red woolen socks for Griffin. It was said that Gammarelli's always kept three sizes of papal robes – one small, one medium, one large – in preparation for a pope's passing. She was tempted to ask the clerk if the story about the three sets of robes was true, particularly given the fragile health of John Paul II, whose declining condition the newspapers reported on daily. Already crowds gazing up at his apartment windows were beginning to gather in Saint Peter's Square.

On a pedestal in the nearby Piazza della Minerva stood a whimsical statue of a small elephant. On its back was an Egyptian obelisk. A young woman with long dark hair wearing a black baseball cap stood at the statue's base, offering to feed the statue a sprig of green broken off a nearby bush. Her boyfriend snapped pictures of her with his camera. "Closer, Nicole!" he called out. On his black-and-red striped stocking cap were the words *AC Milan*. "Yes!" he shouted. "Yes, yes! Perfetto! That's it!" For a moment Lucy pretended the boy was Griffin and she was the happy, laughing girl in the black baseball cap.

Then a tall striking blonde in a dark sweater, designer jeans, and leather jacket the color of cranberries walked toward Lucy and nodded before turning toward the doorway of the hotel facing the square. Lucy couldn't help but stare at the woman. For several moments their eyes met, as Lucy wondered if there was some connection between them, if she should somehow know the woman, acknowledge her. Then before Lucy could complete the thought a man with slick black hair darted from a doorway and marched briskly, militarily, toward the hotel's entrance. Lucy realized he was following the woman. She was tempted to enter the hotel to warn her but was distracted by the laughing lovers now embracing beneath the little elephant. As the boy kissed Nicole he turned the bill of her San Francisco Giants cap around so that it faced backwards, as he kissed her again and then again.

Lucy walked past the Pantheon's imposing columns and through the next piazza, edged with cafés – gas heaters glowing warmly, a forest of open umbrellas shielding the tables. The street opened into another small square where a few cars were parked beside a hideous mechanical Santa. The upper torso of the figure rocked back and forth as the arms opened stiffly and a speaker inside the freak's belly issued a rolling "Ho, ho, ho."

Lucy turned away. She hated Santas. One of her first memories of her new life in Vancouver was that of a fat man dressed as Santa reaching his gloved hands out to grab her after she'd stood with her new parents in line before him. The man held her waist as he forced her to sit on his knee. A gray tabby cat missing part of one ear strolled past the Santa Claus and up the curved steps of a church, then curled beside its open doorway. Lucy entered the church, Santa Maria Maddalena, known by locals simply as La Maddalena.

The church itself was a splash of gleaming gold and brown and rose. Everywhere Lucy's eyes fell she saw gorgeously textured, mottled marble – gentle pinks and somber grays and blacks, deep siennas and reds dark as congealed blood, swirling sepias and bright forest greens. Each detail in the church attracting her attention led to another detail, and then to yet another, in a marvelously fluid, dynamic way. Lucy stood in the center aisle, turning around and around. The columns drew her gaze to the rows of windows in the clerestory, each made of clear glass broken into rectangular leaded panes. The center of each window was marked by a red cross.

Nearly every image in the church was female. In concave niches above the confessionals stood statues of women portraying the virtues necessary for confession – Sorrow, Fidelity, and Shame on one side, Humility, Secrecy, and Simplicity on the other. A painting of Mary Magdalene gazing up at a wooden cross borne by several angels hung over the main altar. Flanking the painting were bas-relief sculptures of the Magdalene arriving at Christ's tomb, in her hand the jar of oils with which she'd planned to anoint his body, and another of the Magdalene on her knees before the risen Christ.

The late morning sun cast the reflection of the clerestory windows on the church's west walls, and Lucy saw imposed on one of the marble columns a shimmering red cross. She knelt before the cross of light and made the sign of the Cross and said a prayer for the victims of the tsunami. Then she bowed her head and prayed that she herself might be cured, that her sense of smell might be restored, that she might be able to smell the bouquet of flowers she would carry to the altar on the day she married Griffin.

THAT NIGHT AT dinner the conversation wound its way to what everyone had done that day, and Lucy told the group that she'd visited La Maddalena.

"La Maddalena?" Edith Glover said. Immense ornate earrings dangled from her earlobes as she shook her head in disbelief. She sat at the foot of the table with her husband, Duncan, who was cutting the long, soft stem of an artichoke with the side of his fork. On the table before them were platters of bruschetta and grilled mixed vegetables along with green bottles of mineral water and dark bottles of wine and wicker baskets heaped with bread.

"It says here in my guidebook that La Maddalena is a rare example of the rococo," said Vijay Jayaraman. He spoke softly, with a pleasantly lilting British accent, and wore a crisp pink shirt, neatly ironed and open at the neck. His guidebook rested like a faithful companion beneath his hand.

The Chatterjees, Kunwar and Bhavani, who generally accompanied Vijay on the church group trips, agreed. Their faces were clear and round, like winter squash.

"I can't imagine a church named after Mary Magdalene," Iris Mackenzie said. She'd exchanged her snowman sweater for one featuring a herd of reindeer. "After all, and please forgive my language, but wasn't she a whore?"

"She confessed, I believe," Vijay said. His hand made a cross in the air.

"Wasn't she the adulteress the crowd wanted to stone?" Edith said.

"I believe that was someone else, dear," Duncan said as he patted his wife's hand. "You may be confusing all of these women, lumping them all into one."

"'For a prostitute is a deep pit,'" Edith quoted, "'an adulteress a narrow well. Like a bandit she lies in wait and multiplies the unfaithful among men.'" Nodding at everyone to insure that they understood, Edith took a deep drink of her wine. "*Proverbs.*"

"Rococo," Bhavani Chatterjee said, allowing the three syllables to slip slowly from her mouth. "What a lovely word, like some sort of ice cream or crunchy chocolate." She smiled at Vijay and Kunwar, who swung his arm around her shoulders and drew her close.

"Actually," Brian Kent said, "I recall reading that Mary Magdalene was neither a prostitute nor an adulteress. In fact, she was the only person to have witnessed Christ's death, the discovery of his resurrection, and his later ascension. It's said that Christ cleansed her of seven demons, which scholars take to mean that at one point he cured her of some physical disease, but there's certainly no evidence that she was sinful." Brian was an accountant, normally dressed in a blue suit, and served as the parish treasurer. He sat with his wife, Harriet, and the

Cooke sisters, Eileen and Merle. The three had finished their bruschetta and now nibbled on slabs of bread.

"She was called 'the Apostle to the Apostles' by Saint Augustine and even wrote her own gospel," Brian added. "Next to the Virgin Mary, Mary of Magdala is the most important woman in the Bible. Isn't that right, Dan? The early Church suppressed her writings, editing the female principle nearly completely out of the New Testament."

"Editing out the female principle," Eileen Cooke said. "What foolishness. God's word is God's word." She looked around the table for agreement, jerking her head from side to side like a wild bird in a cage. "I think we're going to need more of this marvelous wine."

"She's the reason we dye Easter eggs," Brian said. "Evidently at one point she was a guest of a Roman emperor, proclaiming Christ's resurrection. To illustrate her point she picked up an egg and described how life bursts from it. The emperor said that Christ's resurrection was just as likely as the egg in her hand turning red, which of course it most immediately and miraculously did."

"That adulterous whore certainly wasn't one of the apostles," Iris Mackenzie said. "At least not in the Bible I grew up with."

Father Dan smiled and shrugged. He was a small man with a perfectly round bald spot on the back of his head, which invited many who saw him to wonder if he was a monk. "I leave matters like these to minds greater than my own. Though I do know that La Maddalena is run by an order known as the Camillians, and that the church our dear Lucy visited stands on the site of an ancient hospital."

"Everything here stands on the site of something ancient," Ned Mackenzie said.

"I was able to talk in Italian today with a gladiator outside the Colosseum," Mrs. Fiorello interjected proudly. She had been waiting for a pause in the conversation to share her news. "A young Roman named Massimo. Troubled, I fear, with problems at home, the little missus more than likely, but so handsome and strong."

"Not a gladiator," Duncan said. "A faux centurion. And in the future be careful of them, dear. I hear many of them are thieves."

"No, not Massimo," Mrs. Fiorello said.

"The ones who convince you they aren't are the worst ones."

"No," Mrs. Fiorello said again. "Not my Massimo."

Duncan shrugged. "Did you hear that now apparently there's a costumed character running around Rome threatening crowds with an actual sword?"

"Chameleons," Merle Cooke said suddenly, as if she'd just awakened from a dream. "Aren't they those weird-eyed little creatures that change colors and snatch up things to eat with their indecently long tongues?"

"Oh, I get it," Vijay said. "Camillians, chameleons. Oh ho, that's a good one."

"Speaking of everything standing on the site of something else," Ned said, looking around theatrically, "I wonder what's below our feet right now."

"Likely the wine cellar," Brian said. "Please, someone catch the eye of our waiter."

Father Dan laughed along with the others. He told the group that the Camillians were a holy order that since the sixteenth century ministered to the sick, named after their founder, Saint Camillus de Lellis, whose followers wore bright red crosses on their black cassocks. Centuries later the International Red Cross adopted the red cross as their symbol as they carried out the Camillians' mission and work.

"What is the word I'm thinking of?" Bhavani asked the table. "Don't anyone say anything, please. It's right on the tip of my mind."

"Try thinking of something else, dear," Merle Cooke said.

"Tongue," Kunwar said. "Tip of your tongue."

"Palimpsest," Bhavani said finally. "That's the word." She pronounced it again, slowly, as if she were tasting it, allowing its syllables to roll slowly over her tongue. "Palimpsest. All of Rome is a palimpsest."

"Bravo, dear," Kunwar said.

Then Lucy told the group about the cat sanctuary, as a waiter brought them their orders of pasta. A second waiter followed with more bottles of wine. Lucy didn't appreciate all the earlier talk about adultery. It wouldn't be adultery after they married, she thought. Again she was aware of how separate she felt, not being able to smell the aromas around her. The wine everyone was raving about tasted flat to her. The grilled vegetables she'd tried had only oily texture. After she told the group about Feronia and the sign stapled to the wooden post, Harriet Kent asked what in the world would two homeless men want with a stray cat. If indeed they were homeless, she added, they could hardly keep the animal as a pet.

Vijay reached across the table and stabbed the last piece of roasted red pepper off a platter before the waiter could clear it. He held the pepper up on the tip of his fork as if it were a trophy. "To skin and cook and eat it, of course," he said, then with a grin popped the length of the pepper's seared flesh into his mouth.

AFTER LUCY AGAIN endured the conversation in the breakfast room, she took the pair of buses to Largo Argentina where she met one of Rome's gattare, or cat women. The gattara was working down on the Via Florida side of the sanctuary, carrying buckets from one area to another. Her name was Pina.

Pina told Lucy that the animals originally came from Egypt on the same ships the Romans used to carry their pilfered obelisks. For centuries the cats fed on the rats that ran wild in the city's granaries. When the Black Death began to spread across the land, many of the cats were hunted down and killed. Slaughtering the cats likely contributed to the further spread of the disease, Pina said. She handed Lucy a brochure. Because the Area Sacra borders the site where Julius Caesar was killed, she and other Roman cat lovers believed that some of the emperor's bold spirit lives on in each of the hundred or so animals housed there.

A pair of combs in the shape of small chameleons – multicolored, with protruding curled red tongues – held back Pina's long dark hair. She told Lucy that in Rome cats were protected by law, that a cat born in a courtyard or garden had the legal right to live there. She said that all across Rome there were people like her who cared for cats, that strays weren't thought of as pests but rather as a normal part of everyday life. Everyday Roman life, animals with a right to live wherever they were born, though the ones at the sanctuary could be adopted and would Lucy like to adopt one or at least make a donation toward their care?

Lucy opened her purse and made a donation, then asked about Feronia.

"Oh," Pina said, with a gesture of her hand near the side of her face as if she were brushing away a fly, "of course she's gone."

Already on the slab beneath the sign were the beginnings of a shrine – a bouquet of red roses lying beside a squat candle, a few open tins of cat food, a sonnet about the grace of Roman cats written in precise longhand on deckle-edged linen paper held down by a stone.

THOUGH IT WAS the same time of day as when she'd visited the church the day before, there was no reflection of a red cross on La Maddalena's marble columns. Instead the small church was filled with tourists listening to a tour guide lecture boisterously in German. The guide's oily black hair seemed painted on his skull. The heels of the man's shoes clicked sharply on the marble floor as he strutted back and forth before the altar. Lucy realized he was the same man she'd seen on the Piazza della Minerva following the striking blonde-haired woman into the swank hotel, the stalker she'd wanted to warn the woman about. Some tourists in his group were attending to his every word while others roamed about restlessly, as if the holy church of Santa Maria Maddalena were a department store and they were simply passing time while someone they were with shopped.

Lucy stood at the back door and dipped two fingers into the bowl of holy water, then crossed herself. She considered leaving and returning later but the holy cards and literature scattered on the table near the doorway caught her eye. For a while she tried to read the many pleas for tsunami aid written in Italian. She dropped several euros into a tsunami-relief donation box and knelt at a back pew and covered her face with her hands. She did her best to clear her mind and pray, but the presence of the others made it nearly impossible to concentrate. She wanted to ask those wandering about to respect her space and obvious purpose. She wanted to ask the guide to use his inside voice.

Lucy prayed for herself, that her anosmia might be cured, then again felt selfish and said several prayers for the victims of the tsunami. It was difficult to focus on them since they seemed more of an abstract concept than something tangible or real. Her thoughts kept sliding back to Feronia's photo and the shrine on the marble slab. It was ridiculous to pray for a dead cat, she thought. Should she pray instead for the two men who'd captured and killed her? Lucy tried to remember the images of the tsunami survivors she'd seen in the newspaper. Wasn't there a picture of a weeping man standing beside a mound of wreckage, another of a woman with open, empty arms? Lucy shut her eyes. She prayed for the weeping man standing by the wreckage, for the woman with open, empty arms.

The tourists were gathering now around the altar as the guide gestured toward the painting of the Magdalene contemplating the Cross. Two men on the far right turned away from the group, laughing loudly at something one of them had said, a joke, as if they were in a tavern, and then the joke-teller raised his foot and placed the sole of his shoe up on the communion rail and leaned over to retie his shoelace.

She ached to be able to smell the church's odors. Tears rushed to her eyes. She stood and walked toward one of the square marble columns, hid her face, and inhaled deeply.

Nothing, again nothing. For months and months, nothing. As if she were not there, not fully present in this, the moments of her life, now passing.

What else was she not detecting? she thought. At that moment the tour group shuffled down the center aisle, everyone talking at once, as if they were children and the teacher had just announced recess.

She shouldn't fault them, she thought. After all, they were here in Rome on holiday, just as she was. Perhaps one of them was like her, suffering from some illness or disease. Perhaps one had recently lost a parent or son or daughter. Perhaps one was confused and sought clarity. Perhaps one walked with shoulders heavy with doubt and despair. Perhaps one was waiting for a phone call from a lover.

Lucy pictured the face of the woman now, the woman in the photograph in the newspaper, her desperate eyes and outstretched arms, the mother who'd lost her baby, who'd felt the tsunami's surging, sucking waters tear her child from her grasp. Lucy crossed herself and prayed fiercely, with red-hot intention, as she had back when she was a child in school, back when she fully and truly believed with the wholeness of her heart in God and his infinite and bountiful mercy and compassion.

SHE RETURNED TO La Maddalena the following day, then the next several mornings after that, each day taking the two buses to Largo Argentina, but on her second-to-last scheduled day in Rome she found that the church's doors were locked.

The gray tabby with the torn ear sat in its usual spot on the church's steps, sunning itself. New Year's weekend had come and passed. Lucy's church group had visited Orvieto and Florence and Assisi – all without her – and this morning was in Naples with plans to lunch at Da Michele, where they'd eat genuine Neapolitan pizza, then tour Naples' harbor and dine at a restaurant overlooking the magnificent blue sea. Lucy stood outside the locked church staring at the sleeping cat, not knowing what she should do, as a bearded beggar approached, holding out a small waxed cup, the kind used for a single scoop of gelato. He rattled the change in his cup as if it were a toy. Lucy opened her purse and gave him several of the coins she'd saved for candles. The man dragged his right foot and oversized shoe as he limped away. Behind him the mechanical Santa rolled his fat belly, spread wide his arms, and laughed.

She'd hated sitting on the strange Santa's lap, and yet she had done it. She'd always tried to do her best to please others. Her therapist suggested that her issues likely stemmed from the fact that she remained aware that she'd been given up for adoption, that as a result she perhaps felt unworthy and, since she was later accepted into a family, compelled to feel grateful. It was why she was so compliant. It was why she was so reluctant to eat. It was why she'd allowed herself to become involved with a married man. It was why she traveled with a parish church group that constantly bored her. Apparently she felt she didn't deserve things. Food. Marriage. Genuine friends. Rubbish, Lucy thought as she'd stared at the therapist's crossed legs, as she looked at the fabric straining at the woman's waist and judged that the woman could stand to lose a good twenty pounds.

The lights from the restaurants beyond the church twinkled as Lucy gazed at them. She took a tissue from her purse and wiped her eyes.

No matter, she decided, as she stood there on the cobblestones of the Piazza della Maddalena as a family walked past, the woman pushing a baby stroller. The child in the stroller clutched a green cloth Tyrannosaurus rex. Of course the toy made Lucy think of Bradley. Then a pair of high-school girls approached, wearing short leather jackets and skin-tight jeans tucked into their high black boots. They stepped over a colorful postcard lying on the sampietrini, an advertisement for a party at a local dance club. Lucy picked the card up. *Capodanno Gitano, Locanda Atlantide,* the card announced alongside a picture of a sexy long-haired brunette, both hands behind her head, a lei covering her breasts, standing on an open scallop shell. A hip take on Botticelli's *The Birth of Venus*.

The robot Santa called out, "Ho, ho, ho." Lucy wiped her eyes again and stared at the trampled postcard, which rather than throw back onto the ground she put into her purse. Silly to let something so trivial as a locked church upset her. Silly not to take advantage of the day. She walked back toward the Piazza della Rotonda as it suddenly began raining.

She shook her head no to several vendors and ran through the rain toward one of the cafés, where she sat at an empty table beneath a wide umbrella. For a while she watched the rain and listened to the calls of the vendors and the various conversations on the square. The rain bounced softly off the top of the umbrella under which she was sitting. The gas heater beside it gently hissed. After a while a waiter took her order. Coffee and a pastry. Lucy didn't want to eat anything but she knew she couldn't occupy a table and not order something.

The day was too gray, the temptation too great, and so as she sat waiting for her coffee and pastry she took out her cell phone. No messages, again. Finally, she pressed the button for Griffin's number.

After some stumbling and a pause, he said What are you thinking? It's the middle of the night. No, nothing's settled. Look, I can't talk now. No, I don't know when things will be settled or if they'll ever. Just a minute, babe. Yeah, the office. I know, I know, at this time of night, what the hell. I'll tell you as soon as I'm back up there. Go back to sleep. Don't wake Brad and Emily. Then, in a lower voice, a voice nearer to a whisper, as the waiter brought Lucy a demitasse of espresso and a gold-edged plate on which rested a glazed fruit tart perfectly centered on a lace paper doily, around which was sprinkled a ring of sliced almonds dusted slightly with powdered sugar, Griffin hissed Luce, this really isn't going to work. At least not now. Don't call me here again.

SHE STOOD FROM her seat at the café and ran across the square, past the pizza and gelato shops, across the Corso del Rinascimento, where she was nearly struck by a motorino, and then down another narrow alleyway that led to the Piazza Navona. The rain was lessening now. People continued to stroll about, bunching near the antique carousel's bright lights as well as beneath the canvas awnings hanging over the Advent fair food and gaming stalls. By the fountain, a crescent of onlookers gathered around the young woman with curly black hair playing the organetto. The musician appeared happy, untroubled, free, as she sat sheltered from the rain by a broad umbrella fastened to the back of her chair.

The red-and-black diamond design on the organetto's bellows stretched back and forth as she played a song that was lively and bright, that many around Lucy recognized. A young American wearing a pink slicker stood at the crowd's edge, clapping her hands in rhythm with the tune. She seemed to notice Lucy's sadness and offered her a wide smile. Lucy realized she was the same girl who'd posed for pictures with her boyfriend near the statue of the little elephant on the Piazza della Minerva.

For a while Lucy watched the organetto's bellows breathe in and out. She thought of the others in the church group, dining that evening in Naples, overlooking the sea. She then reached inside her purse for a few euros and requested the traditional Neapolitan song "Santa Lucia." The organetto player smiled and nodded knowingly at the request.

Why had she been so surprised? Lucy thought. Hadn't it been clear all along? She looked again at the young woman in the pink raincoat and felt envy.

"Sul mare luccica," the musician sang as she played. "l'astro d'argento. Placida è l'onda. Prospero il vento." Upon the glittering sea, a star of silver. Calm is the wave, prosperous the wind.

Rain dripped from the curled beard and wavy hair of one of the statues in the fountain. Rain fell onto his bare chest, down his stomach and dangling arm, down his leg and the toes of his outstretched foot. How blind had she been? Rain dripped from the fronds of the palm tree in the fountain's center and from the mane and nose of the lion crouching in the hollow below. Rain bounced off the heads of the sea dragons rising from the churning water. Rain dripped from the lower foot of the stone figure hiding his face.

The crowd was murmuring happily now, pleased with Lucy's choice, dropping coins into the cap at the organetto player's feet. The girl nodded in appreciation and tapped one foot as she began the third verse. "In fra le tende, bandir la cena. In una sera, così serena." Within the tent, setting aside supper. On such an evening, so serene. "Chi non dimande? Chi non desia?" Who does not ask? Who does not desire?

Lucy turned away then from the fountain and the music and made her way to a familiar place, Largo di Torre Argentina. There she stood beside the iron railing separating the walkway from the Area Sacra, looking down for the cats among the ruins.

Her eyes scanned the ground and weeds and stones. The steps of the ancient temples. The blocks of travertine. The fallen columns of tufa. She saw no movement. Clearly, the cats were taking shelter inside the sanctuary from the rain. Far wiser than she, Lucy thought as she walked toward Feronia's makeshift shrine.

It was then that Lucy thought she smelled Naples and the sea.

Yes, there on the slab beside the squat candle and the poems held down by stones and the now-wilted bouquet of roses were several open tins of fish. Sardines. Anchovies. Pieces of fish from each of the cans were spilled out for the cats onto the slab.

Lucy lifted the bouquet of roses from the slab. Water beaded on the bright red ribbon, tied in a neat, tight knot, that held the bouquet together. The flowers' petals had browned, their edges curled and darkened. And there, Lucy noticed as she again breathed in the distinct, unmistakable scent of fish, was a single white long-stemmed rose. Likely placed there earlier that day, its delicate petals, wet with rain, were still soft and fresh. Lucy tossed the bouquet of dead roses over the railing and down onto the stones in the Area Sacra, then lifted the single rose to her face and smelled it.

Sevdalinka

Dubrovnik, May 1981

When Dubravka and Marija were younger, sometimes they'd play a game about an airplane that was minutes away from crashing. They called it the *Who Would You Save Game*. They'd begin by telling all of their aunts, uncles, and neighbors to buckle their seatbelts, make the plane fly around for a bit, then have the pilot announce that he was sad to inform them that they were going to crash and after counting up the passengers he realized they were one parachute short. The girls would then take turns passing out the parachutes, explaining their reasoning as they went along.

Sometimes the game was about a boat sinking in the ocean and Dubravka and Marija tossed out life preservers. They never included their parents because of Dubravka's mother, how one evening she was there in the house cooking a pot of the father's favorite soup and the next morning she was nowhere to be found. Besides, both girls knew that their mothers were certain to be given a parachute or a life preserver. Who could deny their own mother? Dubravka and Marija also knew they would never rescue their fathers. Both men would always end up literally dead last, destined to go down with the airplane and be burned to a coal-black crisp or be left to thrash alone in the dark wild sea, circled by hungry sharks.

Sometimes when they played, Dubravka was excited beyond measure. The game allowed her to pretend for a few moments that she was God. And sometimes she felt horrible, even sinful, for pretending to be the Almighty. I can't decide, she'd tell Marija in the middle of a tense scenario involving an erupting volcano and two neighbors and only one lava-free spot on which to stand. Marija would tell Dubravka that she was stupid and a big baby.

So at first Dubravka tried not to blame Marija for what she did because part of Dubravka understood that in the world there were only so many parachutes, only so many life preservers, only so many safe places that offered shelter. Another part of Dubravka entertained thoughts so dark she knew she couldn't even whisper them to Father Josip in the shadows of the confessional box, so she kept them hidden inside herself.

It was impossible for Dubravka to talk to Marija after that. They still drank secret glasses of slivovitz, but since Marija found the net shed before Dubravka did the two young women worked together in the kitchen in uneasy silence.

Practice for life in the convent, Dubravka would think later, though at the time Dubravka hoped Stanislav would tire of her cousin and admit his mistake, and Marija would take care of things. Stanislav would bathe and wear fresh clothes and stand outside the restaurant's back door as he apologized. Then they'd talk and once again hold hands as they walked along the harbor. Marija would do what needed to be done and become her old self again. But then Marija vanished, like Dubravka's mother – there one day, gone the next – and Dubravka found herself making the restaurant's puffy flatbread all by herself.

THE COUSINS HAD played another game – the *Wait for the Reward Game*. This game started one afternoon when they each had a bit of money and decided to go to one of the Old City's finest bakeries and each select a favorite treat, then bring their sweets back to the kitchen where they'd compete to see which one could wait longer to eat theirs. To make the game more interesting, each girl put up a few dinars, winner takes all. Marija would resist eating her pastry for an hour or two, sometimes for the remainder of the afternoon, but by nightfall she'd always surrender. I'll get you next time, she'd tell Dubravka as she licked crumbs from her lips and fingers, but she hardly ever did.

Dubravka kept her growing winnings in a jar she kept hidden in a spot in the kitchen where she hoped Marija wouldn't be able to find it. While Marija said the game was a way of sharpening their self-control so that they wouldn't grow up to be like Marija's mother and aunts, plump cows with dangling udders swinging beneath their sack-like housedresses, Dubravka took a different approach to the game. She pretended that the treats were symbols of a lifetime of earthly pleasure, and the dinars were tickets to Heaven. Whenever she was tempted to eat her treat, Dubravka would press her fingernails into her palms until her hands stung with pain. Then her mind would weigh the seventy-five or eighty years she figured she'd live in Dubrovnik against her approximate concept of eternity, which she calculated was at least a million years multiplied by another million at least a million times, and then a million times again, until even God would admit that he'd created no higher numbers.

Marija grew wiser as the two girls matured, as Dubravka's winnings grew to ever more significant amounts. Marija chose less and less desirable sweets from the Old City's bakeries. She requested broken or stale cookies – sweets she could easily resist – then with the money she didn't spend she'd purchase the most exotic pastries for Dubravka. Chocolate chestnut cream tortes, cinnamon apple strudels, sweet Croatian zlevanka, jelly-filled krafne, sponge cakes with custard, crème caramel rozata, tantalizing squares of nine-layer filo pies. Marija would watch Dubravka eye the treats as they waited patiently for her on their dainty paper doilies. Dubravka would gaze longingly at them, bite her lower lip, clench her fists, resist. The pair of sweets would sit for a day, sometimes two. Finally Marija's mother ended the waiting game after noticing that the untouched pastries were attracting ants.

After Marija disappeared, Dubravka thought it best to retrieve her years of winnings, which had far outgrown the reward jar. Dubravka needed a footstool to be able to stand on the counter and then tiptoe her way to reach up and behind the old radio, where she'd hidden her treasure in several tight rolls of dinars bound by elastic hair bands.

Of course Dubravka's hands grasped only the emptiness of air. Of course Marija had discovered and taken the stash of money first.

AND WHAT MIGHT have happened had Dubravka found and opened the right unlocked net shed and gotten there before Marija? Dubravka considered the question when she wasn't parsing the words of some prayer. She'd searched so hard for the right shed that night but in the darkness they all appeared alike, as Stanislav had warned. Finally she simply gave up.

Had she found the unlocked door, Dubravka imagined Stanislav standing patiently inside, arms open, a grin on his face. Perhaps he would have brought along a candle or, better yet, a stick of incense to mask the stink of dried nets and fish and the sea. Dubravka would have smiled at him as she stood at the shed's threshold, deciding whether or not to cross it, to go to his waiting arms.

Would she have gone into the shed? Yes, she thought. Would she have pulled the door closed behind her? Yes. Would she have let Stanislav kiss her in greeting? Yes. Take her hand? Yes. Kiss her like a boy really kisses a girl? Probably. No, yes. Yes, certainly. At least once. Yes. More than once? Probably. No, yes. Yes again to more than once. Touch her in the front over her dress? Yes, again. Yes, yes.

Then Dubravka would remember that when she'd looked for her pink dress she couldn't find it. Later she'd discover that Marija had taken her pink dress as well as her off-white sweater with the plastic heart-shaped buttons and even the twin barrettes she used to hold back her hair. Dubravka would burn with anger all over again. Then feel sad. Then pragmatic. What was the use of thinking about what she would have done since she hadn't been given the opportunity to do it? Besides, Marija was now wearing Stanislav's black nylon racing windbreaker with the cool red stripe wherever she went around town.

Eventually Dubravka realized that the game Marija had played that night was to pretend she was the younger cousin. Unless Stanislav had brought a candle or flashlight, it was likely that at first he'd be unable to tell. The girls were the same height and had similar voices. Do girls have different kisses? Dubravka wondered. She imagined the answer to this was yes, but then she recalled that when she'd told Marija about her walk to the lighthouse with Stanislav and admitted that after hours of conversation they'd kissed, Marija wanted to know how had she'd kissed him back. Was it with soft lips or hard lips and did she part her lips slightly or use the tip of her tongue? Soft lips with a closed mouth only, of course, Dubravka answered. Marija had her illustrate the kiss on the back of Marija's hand. Then Marija tried out the kiss on the back of Dubravka's hand. Not so rough, Dubravka said. Not so eager. Marija kissed the back of Dubravka's hand until Dubravka said Yes, that's it, exactly. So maybe Stanislav thought Marija was Dubravka while they were kissing. At least at first. During the first few kisses. And maybe he thought Marija was Dubravka when they –

No, Dubravka thought. As soon as Stanislav's hands touched the front of Marija's dress he had to realize that the girl in his arms, or perhaps the girl lying beneath him had he thought that night to bring a blanket or tarp to the net shed, wasn't the younger, flatter, shy one he'd waited so patiently for in the alley behind the restaurant.

LATER, WHILE SHE knelt in her usual spot in church trying to concentrate on her prayers, rather than think of Stanislav kissing her Dubravka wondered if perhaps it had all been a trick, a trap, an elaborate and cruel joke played out by both of them. *The Unlocked Net Shed Game.* Marija telling her younger cousin that the handsome young spearfisher waiting outside the restaurant's back door was really waiting for her, then encouraging the naive girl to go out and talk to him, then after their repeated conversations his arranging a date, a walk along the sea's edge and the old harbor, a romance-novel stroll to the Porporela lighthouse, his making plans for the two of them, setting a later date on a moonless night, implying that they could be lovers if she wanted, knowing full well that she'd tell Marija every detail of their plans, knowing in advance that Marija would then step in.

How exciting that must have been for them, Dubravka thought. Marija opening the shed door, wearing Dubravka's finest clothes, pretending to be her younger cousin. For Stanislav it must have been like being in the presence of both young women at once. Holding and kissing both at once. Making love to both at once. And since Dubravka never found the unlocked door, they must have fled to some other secret place near Dubrovnik's Old City Harbor, laughing as they snapped shut the door behind them.

SO IS THERE a sign I'll receive, Dubravka asked, thinking that her best option now was to see if she had a calling. Or a voice that I'll hear?

She was talking to Father Josip, who'd dragged his bad foot up the aisle toward her one afternoon while she prayed in church and asked why was she sitting there crying into the cradle she'd made of her hands. Dubravka posed her question as they walked to the rectory, where once again they sat on the two dusty armchairs in the public room. The priest took out his tobacco pouch and rolling papers from inside his cassock as the housekeeper came in carrying a tray with a bottle and two glasses. Father Josip poured.

Likely you'll decide how you were called long after you've taken the vows, he said. Looking back, you'll pick some moment and twist it around and decide it was then. He spat out a piece of tobacco. Perhaps it will be today, he said, when I came up to you in church and touched your shoulder. Perhaps it will be a moment in the coming year, while working in your uncle's kitchen. Whenever I'm asked I say it was the first day I arrived in Dubrovnik, a boy fresh off my family's farm, as I walked through the Pile Gate. I saw a flock of gray doves by Onofrio's Large Fountain. Standing tall in the middle was a white one. It stood out from the others. I took it as a sign from God. Father Josip laughed. It makes a good story, doesn't it? Its meaning is immediately clear. Priests need to come up with stories with meanings that are immediately clear. The truth is that while I did notice a flock of pigeons by the fountain, there wasn't one any whiter than the others. He nodded to make certain Dubravka understood.

Believe me, Father Josip continued, God seldom announces himself or sends out invitations. You have to be a saint for him to knock you off your horse. If and when God speaks, he only whispers. Faintly. Father Josip sipped his drink. Very faintly.

So there's no moment, Dubravka said.

The priest laughed again. Little chicken, that's something you'll have to learn for yourself. I'm sorry not to be of help. He poured himself more travarica. As I said, at least there wasn't a specific moment for me. Oh, Father Josip added, don't get me wrong, I think that for some our Lord really does tap them on the shoulder. But for me, and I ask that you tell no one, given my options the priesthood was perhaps less a calling than a sensible choice. He nodded as if to agree with himself. I had the bad fortune of being the third-born son of a poor farmer. I don't know if you know what that means. You can divide an already small piece of land into two more or less equal halves, but it makes no sense to chop it even further into thirds. And given my leg – he patted his ankle – what other alternatives did I have? I always knew the priesthood was an option. A guaranteed table to feed me, as well as a warm bed. I'd already decided long before I walked that day through the Pile Gate.

Your foot, Dubravka asked. Likely it was the brandy she was drinking that made her brave. The stories about you saving the farm dog.

Oh, Father Josip said and smiled. How I rescued the pup, fought off the wolf, offered the beast my own leg to chew on while the loyal dog scampered to safety.

Dubravka nodded.

Do you know how hunters set spring traps? Father Josip illustrated his words with his hands. They stretch open the trap's sharp jaws and then hide its steel teeth beneath leaves and twigs in places where wolves or game are known to walk.

You stepped into a spring trap? Dubravka said.

The priest nodded. One set by Satan himself. I was useless on the farm after that. Though the part about my saving the dog is mainly true. I had a sense that something about the ground around us wasn't right and so I called him back to my side just in time, just before I turned after petting him and took the fateful step.

Dubravka declined his offer of a second drink and crossed the room toward the rectory's back windows. Bookcases lined the parlor's rear wall, jammed with volumes long unopened. She looked out the back window and saw a pair of obvious tourists studying a map – a boy and girl wearing matching nylon jackets, neither marked by a cool vertical red racing stripe, who gazed at the Old City as if they'd recently been given the power of sight. Dubravka studied them for a while through the grime on the rectory's window. Father Josip continued telling her about his dog and life on his family's farm as he drank, but she no longer listened. She stared down at the loving couple. They depressed her. For several moments she pretended they were her and Stanislav. It was then that she noticed that on the edge of the window sill lay the corpse of the moljac she'd thought was a hummingbird.

A long-legged spider was busily lacing the lovely winged insect's body with cobwebs. Dubravka's fingertips brushed the checkered stump of the moth's still body, the tissue-thin span of the moljac's wings. Outside the window, the couple folded their map and then the boy embraced the girl and once again they kissed.

Dubravka and Father Josip walked along the Stradun, past the Dominican Monastery and the Ploce Gate, past Orlando's Column and the Town Hall and Clock Tower, past Onofrio's Little Fountain and the Sponza Palace, the shops and restaurants and taverns, past the Franciscan Church and Monastery to the ornate circular concrete dome that was Onofrio's Large Fountain, the city's source of water during the Middle Ages, where the priest asked Dubravka if they might sit so he could rest his aching leg.

Dubravka thought about the white pigeon that really was as gray as the others, the spring trap hidden in the leaves, the locks on the doors of the net sheds. Were the locked padlocks her sign? She knew that if she had gotten there first and found the shed in which Stanislav was waiting she would have done everything he asked of her. And having done that, she probably would have done everything she could do to stay with him. Or at least she would have been given the choice. But Marija stole away from her that choice.

Was that the sign?

Dubravka thought about the dead moth. Was it the same moth that was trapped in the room when she was last there? Or was it another? Hadn't Father Josip opened the window wider to let the first poor creature out?

The priest stood and with the scoop of one hand drank from one of the spigots on the side of Onofrio's Large Fountain. So was the moljac the sign? Should she run from the idea of a calling before she ended up like the moth, furiously beating itself against the glass of an unwashed window, only to tumble down in exhaustion and die and be buried over by a spider's cobwebs? Was that what it would be like inside a convent?

Of course she would end up being buried over, Dubravka realized. She smiled at Father Josip, drinking from the fountain as if he were a boy, looking even sillier now as water splashed down his chin and onto his Roman collar. He needed a shave. And someone should tell him his cassock nearly always appeared in need of a washing.

Whether it be dust or cobwebs, she thought, we all end up being buried over.

THEN FATHER JOSIP said that all he could tell Dubravka to do was what she was already doing. She should pray. As her confessor he suggested she pray in each of Dubrovnik's churches. Start here, he said, by the Pile Gate, at the Church of Saint Saviour. He pointed at the ancient church and began telling her its history, how it had been built by the town's women and how it protected Dubrovnik from earthquakes. Dubravka already knew the story. She knew most of the stories but nonetheless acted as if she were listening.

Then he mentioned something new, the Church of Saint Ignatius of Loyola, in the southern part of the Old City. Be sure not to miss it, he said. It was built by the Jesuits in honor of its founder, Saint Ignatius. The Jesuits even brought in a famous Italian lay brother from Rome, Andrea Pozzo, the artist and architect who'd built a similar church in the Eternal City, to paint a special kind of fresco that would make the church's flat ceiling resemble the round interior of a dome. It's two things at once, the priest said. A trick of the eye. One thing pretending to be something else. It's up to you to decide which image is true.

DUBRAVKA MADE A list of Dubrovnik's churches, including the Serbian Orthodox Church of the Holy Annunciation. She worked alone in the kitchen now, each day rolling out the dough for lepinja. She began the task Father Josip had assigned her, to pray in each of the city's churches. And when she was in Zagorac's kitchen, Dubravka had the chance to search the cupboards for Marija's hidden bottles. Dubravka found just one, a bottle with only a small remaining splash, barely enough to moisten one's tongue. Without considering what she might say if she were caught, she grabbed a spare apron to conceal what she wanted and walked nonchalantly into the restaurant and behind its small bar. She hid the bottle – an unopened silver fifth of Maraska šljivovica – in one of Marija's favorite hiding places.

From up high on the cupboards the old radio played sevdalinka, traditional music from Bosnia and Herzegovina. Several songs were somber ballads that included a tamburica or saz, often an accordion, violin, flute. Dubravka loved somber ballads. Sevdah usually began softly, with a melancholy air, then gently grew faster in tempo until the music rose to an emotional frenzy of pain and anguish, leaving Dubravka with a sense of aching longing. Often sevdah told stories about unhappy love. They filled Dubravka with a beautiful sadness. The radio worked its way through songs sung by the classic sevdalinka artists – Himzo Polovina, Zaim Imamović, Nada Mamula, others.

Dubravka danced a bit as she drank and listened to the sevdalinka and prepared the evening's bread. She wiped away the tears that fell on her bread board. It should have been me, she thought. Yes, it was meant to be me. As the lepinja baked, Dubravka did her best to skip around the kitchen, to keep time, to try to make herself happy, as she cried and danced and drank a little more and cried some more and softly clapped her hands.

Your work is much better now that the whore's gone, Marija's mother told Dubravka later that night, as they were clearing the restaurant's tables. There was no sadness in the woman's eyes for her missing daughter, only simmering anger. On their way out, Marija's mother added, the customers told me they couldn't remember a time when the lepinja had been more delicious.

Sant'Ignazio di Loyola

Rome, December 2004 / January 2005

It was by the Fountain of the Four Rivers that Allison first saw the woman with the tattered cloth coat and azure scarf. The woman moved among the crowds deliberately, meeting the eyes of nearly everyone she passed, offering each person something that she carried before her, something small, made of wood, as if it were a gift. By the time Allison had worked her way toward her, the woman had disappeared.

There was something immediately attractive about the woman, something foreign and yet at the same time familiar. At once Allison thought of Krzysztof Kieślowski's film *The Double Life of Véronique*, the scene in which the Polish soprano Weronika sees her double, the French music teacher Véronique, boarding a tour bus on Krakow Square. Weronika slumps and dies the next evening while performing, and as her coffin is covered over with dirt Véronique in France is overcome by an inexplicable sadness. It wasn't so much that the woman with the collection box physically resembled the actress who played both roles but that the woman by the fountain embodied some of Véronique's essence, her carriage and sure sense of self, her soft, wide-eyed expression – a distinct clarity of vision – a thoughtful attitude of melancholy tinged with vulnerability and intelligence.

Since leaving Japan Allison was immersing herself in Western films, watching DVDs nightly on her laptop as she lay in bed waiting for sleep in her posh hotel room near Bernini's playful little elephant and the Pantheon. Last night she passed the halfway point in the Ten Commandments dramatized in Kieślowski's series *The Decalogue*. Each of the films in *The Decalogue* offered a tale triggered by one of the commandments. One of the women who worked with Allison at the Doll Shop, who'd traveled to Tokyo from a town outside Warsaw, had recommended Kieślowski's work. Allison also watched his trilogy, *Three Colors*, admiring their beauty and interconnectivity. Though each of the three films was able to be appreciated independently, their stories ultimately overlapped and connected, like the waves of a sea. The ten films that made up *The Decalogue* worked in the same fashion. They shared a common setting and timeline as well as the reappearance of several characters who at first glance seemed minor – simple passersby – but who emerged later on as central figures with stories of their own. In the end, Allison concluded, Kieślowski's work was perhaps more about community than the struggles of a single character. All of this made Allison wonder if perhaps everything in life was somehow linked, somehow interconnected.

The Double Life of Véronique offered a slightly different vision, as if the thread of one's life might also be lived by another, as if life offered duplications, repetitions, rhymes, returns. As Allison traveled about Rome, she began seeing impossible doubles of several of the actors who were featured in her collection of Western DVDs. No doubt it was because of what she'd done with her mother as a child. No doubt Allison now wasn't used to seeing so many Western faces. In the Roman forum and then again by the Colosseum Allison saw Cary Grant pause to check his wristwatch, then have a conversation with a faux centurion, a muscular Roman explaining the symbols on his Twin Legion flag. Grant nodded, laughed, then put an arm around the centurion's broad shoulders as a woman – was it Michelle Pfeifer? – snapped their photograph. Outside the Basilica of Santa Maria Maggiore, in the shadow of the imposing Column of Peace, Juliette Binoche leaned elegantly toward a man's cupped palms to light her cigarette. Later that same day, descending the Spanish Steps on his way to the Babbington Tea Room, Allison saw a pouty man whose profile was exactly like Alfred Hitchcock's. Leaving the Antico Caffè Greco and walking jauntily down Via dei Condotti in a black sweater and faded jeans was Brad Pitt.

Allison stood beside the Fountain of the Four Rivers, listening to its soft and furious rushing. She stared up at the figure representing the River Ganges. On a pedestal nearby, a stark-white living statue in a tuxedo and top hat came alive whenever a young female passed, transforming from unhappy to smiling, then pretending to offer the girl the long-stemmed rose he held against his chest. A vendor with skin the color of bitter chocolate worked the crowds, extending one arm inside a long cardboard tube on which was displayed a variety of beaded bracelets. A noisy huckster in a Renaissance costume hissed at her and muttered, then slashed the air with an imitation antique sword, causing the crowds around him to buckle and part. There was something not quite right about him, Allison thought, as if his presence on the piazza was more threat than entertainment.

Allison knew all too well the burden of a life whose purpose was to entertain. But by doing that, and doing it well, one received money, which in turn could be used to purchase options, which were a form of power. For a moment Allison thought she could smell money. Instead the smell was that of chestnuts roasting on a grill. The man roasting the marroni wore a torn jacket and peasant's cap and was unshaven, with a complexion the color of burnt mahogany. He offered Allison a slight bow of his head along with a toothless leer. Then Allison saw the dark-haired woman with the azure scarf again. Indeed, in her hands was the worn wooden box, and on the box a handwritten sign, *S.O.S., Tragedia Sud-Est Asiatico!*

"Here," Allison said at once, reaching into the pocket of her jacket and offering the woman a blue twenty-euro bill. "Here, please, let me give this to you."

"Thank you," the woman said. "You're quite generous."

Allison reached out an arm as if to hold her. "What you're doing" – she gestured toward the holiday crowds around them, then at the collection box – "it's really pretty admirable."

The woman shook her head.

"Forgive me," Allison said as the woman began to turn away, "but may I ask you a question?" Without giving Dubravka time to respond, Allison said, "Have you ever seen the films of Krzysztof Kieślowski?"

"I'm sorry," Dubravka said over the roar of the fountain.

"No," Allison said, "it's just that" – she paused – "it's just that you remind me of an actress in one of his movies. I can't explain exactly why. It's a compliment, really."

"Thank you," Dubravka said again. "I regret to tell you I live very simply." She hesitated. "I don't view many films."

"Ever since I left Japan, it seems that everywhere here, out on the streets of Rome I mean, I keep seeing coincidences, in a way. Doubles."

"You're from Japan? You don't look –"

"No, originally I'm from the States. Chicago. The South Side." She shook her head. "I just flew here from Tokyo. I left the day after the tsunami."

"Yes," Dubravka said, nodding. She touched Allison's arm, then held her eyes. "Thank you, and may the Almighty bless and keep you safe during your stay."

There was nothing more to say, Allison realized. Despite having just been blessed, talking about herself so much, she feared she'd presented herself as a fool. She saw she was hungry for talk, talk with Westerners. The woman with the tattered cloth coat nodded, lips whispering a prayer, then moved on with her collection box. The fellow with the striped shirt and feathered cap shouted something about true beauty as he brandished his sword – Allison saw now that it was a real sword – and the elderly man roasting chestnuts again caught Allison's eyes and bowed. The sweet organetto player by the fountain laughed at something told her by a monk or priest, his bald spot shining in the late morning sun, who stood with a middle-aged couple in matching holiday sweaters. Now a boy in a blue nylon jacket – an Italian who couldn't be much older than sixteen – was grinning at Allison as he snapped her photo with his cell phone. The vendor with the bracelets closed in on her, offering his stiff jeweled arm. A mime approached, mirroring Allison's movements. Behind Allison, the waters of the fountain spilled from their slits in the marble, then splashed down a progression of protruding steps. Water gushed from the open neck of a hidden pipe. Around the heads of the sea dragons, the fountain's waters foamed and churned.

THEY CALLED IT mizu-shōbai, or the water trade.

Allison was told that the Japanese historically associated pleasure with water, with bathing and the islands' numerous natural hot springs, with the many bath houses and inns dotting each road and highway. She was told that in Japan a man could never really know or understand his business clients or associates until they sat down together and drank until they were drunk. Only then, under the dizzy, permissive waves of drink, could a man be freed of the bonds of social expectations and unleash his inner self. To properly conduct business with someone, one must first come to know the other man's essence.

Allison had met all types of men, men who brought their clients each evening to the club where she worked, where they could drink and snack and sing karaoke and talk business as they tested one another's mettle, since in Japan business and entertainment and the pursuit of male pleasure intertwined. Because it was traditional within the water trade that a man be served by a woman, and because the presence of women brought out the best as well as the worst in men, each club offered its own cadre of women, or hostesses, as they were called, to sit with the men and smile, talk, light cigarettes, fetch snacks, pour drinks. Allison was a hostess at the Doll Shop, a kyabakura in Tokyo's Roppongi district featuring gaijin – women from Europe and Australia and North America. The coming April would mark the end of her second year, and now, having taken a leave on the day of the horrific South-Asian tsunami, she found herself in Rome teetering on a cusp, trying to determine where to go next in life.

She turned away from the fountain and walked back to her hotel, then decided against going up to her room to watch more Kieślowski and on impulse continued walking. Before her stood an Egyptian obelisk on the back of a small elephant. In the doorway of the adjacent church, Santa Maria sopra Minerva, an elderly woman wearing a faded headscarf sat begging with a sleeping child on her lap. Allison passed a pair of stationery stores and then a shop selling hand-made chocolates. The candy's scent hung lightly in the air. As she walked along the cobblestones that paved the Piazza del Collegio Romano, its splendor ruined by packed rows of Vespas and parked cars, she looked for an open door of a church, somewhere quiet where she could sit for a few moments and gather her thoughts.

Despite her decision to wear black ballet flats and jeans and act exactly like everyone else visiting Rome, her height and long blonde hair drew the attention of others, the stares of men idling in the doorways of their shops, appreciative nods and smiles from taxi drivers, actual hand waves from carabinieri. Even by Roman standards Allison was stylish – she was willowy and fair, a taller than average blue-eyed blonde with a thin nose and long, straight hair that fell with a slight bounce across the back of her leather jacket, a rich cranberry Pierotucci, despite the clerk in the swank shop on tree-lined Omotesandō who insisted that its color was burgundy. The jacket's cranberry, Allison told the clerk. Don't tell me otherwise. I know my colors. Because she was in — and often fell out of — a recovery program, she didn't want to own a jacket whose color was the name of a wine.

Other than mascara and eyeliner she didn't wear much makeup. She knew that in Rome one's public image was everything. She knew that the philosophy of la bella figura extended down even to the soul. She knew that she should have been wearing sunglasses and leather boots that matched her jacket as well as a more obvious lipstick. But then she'd have to stare straight ahead as she walked, act as if everything around her was a mild annoyance or at best a momentary amusement. Her years of living in Japan had made her used to being stared at, and though sometimes she didn't mind being the object of admiring gazes she no longer found them flattering. She knew that the men who looked at her saw mainly what they wanted to see.

She felt she could seldom escape the duties of her work, and she was beginning to deeply resent the continual obligation of having to play the supporting role in someone else's drama. The images she'd seen on television of the bodies swept up in the debris — uprooted tree branches and chunks of concrete studded with protruding rebar, oil drums and splintered boards along with sections of what had once been a building's roof, corpses lying motionless, snagged, face down in the dark mud, outstretched legs and arms locked in the muck, everything baking beneath the abject sun — had changed all that.

Initially she had a five-year plan. She'd work as a hostess, save all she could, then parlay the money into something bigger. She knew there was a lifespan to her job, a ticking clock. Only so many years when she'd be at her most attractive. She'd get out just before she reached that point. Wasn't there a famous book that featured a male character who described to his lover the right way to eat sugar cane, that it was best to stop just before the last sweet bite lest you take the one after that and fill your mouth with straw? Well, Allison thought, she'd be like that man and not fill her mouth with straw.

Every other day a new girl waltzed into the Doll Shop, long-legged, saucer-eyed, asking to speak to the mama-san. No matter. Allison was aware that sooner or later one would take her job. At least for now she felt her position at the club was stable. She was popular and very much in demand. When her time came she'd return to the States – New York or San Francisco or Los Angeles, she could take her pick – where, with her experience of having lived and worked overseas, she'd have more options than one could imagine. She could go into business or public relations. Three more years wouldn't be that long a time, she told herself. But then she learned about the tsunami, listened to the broadcasted cries of the bereaved, watched the living toil about the wreckage retrieving bodies floating among the ruins, witnessed the anguish of those examining the bulletin boards pinned with endless rows of photos of the missing and the confirmed dead.

If she had courage, she thought, she would have flown that day to one of the disaster sites and volunteered her help. Or at least she would be out on the streets collecting money for the survivors, like the woman with the cloth coat and blue scarf.

SHE FELT SHE should continue walking. A man standing idly in the doorway of a pub called out to her as she passed. Allison gave him a cold stare. Ahead was a pair of round blue signs with arrows pointing left, and so Allison turned left. She found herself on another piazza enclosed by an open triangle of matching buildings, their curved façades a warm, inviting peach. The buildings gave Allison the impression of serenity and order – a repeated pattern of framed rectangles – as each painted section of each storey of each house and each shuttered blue-gray window and arched doorway was outlined in unpainted stone. A row of sturdy shrubs in concrete planters prevented motorcycles and cars from cluttering the square. A dozen or so pigeons – stocky and officious, fat bankers in gray suits – pecked the cracks between the piazza's cobblestones.

On the left side of the square stood the towering façade of Sant'Ignazio di Loyola. Allison walked up the steps and entered the dark church.

SHE DIPPED TWO fingers into the holy water font and genuflected while crossing herself. The church itself was a baroque gift – a wide, tall, dizzy array of multicolored marble and plaster, decorative stucco, lavishly textured, with hardly a corner untouched. Everything in the church appeared positioned for the viewer's consideration, each detail part of an elaborately staged design. Winged angels thrust themselves dramatically from chapel walls. Putti flew alongside banners, faces bursting with glee. Glistening marble statues gazed down at Allison, beckoning. Before each side chapel stood tiers of candles, flames quivering in devotion.

Allison walked slowly toward the main altar, gazing up at the church's ceiling. It depicted joyful figures of the faithful ascending triumphantly into the heavens, aided by chubby cherubs and more angels, while several of the less fortunate – sinners, skeptics, unbelievers – plunged gracelessly downward, desperately grasping the sides of the church's vaulted ceiling as they fell. Though it seemed less impressive, even flat, when she'd first entered, Allison saw now that the ceiling was indeed vaulted and that the steep sides of its rather magnificent clerestory were further adorned with windows and pillars and arches and statues reaching up into the church's heights. As she neared the arms of the transept, the dark belly of the church's cupola opened above her, and for several moments Allison stared up and into the round dome, at the gold circle of sunlight emanating from its lantern.

"Step more close to the disc," said a man in a raw voice. The man stood in the shadows at the edge of the main altar, stretching out an arm. His English was edged with a German accent. "If you stand more close, yes, directly on the gold disc there at your feet, you may appreciate the illusion even more."

"The illusion?" Allison said. She looked at where the man pointed. Set nearby in the marble floor was a winged skull, but a half-step away, nearly the size of a basketball, was the yellow disc the man referred to.

The heels of his boots rang out as he approached. He wore a dark overcoat, open and unbuttoned, over a smoky gray jacket and vest and matching wide-cuffed trousers. His thin hair was unnaturally black – obviously dyed – and combed back sternly away from his face. As he approached, Allison could smell his cologne, something sharp, chemical. Its intensity made her pull away.

"I don't understand," Allison said.

"I serve as a guide," the man told her and reached out to shake her hand. Allison took a step backward, declining his touch. "In a few moments, or two or three if they are on time, here will be coming my tour group." He paused. "Who so very kindly arranged, how shall I say, my services." The man glanced up and away, as if searching the air for the right word. "My expertise, you understand, yes, to present historical explanations. Backgrounds and hidden truths, all concerning the great Roman past. The sort of information one does not find in guidebooks. In this instance I tell of one of Andrea Pozzo's grand creations."

"Andrea Pozzo," Allison said.

The guide smiled and nodded, as if Allison had said something that made him proud.

"Very certainly, yes." His outstretched hand tapped Allison's arm. "Brother Andrea Pozzo, the seventeenth-century lay brother of the most sacred Society of Jesus, or Jesuits, as they are known, who himself painted both this church's apse and ceiling. A great artist, a true master of perspective. Perhaps in all of Rome, Andrea Pozzo was the most famous of quadraturisti."

Allison stood on the gold disc and gazed up at the church's ribbed, coffered dome, then back at the dark-haired man. "Thank you," she said.

"Quadratura is a variation, a further adaption, if you will, of trompe-l'oeil. What you are looking at" – he waved a practiced hand toward the illusion of a dome – "is actually two-dimensional, mere paint, do you understand, artfully applied to a flat surface." He spread the palm of one hand evenly in the air. "The eye imagines it sees depth, but there is none. None. No depth at all. Flat. Do you see it now?" He laughed. "All is illusion, deception. Trompe-l'oeil, a trick of the eye. What the eighteenth-century historian Francesco Milizia called a *diavoleria*. A devil's trick. Stand back, yes, that's it, now come closer. Now you see, no? Yes? Yes? As is the case of the first painting" – again he pointed, this time toward the church's ceiling – "which offers to the eye the illusion of a vaulted ceiling. That painting, too" – again he spread out his hands, as if smoothing a wrinkled bed sheet – "is perfectly flat. Quadratura simulates the depth of actual architecture from a single point of perspective, as marked by the disc on the floor."

Allison nodded.

"It began like so many other things, with the ancient Greeks." He leaned toward Allison and nodded as if sharing a family secret, then launched into another prepared speech. "As the old tale goes, two of Greece's most famous of artists held a competition – yes? – to determine which could paint the more convincing trompe-l'oeil. One day they met in the village courtyard before a large crowd who would serve as their judge. The first artist painted a table on which was a display of fruits. The fruits were so vivid and true that the birds of the air flew down from the sky to pluck them. Certain that he had won, the first painter turned to the second artist's canvas, which was hidden by a tattered curtain. 'Unwrap your painting and show us your work,' he said, only to realize as his words left his mouth that the painting of his competitor was of a canvas hidden by a curtain."

Allison smiled.

"The crowd cheered, and the first painter acknowledged his defeat. 'My work may have deceived the birds,' he said, 'but your work has deceived me.'"

By now a noisy throng of tourists was filing into the church, laminated tags dangling from their lanyards. They milled about the holy water font, staring around, lost sheep in search of a shepherd.

"If you'll forgive me," the man said in a low voice, "my group awaits. But my service as a guide, it does not take up the whole day. Perhaps later this evening" – he tipped back his head and grinned broadly – "we could meet for a drink. Perhaps, yes?"

"Thank you," Allison said in a firm voice. "No."

ONE DETAIL ABOUT the South-Asian tsunami that Allison couldn't shake was how the sea off Thailand receded before the first of the great waves hit. Allison knew that *tsunami* was a Japanese word that meant *harbor wave*. When the massive underwater earthquake off the coast of Sumatra struck a minute before eight on the morning of 26 December, the sudden lurching of the Earth's tectonic plates, pressing mightily against one another for centuries, shot untold tons of rock into the ocean above, causing the water to swell upwards with tremendous urgency and power. Gravity then pulled the rock back down to the seabed, forcing the energy to disperse itself horizontally, out along the ocean's surface. The result was similar to tossing a stone into a pool of water and observing the subsequent ripples, the only difference being that in a tsunami the stone is tossed in reverse, thrust up from beneath the sea's surface. During the quake a section of one of the plates nearly twelve hundred kilometers long plunged nine meters beneath another plate, generating the energy equivalent to a million Hiroshima bombs.

As the great wave grows in the deep ocean, it gathers incredible speed, then slows and attains height as it nears land. One television analyst claimed the tsunami's speed as it hit land was faster than Japan's bullet train. As a tsunami nears shore, it encounters increasingly shallow water, which compresses the force of its energy and draws even more water upward toward its crest. Sometimes the coastal waters disappear completely as they are drawn back up into the approaching wave. This is what happened that December morning in Thailand, when the sea suddenly receded, pulling itself back from the shoreline, like a deadly lover drawing back a bed's top sheet.

How inviting it must have been to see the ocean suddenly pull itself back, Allison thought. Who wouldn't rush out onto the newly naked ocean floor to observe the effects of the phenomenon? Allison knew that if she had been on the shore and had seen the tide reverse itself she would have eagerly run after it. She understood the ploy all too well, how a calculated retreat served only to heighten and encourage the pursuit.

LATER THAT EVENING, after watching more Kieślowski and searching the internet for a schedule of Rome's AA meetings, Allison took a taxi that dropped her off at the intersection of Via Nazionale and Via Napoli. There on the corner opposite the church where the AA meetings were held was an Irish pub, neon Harp and Guinness signs glowing in its windows, a row of green shamrocks cheerfully spotting the dark glass above the signs.

The pub reminded Allison of her native Chicago, any one of a thousand and one corner taverns, the yeasty smell of beer so thick that once you walked in the door you could nearly taste it. Mounted high in one corner a TV set would be showing the latest White Sox, Cubs, or Bulls game. On the wall opposite the bar would hang framed photos of Chicago's two Irish-Catholic heroes – Richard J. Daley and John F. Kennedy – the beloved mayor and the martyred president. Hard-knuckled union men would straddle the barstools, smoking cigarettes or panatelas, talking politics and sports, work and the demands and grinds of family life. They'd knock back shots of Jack Daniels chased by glasses of cold beer.

Her father owned such a bar, a few blocks from the old stockyards on Chicago's South Side. Stormy, husky, brawling Chicago. City of the big shoulders. Her family lived upstairs in a two-bedroom flat, the five of them – her three brothers, her father, and herself. The mother gone, buried in a plot on the city's far Southwest Side beneath a stone slab with a weeping Angel of Grief slumped over the headstone, arms folded, obscuring her face, wings drooping on either side of the slab. A donation from the bar's regulars.

Allison hesitated at the pub's doorway, tempted to go inside if only for a moment to smell the air. No, she told herself. No. She wouldn't give in to the temptation. The place she needed to go was across the street. Several men stood there by a gangway, talking and smoking cigarettes. Sure sign of a meeting. They grew silent as she approached.

She descended the back stairs. There on the concrete wall in front of her was a plaque bearing the familiar circle enclosing a triangle. She stepped down another flight of steps and then down a hallway that led to an arched doorway where she heard muffled voices coming from a basement room. Yes, there on the walls were the Serenity Prayer in Italian, the Twelve Steps and Traditions in English, the Steps and Traditions in Italian, and the usual assortment of signs.

Easy Does It. First Things First. Keep It Simple. One Day At A Time.

And sitting by herself in a chair against the wall was the woman Allison had seen earlier that day by the Fountain of the Four Rivers, the woman with the azure scarf. As Allison rounded the corner their eyes met, and the two women smiled nearly identical smiles.

SHE WAS BORN in the former republic of Yugoslavia, Dubravka told Allison the next day as they met for coffee near the Piazza Venezia. Allison insisted they sit at a table rather than stand at the bar. In

Croatia, the woman continued, in Dubrovnik, where she'd worked in her uncle's restaurant until she was sixteen. Then she traveled north, to Bosnia and Herzegovina. At eighteen she returned to Croatia and entered a convent, leading the simplest of lives.

"A simple life," Allison said. "I can hardly imagine it."

"It was precisely what you'd expect," Dubravka said. "Austere. Insulated. Governed strictly by rule. The outside world blocked out. A life of near-complete silence. A great deal of meditation and prayer, punctuated by work and sleep."

"And yet," Allison began.

"And yet you'd like to know how someone could be a sister in a cloistered convent and at the same time maintain the habits of an alcoholic."

Allison nodded.

"Well," Dubravka said, smiling, "you start by working in the kitchen because its back door is the one place in the convent open to the larger world. Because of my work in my uncle's restaurant, my superiors were more than happy to place me there. Of course the convent had a rigid hierarchy. At the top were the choir sisters, who came from wealthy families and therefore were taught to read Latin. They were the ones in charge, the ones who chanted vespers and each day's Divine Office. At the bottom were a few paid lay servants and the unpaid women like me, the ones from poor families, who did the convent's domestic work. The servant sisters, or sometimes they called us kitchen sisters."

"And the convent served alcohol?"

Dubravka laughed. "Do you think everyone who cinches a rope around their waist is a saint? Far from it. The priests here in Rome, they hold their own AA meetings. Quite large ones from what I hear. And of course absolutely closed to outsiders."

"Of course," Allison said.

"Being a member of the clergy," Dubravka continued, "one is prone to sins of the flesh. Prohibit some desires, others emerge in their place. Sins of excess. For many, it's food. Look at all the fat priests you see walking about. With others, it's drink. An aperitif as the sun nears the horizon, another just before dinner, followed by wine with the evening meal, then Scotch or sherry. Of course our convent had wine as well as a small supply of spirits. I always found ways to get what I wanted. I had very little problem with access."

"And no one suspected you?"

"They more than suspected me but what could they do, cast me out? Our numbers had been in decline for years. Besides, I was an excellent worker. I was advised to take up the problem with my confessor, who himself drank even more than I did. He told me to pray and exercise control."

"Control?" Allison said. "By yourself?"

"He left things up to me. At the time I was certain I could keep the ship from sinking. I didn't cause anyone serious problems." She paused, then forged ahead with the sanitized version of her life in the convent as a drunk. Dubravka often had difficulty admitting the truth even to herself. "I was never sloppy. Everyone enjoyed the food I made. And if now and then something came out a bit burnt, well, you scraped off the part that was inedible and did your best to appreciate the rest. So you could say that at times I offered others in my community the opportunity to cultivate forgiveness. I was an exceptionally clean drunk. Neat, organized, attentive."

The women sipped their coffee and sat for several moments in silence.

"So why did you quit?" Allison asked after a while.

Dubravka seemed to be thinking of something else. "Drinking? Or remaining in the convent?"

Allison stared at Dubravka's face, which in its character still reminded her of Véronique's. "Either. Both."

The woman looked away, then down at her hands. "Because I missed the world – all of its flaws and clutter and beauty." She gazed out the window for several moments, then back at Allison as she nodded. "At least that's what I tell people when I'm asked."

"And what don't you tell people?"

Dubravka laughed. She shook a packet of sugar, then spilled it into what remained of her coffee. "You have a way in conversations of asking questions."

"I'm sorry," Allison said. "It's a habit, I guess. I learned where I work how to extend conversations. I listen, then ask questions."

Dubravka wagged her head. "There's no reason for you to apologize. To answer your question, I became proud and increasingly resentful."

"Go on."

Dubravka shrugged. "Personal stuff. Too much to go into." She was being honest now. She didn't want to talk about Marija or the dying pope. "But to give you an idea of the big picture, over time I became judgmental. I thought, simultaneously, that I was better than the average person, that I was a part of something somehow helping to save the world while everyone else was free to do whatever they wanted, and at the same time I felt incredibly inferior. Sometimes the silence in the convent became so unbearable that I stopped whatever I was doing and screamed." She sipped her coffee. "Likely the others imagined that I'd stepped too near the stove and burned myself."

Outside the bar's window, a young man on an idling motorcycle caught Allison's eye and smiled, then kissed his thumb and first two fingers and popped them hungrily before his face. Behind him, passing through the crowds crossing the congested corner, Spencer Tracy paused near the curb and bent and picked up a piece of paper – a crumpled euro? a fallen matchbook? – from the sidewalk.

"And you," Dubravka said. "What type of work do you do in Japan?"

"Nothing too special," Allison answered. "I'm a waitress." Spencer Tracy was wearing a tan double-breasted suit, a silk tie the soft color of caramel. No hat. His thick silver hair was combed to one side and flapped slightly in the breeze. Allison scanned the faces of the others in the crowd, expecting to see Katherine Hepburn. The man on the motorcycle was still smiling. Then with a roar and a wink and a wave he sped away.

"A waitress," Dubravka said, nodding. "Another kitchen worker." She gazed at Allison and then reached out and touched her hand. "That makes us comrades. Yes?"

AFTER HER COFFEE with Dubravka, after she walked up Via del Corso and then through a maze of side streets looking for Via del Piè di Marmo and its gigantic marble foot, after she passed the corner that smelled of chocolates and the pair of stationery stores and neared the entrance to her hotel, Allison noticed a young woman who stood below a shrine to the Madonna hanging over the papal shop, Gammarelli's. The woman was slight, dark-haired, Asian. Her eyes looked back at Allison and seemed to be asking a question, inviting conversation. Allison knew the look. She nearly approached the woman but was distracted by a pair of lovers – a girl wearing a baseball cap, obviously North American, joking with an Italian boy near the statue of the elephant. The woman beneath the shrine continued to stare at her, as if Allison reminded her of someone she knew. Allison turned, entered her hotel.

As she approached the front desk she saw that the guide who'd spoken to her in Sant'Ignazio was now standing behind her in the hotel lobby. The lobby was a vast place, extravagantly appointed, named for Minerva, the vengeful daughter of a Greek god.

"Permit me to introduce myself," the guide said as Allison turned. The man puffed out his chest – a male bird beginning its display. "My name is Helmut, and I am agreeable, yes, I am most agreeable to place myself at your service." He extended a hand so as to draw her further into the hotel's expansive lounge. "Perhaps you and I may speak privately?"

His eyes were red – glassy – and his breath smelled of something sweet. Mint or anise, Allison thought. Whatever, it was more than obvious that he'd been drinking. As he talked, he brushed the lapels of his overcoat and bounced slightly up and down on his toes.

"I'm sorry," Allison said as kindly and firmly as she could. "When we met you must have misunderstood me. I don't have any need for your services."

"But this ancient city and its many churches and ruins," the man said. "Without someone knowledgeable to guide you, to explain." He tossed his hands in the air. "Rome's secrets are like a locked door, and you come here as a stranger, a foreign guest, alone and without a key." He grinned. "You are here for only how long? One more day? Two, three? Or perhaps a week or fortnight?"

"Thank you, but no. I've just told you, I'm not at all interested."

"That's only what you say now. I beg of you" – he reached toward the arm of her cranberry jacket, then gestured toward the armchairs in the lounge – "please, let us sit. Allow me to more fully introduce myself."

"No, really. Thank you."

"How can you not be interested – "

"Enough," Allison said. "Don't invite me to be rude. My husband is waiting for me upstairs. Would you prefer for me to call him down here so that he can explain?" She paused for effect. "Neither he nor I are interested."

"Your husband. I did not know." The guide blinked several times. "I would be most happy to speak with him."

"This afternoon he asked not to be disturbed."

"In that case," Helmut said, stepping back and nearly clicking together his heels, "I shall leave you. I wanted only to avail myself – "

"Thank you," Allison said as she turned away. She made certain the man had walked out of the hotel's glass doors and onto the piazza before approaching the clerk at the front desk and requesting her room key.

"It was always 'Little Allie, Little Allie, where's Little Allie? Get Little Allie. Why isn't Little Allie down here?' Let me tell you, over time I came to despise that name."

Allison was eating lunch with Dubravka at a trattoria a half block down from Via dei Farnesi, a simple place with checkered paper tablecloths, where the day's menu was scrawled in Italian on a chalkboard. On the walls alongside and opposite the chalkboard were displays of decidedly mediocre art – landscapes depicting places not terribly memorable, still lifes that shifted perspective in less than graceful ways – along with a dozen or so faded photographs of the generations of the establishment's owners posing with friends and families as well as yellowing newspaper clippings of past reviews, each in a dusty frame. Of course the vegetables were perfectly seasoned and grilled, the bread in the basket fresh and crisp, the homemade pasta utterly perfect. Bad art on the walls insures that what is served on the paper tablecloths is outstanding.

Living above the tavern, having a young girl around, even if she was an underaged string bean, all of it was good for business, Allison explained. Her father noticed that customers would ask about her whenever she wasn't there, and stay longer and drink more when she was. To appease him, she'd consent to sit on a barstool in a far corner, where she tried to do her homework. Even then the men would call out to her, ask her opinion about whatever ballgame was playing on the TV. The men grew happy whenever she listened to them and answered, whenever she passed by their tables and carried away their bottles – *dead soldiers*, the men called them. They grew happy when she emptied their overflowing ashtrays. No funny stuff, of course, no off-color comments or jokes, since her father and usually at least one of her brothers were always around, but always a few winks, lingering pats on her hand, grins and plenty of tips dropped into a wide-mouthed pickle jar labeled *Little Allie's College Fund*, every penny of which went into her father's pockets, until catering to the tavern's customers became an expected duty, a routine part of the girl's life.

Dubravka nodded. "The girls here today, in Rome and throughout much of Italy, all of them nowadays they want to become veline."

"Veline?" said Allison.

Dubravka nodded again and explained that veline were the young women who assisted the male host of a television show, often by reading something from a card and then performing a stacchetto, or brief dance. Originally the term *velina* referred to the thin paper on which a press release was printed and, during Mussolini's era of power, was allowed to be read on the news. Then a TV show that parodied reading the news introduced a pair of sexy young women – one blonde, the other brunette – who handed two veline to the host as they performed a seductive dance. Soon the term came to refer to the young women themselves. You can blame Berlusconi, Dubravka said. Now nearly every show on Italian television featured its own stable of scantily clad veline, suggestively writhing across the screen.

"I've seen them," Allison said. "'Baci, baci,' They wear next to nothing and dance and throw kisses to the audience."

"Roman girls actually compete with one another," Dubravka said, "hoping to become one. As if acting mindless in public is something to strive for."

The pair grew silent as a woman selling red roses entered the trattoria and began moving from one table to the next. Dubravka spoke to her in soft, rapid Italian, and the woman walked away. Then a tall North American with sad, heavy eyes approached their table and begged their forgiveness for the intrusion but might Dubravka be the woman who'd been collecting money by the Piazza Navona fountain on the day of the tsunami? The man wore an expensive sweater and jacket and spoke with a slight accent. After Dubravka nodded, the man pressed two twenty-euro notes next to their basket of bread.

"You could have put this in any donation box in any church," Dubravka said. She remembered seeing the man, noticing him, praying for him.

"I have," Ben said. "I have in several, but I felt I needed to find you. Because I walked past you that day. With my wife. We were in a rush." He paused. "I saw you but I didn't stop. I wasn't paying attention."

"And now you are." Dubravka nodded. "Thank you."

"You're welcome," Ben said. "And now I am. Now I'm paying attention." He looked around, as if suddenly embarrassed. "Here in Italy now, we're not rushing. We're staying a while longer." He seemed to want to say more but then smiled at the two women and nodded and turned and walked away.

THE PAIR ATE in silence. After a while Dubravka said, "Given all you've told me, what drew you to Japan?"

Allison shrugged. To admit it was the promise of money would expose her, but the promise lay at the base of her motives. Still, Tokyo was considerably more expensive than she'd anticipated. There was the constant need for new clothes, shoes, and makeup. She was expected to wear a different outfit every night and never travel to and from the club in public transportation, which meant she always had to take taxis.

Since a good hostess made her guest feel not only like a man but also like a man who might get somewhere, her job was based largely on guile. A good hostess in a Japanese club never said yes and never said no – the answer to every question always had to be *perhaps* or *maybe*. The window of possibility always needed to remain open, just as it was her duty to jump up and shout "Irasshaimase!" as the Doll Shop door swung open and the first guests of the evening arrived. It was her duty to fetch hot wet flannel cloths and the first round of snacks. It was her duty to drop ice cubes into glasses, pour drinks, light cigarettes.

It was her duty to assure each man that he was attractive, intelligent, witty, even when he was as dull as last year's newspaper. To keep up the flow of conversation and attend to each of the guest's words, even when the talk grew personal and bawdy. To never answer any question directly or admit to having done any specific thing. To always agree that anything hinted at, even the grossest suggestion, sounded interesting, was a possibility. To laugh with surprise each time a hand dipped below the table. To gently slap the offending hand and return it to where it belonged, then act as if nothing inappropriate had happened. To defer everything to the realm of *perhaps*, the territory of *maybe*.

And if a hostess wanted to earn money – real money – she had to entice men to invite her on a dohan, either to dinner before the club opened or for drinks after the club closed. In addition to paying the club a fee for the dohan, the client normally gave the woman cash or a gift, most often jewelry, which she could later sell. Of course the expectation was eventual intimacy, though if the mama-san discovered that a worker was having actual sexual contact with a guest – *pillow business*, it was called – the hostess would be fired. The dohan meant always walking the fine line between promise and fulfillment. The women at the Doll Shop were expected to arrange and go out on at least several dohans each month.

"Looking back," Allison said, "I guess what attracted me was the idea of escape. Japan was as far away from Chicago as I could imagine. At the time, had there been a way to get there, I would have gone to the dark side of the moon."

"And you go to meetings there?"

"A few. When I can. The women's meetings mainly, on Fridays. Two years now. But I never make it very long." She hesitated. "My work continually compromises me."

Dubravka smiled. "Then maybe you should change your work."

"Yeah," Allison said. She shook her hair and laughed, then poured herself some of the sparkling mineral water from the tall green bottle that stood on the table. "I don't know." She sighed. "I get so tired of myself sometimes. I'm never really where I want to be. It's like I'm between things, if that makes any sense. Sometimes I think that if you took a photograph of my life the real me wouldn't even be in the picture."

Dubravka nodded. "I know how that feels. To be on the side of things, between the mountains. So far down you can't even gaze up and see the mountains' peaks, and yet you know that somehow you need to see them, to climb up and beyond them, or rush down the rocks to the valley and the sea." While she talked, her hands outlined the shape of mountains. "But one morning the fog lifts, and you recognize things as if you hadn't seen them before, and you realize where you stand."

"Between the mountains," Allison said. "Yes. That's exactly how I feel."

FOR A WHILE Dubravka sat silently. "You know," she said as a waitress cleared their plates, "the first time we met, I told you how in the convent I became prideful. Later I thought I should explain. It began when I tried to figure out when is the start of life."

"Big question," Allison said.

Dubravka nodded. "I don't mean biological. We all know the answer to that, when the cells grow and divide. I mean the soul. The divine essence. The question of when the soul inhabits the physical body. Whether it's the very moment of conception, as the Church tells us to believe, or three or four months later, when the fetus quickens in the womb, or perhaps still later, when the child is actually born." She paused.

"There was a woman in the convent, one of the kitchen sisters, who was repeatedly raped by her brother. A brutal story. After two months she had the fetus aborted, then came to the convent to pray. Not for God's forgiveness, mind you. She felt she'd done nothing wrong. She told us she was certain that the cells growing inside her didn't yet have a soul. She neither loved nor hated them. She believed they were merely multiplying cells. She said she knew women who claimed they could feel a child in their womb the week after it was conceived, but she felt only a void. Emptiness. She said she came to the convent to pray for the others like her. Women who are raped and become pregnant by rape, that they find peace, no matter what decision they make."

"So you believe in abortion?"

"I believe the decision should belong to the woman. I believe that since it's her body she would know best. Whether a fetus is merely a mass of growing cells or something with a divine soul, I'd trust the woman to be able to tell. Consider that miscarriages are not named, baptized, or buried. It's only after a birth or sometimes even longer that a name is given and a soul is blessed. You'd be surprised what the mind in a cloistered convent can think of, what algebras it chooses to invent and work out once the hands are made busy with work and the tongue is shackled. Your thoughts, like horses free of fences, run wild."

Dubravka refilled her glass with mineral water, then took in a deep breath. "My cousin became pregnant a few months before I left Dubrovnik. Everyone knew it was by a Serb. Her family disowned her, vowed to never again speak of her. I spent years hating her for what she'd taken from me. I searched for her, for him, simply to be able to stand before them, to show them my face. To remind them both of my existence."

"I'm not sure I follow."

"I didn't know exactly what I wanted from them, but I did want something. Particularly if it had all been a mean trick. I didn't want them to think they'd gotten away with it. But then over time, as I searched street after street not finding them, my anger turned toward the realization that had they only made use of a contraceptive my cousin likely wouldn't have become pregnant. I even thought that had she aborted the fetus no one would ever have needed to know." Dubravka stared at Allison, trying to read her face. "Do you find that shocking?"

"No," Allison said.

"I often had that thought while we worked together in the kitchen. I could see it before the others did. Everyone knew of a woman in town who took care of such things. I would look at my cousin and imagine her and the woman taking care of it. I was certain then that he'd tire of her, since I was – " She hesitated.

"Since you were what?"

"Since I was young. Since at the time I had a lot of foolish, selfish thoughts."

"That he'd leave her for you?"

Dubravka didn't answer. With one hand she waved the question away. "I was young. My cousin would never have thought to go to the woman, and the Serb would never have considered using a contraceptive. We were all taught that condoms are a device beloved by Satan. The Church's rationale? Condoms both invite and facilitate mortal sin as well as interfere with sex's true purpose, which is procreation. Nothing here about love or emotions or protection against disease. One of the causes our Mother Superior had us pray for was an end to the spread of the HIV virus, particularly in Africa. Hundreds of thousands of Africans die from AIDS every year."

"It's a tragedy," Allison said.

"John Paul went to Africa in 1990, when HIV was raging across the continent, and instead of speaking out in favor of contraceptives he told the crowds that the use of condoms was the gravest sin. People who came to see and hear him already believed the disease was a punishment from God. They wanted to hear from this holy man from Rome that it was not. They looked to him for the affirmation that the advice the foreign aid workers were giving them, that they should make regular use of condoms, was the best way to prevent the disease. Instead, John Paul told them to practice abstinence. His speeches set the cause of AIDS and HIV education back by more than a generation."

"Well, wasn't that what the pope was supposed to say?"

Dubravka shook her head. "Not if he had compassion. Not if he put himself for one moment in their place. Here he was, telling an impoverished continent to give up one of their lives' only comforts. Do you know that it's impossible today to find anyone in Africa whose family hasn't been affected by the disease? I came to judge the man not only as wrong but indirectly responsible for the deaths of millions. Can we even begin to hold that number in our minds? It's like trying to imagine how many were slaughtered during the Holocaust. All because birth control is forbidden by a celibate pope." She shook her head. "Years later my parish priest sent me a letter saying rumor had it that my cousin had contracted the same disease. There are times I think I should have been her."

"I'm glad you were not."

Dubravka raised her eyebrows. "Oh, none of it really matters now, does it? I say rosaries for their souls, and sometimes I imagine a poor child somewhere wandering the streets. For some reason I sense the child, had she lived, was a girl. She'd be in her twenties now."

Allison reached forward and placed her hands on Dubravka's.

"I tell you, my mind runs around in circles. I put myself in my cousin's place and wonder what I would have done. I'm sure that had I been in her shoes, things would have ended differently. I'm certain there would have been times when she failed to do something I would have, or times when she did something I wouldn't have done." She dropped the flat of her hand firmly down onto the table. "And even now my daring to judge the pope makes me feel uneasy. This is where my defect of pride comes in. Who am I to think such thoughts? In the world's order I'm hardly more than a crumb. A worm. As the prayer goes, in God's eyes I'm his poorest and meanest servant." Dubravka laughed. "I'm certainly no one to measure someone else, and yet another part of me" – she took in a deep breath – "another part of me is more than willing to use my ability to reason. To think things through to conclusions." She nodded. "Bruno's statue stands in the square where I live. I don't think it's an accident my life has led me here. Each day I look up at his hooded face and cross myself. I consider him both a martyr and a saint. His courage gives me strength and makes me proud."

"You give me strength and make me proud," Allison said, eyes wide.

Dubravka's face softened. "I'm nothing special. All I do is try to think things out. Like a child in school assigned an arithmetic problem by her teacher. Convent life gives one's mind ample time to do the mathematics."

THAT AFTERNOON ALLISON walked about the piazza outside the Pantheon. She watched a flock of pigeons gather to peck whatever had fallen between the sampietrini. As passersby neared, the birds spread wide their wings, slapped them back sharply to their bodies, and took flight. Allison watched the vendors – recent immigrants, each man dark-skinned, wearing nylon jackets that seemed far too thin for the season – do much the same. The vendors placed a blanket or tarp down on the stones, on which they displayed whatever it was they were selling. Some vendors used cleverly folded cardboard sheets they could snap open into waist-high, make-shift stands. They positioned themselves along the most frequented walkways. Whenever the carabinieri approached, the nearest vendor let out a whistle and the others gathered up their wares and scattered like the birds. Then as soon as the carabinieri strolled out of sight the birds settled again on the cobblestones and the vendors set up shop.

She craved a drink. There, in each of the cafés lining the piazza, waiters carried trays bearing glasses of red wine that glistened like inviting jewels.

Drinking took the edge off things, fuzzed the lines, eased life's harshness. Drinking clicked the switch that flooded the room with a warm, all-encompassing glow. Stealing sips from the many shiny bottles downstairs in the tavern made living upstairs with her father and brothers more bearable. Allison walked back to her hotel and then, deciding against another afternoon watching DVDs, continued walking until she found herself again on the square that fronted Sant'Ignazio. A woman squatted outside the church's doorway, holding out a wooden bowl. Allison dropped a few coins into the bowl and entered the dark church.

She stared up at the ceiling and made it go flat and then pop back up toward the sky. Then she did the same with Pozzo's dome. One moment it was one thing – the next, something else. Just like her in Japan. The trick was easy once you knew how to do it. In the Doll Shop Allison was even known by another name. It was the same with the doubles she could see. You stared at a crowd until a detail about a person triggered some switch in your mind, and then you surrendered and let your imagination take control, blur what was there before you, fill the necessary gaps. Do it often enough and you didn't even have to think about it. It would simply happen by itself.

After her mother's death, Allison mastered the trick in Marshall Field's, the massive downtown department store on Chicago's State Street. The girl would think she saw her dead mother browsing or purchasing something – a new scarf or a pair of gloves, a green box of Frango mints. Allison would free herself from her father's grasp and rush toward her mother, try to grab the back of her coat and pull, but she was never quite fast enough. She would always end up tugging the back of the wrong coat, as the wrong woman with the wrong face turned and stared strangely down at her while Allison's real mother slipped away, deeper into the recesses of the immense store. Her father always apologized to the woman and later chided Allison, the skinny stupid daughter he could never take anywhere without her causing an embarrassing scene.

At home she would sulk. At night she'd lie in bed and talk to herself, create imaginary conversations between herself and the false mothers in the store, who would try to explain why they weren't at home with her. Sometimes they had to cook something – a chicken or a pot roast – in someone else's kitchen. Why? the girl would ask. The women would explain that they'd made a promise to another family, and when you make a promise you have to keep it. But what about the promise you made to us? Allison would ask.

After a while she kept the sightings to herself. Then *Full House* debuted on TV. Of course her father was Danny, though much older and more grumpy, and her two brothers were less fashionable versions of Joey and Jesse. She was the middle girl, the thin blonde, Stephanie. Allison spent hours writing the name *Stephanie* inside her school notebooks. She wrote the name in fat overlapping letters that resembled balloons. Stephanie was Allison's name at the Doll Shop. When people asked young Allison about *Full House*, she said the main reason she liked the show was because it didn't have a mother, that in the show not having a mother didn't matter, not one single bit! If anything, the family didn't need a silly mother. And even an idiot could see that the show wasn't named *Empty House* or *Empty Sad House* or *Empty Stupid Horrible Sad House Where Downstairs Was a Disgusting Smelly Tavern Full of Disgusting Smelly Men*. No, this was a full house, so full that there were even two of the youngest daughter, cute little Michelle, though on TV you saw only one at a time. It was just like that with her mother, Allison believed. There were two of them as well – one sleeping beneath the cold gray stone topped by the grieving angel, the other somewhere out in the real world, shopping for a new blouse or skirt or making pork chops or meatloaf or spaghetti for some other family.

Young Allison didn't know why, but that was the rule. It was like all of the other things she didn't understand. The world was full of stupid rules. It was then that she began spending less time doing the pathetic things – inventing endless dialogues with her mother as the pair sat on the girl's bed, opening and closing her mother's dresser drawers so Allison could catch the fading whispers of her mother's smell, crying and sucking her thumb as she lay curled like a forgotten sock on the floor of what was once her mother's closet – and more time downstairs on the barstool being told she was pretty by strange men.

Near the painting of the dome stood a wooden confessional box – a shrine to a deceased priest, Father Felice Cappello. Hanging inside the confessional were the priest's portrait, black cassock, purple stole. His Roman collar rested on a worn cushion on his chair. The confessional's inner walls were lined with scores of silver hearts topped by flames and a cross, tokens offered in gratitude for favors granted.

The sympathetic expression on the Jesuit's face in the portrait invited Allison to cross herself, then step around and kneel on the wooden plank at the side of the confessional as if the good priest were still there.

She decided to surrender. For a moment she rested her forehead against the grid separating the priest from the penitent. On the grid was the embossed outline of a crucifix standing atop a bank of clouds. She folded her hands and leaned them on the wooden ledge. "Bless me, Father," she whispered into the metal grate, as if the priest were still there.

IN THE PIAZZA outside Sant'Ignazio, the foreign guide stood by one of the concrete planters, smoking a cigarette. On the sampietrini near his black boots were several crushed butts. "Ha," he cried when Allison stepped through the side door. "I knew you would return."

Allison saw that he had been waiting for her. She said nothing.

"I've followed you," the man said with a knowing nod. "I've watched your every move. You aren't what you pretend to be. You have no husband."

Allison froze.

"I know what path you've chosen," the man told her. "The image of you, I tell you, in my mind it does not go away."

Allison took in a breath and thought of herself in her father's bar, clearing the booths of empty bottles. She thought of the tables in the Doll Shop, how she'd carefully stack the plates. She thought of *The Double Life of Véronique*, the scene near the film's ending, when Véronique spills the contents of her purse onto her bed and sees the photographs she'd taken from the windows of the tour bus and notices there in the crowd on Krakow Square her double, a woman dressed as she herself that day was dressed, standing on the square gazing back at her, caught in the moment of recognizing her own image, as if seeing herself for the first time.

"All a man has to do is look at you," the guide said. "The way you walk down the street. The clothing that you wear. You know what you are, what you pretend."

"I don't care what you think you see," Allison said as she walked away.

It was only later, after she returned to her hotel room with scissors that she bought at one of the stationery shops near the store that smelled so darkly of chocolate, and then hair clippers at a pharmacy on Corso Vittorio, that she understood what she was about to do. This was before she removed her eyeliner and mascara with a cotton pad, before she showered, before she dried herself with one of the hotel's plush towels and stood naked before the bathroom mirror taking measure of herself. Before she took the scissors to her long hair and hacked as much as she could away, then lowered the setting on the hair clippers and gently buzzed her skull, feeling the clippings fall softly on her shoulders and breasts. Before she gathered the fallen hair and wiped the floor with tissues and cleaned the hair from the sink so that some poor maid wouldn't have to do it. Before she showered a second time and then decided on a bath. Before she lay in the tub's hot water until it grew cool as the light from the windows in her hotel room grew faint and then dark. Before she wrapped herself in another of the hotel's towels and drew out her laptop. Before she made the telephone calls to the relief agency and left her name and a detailed message. Before she booked a one-way ticket to Soekarno-Hatta, Jakarta's international airport, where she would join the other tsunami-relief volunteers. Before she finally went to bed and slept a deep sleep and then woke and ventured out into the streets of Rome searching for Dubravka, who, reliably, was offering her wooden collection box to the holiday crowds by the Fountain of the Four Rivers.

"Good Lord," Dubravka said. "Is that you?"

"Don't be surprised." Allison ran her hand over the top of her head, feeling the soft stubble. "Do you like it?"

"I nearly didn't recognize you. You look like someone else."

"I am someone else," Allison said.

"Aren't you cold?"

"Yes. Unbelievably so." She shivered and laughed.

The women talked as the waters in the fountain swirled and splashed, and then Allison slipped her arms out of her cranberry Pierotucci jacket and offered it to Dubravka. "I think we're close to the same size. I would love it if you kept this for yourself."

"No, I couldn't," Dubravka said.

"Here, as a favor to me. I want you to have it. Just try it on for a moment, please, to see how it fits."

"And what will you wear?" Dubravka asked.

Then, seeing that the answer was obvious, Dubravka handed Allison her tattered coat, then draped her azure scarf around Allison's shoulders and head.

Zagorska Juha

Dubrovnik, May 1981

You filthy whore, Dubravka's father roared as he stumbled through the door, more drunk this night than usual. The girl was sitting at the table, mending a tear in one of his shirts. Don't tell me you're still pure. You miserable slut, you were seen. Three months ago. Seen by two fishermen from Split. And now everyone knows you were with that boy too.

Dubravka placed the shirt and needle and thread down on the table. I did nothing to be ashamed of or to dishonor you. She tried to still herself. Breathe. Remain calm.

Her father lurched toward her, reaching for one of the bottles of slivovitz that stood on the table. Lately there were always a few bottles of slivovitz on the table. That was where the man left them. He lifted the bottle to his lips and slurped. Do you deny walking with him along the harbor, in front of everyone, holding his hand?

There was no harm in that, Dubravka said.

At least your cunt of a cousin had the good sense to run away.

Dubravka took in another breath. So you'd have me run away?

With the back of his hand he slapped her. Blinding light, dizzy shock. The slap knocked the girl as well as the wooden chair on which she was sitting backward and onto the floor. Just like your mother, the father said, standing over her. The bottle in one hand, he raised the other to hit her again as soon as she began to stand. Spreading your legs for a Serb. A whore dropped from the slit of another whore.

Dubravka knew from the bits and pieces of her aunts' stories, related while the women worked in Zagorac's kitchen, that when Dubravka was a child one night her mother had run away. Or was it more accurate to say that Dubravka's father had cast the woman out? Apparently it was because her mother had befriended a Serb. According to the aunts, the man was new to the city and in need of something, and her mother had agreed to help him. The details of the request were left to conjecture. Most of the women guessed the Serb was searching for work. His pockets were not only empty, the women said, they had holes. His family was from the same town near the Bosnia and Herzegovina border where her mother's parents were born, the women said. Whatever the specifics, the women claimed, Dubravka's mother met with him and somehow gave him aid.

Dubravka's parents argued then, the girl faintly remembered, shouting at each other for days. She could remember the terror she felt because of their screaming. Then came the evening her mother made the pot of soup – zagorska juha – a hearty soup said to be the cure for hangovers, made of potatoes and onions and bacon and mushrooms and carrots and paprika and other spices, finished off with a dollop of sour cream. The soup was from the region of Croatia where Dubravka's father was born. Her mother made it on each of the man's name days. As the stories related in Zagorac's kitchen had it, the next morning a simmering pot of zagorska juha sat waiting for him on the stove, but the wife was nowhere to be found. Some goodbye! the aunts agreed. It was a way to tell someone two distinct things at once – that you possessed the power both to give and to take, to please a man with his favorite dish as well as to deprive him for the rest of his days of your presence.

The women cautioned Dubravka never to make the soup. After your mother left him, they told Dubravka, he asked that we no longer serve it here in the restaurant or even make it for ourselves at home. He didn't even want to smell it. For the rest of his life the soup would be a reminder of that night, of their arguments and fights, of what he'd had and lost.

Dubravka remembered that in the days after her mother's disappearance she fell ill with a high fever that nearly killed her. Or that actually did kill her, as the kitchen stories had it. She was only a child, nearly three. She lay in bed burning like the glowing embers beneath a grate. Her skin was so hot it melted the blocks of ice they packed around her. After the fever broke, her body went cold and she ceased breathing. She grew so cold that they grieved and did what was necessary to prepare her for burial. They washed her body and wrapped it in white cloth. They covered her face with a sheet. But then by morning, the women claimed, the girl returned to life and the grieving father's tears fell on the child's face as the father fed her spoonful after spoonful of her mother's soup until the pot the woman had left them was empty, and the child survived.

DUBRAVKA STOOD OVER the sink rinsing off the blood running from her nose and cracked lip. She hoped her nose wasn't broken. Ever so slowly she ran her tongue up and over her teeth. She thanked God none felt smashed or chipped. She'd bitten the side of her tongue and spat blood and a bit of her flesh into the sink. Her blood tasted of iron. Thank God her father had used only his fists and not the bottle, she thought. She looked down at the bright splashes of blood staining her blouse. She hoped she could wash it out of the fabric. The blouse was one of her favorites, one with cross-stitched patterns of rosettes and triangles on its collar and down across its front and its long sleeves.

Her father was at the table, slumped in his chair, still drinking, acting as if nothing had just occurred. He'd opened a new bottle. Now he drank from a glass. The bottle he didn't hit her with lay empty on its side on the floor.

You know, Dubravka said, turning toward him. She hoped he'd look at her bloody face. She hoped he'd understand what he'd just done to her. When I was a child you could have made your life much easier. You could have just let me die.

Her father didn't respond.

After my fever broke. She looked back at the mirror and carefully touched the bridge of her nose, then gave it a slight wiggle. The pain was bearable She spat out a bit more blood. After they washed my body, she said, spitting, and swaddled me.

He said something and grunted, like a rooting pig.

What? she said. So you agree with me?

He stared at her now. I said your mother wouldn't have it.

Dubravka faced him. No. She took a step back. Don't give me your stories. I know the truth. I remember what happened. By then my mother was gone.

You know nothing, the father said. He looked around the room and let out a long sigh.

So tell me what I don't know. Since you say I know nothing.

Again he grunted. You could barely sleep through the night without pissing a pond in your bed. Your mother stayed until after the priest left.

The priest?

Yes, the priest. The young one with the limp, the one you favor. The one stupid enough to sacrifice a perfectly good leg for a dog. He was still new to the city, the only one from the church willing to come out that night to bless you. Your mother insisted a priest bless you. He gave you the deathbed blessing.

Dubravka didn't know anything about this. Did Father Josip give me the Last Rites?

Her father waved a hand in the air. He spent the longest time on you. A good half hour. Rubbing oils on your forehead, your eyes, your nose, ears, lips. All the time praying over you, as if it would mean something. We were already grieving since you were so cold to the touch. He made us undo the cloths the women wrapped you in so he could anoint your hands and feet. What was the use since your soul was already gone? Even an idiot could see it. Through it all your body was still, cold, though he claimed that when he was alone with you you had a seizure. We didn't believe him since he'd been drinking. He's a drunk, you know. Besides, anyone with sense could tell you were already dead. The man shook his head. That was before your slut of a mother ran away.

No, Dubravka said. You're wrong. I came down with the fever after she left us.

Before, the father said. Before, before. On the night of. And believe me, there are a good many things in this God-fucked life that I don't remember but that night I do remember. Clearly. He poured himself another glass of slivovitz. And then, the next morning –

Go on. And then the next morning –

That was the night the whore left the burial up to us and made the soup.

She left thinking I was dead?

How many times do you want me to say it? You were dead. We all thought you were dead. Even the priest. He pronounced you dead. Your mother agreed. She closed your eyes and covered your face with the sheet.

Dubravka said nothing for a while, trying to think. She knew that the old custom was to bury the dead on the day they died, though now there were laws to wait for at least a day. Dubravka wondered if, before leaving, her mother had followed the other customs, if she had let down her long hair and closed the house's shutters. She wondered if her mother had hung a black shawl on the outside of the door. If her mother had wept over her. She stared at her father. I can remember you feeding me soup.

The soup she made that night, he said, to goad me. So you see, shit for brains, I'm right.

Dubravka nodded.

The man paused to drink, then spat on the floor and refilled his glass. I can still picture the pot there on the stove. He pointed. The next morning. The smell of it filling the air, like in my childhood. Wondering where your mother was until I noticed she'd taken her clothes. That was when I saw the sheet covering your face moving. The doctor said a child sometimes can go stone cold after a high fever breaks. He said all the while you must have been unconscious. What did we know, we weren't doctors. Besides, all of us, your mother and the priest included, we were drinking, and then after you died we drank even more. He tilted his head back as he downed his glass. When I told the doctor we were certain you'd stopped breathing, he said you had to have been taking shallow breaths. None that we noticed. Take it from me, you were dead. As you are now again to me.

Think of it, he said, as he stood before leaving the house, to go through all of that, for all these years, and then for you to turn out to be just like her.

DUBRAVKA KNEW HE'D be gone until morning. She stared at her reflection in the mirror that hung near the sink and saw that he'd blackened her left eye. Her bottom lip was cracked and swollen but had stopped bleeding. Did he beat her mother too? Probably. When he returned in the morning, Dubravka thought, he'd either be penitent or not remember a thing he had done. Or he'd beat her again. She tried to remember if she'd seen him beating her mother. She gazed at her image in the mirror. She still felt terrible about her ruined blouse.

Then Dubravka prayed, thanking the Almighty and the Virgin Mary for the blessing of now understanding that her mother hadn't simply abandoned her. Her mother had likely left the city because now that her child was dead there was nothing left to keep her here. She must have wanted to leave for a long time, Dubravka thought. She must have seen the child's death as her chance to escape.

Did she stand over me and kiss me as she made the pot of soup, as I lay in bed breathing so slightly no one could notice? Dubravka had a faint memory of that, a face hovering over her as she lay on her back, burning. She'd always thought that had been her father. Now she imagined the face above her as her mother's.

Dubravka wept as she took out the soup pot, as she did her best to remember the recipe. So it was Father Josip who'd anointed her, she thought as she diced the vegetables and looked for a slab of bacon or pršut and took out the paprika and other spices from the cupboards.

She knew her father hadn't eaten this soup since her mother left him. Now, Dubravka thought as she packed a bag of her clothes, as she set the pot to a low simmer on the stove, now in the morning when he stumbles home he'll once again be greeted by both an empty house and another simmering pot of zagorska juha.

Stari Most

Mostar, May 1981 / February 1983

She headed north to Bosnia and Herzegovina, to Mostar, where even though Dubravka had never been ten kilometers away from Dubrovnik she planned to search the city for Marija and Stanislav. They couldn't have gone far. Dubravka sat on the left side of the bus so she could enjoy the view as the bus made its slow way through the Croatian hillside. In the valley below a man drove two oxen as the beasts worked his field.

She wasn't sure what she'd say to Marija and Stanislav when she found them. Perhaps they'd only stare at her, see her swollen lip, her blackened eye. She'd tell them she'd taken the beating for them both, though in truth she thought only of Marija and how she still was jealous and angry. Dubravka felt as if she'd been robbed. Doubly robbed, when she thought of her rolls of dinars hidden behind the old radio.

An older man in a long overcoat took the seat next to her, then as the bus drove on he began nudging her with his elbow, asking for her pardon each time she turned. He smelled of something bitter and citrusy. Aftershave, likely. Finally he spoke.

Running away, I see. He spoke in a soft voice, as if they were in a confessional, nodding with each word. Your husband, the man said softly. He must be a fool.

Dubravka said nothing.

Mostar, he said after a while. I know it well. I'm guessing you've never been. He began describing the city to her, its serpentine cobbled lanes and alleyways, Turkish bazaars, Ottoman architecture, the towering minarets of its mosques, the town's various cafés and bars and restaurants. Where to purchase the best carpets, the finest items fashioned of copper and bronze. How the river – the Neretva – slices the city in two, with the bank on the west more flat, spacious, and developed, the bank on the east smaller and more ancient and steep. No need for you to be concerned, he told Dubravka. I can show you around. We'll walk together across the Old Bridge, and what a jewel it is! the man said, talking loudly enough now for others to overhear him. The Stari Most, built, I believe, in the sixteenth century. Passengers in the nearby seats nodded and smiled, and the man continued to show off his knowledge. The Old Bridge spans the narrowest point between the Neretva's banks. You can look at it from a distance and see that it forms the top half of a perfect circle. Perfect, he repeated with a slight shake of his head. Its reflection in the water – he raised a hand as if he could see the bridge there on the bus before him – coupled with its stone arch form the whole of a perfect circle. A supreme example of Balkan Islamic architecture. A desire for ideal form.

When he reached his hand to touch hers, Dubravka pulled her hand away and told the man so firmly and loudly to stop that others on the bus turned to look at them, and then there was shouting as the passengers on the bus noticed Dubravka's bruised face, and the man in the long overcoat who smelled of rotting lemons nodded in apology. After Dubravka stared at him fiercely, he stood and walked to the back of the bus, where he took an empty seat.

NEARLY EVERY YOUNG man on the streets of Mostar's Old City looked like Stanislav, and of course none of them were. Dubravka walked up and down Mostar's lanes until she grew weary, and then she paused by a small restaurant on Braće Fejića, a street not far from the Old Bridge, full of café bars and restaurants. From the look of the plump cartoon chef twirling a pizza on its sign, the restaurant – Ukusno's, *tasty* in Serbian – offered a rare Italian flair in addition to the usual items. Its portion of busy Braće Fejića stretched between the slender minarets of a pair of mosques, the Koski Mehmed Pasha and the Karađoz Bey.

The number of the Ukusno's vacant tables that were yet to be cleared and wiped down suggested to Dubravka that the young waitress toiling there alone was in need of help, and so Dubravka set down her bag near the kitchen's doorway and immediately began clearing tables of their used plates and dirty glasses and empty bottles.

The waitress had Stanislav's tanned, glowing skin and wore a nose ring and dainty teardrop earrings. She'd pulled back her thick hair into a low ponytail. She nodded as Dubravka worked, and then a man in a tomato-stained apron smoking a cigarette came out of the kitchen doorway and with a jerking motion of his head called Dubravka over. As she approached he asked her loudly what she thought she was doing. His expression shifted as she neared, as he saw her bruised, battered face.

Clearing the tables, Dubravka said. She paused. Since they're hardly capable of doing it themselves.

Come inside, the man said, his expression softening. Don't be afraid. You won't be hurt here. We'll give you something to eat, and then you can be on your way.

No, Dubravka told him. I don't want a handout. She followed the man into the kitchen as he walked away from her. I want work. All I ask for in return is shelter, a safe place at night to sleep. I come from Dubrovnik, she said, the Old City, where I worked in a small restaurant. She told the man she could clear tables, wash dishes and pots and pans, roast vegetables, bake bread, make soup, prepare and grill meat. She would eat only what others left on their plates – she did her best to smile – and would otherwise be thrown away or given to the pigs or dogs.

The man took his cigarette out of the side of his mouth and returned her smile. Dubravka saw his missing teeth. Like most kitchen workers he needed a shave, and his breath smelled of his most recent drink. If you work as good as you talk, the man said, you won't have to eat what we toss to the pigs and dogs.

She thanked him and asked if he knew a young man named Stanislav. He catches fish, she said.

The cook grinned, then laughed. If you're looking for him I'll wager he catches more than just fish. For a while the cook chuckled softly at his joke. Besides, he added, puffing again on his cigarette, at least half of the young men here are named Stanislav.

DUBRAVKA WORKED AT Ukusno's for the next two years, serving beer and wine and coffee, sausages and fries, pizza and panini. She slept in a small room off the kitchen and was often up late since it was nearly a written rule that if you worked in a kitchen you drank after the last customers had settled their bills, drank with your fellow restaurant comrades deep into the night, often while one or more of the cooks prepared something for the staff to eat. She wrote letters to Father

Josip telling him not to worry about her, that she could be reached at the restaurant. For the first few weeks early each morning before she began her shift she walked down to the Old Catholic Church near the bridge to say her morning prayers, until one day she was attracted by the women gathered in the courtyard outside the Koski Mehmed Pasha Mosque, which was only a handful of steps from Ukusno's and open to non-Muslims. One woman took notice of Dubravka standing there watching them, then nodded and gestured to her to join.

Like the others who prayed at the mosque, Dubravka washed her face and hands in the circular ablutions fountain in the courtyard before entering. She imitated the women, starting with her right hand, washing it up to the wrist three times, then the left hand, again three times, then her mouth, nose, face, forearms, head, neck, ears, feet. At first Dubravka missed the glowing red presence of a sanctuary lamp hanging down from the right side of the mihrab, but after several days she came to recognize that in the elegantly designed Ottoman mosque – its stone floor covered by a soft mosaic of worn carpets, its off-white walls and dome painted with a lovely series of arches and ornate designs along with a fine display of native plants and trees – there was the distinct, absolutely undeniable presence of the divine. Soon Dubravka adopted some of the ways the Muslim women who prayed beside her dressed, wearing longer skirts and a black headscarf. She also learned that wearing a black scarf on her head made it easier to walk about the city unbothered.

After a few months she was issued a cook's apron and asked to make the day's pizza dough as well as other breads. Over time she was put in charge of filling and baking the calzone and mastering the intricacies of the temperamental espresso machine.

Even though she spent much of her spare time walking Mostar's ancient streets, looking into faces, she never found Stanislav and Marija. Dubravka worked at Ukusno's until she was eighteen, until a couple of months after she leapt from the Old Bridge.

SHE FOUND THAT working up the courage to make the jump was more difficult than doing it. The actual thought of jumping seemed so frightening to Dubravka that she was certain she would die, and yet she felt that if she worked hard enough preparing for the leap she'd live through it. And if she did die, well, she prayed God would understand.

A part of her looked forward to her death because, in a way, it would be a comfort. She was also sure that immediately afterward she'd see some form of God. Not the Almighty as such – not the one true God – but likely one of God's manifestations. A spirit or some sort of angel. An entity that would tell her she was in fact dead and would soon be judged. She imagined the spirit's form would be something similar to smoke, maybe like the singular spiraling ribbon of smoke rising from the head cook's cigarette left to burn in the kitchen's ashtray.

No doubt she'd have to suffer for some period of time in something that resembled purgatory, which Dubravka believed was less like a waiting room and perhaps more like a place where she'd have to work to be cleansed. Less like the fires of an oven and more like the wudu, the ritual washing before prayer. She guessed she'd be asked to confront each of her life's many transgressions. She'd be made to relive them, then be challenged to make amends. Dubravka was certain she wouldn't be immediately granted the beatific vision, but she was vain enough to think that even if the jump off the bridge took her life she wouldn't be condemned to an eternity in Hell. She imagined Hell as sheer and utter emptiness, a void of all things known as well as all things possibly imagined, where all that existed was your soul's constant awareness that for all of unending time you would be alone. Unheard. Unacknowledged. Untouched. Unloved. Perhaps the most evil souls would be made to relive a never-ending barrage of their lifetime's sins, but from the side of their victims, those they'd transgressed against. A thief would be eternally stolen from. A murderer, each passing moment murdered. A torturer, continually given unrelenting brutality and unbearable pain.

On a very basic level, Dubravka thought, dying would be like finding out from the teacher how you did on a test. The final test. The only test, really. Which puts life into a rather different context. As she walked about the streets of Mostar, Dubravka sometimes shook her head at the way others appeared to be taking the test. Still, who was she to judge? She looked forward to the moment of her death and, in the meantime, would be sure to follow God's plan. She still very much believed in the idea that there was a plan for her. Why else had she been reborn after she'd died of a fever?

Though when Dubravka was bold enough to share the story of her death from fever with the others in Ukusno's kitchen, everyone laughed at her. Dubravka's story was the funniest thing they'd ever heard. Of course she hadn't actually died and come back to life. Of course a body feels cold after a high fever breaks, particularly if the body was packed with ice. Particularly if the body is then washed and tightly swaddled. And you said everyone was drinking? They must have been so drunk they couldn't even tell if they were still breathing. Even the priest, who you admitted was more than fond of a sip. He must have oiled you up like sliced zucchini, they said, still laughing. And besides, what do priests know anyway? If priests were good at anything, they'd be doing something else. Believe us, Dubravka, you were lucky that night they didn't dig a hole out back and bury you. You were lucky you didn't wake up the next morning inside a wooden box covered with stones.

Still, Dubravka thought, why else had God sent Stanislav to Zagorac's back door, and why else had God had Stanislav tell her so much about Mostar and offer her so many details about jumping off the Old Bridge? Why had God allowed Stanislav to describe the act so perfectly that at night as Dubravka slept in the small room off the kitchen where they stored white sacks of flour and big cans of peeled tomatoes she could imagine the act clearly in her mind? Why else had she been allowed to work at a café so close to the bridge that if she took a short walk she could watch boys leaping off it? That was why she'd been given a mind, she thought. To form pictures of things as they might happen, just as she'd learned to form and fill calzone, just as she learned to work the dough in the ciabatta so that the yeast would be able to breathe as it baked and force the bread surrounding it to rise.

THOUGHT WAS PARENT to action.

So when she wasn't looking for Stanislav and Marija, Dubravka went to the river to study the other jumpers. She saw that to begin she must become accustomed to the water. The Neretva was fast-flowing and cold, even in the summer months. Dubravka began by submerging herself into it. Leaping into it from the shore. Swimming. Then forcibly pushing her body down into the river as low as her body would go. She'd let the Neretva play with her. Push her this way, push her that way. Then she'd push the river back. She did her best to make the river her friend or, at the very least, a familiar acquaintance.

It was rare in Mostar in the early 1980s for a young woman to attempt a jump off the Stari Most. Even though she knew the Neretva would be cold, Dubravka picked a date in early February. As she undressed in preparation for the jump, a crowd of locals and tourists gathered. A few knew Dubravka from her work at Ukusno's. She was the quiet one, not the cute one with the ready smile and nose ring.

Dubravka wore a modest swimsuit beneath a wetsuit and stepped over the stone railing. She kept her arms straight down at her sides. She looked out as calmly as she could at the horizon. She knew that the drop to the water was at least seven storeys high. Seven storeys! she thought. No, she chided herself, she shouldn't think of the height. She should focus on what she'd practiced. How the next step was to will herself not to look down, and so she ceased looking down, and as she did the voices from those clustered behind her on the bridge and on the banks of the river below fell away. Dubravka felt a slight breeze, and then all she could hear was the quick suck-and-push of her lungs and the throbbing hard lub-dub of her heart. She counted to three, then stepped off the Old Bridge's narrow ledge.

Those watching her from down on the shorelines saw her open her arms straight out to each side as she fell, then drop her arms down below her waist, her right hand grasping her left. Dubravka had no awareness that her body was doing this. She was concentrating on her legs and feet, keeping them straight, pointing her toes down toward the river so that their narrow width would be the first part of her body to pierce the hard surface of the water, slice an opening through which her legs would follow, which would allow the rest of her body to slip into the river with ease and grace. Her ears did hear the splash. Then her whole body felt the sudden freezing pressure of the water along with a terrible confusing darkness engulfing her as she plunged more deeply toward the river's rocky bottom, twisting now in the current and in response to the unbearable cold, until she remembered that she'd worked on making the Neretva her friend. Still holding her breath, untwisting herself, wondering why she'd opened her eyes, doing her best not to panic, momentarily unsure about which way was up and which way was down. Wanting now to breathe, suck in breath, just one breath, just for a moment, but sensing that she mustn't, no, not yet, not quite yet. Willing herself to hold her breath and then realizing that her arms and hands were somehow remembering all by themselves to do what she'd repeatedly practiced – to point up and then spread themselves out wide and flap downward like winged paddles – and then Dubravka broke surface and felt the afternoon sun on her face as her mouth gaped wide open and she took in a great gasp of air and heard the sounds of cheering.

Santa Maria in Aracoeli

Rome, February 2005

"You have a hole in your heart," the old woman said.

On the table before her the cards were spread like a cross within a half-circle, with some figures sideways and others upside down. The old woman from Napoli smelled of ground peppercorns and some lotion or ointment Massimo's nose couldn't place. Her face was like an overripe apple left to bake in the sun. She wore a widow's dress and shawl and, on her second finger, a ring with an oval stone the color of smoke. A friend of a friend of Massimo's mother, the woman was visiting Rome for a few days and reputed to be so accurate reading the cards that when she was younger crowds waited in line wherever she ventured, bearing money and gifts. Of course since she was from the South the woman was in touch with these things. All she asked for in return was caffè corretto and, if it wasn't too much trouble, some nice pasticcini for her sweet tooth. That and a modest donation, a few coins, for the care and well-being of her dog.

She gazed up from the cards and smacked her lips several times, eyelids fluttering like butterfly wings. "I see that you're often misunderstood, mistaken for someone else."

"That's true," Massimo said. An ox of a man, with wide shoulders and soft eyes, he was dressed casually, in blue jeans pressed with a knife-sharp crease and a cotton sweater the color of desert sand. He'd just come from work, from his station outside the Colosseum, and had plans to go out on the town after he walked his mother back to their apartment.

"A shame," the old woman said. "You'd be much happier if people could see you as you really are. So many secrets. Like locked rooms in a big house. Not common in a man so young. It would be better if you threw open the shutters, let in the air and light."

Massimo said nothing.

"No matter. All will clear in time. For some things, soon. I see you meeting a man. Someone who will give you advice, which you must follow or else there will be a great calamity. He'll be sent by a woman in red who will give you a blessing. But here" – with a long, yellowed fingernail she tapped one of the upside-down cards – "here, deep inside you, I see an old, simmering anger. A powerful acid, burning all it touches. It wants to bubble up from where you've buried it. And here" – again she paused – "here there's an abiding sadness. This card shows the wound. For a young man, you've suffered greatly."

Massimo's face remained calm and unchanged.

"Here I see someone else, someone close to you, taking a journey. Is one of your relatives or friends on a trip? Or perhaps that person is lost? You too, I think, will soon take a trip, but not the same one as this relative. I see a long road stretching out ahead of you. A hill with many rocks. A steep mountain you'll be challenged to climb. I see you carrying some sort of weapon, perhaps a sword or knife or club, to protect yourself from being wounded again."

The pair was sitting at the kitchen table in the friend's apartment. A plate of frappe – deep-fried ribbons of crumbly pastry sprinkled with powdered sugar – lay beside their coffee cups and bottle of grappa. Though it was the week before Martedì Grasso, Massimo was not in a carnival mood. He knew his mother, Renata, was in the next room pretending not to overhear what the old woman had to tell him. He'd consented to see the Napoletana only to please his mother. She was sick with worry about his father, who seemed to be living backward in time. Still, Massimo didn't want all of his secrets exposed.

On the stove's front burner behind them squatted a well-used Moka Express, its bottom blackened, a smudge of coffee darkening the lip of its spout. At the foot of the stove slept the woman's ancient dog. Across the room, gazing down on Massimo and the old woman, was a silent Jesus Christ pinned to a dusty wooden cross.

It was the story about the dog that had attracted Renata's attention. Her friend claimed the dog was even more talented than the old woman. Apparently the dog's sense of smell was so keen it could detect sickness. All one had to do was bring the dog into a room with sick people and it would sniff here, sniff there, and if deep inside someone's chest or leg or armpit a cancerous tumor was hiding like an onion or a beet the dog would let out a howl and push its nose into the skin beneath which the tumor was thriving. The dog was also able to see souls as they passed from the body. More than once the dog sat at attention before someone about to die, resisting all commands, foregoing all food and water, remaining still, eyes unblinking, often for hours, twice for more than a day, occasionally giving the air a series of sharp yips, until the moment the dying person let out a final breath. The dog would then slowly lift its head, its eyes fixed on the space immediately above the body where the dead person's soul would hover, like an uncertain cloud waiting for a decisive wind. Once the spirit began moving, the dog would track it until it flew up through the ceiling or down through the floorboards, and then the dog would sleep.

"This wound, I see it lying near the area of love. There, you sometimes struggle in the darkness, nearly as if you're fighting. In the area of love, you've been hurt deeply, yes?"

"Who hasn't?" Massimo said.

The old woman's eyes held him. For a long moment neither said anything or moved, and Massimo sensed she understood. "Such big hands," the old woman said finally as her arms reached across the table toward him. "So callused and rough. Such shoulders and arms. You're a Hercules. Yet I don't see that you're a common laborer."

From the other room came Massimo's mother's laugh.

"You work outside in the sun and rain, but there's something on your head."

Massimo stared at the sad-eyed figure on the cross.

The old woman released his hands and reached for one of the frappe and broke it in half. Powdered sugar feathered down to the tabletop. "You're like this," she said, thrusting one section of the sweet toward him. "A part of something that once was whole. Now" – she gave Massimo a shrug – "something broken." She ate the part that wasn't Massimo, then sipped her coffee and ate the part that was too.

"He needs a wife," came his mother's voice from the next room.

"She wants me to marry a second cousin," Massimo said.

The old woman turned her head to the wall, as if listening. Her eyelids fluttered wildly once again. At the same time the dog lifted its head as well. After many moments the woman looked back at the cards and added, "You won't marry this cousin." She hesitated, then poured some grappa into the coffee remaining in her cup and drank it, then refilled her cup with grappa and took a deep sip. "Understand, I make no judgment, though I caution you to take care." She gestured to the air for more coffee. Massimo stood and refilled her cup.

"I know others are waiting and you need to leave," the old woman said. "But still, I see you with a baby in your arms. Yes, un bambino. A very old and gentle soul, deserving to be swaddled in the finest cloth, covered head to feet with gold and jewels."

CERTAINLY PART, IF not all, of what the old woman from the South revealed was true.

Nearly everyone who saw Massimo at work as he paced outside the crumbling walls of the Colosseum thought he was a gladiator. They looked at his red cape and tunic, his shining steel breastplate, his leather cingulum belt studded with grommets and gold coin accents that glistened as he moved in the sunlight, and imagined him inside the Colosseum's pitted walls, sword raised. Only later as they noticed his ringed bracers, the leather sandals that he carefully crosslaced from ankle to knee, his steel helmet with its curved red horsehair plume, did it occur to them that perhaps he was dressed as a Roman soldier, a legionnaire perhaps, or a centurion. If they were familiar with Roman history they knew Massimo's helmet was worn by centurions, though rather than wear the plume from ear to ear, like a partial halo, as true Roman centurions did two thousand years ago, Massimo wore the plume forehead to neck, like Russell Crowe and the other men in the opening battle scenes of the famous North American movie *Gladiator*. *Il Gladiatore* was Massimo's favorite movie, even more than Luchino Visconti's *Rocco and His Brothers*, though only a blind man could deny the breathtaking beauty of the young Alain Delon. If Crowe and Delon ever walked past the Colosseum, Massimo knew which one he'd follow.

Regardless of accuracy he was something from history, or at least he pretended to be, and everyone who came to Rome knew the place had history in spades. Nearly every tourist wanted to be photographed in front of Rome's ruins, to be able to show their friends and families back home that they'd stood in the presence of the truly ancient. Was there a greater symbol of the ancient world than the Roman Colosseum?

This was the service Massimo provided. For only a few euros he offered tourists the chance to be photographed beside him, with the pocked travertine walls of the towering amphitheater in the background.

He kept a pair of Roman legion flags braided with gold rope on wooden dowels for added authenticity. One flag bore the letters SPQR inside a laurel wreath. The other was from Legio XIII Gemina and featured a golden lion. The thirteenth legion was recruited by Julius Caesar himself and was known as the Twin Legion. Massimo had selected the thirteenth legion because he believed Dario, his deceased childhood friend, was his twin.

Massimo allowed the tourists to wield his wooden short sword and wear his plumed helmet in the photographs. The men, particularly if they were with their girlfriends or wives, nearly always wanted to wear his helmet. The girlfriends often chose to stand beside him and smile, though Massimo was frequently instructed by their boyfriends to look menacing, to raise his sword and pretend that he was about to slash the young woman's throat. Groups of women sometimes wanted to hold the sword to his throat or have him kneel on the ground before them in submission, helmet in hand. That tableau Massimo could understand. And a few simply wanted to talk to him, practice their rusty Italian, like that sweet older woman he'd met a few weeks ago from Canada, here in Rome with her church group, who told him that when her feet touched Italy's ground she couldn't help but burst into tears.

Massimo was an honest centurion, unlike some of the other costumed characters who roamed Via dei Fori Imperiali, particularly the stretch by the busy Metro station. They donned cheap plastic breastplates and ripped off anyone unfortunate enough to trust them. Usually they worked in pairs, with one volunteering to take the photograph. No sooner would one have his hands on the tourist's camera than both would run off. The previous spring Rome's Ministry of Culture ordered all of them away, saying they were a disgrace, a blight on the city's reputation. Massimo and his fellow honest centurions demonstrated.

We have the right to work, they shouted as they marched. We're no more a blight than the souvenir stands, which exist all across the city. In addition, we educate as well as entertain. The tourists wandering outside the Colosseum's walls cheered them. The next day Rome's newspapers splashed word of their actions in headlines in bold type.

MODERN DAY GLADIATORS
BATTLE OUTSIDE THE COLOSSEUM

Their demonstrations were broadcast on the national news, and after a while the ministry relented, though from that point on the centurions were to be regulated, licensed, and taxed. There were rules about their costumes as well as tests on basic language skills and a rough knowledge of Rome's history. Massimo's grades ranked among the best.

When tourists understood some Italian, Massimo would tell them that in ancient times the Colosseum was known as the Flavian Amphitheater, named for the three emperors – Vespasian, Titus, and Domitian – who built it, and that the name *Colosseum* derived from a huge bronze statue of Nero known as the Colossus Neronis. Massimo would explain how the great arena stood on the site of Nero's decadent Domus Aurea, or Golden House, how erecting the amphitheater was a way for Vespasian to distinguish his rule from Nero's and at the same time return some of Rome's wealth to its people. Massimo would draw out his short sword, or gladius, and tell people that was how gladiators got their name.

Though he was not a tall man Massimo was fit and powerfully built, thickly muscled from the many evenings he spent in his neighborhood's palestra, where he lifted iron weights and played catch with a medicine ball, holding the weighted ball up to his chest and then heaving it toward a fellow weightlifter, who caught it and lifted it to chest level and returned the throw, then heaved it again, back and forth, forth and back, until their muscles throbbed. Only after Massimo had physically spent himself would he return to his parents' apartment in Testaccio and eat a bit of whatever was in the oven or a pan atop the stove and bathe and then fall asleep. And even then dreams of his beloved Dario filled with images of the traitor, the Santo Bambino of Aracoeli, nagged at him, trailing his steps like a pack of wild dogs, snapping at his ankles and the hem of his red cape.

Unsettled by the old woman's reading of his cards, after Massimo walked his mother back to their apartment and checked on his father to see if he was still in the chair where they'd tied him, Massimo hopped on his Vespa. The golden walls of the Colosseum, splashed with powerful floodlights, loomed behind him as he sped down Via dei Fori Imperiali. Near the Piazza d'Aracoeli he parked his scooter and approached the gently sloping Cordonata Capitolina – the ramped steps built by Michelangelo marking the path to the Piazza del Campidoglio, Massimo's favorite place in Rome.

Standing next to the Cordonata Capitolina, beside the steep stairs that led up to the Church of Santa Maria in Aracoeli, was a figure in a long gray skirt and top, wearing an unzipped cranberry-colored jacket. Massimo could see the woman was waiting for someone. He took note of the disparity in her clothing – the opulence of her jacket's fine leather, the obvious humility of her skirt and blouse. As Massimo nodded to her in greeting the woman's dark eyes fixed on him and held him, and for a moment Massimo was certain he was the very person she was waiting for. He also had the sense she had something important to say. For a few long moments she stared at him and then glanced up at the church over his shoulder. Then her gaze released him as another man – small, dark, with a gray mustache, dressed in a coal-black suit and blinding white shirt buttoned all the way up to the neck – shouted her name as he crossed the street. The woman called out his name, and the pair smiled at Massimo as he again nodded, politely, and wished them both a good evening. Massimo then rushed up the Cordonata Capitolina toward the area by the Rocca Tarpea, where other men like him idled, lit cigarettes in hand.

There was a formality about meeting other men, a sort of dance involving distance and eye contact and the angle of one's shoulders, as well as the absence of any rules at all. Massimo wasn't even sure he wanted the company of someone else, and since he didn't smoke he thrust his hands into his jacket pockets and stood leaning against a stone wall, bracing himself against the crisp night breeze and the sounds of the others. He listened to their muted conversations, their whispers and laughter, the scrape and shuffle of their boots against gravel and stone. No, tonight he would go home early, check on his poor father, do his best to avoid talking to his mother about the old woman from the South.

"I know just how you feel," a man said as he approached.

"What?"

"You know," the man said. "I know how you feel deep inside."

"I doubt that," Massimo said with a shake of his head. "And I've already had my fortune read once tonight."

"Lucky you," the man said. He was thin, light-haired, dressed entirely in black. By his accent Massimo could tell he was from the North. The man had clear blue eyes and a full, soft mouth. Along his jawline was a small scrape where he'd cut himself shaving. "I think if I knew my future," the man continued, "I'd run and hide."

"Fate runs faster. You're from the North?"

"Lugano," the man said and smiled with pride.

"Switzerland. I've never been."

"Oh, you'd adore it. Lugano is an absolutely beautiful place, quite peaceful once you get outside the city and its traffic, particularly in the spring." The man then went on about the region's lakes and hills and outlying mountains.

After a while Massimo asked, "So what brings you to Rome?"

The man from Lugano laughed and raised his arms as if the answer were obvious. "What brings anyone to Rome? It's the true center. Of everything that exists."

By then Massimo and the man from the North were walking back toward the Piazza del Campidoglio, with the man's thin fingers lightly brushing Massimo's hand. Maybe he'd spend an hour or two with this fellow, Massimo thought as they walked. The pair strolled past the Palazzo Senatorio, floodlights bathing its tangerine-colored walls, and then they wound their way to its left where they approached a copy of the Capitoline She-wolf suckling Romulus and Remus. The statue stood on top of a tall pillar, and as the man from the North paused to examine it Massimo's face fell, and his heart grew heavy and sad.

"What troubles you?" the man asked. "Is it me? Do you want me to leave?"

"No," Massimo said. "It's the statue. I forgot it was here."

The man from Lugano said nothing.

"You see," Massimo heard himself saying, "no, never mind."

"Tell me."

"No," Massimo said again, but then he thought he might enjoy the pain of telling the story to the stranger. "I once had a young friend named Dario."

Massimo and Dario met when both were children, in scuola elementare. As part of their curriculum, their teacher had the class perform dramas that reenacted famous scenes from Rome's history. Because Massimo was the strongest child in class, he was chosen to play Romulus in a play about Rome's birth. Selected to portray Remus was Dario, who was small and blond and brittle as a dry stick, with large, piercing eyes framed by long lashes and skin so fair it resembled English china. A web of blue veins pulsed beneath the child's skin, like the tributaries on the maps that hung on the classroom's wall.

In the play a servant is ordered to kill the pair of newborn twins because an evil king fears that when they mature they'll overthrow his rule. The servant disobeys and sets the basket in which the twins lie into the Tiber's surging waters. The river carries the boys away until Romulus raises a hand and grabs the branch of a fig tree growing along the bank. He and Remus crawl out of the basket. A friendly wolf offers them bowls of milk.

The boys frolic beneath the tree and fall asleep, and when they awake they tell the audience they are grown men now. They march back to Rome, slay the evil ruler, then walk to Palantine Hill where Romulus says he will build a mighty city. Remus argues, saying that he'll be the one to build the city, and it will be on Aventine Hill. An augur steps between them and suggests they leave the matter to the gods. Soon six eagles fly over the Aventine, and the brothers understand that Remus has been preferred. Then twelve eagles appear over the Palantine and circle Romulus's head. He begins to erect the city walls but jealous Remus taunts him, knocking down what Romulus has built.

The image of young Dario gleefully laughing, leaping back and forth over the cardboard boxes painted to resemble stones, is as fixed as an ancient carving in Massimo's memory. Romulus then draws out his sword and slays Remus. Remus issues a small cry and falls dead. The auger announces that the new city will be named Roma, after Romulus, and he will be known as Rome's first king throughout the ages.

Young Massimo took the role given him by the teacher seriously, though whenever he had to stab Dario he felt like crying. Even now, as he relates the story to the man from the North, tears brim in his eyes. Dario had spoken his lines with such conviction that Massimo was tempted to stray from the script and tell Dario that if he wanted to build the new city he could do so. What would it matter who decides where a city is built? Massimo would have preferred Dario to have ordered him to be silent. He would have been ecstatic if Dario had commanded him to be his servant. But of course at the time this couldn't be said, let alone performed. All remained on the edge of desire.

Over the next year Massimo and Dario because fierce friends. At night, as Massimo fell asleep, images of Dario's face filled Massimo's mind. Then Dario became ill and could no longer attend school. For several months Massimo went to Dario's apartment and sat beside him as the boy lay in bed, until the afternoon Dario was taken to the Fatebenefratelli Hospital on Tiber Island. Something was wrong with the child's blood. Gradually Massimo came to understand that Dario was dying.

The priests in charge of the great church that stood on the summit of the Capitoline Hill, Santa Maria in Aracoeli, decided to bring the famous Santo Bambino of Aracoeli to Dario's bedside. The Santo Bambino was a small wooden statue of the infant Jesus, carved by a Franciscan friar during the fifteenth century. Made from an olive tree that grew in the Garden of Gethsemane, the carving was said to have been painted by an angel who came to the friar's cell one night while he slept. After the image of the infant Jesus was brought to Rome, many who prayed before it were cured, so many that the Franciscans began bringing the statue to the bedsides of the sick and dying. More miracles followed. For years the Bambino had his own carriage that would race through Rome's streets, stopping all traffic in its path. It was said that even Mussolini's long black limousine once stopped at an intersection to allow the Santo Bambino's carriage to pass.

"Your friend," the man from the North said, "after he was visited by the Santo Bambino, was his disease of the blood cured?"

Massimo wagged his head. "How the little Judas could save so many doddering old women and senile, piss-stained old men, all who had already lived an entire life, yet allow young Dario to die, I'll never understand."

The man from the North appeared shocked. "You call the Infant a little Judas?"

Massimo nodded. "Betrayal is betrayal."

"You blaspheme."

Massimo gave the cool night air a shrug.

"But certainly you know that Christ makes no promises other than the possibility of redemption for one's soul."

"He was only a child. You don't know how often I fell to my knees and prayed."

By now the pair had walked down the Cordonata and stood by the steep bank of steps leading up to the church standing atop Capitoline Hill. The two sets of steps, one so inviting and easy to ascend, the other so demanding and stern, were said to suggest the relative paths one might take in life, the former leading to the worldly, the latter to the sacred and divine.

"Forgive me for saying this, my friend, but you have a hard heart."

"No," Massimo said, "I have a heart with a hole in it." He took the other man's hand into his and drew him closer. "Now let's not waste time while the night is still young."

"THIS CAN'T BE true," Massimo said as he picked up his sweater and jeans from the floor and was preparing to leave the small room in the B&B where the man from the North was staying. "Stop this charade. Please assure me this is a mistake."

On the wooden desk near the narrow bed lay the ivory beads of a rosary and an open notebook and breviary along with a stiff Roman collar, round and white like a halo. Hanging from a nail in the wall on a hanger was a black tab-collar shirt. "For the love of God," Massimo said, "tell me you're not a priest."

"You never asked," the priest from the North said. "And in all truth I didn't think it was relevant."

"You didn't think it was relevant?" Massimo rushed to clothe himself. "Don't you have any concern for my soul?"

The priest smiled. "But of course."

"Yet to do," Massimo began, then hesitated, "with an actual priest. Now I'm sure to be damned."

The priest from Lugano let out a long sigh. He reached for his underwear, which lay bunched at the bottom of the bed, then lay back in the bed again. "I'm certain you won't be, at least not for any action we've taken tonight." His face eased into a smile. "But if you think it will be any consolation, kneel and I'll hear your confession."

"After what we just did? You're in the state of the darkest sin too."

The priest laughed. "I'm only jesting. Of course, do as you like. Find another priest in the morning. Certainly here in Rome there's no shortage. And please know that you'll be in my prayers. Tomorrow morning, and all the mornings thereafter." His nodded his head and smiled.

"You should have been wearing your collar, you know. You shouldn't have been out on the street in disguise."

"To be honest, the collar attracts the sort of man I'm not interested in spending my time with."

"A man of the cloth." Massimo shook his head as he crossed himself, then raised his eyes to the heavens. "May I live until daylight, long enough to confess."

"Listen to me," the priest said. "What we did was no sin. At least not in the eyes of the one true God who made each of us in all of our variations in his blessed image and likeness. Though, if you're looking to confess something, you might consider coming to terms, so to speak, with the anger and resentment you hold against our Savior."

Another of the priest's black shirts was hanging on a cord stretched across the tub in the bathroom. "Don't preach to me," Massimo said.

"Forgive me, I don't mean to preach. I'm only trying to help."

"You could have told me you were a priest. That would have been of help."

"You're quite deft at evasion."

By now Massimo was fully dressed. "All right," he said, "since you bring up the subject let me ask you this." He pulled out the chair from beside the wooden desk and sat on it backward, with his thick arms resting on its back. "If there is a God and God isn't a truly sadistic son of a bitch, why does he allow people to suffer and die?"

"Why does suffering exist in the world? An excellent question." The priest paused, then stood and pulled on his black trousers. "Suffering exists as a result of free will because just as man is free to worship the Creator and lead a moral and virtuous life, man is also free to turn away from our Savior and embrace evil. God, therefore, allows people to suffer as a punishment for their sins. You're familiar with the story of Adam and Eve. Their decision in the Garden is representative of the daily choices each of us makes. And as we see elsewhere in the Bible, suffering is often a test."

"You make it sound like a subject in school. The ones who study receive a good life, and the ones who don't – " Massimo shrugged and threw up his hands. "But, tell me, what about the children? The innocents? What about the young, the newly born? Certainly my friend Dario committed no sin."

The priest sat on the edge of the bed across the room from Massimo. "As descendants of Adam and Eve, none of us are innocent."

"Meh," Massimo said. "A child's pap. Only a few weeks ago, just before the new year, an earthquake that lasted a full ten minutes ripped open the sea floor and created a series of mighty waves that killed hundreds of thousands of innocent people. How could a merciful and loving God have permitted that?"

"The Earth isn't Heaven."

"To God, preventing such a calamity would have been nothing. All he would have had to do was lift the least of his fingers."

"And then he would have to prevent the next catastrophe, and then the next one, and then the one after that. And who is to say that at this very moment, as we discuss his divine nature in this room, he isn't preventing a disaster that would reduce every stone in Rome to dust? No, my friend, as for tragedies like the tsunami or even the Holocaust, all we mortals can say is that God's will is beyond our comprehension. Imagine an ant struggling to climb a blade of grass, trying to understand the workings of the sun and moon and stars." The priest raised a hand. "It's a mystery. Christ's sacrifice for our sins is the only constant, the sole beacon of light on life's rocky shore."

"You've heard the one about the Holocaust survivor who dies and goes to Heaven," Massimo said. "When it's his turn to face judgment, he begins by telling God a Holocaust joke. God says, 'That isn't very funny.' The Holocaust survivor replies, 'Well, you had to be there.'" Massimo shook his head. "Because, of course, God wasn't there. So go ahead, write a sermon about that."

Massimo stood in the center of the room, smoothing the wrinkles in his sand-colored sweater with his hands. "It's shit is what it is. Ants climbing blades of grass. Beacons of light on life's rocky shore. Complete and utter shit. What do you priests do? Take a Vatican-approved course on how to spew shit whenever people ask you intelligent questions?"

"You guessed it," the priest said. "Our secret is out."

"You know, years later, when I heard that the figure of the Santo Bambino had been stolen and all of Rome was in an uproar, I was ecstatic."

"Now who's blaspheming?"

"I speak from the heart. He deserved it. I hope the true Bambinello is never found."

"When did you say this happened?"

"I don't know exactly. When I was a teen. Ten or eleven years ago."

"But the statue in the church on the hill," the priest began.

"It's a copy. Something for the tourists from England. Supposedly it, too, is carved from the hard wood of a tree that once grew in the Garden of Gethsemane but" – Massimo laughed – "at night so is my cock." He patted the front of his pants. "And I suppose the Franciscans found another angel with a paintbrush."

"It's not the wood or the paint that makes an object holy," the priest said. "All of what we experience, the entire material world, is only an illusion passing before our senses. What makes the Bambino Gesù di Aracoeli sacred is the belief people have in it, and in Jesus Christ himself. True holiness lies not in the object but in the person's perception of it, in the individual's strong and abiding faith."

"A fake is still a fake. Just like God is a fake."

"Nothing on Earth is perfect, at least since the time of the fall of man." The priest paused. "You know the statue you're so fond of, that brings tears to your eyes, the figures of Romulus and Remus and the She-wolf?"

"The Capitoline wolf," Massimo said. "Yes, of course I know it. And I know that the one we looked at atop the pillar, it's a copy. The original is kept under lock and key inside the Capitoline Museum."

"It's more than that. The wolf is said to be Etruscan, sixth or fifth century BCE, if I remember correctly, but the twin figures of Romulus and Remus beneath it were added centuries later, sometime during the Renaissance."

"No," Massimo said, wounded.

"Yes," the priest said. "Like nearly everything else in Rome, it's a palimpsest. And yet when we see it we accept it for what it represents, and we believe it's whole and true. Our belief in the image defines it."

Then the priest suggested that just as Romulus went on to build a great city after Remus's death, Massimo should set his grief for Dario aside and give the Santo Bambino a second invitation to dwell within his heart. To do this, the priest advised, Massimo should visit the Bambino on seven consecutive days, each time asking for forgiveness. In addition he should pray for Dario's eternal salvation. Each day Massimo should make an offering of part of his wages to some worthy cause, giving as much as he could afford. "Pray for guidance as you ascend the stairs," the priest added. "You don't have to climb them on your knees – this isn't the Scala Sancta – but don't rush up them like a tourist. Walk slowly, in meditation, and with each step ask that bitterness be lifted from your heart. Pray for enlightenment. Take it as penance, as we near the sacred season of Lent. Understand that when the original statue was stolen, the last remnants of your faith were taken too."

"You can't be serious."

The priest said nothing, though his lips appeared to move. After several moments Massimo realized the man was praying.

"But that would have me completing my penance on Fat Tuesday."

"So you miss a bit of Carnevale," the priest said with a shrug. "So much the better. Begin tomorrow, nonetheless. You realize this reconciliation, it's what you've wanted to do your entire life. You wouldn't still be here talking to me if that weren't true."

Massimo said nothing, nodding imperceptibly.

"Think of the relief you'll feel after you've finished."

Massimo still said nothing.

"Seven consecutive days," the priest from the North said. "Without fail."

WHEN MASSIMO ARRIVED home he found his father still awake, sitting at the table in their tiny tinello, his left foot tethered to a heavy chair. He'd silenced the clapper of the bell around his neck with the sock from his right foot and was bent over the table, alternately writing lines on a pad of paper and lifting his head and whispering phrases into the air.

For the past year or so Massimo's father had begun to wander, and Massimo and his mother had taken to securing him to chairs. They used soft, furry handcuffs – *love cuffs*, the man in the adult store called them – padded with faux sheepskin, and hung bells on the door so that they could tell whenever it opened or closed. It was as if Massimo's father was losing all sense of boundary. If a neighbor's door was unlocked, he would wander into the apartment and make himself at home, pull open drawers and paw through their things, help himself to whatever was in their refrigerator or cooking on their stove, then take off his shoes and pants and curl like a child upon their sofa. Sometimes he'd forget what purpose objects had and would sit for long, angry minutes with the television remote control in his hand staring at the glass door of the microwave, demanding that the machine come to life and show him the latest episode of *L'eredità* or *Grande Fratello*. He'd lather his face and neck with soap and stand over the kitchen sink shaving himself with a spoon. He needed to be reminded each morning how to put on a shirt and which buttons went into which holes. He never harmed anyone or raised his voice when corrected, and for a while everyone was kind to him, leading him back to his apartment as if he were a lost lamb, but after several months the neighbors grew weary of playing the dutiful sheepdog.

Can't you keep him inside his own house? they asked Massimo and his mother. Of course the dear soul is more than welcome to share whatever we have, but it's no fun when in the middle of supper he walks in like a long-lost relative and takes off his pants. It makes the dog bark and upsets the children. They're too young to have to witness something like that. We've tried bolting the door and ignoring him, but he rattles the knob like a woodpecker and scrapes the keyhole with his belt buckle. That was when Massimo and Renata decided to hang the cowbell around his neck and use the padded hand- and ankle-cuffs.

"How are you, Papa?" Massimo said, kissing the man's unshaven cheeks.

"What rhymes with *struggimento*?" his father answered.

Scrawled on the paper before him were alternating runs of looped, jagged lines, some spiked like the tips of an iron fence. "Ahh, Papa, I see you're writing a list for the grocery."

"It's a love poem," the father said. He was a thin man with unruly gray hair and a silver beard and mustache, the upturned ends of which he was fond of twirling whenever he was in deep thought or confused. Some in the apartment building said he resembled Don Quixote. He raised a finger to his lips. "For my Giuliana."

Giuliana was the thirteen-year-old girl who lived in one of the downstairs apartments. She was a pleasant enough child, overly enamored with eyeliner, with long dark hair and eyes big as a hoot owl's. Her ears were nearly always glued to her pink cell phone. "That's very nice, Papa," Massimo said. "I'm certain she'll like it."

"But first I need to capture the rhyme scheme. I know the first part is the octave, the second the sestet. Last week we were tested on it in school. But now I can't remember what follows the volta. Is the scheme cde-cde or cd-cd-cd?"

Massimo had no idea what the man was talking about. "I'm sure either one would be fine." He patted his father's head affectionately. "As for poetry, do as you like. I don't think there are many rules."

"Oh no," the man said, wagging his head. "No, now there you're wrong. There are many rules, particularly for love poetry. Of all forms, getting the poetry of love right is by far the most difficult." The man paused and gazed into the empty air. "Without doubt" – he stroked his beard and bent his head over the paper as he licked the point of his pencil and went back to his furious scratching – "the poetry of love is the most difficult."

From the next room came the squeak of bedsprings, the thump of footsteps, the flushing of a toilet, the yawning of an opening door. After several moments Massimo's mother, clad in a polyester robe over her nightgown, walked into the room. Renata was a sturdy woman, thick as a wrestler. Looking at her one could see where Massimo got his muscles. Her robe bore a repeating jungle theme, featuring a pack of growling lions pursuing a herd of terrified gazelles desperately leaping toward a stand of acacia trees.

Massimo kissed his mother on both cheeks. "I'm getting a lesson on love poetry. He's writing a poem to the little girl who lives downstairs."

"Oh," the woman said, turning toward her husband and nodding. "Giuliana. He's gotten it into his head they're classmates. When she goes off to school he stands by the window and looks down at her on the street and cries."

Massimo's father hid his poem with his arms.

"Take your sock out of that bell at once," Renata said sharply. "Put it back on your foot where it belongs."

The man did as he was told.

"There's soup on the stove if you're hungry," the woman told Massimo as the pair walked into the kitchen. On the wall hung a gaudy crucifix. Beneath it on the counter stood a ceramic rooster, its serrated comb a brilliant red, its head tilted back, beak wide open, as if perpetually announcing the new day.

"Tell me, now that you've had some time on your own to think, what were your impressions of Peppina?" Renata said as she reached for a ladle. "And did you let the dog inspect you?"

"She smelled of ground peppercorns."

"I noticed that too."

"I think it was a waste of good money, Mamma." Massimo held up his spoon. "This isn't one of the ones he uses for shaving?"

"No. I keep his spoon-razors next to the soap." Renata pointed. "I had the dog sniff me all over, twice. I'm happy to say I'm cancer-free."

"But at least she could see that I'm not meant to marry Iolanda. You heard her with your own ears."

"Iolanda has a younger cousin, a virtuous girl as I remember, named Livia."

"Mamma," Massimo said, "don't."

"Don't what? Don't try to help my son? Don't do what I can to insure that one day he'll be content?"

"Struggimento e dolore!" cried Massimo's father from the other room.

"I'm already content, Mamma," Massimo said. "Can't you see? I'm so content that one hundred percent pure contentment bursts each moment from my pores."

Renata filled his bowl with warm soup, then grated on some pecorino. The flakes of the cheese fell softly to the soup's surface, like winter snow, then swelled within the broth and drifted slowly toward the vegetables lying on the bowl's bottom. "No matter what you may think or feel," the woman said, "you need a wife and children. You never know what will happen in life, what the next day brings, what the day after that takes away. Just look at what your father has become."

"He seems happy enough," Massimo replied. "Look at him now as he writes. He makes no complaint."

"He's happier now than he's ever been, I think. Though I fear it won't last. You see how frustrated he gets sometimes. Sometimes he flies off into frightening rages. But that's not the point. We're talking about you."

"I told you, Mamma. I'm content. I'm content."

"I know more than you think," Massimo's mother said slowly. "Every day I thank the Virgin that she blessed me with a son, just as she herself was blessed. And please know that I wouldn't change you for an emperor's chest full of gold and jewels."

"I'm content, Mamma."

"Still, I heard Peppina's words. Inside of your heart there is a hole."

"And you think that Iolanda or Livia – "

"Who she is doesn't matter. But that there is a *she* in your life does. You know of what I'm speaking." The woman paused. "Instead of going to the gymnasium every night and spending your time among other men, you should be the one sitting by the window writing love poems."

"Get me a pencil and paper, Mamma. I'll begin at once."

"Don't humor me. I only want what's best for you."

"As do I, Mamma. As do I."

Renata said nothing then. The packs of lions on her robe shifted as she moved, drawing closer to the herd of wild-eyed gazelles, then falling back in the chase as the crazed creatures raised their great horns toward the sky and stretched their hooves toward the safety of the acacia trees. Pinned to the cupboard over the sink hung several plastic charms – a bright red cornicello, big as a hot pepper, a smaller gold-plated mano cornuto, and a red, black, and white Gobbo, the smiling, dapper hunchback. From the next room came the occasional soft ringing of Massimo's father's bell.

"Did you have time to sew the torn braiding on my legionnaire flag?"

Renata nodded. "I also replaced one of the grommets on your belt and washed your cape and tunic. Everything's folded in your room, by your breastplate and sandals."

"I don't know what I'd do without you, Mamma."

The woman said nothing.

"Believe me, Mamma. I'm fine. I'm content."

"Of course you are." She patted the back of her son's hand and then picked up his empty bowl and turned to the sink to wash it. "Of course you are."

AFTER WORKING OUTSIDE the Colosseum the next day, Massimo rode his scooter down Via dei Fori Imperiali and its elegant rows of umbrella pines and past the weaving snarls of traffic by the Piazza Venezia and the filthy glacier Il Vittoriano, which always looked wrong to him, both misplaced and out of proportion with the rest of Rome. Massimo searched for a place to park by the Piazza d'Aracoeli, near the base of the Capitoline Hill. He'd left his centurion outfit, which he normally took home each evening, in a locker in the Colosseum. He thought the priests in the church wouldn't appreciate him coming in with a bulky duffel bag. These days someone might think him a thief planning to rob the place or an anarchist carrying a bomb. He wore his usual street clothing – a cotton sweater and pressed jeans along with his black jacket and a soft red scarf looped casually around his neck.

He walked past the Cordonata and paused at the base of the steep staircase leading up to the basilica's open doorway. Better to carry out this penance, Massimo decided, than suffer for all of eternity in Hell. Particularly after getting in bed with a priest. Massimo genuflected on the first of the church's steps and crossed himself, then stood and began his way up the steps slowly, reverently, as if he were part of a funeral procession. As he ascended the stairs he mumbled a half-hearted prayer.

Like so many other churches in Rome, Santa Maria in Aracoeli was built on the site of a temple devoted to an ancient Roman sect. Legend had it that the Emperor Caesar Octavian Augustus, nephew of Julius Caesar, had a vision of the Virgin standing near the temple on top of the hill. She appeared in a wash of dazzling white light with the infant Jesus, the Santo Bambino, in her arms. "This is the altar of the Son of God," announced a voice from above, and so Octavian commanded that an altar be erected on the temple's site, an *ara coeli*, or altar of the heavens. Soon a church was built over the site of the altar, a visible display of Christianity's triumph over paganism.

Massimo had genuine admiration for Octavian, who, with Mark Antony, remained loyal to the emperor Caesar and later avenged his death. Whenever Massimo walked by the bronze statue of Caesar overlooking the Roman forum, or the cat sanctuary at the Area Sacra at Largo di Torre Argentina, the site where Caesar was viciously murdered, he wondered how history might have been different had he been there at Caesar's side. Even now on every Ides of March Rome's citizens brought flowers to the base of Caesar's statue. Little did the senators who assassinated Caesar know that by killing him they'd bring about precisely what they protested against – centuries of rule by emperors – as well as their own deaths. Massimo believed in the rule of gods and emperors and would happily serve in an army led by any of them. Moreover, he felt he would gladly die fighting in their defense. In his imagination Massimo marched in the Legio XIII Gemina, the Thirteenth Legion, which Julius Caesar himself recruited, and which crossed the Rubicon under his command.

The grand basilica was as Massimo remembered it. There near the doorway was a table, normally littered with church-related pamphlets and appeals for this and that cause. Today's flyers solicited donations for tsunami relief. One flyer showed a picture of a man carrying a dead child, arms and head limp, dangling. Massimo paused and slipped several euros into the nearby donation box, then made the sign of the Cross.

As Massimo looked at the church again, a swell of emotion pressed at his eyes. Santa Maria in Aracoeli was constructed in the classic form, with a great nave and twin rows of marble pillars, each different in design, each plundered from the ruins of other buildings. That was the way of the world, Massimo believed – the strong took what they needed from the weak. The church gave its visitors the impression of being inside a spacious meeting hall, one filled with golden light. The vast nave held a rare, noble eloquence. Massimo looked toward the chancel, then lifted his eyes to the coffered ceiling – a rich mix of sorrels and cinnamons and chestnuts, carved into protruding rectangles and squares, their edges gilded brilliantly in gold filigree, arranged to make a series of interconnected crosses in the center of which was an oval bottomed and topped by winged angels, in which the Madonna and Child stood on a gold cloud.

His steps echoed on the marble floor, mottled with variously colored slabs of stone, several of which topped graves. Trying not to appear like a child performing a silly dance, Massimo stepped gingerly around each of the gravestones as he made his way to the intimate chapel housing the Santo Bambino. Above the door to the hallway leading to the chapel was a small figure of the martyr Saint Sebastian – hands tied behind his back – his chest, neck, abdomen, and legs pierced by arrows. Massimo admired Sebastian, a brave soldier who'd endured great suffering. The figure's pained eyes gazed upwards toward the sky.

Unlike Sebastian, the Santo Bambino stood peacefully on an altar beneath a semicircular apse built to resemble a miniature temple, complete with golden pillars topped by angels, their silver wings lying flat against each side of the shrine. The statue stood inside a protective glass case atop a satin pillow embroidered with gold thread. The Child's stocky body was swathed in a shiny robe covered with jewels and gold chains, and on his head was an imposing gold-plated crown bearing a round gemstone. On both sides of the glass case were frescoes of the Holy Family, and above, looking down from a white cloud, God the Father. Next to the case were baskets overflowing with letters, each imploring the Santo Bambino to grant a special favor. The figure stood confidently, dark eyes wide, mouth turned down slightly into a frown, as if he were a little judge standing before his throne, abjectly considering the merits of each request brought before him.

Massimo stared at the doll. "I see you're still here," he whispered. "Fat and happy there in your glass box, wearing your little gold slippers, looking smug as always."

The Santo Bambino said nothing.

"No," Massimo said, "I must be mistaken. You're not Christ. You're not the Holy Child I prayed to as a child, the chosen one the priests unveil on Christmas Eve, the one in whose honor the shepherds from Calabria and Abruzzo play their bagpipes, the one who stands on his mother's knee in the Chapel of the Presepio each Christmas listening to the children's prayers and poems, the one the priests carry outside on the morning of l'Epifania to bless all of Rome. You're the replacement. The substitute. The True One's kid brother or cousin." Massimo paused and wiped his mouth as he gazed at the figure. "You know, now that I look at you I can see that he was the more handsome. A bit taller. More manly. With wider shoulders, larger eyes, a stronger jaw. I bet you envy him. I bet you don't even know where he is now."

The Infant remained unmoved.

"Of course you don't know," Massimo whispered, "because God knows everything, every single thought and desire in the world, and you're not God."

A sparkle of light reflected from the Child's crown.

"Did you hear me? I just said that you're not God."

The chapel's silence was broken only by the sound of Massimo's heavy breathing.

"The world's collapsing around us, falling into shit." Massimo took in a breath, then let out a long sigh. "OK, I get it. Stand there inside your little gold box, staring out at this room as if you're dead. When it would mean nothing to you to lift a hand and spare a dying child, or stop the tremendous waves from sweeping thousands of people to their deaths."

The Infant remained expressionless.

"Still," Massimo continued, "I suppose you could strike me dead right now if you wanted. You could do it with a flick of your little finger." Massimo shut his eyes. "So, go ahead. Do it. I dare you. Kill me. Hear me, as I stand before you and blaspheme." He paused. "I'm not afraid. I already know that I deserve to spend eternity in Hell because at least twice a week – twice a week! – I commit an act that you find offensive. I live in the constant state of the darkest sin. Worse, I understand that my sin is unforgivable since it's not my intention to stop committing it. Do you hear me? I'm not in the mood to stop committing my sin! It's the way I was made. The way you made me. But of course you're a mere child, an innocent who knows nothing about the desires of the flesh."

Again the Santo Bambino of Aracoeli said nothing.

"Can't you understand that when I was younger I believed in you with all of my heart? I would have given you my life in exchange for his. I *begged* you to take me instead of him. I *implored* you, on my hands and knees. I *praised* you. I *worshiped* you. Why weren't my prayers good enough? Why did you refuse what I was willing to sacrifice?"

The Child stood still as stone.

"You, who would grow up to be the Prince of Peace, the Good Shepherd, the Joy of Angels, the Lamb of God, the Son of Man, the True Bread, the Blessed Redeemer, how could you have let Dario die?" Massimo was shouting now. "For the love of God, he was only a child! Ahead of him were the days of a long life! Given all the sin and evil in the world, how could you let him perish? What would it have mattered had you allowed him to live?"

Massimo held his face in his hands, and as a tear made its way down his cheek he was distracted by a sound – the click of metal striking metal, followed by footsteps – from the sacristy. Likely the sacristan or one of the gray-haired Franciscans, alarmed to hear someone yelling in the church. Massimo wondered if all he had said inside the small chapel had been overheard, and then he realized that of course the True Child as well as God the Father and the Holy Spirit and the Blessed Virgin had heard and understood everything, even the darkest thoughts that Massimo knew dwelled deep within the hole in his heart.

On his way out of the church he ignored the many tombstones as he stepped on them, staring up instead at the heart-shaped blue window on the basilica's rear wall. Displayed there was the Barberini family's trio of golden bees. Massimo turned back toward the main altar and genuflected. The church was vast and cold, empty save for the old sacristan who was meticulously spreading on the main altar a cloth the color of December frost.

That night at the palestra Massimo exercised with so much vigor that several men noticed him and asked him out for a drink or a stroll to the baths – whatever might be his preference – but Massimo shook his head grimly, declining each invitation.

AFTER HE ARRIVED home, Massimo learned that his father had slipped free of his shackles.

"One minute he was here," Renata told Massimo as she took from the oven a bowl of something warm for him to eat, "and then the next – " She tossed a hand into the air and shrugged. "I tell you, sometimes I can't keep up with him. I didn't even hear the bells."

Massimo grabbed a fork and spoon, then walked over to the sink to check that it wasn't one of his father's shaving spoons. "Do you know where he went?"

"Where do you think?" The woman brought out a grater and a wedge of pecorino, along with a length of bread. Tonight she wore a robe pattered with the silhouettes of open flowers trembling beneath a pair of hovering hummingbirds, their prominent beaks long and needle-sharp. "To find the girl, Giuliana." Heaped in the bowl were peppers and sausage mixed with triangular wedges of tomato and fennel and onion.

"But wasn't she in school?"

"Of course she was in school. Still, your father managed somehow to open their apartment door and make his way into her room. I tell you, that man has learned his way around locks. They found him in the middle of her bedroom, sitting on the rug, pants off, playing with her little barbarians."

"Barbarians?" Massimo said, as he blew on the first spoonful of hot food before putting it into his mouth. "Barbarians?"

"You know," Renata said, "those skinny little dolls with the long hair that come from America. Both the girl and her parents collect them."

"Barbies," Massimo said after a beat. "Mamma, those little dolls are called Barbies."

"Barbies, barbarians, what difference does it make? They're little dolls. The parents allow the girl to play with a few, and the others they keep hidden away, untouched, in their boxes. Unopened, as an investment for when they grow old. Oh, you should have heard the girl's mother scream when she discovered that your father had torn some of them open."

"So?" Massimo said as he ate. "Can't the woman put them back inside?"

"That's what I said too, but she told me now they're ruined. He ripped the cardboard and broke the little cellophane windows behind which the dolls stand. She said these were originals, decades old. You buy them new and keep them long enough in a dark closet and apparently over time they're worth a fortune."

"They're only plastic," Massimo said as he tore off a piece of bread and made a little shoe, mopping up the remaining bits of vegetable and sauce in his bowl. "Plastic and a silly costume and pretend hair."

"No," his mother said, "not to the collectors. To the collectors the ones still in their boxes, untouched, are worth more than gold. She said that the barbarians are so popular – "

"Barbies, Mamma. Barbies."

" – the Barbies are so popular there are more Barbies here in Italy than there are Canadians in all of Canada."

Massimo walked to his father's chair. On the floor beneath it lay the man's cowbell and a broken pair of faux sheepskin ankle cuffs. "Where is he now?"

Renata frowned. "Sleeping in my bed." She shook her head sadly. "I tell you, he hardly recognizes me anymore. Tonight he thought I was a stranger. Earlier he insisted I was his mother." Renata threw one hand into the air. "So tonight I told him I was a nurse and had him take one of my pills." She carried Massimo's bowl and cutlery to the sink, then ran water from the tap as she rinsed them. "At least he'll sleep tonight."

"He's growing worse, isn't he?"

Massimo's mother said nothing.

"A grown man," Massimo said, "breaking into houses, playing with dolls."

"At least he's alive."

"I'll talk to the mother," Massimo said. "As for the Barbies, I'll give her whatever she wants to buy some new old ones." He picked up the broken cuffs from the carpet near the desk where they lay.

"And where were you tonight?" Renata asked. Wings spread wide, the hummingbirds fluttered menacingly over the open flowers, their beaks like eager daggers. "Sweating again at the palestra with the other single men?"

"I went to church, Mamma." The clasps on the cuffs were broken, sheared open, as if by a strongman. "Up on the Capitoline Hill. Santa Maria in Aracoeli."

Renata continued wiping the table, scooping the crumbs with a damp rag into the hollow of her open hand. "Ahh, so now you're religious. Praying to the little Jesus in the glass box for your father's cure."

"I went there to say a prayer for Dario," Massimo said. He frowned and shook the broken cuffs in the air. "I'll take these back tomorrow and get a few new pairs. Maybe they'll have ones that are stronger."

The woman appeared on the verge of tears. "You should have seen him as we walked up the stairs. He was sobbing like a wayward child. He didn't have any idea who I was."

"New cuffs will buy us a bit more time, Mamma. And I'll speak with the girl's parents and apologize and pay them whatever they want."

Renata exhaled a deep breath. "I live with one man who can't remember, another who can't forget."

"True," Massimo said, "but you, with your cards and amulets" – he pointed at the cupboard and the plastic figure of Gobbo, the grinning hunchback in the black top hat and vest, who bore not only a lucky hump to rub but whose right hand made the corno and whose left hand held out a horseshoe, and whose legs were fused to make a thick red horn – "and your insistence that I sit down and talk with old women who claim to have a cancer-smelling dog who can see death, it seems all you're concerned with is the future."

"And why shouldn't I be?" Renata said. "Do you think living each day without hope and prayer is worth it?"

"And what do you hope and pray tomorrow will bring, Mamma?"

"Stupid boy, what's in your head? I hope and pray for a husband who recognizes and loves me, and a son who brings home a young wife who will give me many grandchildren. Like Peppina said, I want to see you with a child in your arms."

"And if you don't get what you want, Mamma? What do you do then?"

The woman brought her hands together, as if in prayer, and swung them up and down. "I do what all those who walk this Earth have done since the first moment of time. I live another day and hope for better. I work and hope and pray and go to bed, then wake up and live another day and work and hope and pray."

OVER THE NEXT week Massimo continued to visit the church, each evening praying before the statue and making an offering to various relief agencies aiding the tsunami survivors. On the evening of the last day, the height of Carnevale, Massimo made his way to the church on his Vespa down Via dei Fori Imperiali. He kept his centurion costume on, not because he was hopeful of earning money from tourists wishing to pose with him but in keeping with the spirit of the day.

The crossways and sidewalks around him were sprinkled with coriandoli – colored bits of paper in the shape of circles and stars – that the children threw at costumes they were especially amused by. Though Rome certainly was not Venice, at least a few in the crowds wore capes and masks, both the traditional white Venetian bautta and the oval black moretta. Others were dressed in the old style, as figures out of the pages of Goldoni – as Arlecchino, Brighella, the lean and scrawny Pantalone. Massimo guessed they were actors on their way to a performance or individuals parading down the wide avenue to some private party where they'd celebrate raucously until dawn.

Near one intersection Il Capitano strolled arm in arm with the high-spirited servant Smeraldina and a fat Il Dottore. A few steps behind them trailed a particularly long-nosed Pulcinella, his floppy white hat dangling like an empty sock. Beside the Piazza Venezia, Massimo spotted the rascal policeman Rugantino accompanied by a black-hooded Mastro Titta, Rome's famous executioner. And there, on the center of the piazza, encircled by the endless ring of traffic rattling its way over Rome's cobbled streets, was the curious character Massimo had heard talk about, Rome's reborn Caravaggio, wearing a feathered cap and striped shirt and skin-tight leggings, in his hand a fancy sword – a basket-hilted schiavona, Massimo realized as he drove around the circle a second time so as to give the performer a closer look – ranting like a rock star in a mix of Italian and English, occasionally pausing to lunge his sword forward in mock battle with his opponent, an apparently angry man, clearly another actor, whose sole defense against the sword was a tennis racket.

As Massimo crossed himself and genuflected at the bottom of the steep stairway leading up to Santa Maria in Aracoeli, men strolling on the nearby Cordonata called out to him. They reminded Massimo that the season of Lent began tomorrow, and if he was wise he'd wait until then to put on the sackcloth and ashes.

There's plenty of time later to atone for your sins! the men shouted. Tonight, Fat Tuesday, is a time for indulgence! A night for pleasure! For food! For drink! The delights of the flesh! Come down and join us, my friend! Join us!

But Massimo continued his slow ascent, thinking of Christ and the unimaginable torture he must have experienced when he was crucified. Massimo wondered how much the Infant knew about his imminent death. Even as a bambino the Child must have realized how much suffering and humiliation it would be his task to endure. He must have carried within him the ringing sense of each moment of excruciating pain his flesh would later be made to experience. Maybe that was why the Infant's eyes were so wide and dark, Massimo thought. Perhaps what Massimo had judged as smugness was actually the consequence of knowledge, the weight of genuine sadness, the realization of what being the son of God sent to redeem the world's sins actually entailed.

Massimo sensed something wasn't quite right as soon as he pushed his way into the church. The wooden table that held the church's pamphlets and donation boxes had been shoved back against the doorway in an attempt to block it, and the pamphlets and holy cards that normally lay on the table were scattered like coriandoli on the floor. The side door on the far side of the nave, leading to the walkway behind the Palazzo Nuovo and the expanse of the Piazza del Campidoglio, was propped open with a paving stone. Muffled sounds came from the sacristy, followed by a cry and a dull thud. On the floor of the hallway outside the Santo Bambino's chapel lay the prone figure of a man – the church's old, white-haired sacristan – groaning, his hands holding his broken, bleeding head.

The invader inside the chapel was dressed as the servant Zanni, in a peaked hat and baggy white shirt and pants, along with a dark mask with a wrinkled brow and an immensely long, pointed nose. With the base of one of the heavy gold candlesticks – it lay on its side on the altar amid a smattering of glittering glass shards – the thief had apparently smashed the door of the case in which the Bambino stood and was now stripping the wooden carving of its gold chains and jewels, dropping the bounty into the open mouth of his cloth bag.

Without thinking the centurion drew his short sword from its scabbard and with the flat of the weapon whacked the figure's back and head until he turned and cried out in pain. Then Massimo dropped his sword and slapped the man's mask away and bull-rushed him, circling the robber's chest with his arms as he bounced the man up and against the chapel's wall – once, twice, three times, four – until the man's breath gave out and his throat issued a squeak. Massimo's hands then curled into fists and beat the scoundrel's chest and abdomen with crisp combinations, like he routinely punished the heavy punching bags hanging from the palestra's ceiling, until the thief's twitching legs grew still.

The rogue slumped into a heap. On the altar steps beside him lay the open sack, stuffed with the other candlesticks and the Bambino's golden crown and jewels. Massimo stood over the man, heart pounding. In his heart he felt a mix of rage and joy. He removed his plumed helmet and set it carefully on the altar beside the smashed glass case.

By now the moaning sacristan in the hallway had crawled inside the doorway. Blood ran down his forehead from the broken patch in his white hair. He stretched forward a hand and cried out, "Our Savior."

Massimo turned and nodded, thinking he was the one being addressed, then picked the near-naked Infant up from the floor where he'd been thrown and cradled him tenderly against his shining breastplate.

Gospa

Međugorje, April 1983

The six children ran in fear the first time they saw her. She was standing on the side of Mount Crnica, a rocky hill overlooking the hamlet of Podbrdo, near the village of Međugorje in southwestern Bosnia and Herzegovina. Teens, mainly. They said they saw a sudden shining light and in its center a young woman in a gray robe, her head covered by a scarf, holding what looked like a lamb or a baby in her arms while gesturing to them to come to her. After they returned to town they referred to her as the Gospa, which meant the Lady. We were up on Crnica tending our sheep, they said, when she suddenly appeared. Later one of the six admitted that they'd actually climbed the hillside to smoke cigarettes.

The following day, 25 June 1981, four of the six hiked back up the hill to the vision's site. They were joined by two others from the village – curious friends, one a boy who was only ten, the other a young girl named Marija. The Gospa appeared again, this time with empty arms, speaking to the children as they dropped before her to their knees. One girl whose mother had died two months before was bold enough to ask the vision about her dead mother. She is with me, the Gospa answered. She is happy. Give us a sign, another girl said, so the people in town won't think we're lying or crazy. The girl's wristwatch immediately stopped. Will you come back here tomorrow? the children asked. The Gospa nodded. Goodbye, my angels, she said as the children stood to leave. Go in the peace of God.

On the third day the children asked the Gospa why out of all the places in the world she chose this place to appear. I've come to Međugorje because here there are many true believers, she said. The girl whose mother had died asked if her mother had anything to tell her. Obey your grandmother, the Gospa replied. Help her because she is old. Then one of the children slowly approached the apparition and splashed her with holy water – this, at the urging of the parish priest – and recited what she was taught her to say. Stay with us if you are the Gospa. If not, I banish you, go away!

The Gospa only smiled and remained.

Why appear to us? the children asked. We're far from the best. I don't necessarily choose the best in the world, the Gospa told them. Why don't you appear down in the parish church for everyone else to see? the teens suggested. Blessed are those who have not witnessed and yet believe, the Gospa replied. She then gave the visionaries the first of what would be several messages – a plea for peace. Peace, peace! she told the children. Be reconciled. Carry this message down to the village. Make peace with the Lord, and make peace among yourselves.

From then on the half dozen who saw and prayed with the Lady continued to see her, while the two who glimpsed her on the first day but decided not to return on the second never saw her again. After listening to the children's reports, the local priest who designed the holy water test proclaimed the Gospa was the Blessed Virgin. Soon the Marian apparition on Mount Crnica became known as Our Lady of Međugorje, and the rock-strewn hillside was quickly called Apparition Hill.

The six visionaries were then taken in by the police and questioned. Then the police drove the children north to Mostar for psychiatric evaluations. All six were found sane, healthy, sound. By the fifth day over a thousand people joined the six children as they knelt on the hill before the Lady, and the next day even more thousands made the pilgrimage to Međugorje, and the following day again there arrived more thousands, all coming to Međugorje to witness the visionaries as they walked from their humble houses to the hill where they knelt and prayed at the site, which was now marked with a cross.

Yugoslavia's communist authorities quickly closed off access to Apparition Hill, seized the money donated to the parish by the now overwhelming congregation of pilgrims, and arrested the priest who'd given the children his counsel. The priest was sentenced to three and a half years of imprisonment with hard labor. His charge – participation in a nationalistic plot. Without doubt, the authorities maintained, the claim of apparitions was a ploy designed by a predominately Roman Catholic pro-Croatian village to stir up anti-government sentiment. The fear was a return to Croatian nationalism.

With access to Apparition Hill now blocked, the visionaries gathered in a room adjacent to the church's sanctuary, where the

Lady began to appear. She assured the children that the priest who'd been jailed would be all right, and the police would soon leave. She instructed the seers to pray. She stressed the need for prayer and peace. Pray without ceasing, she instructed the children. The road to peace is through prayer. She then proclaimed herself as the Mother of the Redeemer and the Queen of Peace.

AT THE FOOT of the other side of Apparition Hill lay the Serbian Orthodox village of Šurmanci, where, in 1941, the Ustaše massacred over six hundred Serbian Orthodox Christians who had lived in the village of Prebilovci. The men, women, and children were kidnapped, put in rail cars, brought to Šurmanci, then marched up the hill overlooking the Golubinka pit where they were knifed and bludgeoned and shoved over the edge while nearly all were still alive. Hand grenades were then tossed down onto the bodies. The Ustaše was a fascist group of Croatian Roman Catholic ultranationalists who fought for the creation of a Greater Croatia and maintained that Catholicism and Islam were the only acceptable religions.

It was years later that Dubravka would learn this. Years later she would study the details of her homeland's long history of struggles, its battles with the Ottoman Empire, with Austria and Hungary, Germany, the Communist-led Yugoslav Partisans. Years later she'd wonder why the Virgin Mary had chosen Mount Crnica as the site of her appearances since it overlooked the Golubinka pit and the nearly three thousand bodies buried in the nearby area, each a victim of the Ustaše's mass murders.

DURING THE FOUR-YEAR-LONG Croatian War for Independence, when Croat forces fought against the Socialist Federal Republic of Yugoslavia and the Serb-controlled Yugoslav People's Army, bombs darkened the skies throughout Croatia. The Yugoslav Navy blockaded Dubrovnik, and for eight months rockets and mortars screeched down onto the town, concentrating on the Old City and the Stradun, damaging over eleven thousand buildings including Zagorac's and Onofrio's Large Fountain along with the Franciscan Monastery, the Church of Saint Saviour, and the Church of Saint

Blaise. Father Josip would be among those who were killed, crushed by a falling wall, his bad leg slowing him down as he tried to flee. In response, Croatian bombs would descend on Ukusno's and the Koski Mehmed Pasha Mosque and the Karađoz Bey Mosque as well as nearly the entire city of Mostar. Over sixty shells would be deliberately targeted to strike the Stari Most, shattering the Old Bridge's ancient stones, cracking and dropping them chunk by chunk into the Neretva, destroying the magnificent, perfectly formed sixteenth-century bridge completely.

But for now, the spring of 1983, eight years before the beginning of the Yugoslav Wars, Dubravka knew only that for well over the past year she'd heard talk that a half dozen children in a village in the south were claiming they were visited each day by the Blessed Virgin, and so Dubravka wrapped herself in a black cloak and headscarf and made her way from Mostar to Međugorje.

PART OF WHY Dubravka decided to leave Mostar was because her jump off the bridge had turned her into a sort of celebrity. She'd become something she didn't want to be – a tourist attraction. Not too different from a circus freak, she thought. Something popular enough for foreigners visiting Mostar to seek out, to want to talk to, quiz her about the jump, how it felt, how she'd trained, whether or not she'd been afraid. Scores of boys were eager to leap off the bridge for a portion of the tourists' bulging pockets of coins. But few girls. And now the young waitress who bakes the bread and calzone in the kitchen of one of the restaurants on Braće Fejića – the café with the fat cartoon chef twirling a pizza above his head on its sign, the one standing between the slender minarets of the two mosques near the riverbank – had made the jump and survived.

Dubravka was also certain that Marija and Stanislav were nowhere to be found in the city. That Dubravka now wore a headscarf and continued to pray each morning at the Koski Mehmed Pasha Mosque and yet insisted to anyone who asked that she was Roman Catholic made her even more exotic and strange. It was as if not wanting an identity imposed on you made it all the more likely that one would be.

Dubravka wasn't overly fond of talking to people. She disliked tourists snapping her picture while she served the restaurant's outdoor tables, and she was less than pleased when someone asked her to stop what she was doing and smile for the camera and pose. What did they think she was? A dancing dog? Even while she worked in Ukusno's kitchen the curious would stick their heads in the doorway, calling to her to kindly step out into the sunlight so they could take a snapshot. We came here especially to meet you! Please, come out and talk to us. Of course the head cook, a lit cigarette perpetually dangling from the side of his mouth, encouraged all of this. He led the curious to open tables, handed them menus, told them she'd be happy to speak with them. Her fame was clearly good for the modest restaurant's sales.

She was still hoping to receive a sign. Or had she already been given a sign, she wondered. She remembered Father Josip's words, that if she were to be given a calling it would likely be only later that she'd realize when the exact moment had come. She was certain it hadn't been the moonless night by Dubrovnik's harbor, as she'd searched in the darkness for the unlocked net shed. She was ashamed now even to think about it. How she'd tugged on each lock with the expectation it would open. Dubravka decided now to think that it hadn't been a game or a trick on Marija or Stanislav's part, that Stanislav had really wanted her, though Dubravka did her best to convince herself that it would have been only for an hour or two. It hurt her too deeply to think otherwise. She was to have been like a bar of Swiss chocolate. Something you enjoy in the moment and then forget.

She liked the promise of Međugorje, though she was less than sure about all of the excited, frenetic talk the apparitions had generated. It was said that while praying the faithful would sometimes see the sun grow large and spin like a pinwheel. Triple rainbows would arc across the horizon. Some claimed the metals linking the beads of their rosaries would turn to gold. Pilgrims were now taking dirt from the hillside where the visions began and mixing it with holy water from the fonts in Međugorje's church. They'd rub the mud on their lame legs, push it into their unhearing ears, spread it over the lids of their blind eyes.

There was another mountain near the town, the highest peak in the region, Križevac, the Mount of the Cross, named for the twelve-meter-tall cross erected there in the early 1930s. Along the steep, rocky path to the cross, the parish had put up the fourteen Stations of the Cross. Many who made the climb up to the cross's base later claimed that after they returned to the valley the cross sometimes appeared illuminated by bright lights, even on the darkest of nights, and even though Mount Križevac wasn't equipped with electricity. It was also said that on one afternoon during the first year of the apparitions the word *MIR*, Croatian for *PEACE*, appeared in the sky, formed by clouds, over the mountain.

Dubravka didn't really care about the visions since she believed that God existed in all places and was particularly present in places of prayer, and she felt she didn't need to see an apparition of the Blessed Virgin in order to believe in her. She didn't need clouds to spell out what should be obvious to anyone with common sense. That was one of the reasons why she'd stayed away until now. That and the work she'd been doing in Mostar – readying her body for the Neretva's icy waters, preparing herself for the leap she'd make once winter broke. Perhaps the jump was selfish, she sometimes thought. To choose to commit an act so public, so worldly. Still, it seemed vital, central to her life, something to connect her life with the spearfisher's, though her doubts about having made the jump increased as more tourists asked her to talk and pose for pictures.

She was now eighteen. Plain, but with the true beauty every young girl possesses, even though Dubravka hardly valued it. The Ukusno's other waitress, the one with the tanned skin and nose ring and teardrop earrings, volunteered to take Dubravka home and make her up – cut off her split ends, pull her hair into a high ponytail wrapped tight with a scrunchie, emphasize her eyes with liner and mascara, dash on a touch of lipstick. If you smiled more often and wore a tight T-shirt and jeans like me you'd make much better tips, she told Dubravka. Many travel here to relax and enjoy a bit of life. No one likes looking at a dour young woman in a long dress. You could be pretty, the waitress told Dubravka. Maybe not movie-star pretty, but fair enough to make the men and boys want to look at you more than once. This was before Dubravka's jump from the Old Bridge.

No, what piqued Dubravka's interest now was that the word *Medugorje* was Slavic for *an area between mountains*. While working in the Ukusno's kitchen she began to roll the word *Međugorje* around in her mouth. Saying it was like a kiss. It was exactly the way she felt.

Between mountains, yes.

Going south to Međugorje seemed like the next step in God's plan. Dubravka was certain the sign she expected she'd receive would be given to her while she was there, where she felt her soul now was – between mountains.

MEĐUGORJE WAS A crowded, palpably anxious place. On the plaza outside the Church of Saint James pilgrims wandered about, lips moving, rosary beads swaying from their hands. Some of the faithful stood still as statues, eyes shut, heads tilted back, arms outstretched like Christ on the cross, as they prayed loudly enough for everyone to hear them. Others knelt silently on the plaza's stones, heads bowed. The weak and infirm made their way through the plaza in measured steps. The air was tinged with desperation mixed with hopeful commerce. Beggars called out from the lawns near the rows of priests hearing confessions. Hawkers offered silver and gold-plated medals and pendants, crosses, plastic miniature blue statues of the Lady. Tour group leaders shouted out orders in a variety of languages as they waved their colored flags. Dubravka felt overwhelmed by all of it. She could feel her soul sucking up Međugorje's throbbing, conflicting energy as if she were a sponge. There were moments when she cringed in response to all of the desire and need surrounding her. Only drink muffled the feelings, ground off the roughest edges.

Rather than join the pilgrims praying with the visionaries at the base of Apparition Hill, Dubravka decided to climb Mount Križevac and perform the Stations of the Cross.

As she blended into the knots of people gathering at the mount's base, a woman touched Dubravka's arm and asked if she might assist her during the climb. The woman's name was Anđela. She appeared to be several years older than Dubravka. Apparently she'd just come from church, Dubravka thought, because about her was the distinct, inviting smell of incense. Then she mentioned the name *Marija*, which stirred up Dubravka's memories of Dubrovnik and her work at Zagorac's and Stanislav.

The path was studded with a tumble of rocks and slippery slabs of stone. Above them hung a cloudless blue sky and a pulsing, penetrating orange sun. Around them were the sounds of hushed conversations and prayers in several languages, a music of sorts made up by consonants and vowels, occasionally tumbling in cadence like a poem.

The way up the mountain was arduous. A one-legged man with metal crutches fixed to his arms did his best to keep up. Near him walked a veiled woman with a disfigured face. A friar in a simple brown robe bound with a knotted white cincture was making the painful climb up the path with bare feet. Several pilgrims who spoke French led the pack, urging the group forward, pausing occasionally to give the stragglers time to catch up. Dubravka and Anđela shaded their eyes and looked down on the ground as they walked so that they wouldn't fall. Dubravka's steps were far surer than Anđela's.

Two men just ahead of them were with a woman who'd come to the mountain's base in a wheelchair. By the looks of the men they were her sons, Dubravka thought. The woman sat high in the chair, firmly holding its armrests, legs bandaged and held stiffly to one side. One son hoisted the chair by its wheels, the other the chair's back. The taller son's pants were held up by black suspenders. The men exchanged burdens as the group paused to kneel and pray at each station, marked by a bronze bas-relief depicting a key moment in Christ's Passion. As the group made the climb between stations they recited a decade of the rosary, with those at the head saying the first part – a lovely tangle of languages – and with those at the back of the group responding with the second part of the prayer, again in a variety of tongues, all of which blended splendidly in the air.

Almost halfway up, after the group reached the sixth station, which marked Veronica wiping the face of Jesus, the brother carrying the chair by its wheels asked the other if they might pause for at least several minutes to gather their breath. The pilgrims in the front of the crowd as well as the one-legged man and the woman with the facial deformity and the barefoot friar said they wished to continue. Only Dubravka and Anđela remained with the brothers and their mother. Anđela said she, too, needed rest. Dubravka led Anđela off the path to a spot beneath a tree where they could pause for a few moments in the tree's cool shade.

Though she was a Croat at heart she'd been born in Italy, Anđela told Dubravka. In Molise, in Campobasso, and now she lived in Rome with her younger brother, Giorgio, in a pensione near the Campo de' Fiori. She was here in Međugorje at his bidding. He'd sent her here for a vial of holy water for his dying wife. Of course she wouldn't go to the trouble and expense of traveling from Rome to Međugorje if it were only for herself, but for Giorgio and his wife, Anđela said, she'd do just about anything. At best, she added, the poor soul likely had only months to live. Anđela said she wasn't naive enough to think that the Međugorje water itself would be a cure – rather, the holy water might evoke within the dying woman a belief that she might live a bit longer. That was the trick, Anđela said. The matter would come down to belief. The miracle would be triggered by her faith.

Generations back, Anđela told Dubravka as they sipped from their canteens, her mother's family had lived in Dalmatia but then was forced to flee from the advance of the Ottoman Turks. The family crossed the sea like so many other displaced populations driven from their homelands by war. The family settled in Campobasso, a town that preserved their heritage and language. Others from Dalmatia also settled further north, in Abruzzo.

Italy was my family's salvation, the woman said. Then Anđela coughed and drew a handkerchief out from her purse. In Campobasso her mother met a man whose family owned a Roman pensione. The two married. Of course this was before I and my brother and late sister were born. Anđela coughed again and held her handkerchief up to her mouth.

The pair walked back into the sunlight and knelt before the slab depicting the brave woman Veronica who broke from the cowardly crowd witnessing the cruel spectacle to wipe Christ's bleeding face with her headscarf. Anđela was coughing more deeply now, with a rich throaty wetness. Dubravka felt something surge suddenly within her chest. Hold this for me, please, Anđela said, handing Dubravka her rosary. Anđela opened her purse and took out a card that listed her brother's name and the pensione's address. Let me write a note on the back, Anđela said. That way if you ever find yourself in Rome and need something my brother will know I sent you, that we walked together here, that you helped me.

Anđela's handkerchief then slipped from her hands, splattered with shiny clots of blood. The cloth caught in the air and spread open, as time slowed. Dubravka felt herself nearly pass out from the heat. She hadn't yet eaten that day. She'd had only a cup of sweetened coffee. Later she'd wonder if she did pass out. She stretched out a hand toward the slab to steady herself, as before her eyes the spots of blood on the handkerchief shifted and slid, gathering in the cloth's center in the clear, unmistakable form of a cross.

THE BROTHERS WITH their mother and wheelchair were calling out to the pair to join them. In the rush Dubravka picked the fallen handkerchief up from the ground. Without thinking she slipped it into her pocket as she stood, as she tried to clear her mind. Of course what she'd just seen was a hallucination. A trick of the sun, she thought, as she and Anđela brushed the dust from their skirts and began making their way up the path to the next station. Dubravka guessed that the story about the brother's wife was only that, a story. Likely the holy water was for Anđela herself. Would she be one of the many who'd mix the water with dirt from the site of the first vision, hoping the potion might be a cure?

By now another dozen or so pilgrims had caught up with them, on their way up to the cross on top of Mount Križevac, and the brothers had decided on a new tactic to carry their mother. The taller brother lifted his mother in his arms and carried her cradled like a child. The other brother hoisted the wheelchair onto his back and walked, bent over, with the chair flat against his back. The loose ends of the bandages on the woman's legs fluttered in the wind.

The new cluster of pilgrims mingled with the brothers and Dubravka and Anđela as they climbed, and someone in the crowd took Anđela's other arm. Dubravka walked on, a step or two ahead, still dazed, confused, wondering about what she'd just seen. She felt a slight sense of relief as the group gathered around the slab marking the seventh station. She still held Anđela's rosary. The brother carrying the wheelchair set it down and began leading the group in prayer.

Dubravka looked around for Anđela. She was nowhere to be found.

LATER, AT THE top of Mount Križevac, Dubravka knelt near the base of the cross and stared at the sun as the horizon rose up to meet it. The sun didn't pulse or twirl or change color or form as it set. It merely hovered, a distant, brightly burning star, as the rocky, water-splashed, horribly war-torn Earth abjectly spun on its axis away from it.

Dubravka took Anđela's handkerchief out from her pocket and opened it fully. Yes, there in the cloth's center was a clear and obvious red cross. Dubravka stared at the cross, unable to move or think. Then she folded the handkerchief and held it while she prayed, and then after a while she again opened it. The cross was still there, distinct, bloody.

Yes, she thought as she carefully folded the cloth and put it in the pocket of her skirt, she'd search for Anđela when she returned to town, both to find out how Anđela was feeling and of course to return her handkerchief and rosary.

The rosary was made up of the traditional five decades, with shiny wooden beads, round and hard to the touch, in color a rich black, and separated by knots. Four sturdy knots on each side separated the trio of antiphon beads from the other beads. The single Our Father beads were also separated on either side by four knots. Dubravka remembered Father Josip placing his rosary in her hands when she was a child kneeling in the Church of Saint Blaise. He taught her that the Our Father beads always stood alone, that the Hail Mary beads other than the three antiphon beads were always grouped together in sets of ten. Let your fingertips guide you as you recite the prayers, he taught her. That way you don't need to look down at the beads or keep count. That way you can concentrate more fully on the words of each prayer. Nearly every major religion in the world uses beads in prayers, he told her. Let your fingers guide your mind. Follow the beads and the knots. The knots will always lead you to the next bead, the next prayer.

As she held the rosary between her fingertips Dubravka didn't know the beads were made of jujube, from a tree grown in the Middle East, known as Christ's Thorn, said to be the plant whose branches were used to weave Jesus's spiked crown. She didn't know that Giorgio had selected the rosary from a display case of dozens of rosaries on Via dei Cestari and that he'd had both Anđela's and his initials engraved on the back of the rosary's silver cross.

Santa Maria della Vittoria

Rome, March 2005

He traveled to Rome to walk in her footsteps. Stand where she'd stood. Breathe the same air. Visit the same sites. Get some sort of feel for her last days.

The police in San Francisco allowed Sam to go to her apartment and take her Rome journal – a red Moleskine – as well as her black Giants baseball cap. The journal's red ribbon placeholder dangled from its pages like a tail, reminding Sam of the Marian missal his godmother, Zia Lena, had given him on the morning of his First Holy Communion. Sam used the ribbon to mark the Ordinary of the Mass, which lay precisely in the missal's center – the text of the Latin Mass on the left page, its English translation on the right. Sam wished he knew what had happened to the missal, which he'd carried faithfully through the streets of North Beach, past Valparaiso and Taylor, past Joe DiMaggio's former house, through the old Italian neighborhood back when it was still an actual neighborhood. But like so many other things in his life the missal was gone, like Nicole's mother, Kelly, who lived now with her new family back East, and now Nicole, their only child, their daughter.

The handful of entries in her journal were the usual things – occasional descriptions of people she'd seen, sketchy notes on places she'd visited, what she'd eaten, where she stayed. She'd selected an inexpensive two-star in a noisy part of the city adjacent to the Stazione Termini, Rome's central train station, and so Sam booked the two-star and was able to be given the same room in which she, only weeks before, had lived. The room was on the fourth floor – small, Spartan – with just enough space for a narrow bed, a wooden chair beside a small desk, a wardrobe with three hangers, a tiny bathroom. On the wall above the bed hung a faded print of English country life – a brace of dead pheasants, heads dangling, lying beside a knife on a table's warped wooden planks. The view out the grimy window looked out onto another building, its side darkened by the early March rains. Rain from the building's roof ran down in sheets that narrowed as they fell.

Later Sam would think that his troubles in Rome began with the distraction of the postcard. Resting on the wardrobe's top shelf was a small metal safe, the usual kind guests coded with their own combination of letters or numbers. As Sam reached up to put his wallet and passport into the safe, he found lying next to the safe a postcard for a club, Locanda Atlantide. The card advertised a New Year's Eve party, *Capodanno Gitano*. The card made Sam smile. He immediately sensed it was the sort of event that would have appealed to his daughter. He didn't know that the film student from Milan had given her the card and that the two had gone to the club together – there was nothing about him in her journal – but Sam guessed Nicole had placed the card next to the safe with the intention of taking it home as a souvenir. He figured it must have slipped down onto the shelf where she forgot about it.

The card featured a drawing of a topless brunette in a red Hawaiian skirt – the fat petals of her lei just covering her nipples – dancing barefoot on a scallop shell that sat on top of a black-and-white TV. The rest of the card displayed a merry collage. A pair of pink flamingos, legs stuck in bouquets of red and pink roses lying beside tumbling bowling pins. A monkey in a striped vest and fez beating a drum. A cartoon milkman in a checkerboard suit. Tinker Bell hovering near a sad-eyed tiki. A pair of religious medals – one of the Virgin Mary in a pink gown and blue robe, the other of Elvis Presley in tight swimming trunks, singing as he strummed a guitar. In the smiling dancer's hair was a single flower, and immediately above it the enormous head of a clown, its mouth wide open, eyes X'd out. Inside the clown's mouth a skeleton leaned forward and grinned, playing the xylophone on the clown's flattened bottom teeth. Standing on a stick near the card's top was a green silhouette of a curly-tailed, long-tongued chameleon.

Capodanno Gitano. Gypsy New Year.

Sam propped the postcard on the desk and sat down on the wooden chair. The more he stared at the card the more he noticed, but no matter where he looked his gaze kept returning to the dancer's eyes, her knowing smile, the gold flower in her hair, and the dead clown's open mouth, inside of which the cartoon skeleton merrily played.

SAM CAME TO Rome to gather new memories – his daughter in more happy times – that might ease or erase the more recent ones. Receiving the phone call from the hospital. Identifying her body in the morgue. Being told by the police that they were bound to investigate since it may have been a suicide. Given her journal after they made a copy of it. Allowed to look at a few of his daughter's personal belongings, which smelled of the shampoo she'd used to wash her long hair. Remembering the day he'd taken her to Candlestick Park and bought her the Giants cap. Finding in her closet a wooden crate of her old toys, toys Sam hadn't seen in years, that filled his heart with regret that he hadn't been a more attentive and playful father. Being informed that the probable cause of his daughter's death was pulmonary aspiration, an accident, Sam hoped – an overdose, too many pills mixed with too much alcohol – and then just a few days before his trip being told by his childhood friend Jake that the investigation was going to be held up for a while because of the complication with her laptop.

"Procedural. Just something to check up on," Jake told him. Jake was tall, managerial, born to look good in a suit, one of the North Beach cops – now an inspector – with friends who worked the Wharf and Chinatown, where Nicole had lived. The two stood on the street, lower Russian Hill, outside Sam's pet shop. The bitter late February wind blew around them, catching Sam's tie and tossing it up and back over his shoulder. That morning he had been downtown at his lawyer's office, so instead of his usual shirt and jeans Sam wore a sports coat, dress slacks. Later, whenever he thought of the moment, he would think of the tie as a flagellant's whip, the sky a smudged veil of gray about to burst open with rain. Sam was swarthy, thick, like a prizefighter just past his prime, with a full head of dark hair that he combed back and away from his face. A guy from the old neighborhood who persisted in running a failing pet store in a part of town that no longer had need of one.

Later Sam would remember the sound of their footsteps as they walked toward a nearby diner, as rain started to fall and the newly wet roads began muffling the sounds of the traffic on the streets. He would remember the dirty sky and the sleepy slushy sounds the car tires made on the wet road. He would remember how Jake always smelled like soap. He would remember the overwhelming feeling of impending dread as Jake explained that the prelim had found a video on Nicole's open laptop, a video of her, something likely to have been meant to be private, copied the day before from a site that copied it from another site.

Sam raised a hand and clawed the air – a dark tangle of branches – as if to clear something away from in front of his face. "You mean this was pornography?"

"I'm no one to judge," Jake said. "But in that world this would be baby food."

"And you're sure the video was of her."

Jake nodded.

It took Sam a while to process things. "So you're thinking maybe Nicole saw this video and that was the reason why she accidentally overdosed. Or maybe her seeing it" – Sam paused, not wanting to say it – "you think maybe she took her own life."

"I'm not thinking anything, Sam."

"But if she did take her life" – Sam stared blankly for several moments at the gray, empty sky – "she would have left a note."

Jake gave an unconvincing nod. "That's why this is being ruled preliminarily accidental. But now, in light of the video, they want a little more time. You know how slow things can go. I mean, my heart bleeds to have to tell you this."

"And so that night was when she found out about it?"

"Yeah. Likely a phone call from a friend. They're looking into it."

"And now there's no way, I guess, to somehow delete this."

Jake shook his head. "Sure, we can try our best with that, but you need to know that things like this tend to spread. You get rid of one copy here, two others pop up over there." The inspector wagged his head. "Once something's online it's indelible ink, pretty much permanent. You know the saying about trying to put toothpaste back into the tube."

To escape the dreariness of his hotel room Sam roamed the square outside the Termini, its air thick with exhaust from idling buses and near-endless lines of taxis. Around him crowds rushed toward the station, the wheels of their suitcases click-clacking on the cobblestones. Sudden clusters of nuns and priests hurried past him, identically dressed, like teammates on their way to a game. A boy and a girl in North End jackets talked over an open map. Near the station's doorways, volunteers stood with coin boxes, collecting donations for the victims of the late December tsunami. Sam paused to drop a few coins along with a ten-euro note into one of the boxes. After all, he thought, he was in Rome, and if you couldn't be charitable in Rome, the capital of not only his religion but also his people, where else in the world could he be charitable? As he slipped the volunteer the ten-euro note, he felt that if he were a better person he would give the volunteer all he had.

Lining the street leading the way to the Piazza della Republica, a row of vendors sold souvenir trinkets alongside displays of glossy magazines and old hardback books. Squatting on the sidewalk on flattened pieces of cardboard were the inevitable beggars.

A Romani woman in colorful dress rushed up to him with a handful of flowers – red roses, already beginning to wilt – pressing the flowers against Sam's chest as she said, "Dai! Dai!" This was followed by something sharp in a tongue he didn't understand. As she pushed the flowers against his chest, the woman thrust toward him her open palm.

"No," Sam said, "please." He raised an arm sideways to push the roses away. At the same moment someone else – a man, indistinguishable in the crowd – bumped into him firmly from behind. "No, no," Sam said again, more loudly. He shoved the woman with the flowers away and walked on, patting the right front pocket of his jeans where he'd wisely put his wallet and passport.

He paused by the pitted walls of the church edging the Piazza della Republica, watching the traffic circle the grand fountain in the middle of the square. The traffic flowed counter-clockwise, cars and taxis freely changing lanes in a dance so sudden and chaotic and yet so fluid and accident-free it seemed it somehow had to have been choreographed. A teenaged girl, eyes heavy with liner and mascara, hurried past, chatting away on her pink cell phone, saying ciao ciao ciao ciao ciao as though it were a single word. Just behind her, a man walked his dog, a handsome King Charles Cavalier spaniel. The man and the dog wore matching raincoats. More people rushed by, dragging wheeled suitcases. The girl with the phone frowned at Sam as she passed, her eyes dark as a raccoon's. The Cavalier raised a leg and splashed the base of a lamppost. Everyone in motion, Sam thought, on their way to do something, seemingly untouched, with certain purpose. As if death –

He didn't want to complete the thought. He took in a deep breath and gazed at the pure, routine human activity swirling around him, seemingly oblivious to tragedy, as if only a few months ago there had been no life-shattering tsunami, as if only a few weeks ago Nicole had not died. And now on the world-wide internet there was a pornographic video of his daughter.

The main goal, Nicole had written on one of the pages in her journal, *is to do your best to ease the panic, the ever-increasing hurt of life.*

It pained Sam to think that the words might be more than some dark poetry Nicole was quoting, lyrics from a song written by one of the melancholy-thin female singers she was so fond of, whose CD jewel cases lay scattered about her apartment in towering piles. Sam didn't want to accept the idea that the words were actually his daughter's, the true expression of something she'd felt so deeply that she needed to write it down.

SAM WALKED TOWARD Via Cavour and then over to the Colosseum, where he watched crowds swarm around their tour guides, like worker bees gathering around their queens. The tour guides were cocky little martinets, strutting about in gaudy vests, wielding tall wooden poles on which they displayed colored flags. He shunned the shills who approached him, trying to convince him to join a tour group – immediate entrance, they promised, and at a discount – and instead studied the gladiators and centurions in costume. They seemed a peculiar lot, a mix of nationalities. Each protectively paced the width of their territory, a few smoking cigarettes or small cigars. Others munched a panino or a folded rectangle of pizza as they sipped a canned drink. Still others chatted away on their cell phones.

The one Sam liked most was a sturdy fellow with a massive chest, forearms, and biceps so defined and bulging you'd think he lived in a weight room. The man had clear, soft brown eyes lined by lashes as long and dark as a girl's. He stood beside a pair of legion flags braided elegantly with gold rope and appeared, somehow, as if he actually belonged outside the Colosseum's walls.

One flag bore the letters SPQR inside a laurel wreath. The other flag was from the twin legion, Legio XIII Gemina, and featured a gold lion. The man wore the usual outfit – a shining helmet with a curved red plume, a rich red cape and slightly darker tunic, a glistening steel breastplate and leather belt studded with grommets and gold coin accents – but he wore his costume with a degree of dignity that outshone the others. The centurion held Sam's eyes as he approached. Sam couldn't help but nod, then offer a hint of a smile.

"Hello," Sam said. "No photo. No souvenir." Sam raised both hands to show they were empty. "Just a simple hello."

"Hello," the centurion said.

In the man's eyes there was a darkness, a familiarity that invited kinship. "Parla inglese?" Sam asked, not trusting his Italian.

"A little," the big man responded. He pronounced the word with an elongated "e" that stretched nearly to two syllables.

"You know," Sam said, "when I first saw all of you standing out here, you reminded me of a flock of parrots. Lories, to be exact. Rainbow lorikeets. Back when my store sold exotic birds, I handled a fair number of them."

"La Merica," the centurion said.

Sam nodded. "They're a beautiful bird, lories. Gorgeous plumage, deep blue heads, bright red beaks, green bodies, feathered wonders, really, but so messy you would not believe. Since they eat mainly fruit – well, I'll spare you the details. You need to put skirts around their cages or you'll be scrubbing the walls and floor every minute of the day."

The centurion nodded as if he understood. Sam realized the man was responding more to the pauses and rhythms of his language than to the actual words. "I don't know why I'm telling you any of this," Sam said. "In fact, other than maybe the hotel manager, you're the first person in Rome I've actually said more than a sentence to." Sam hesitated, shrugged, looked up for a moment at the graying sky. Massimo's eyes widened. "So let me tell you that my daughter died." Sam paused, doing his best to rein in his emotions. "And only a few weeks ago she was here in Rome, walking these same streets. Likely she came here to look at the Colosseum. Who wouldn't? Who could resist? Maybe she saw you. Maybe you even saw her, walking past, admiring the ruins. Maybe she smiled at you and you smiled back. Makes you want to turn back the clock, doesn't it? And now she's dead and you and me are here and there's not a goddamn thing anyone can do about it."

The centurion put a big hand on Sam's shoulder and gave it a gentle squeeze.

"You know, there's something about you. I mean your presence, your being here. It's as if you're actually standing guard. Protecting something. How can someone not love the concept?" Sam smiled. "I don't know if you have a daughter but if you do you know what I mean. You'd want a man as big and powerful as you to stand guard over her every moment of every single day, even though you know that could never be possible. Even though it would be the last thing she'd want since she'd find it insulting. Patronizing. She'd want to be her own person. You know what I mean. She'd tell you over and over again that she no longer needs you. That she needs to be herself, free from you, your voice, your opinions, your concern. Still, there's something about being a father." Sam shook his head. "I should rephrase that. There's something about having been a father."

The centurion titled his head slightly and offered a comforting smile.

"I know you're just a working stiff like the rest of us," Sam said. "Likely with a wife and kids, doing your best to scratch out a living the best way you can. I bet you drag yourself out of bed each morning and groan as you think that you have to put on this get-up and stand here. But there's something sort of right about all of this. Sort of true. You're like that lion" – Sam pointed to the Legio XIII Gemina flag – "or now that I think of it, even better, you're like one of those massive, magnificent mastiffs. Don't get me wrong here. Where I come from, comparing a man to a dog is high praise. Mastiffs are a foundation breed, you know. True guardians. And it's said that Julius Caesar himself – "

The centurion's face brightened at the mention of Julius Caesar.

" – Julius Caesar himself praised them for their bravery and brought the dogs right here to fight in the Colosseum. Barons bred mastiffs and used them to protect their estates."

The centurion looked confused.

"Here I am, taking up your time, but oh dear God if I had just one wish, how I wish as a father I could have had someone like you there to guard my girl. When she felt alone, when she felt that panic." Sam paused, trying hard not to surrender to his emotions. "When she felt that hurt. When she must have thought that no one in the world was there for her."

Before walking away Sam wiped his eyes and pulled several bills from the wallet he kept in the right front pocket of his jeans and pressed them into Massimo's hands.

ON ANOTHER PAGE of her journal Nicole had written: *Gian Lorenzo Bernini. Is there anything in Rome that isn't his?* followed by a list of Bernini's creations. Sam vowed he'd visit them all.

In the Piazza della Minerva Sam admired Bernini's little elephant, particularly the heft of its legs, though after inspecting the statue he questioned the length of the creature's trunk. It seemed anatomically inaccurate, inordinately long, something an actual beast might trip on. At the Piazza Navona he walked several times around the Fountain of the Four Rivers, a vibrant centerpiece roaring grandly with life, with a sound so steady and sonorous that it blocked out nearly all of the other sounds in the square. There was something joyous about the raucous, swirling water as it gushed about the fountain's base, but Sam knew deep inside that now was hardly the time for him to feel joy. Standing there with the obviously delighted crowd, listening to the rolling rumble of the surging water, Sam felt deep in grief.

In her journal Nicole had written that late one December day she'd stood by the fountain with a boy she'd met, listening to a young woman play Italian folk songs on her accordion. Nearby, she wrote, a handsome young man in a Renaissance costume performed tricks with his sword. Another journal entry mentioned a time Nicole had stood in a pouring rain listening to the accordionist play "Santa Lucia." A lovely Asian woman who was crying had requested the song and mouthed its words as the music played. Nicole wrote that she'd wanted to talk to the woman, say something, anything, perhaps even offer her a hug since the expression on her face was so forlorn.

Sam looked for the accordion player and the fellow with the sword but the only performers on the piazza were several living statues and a guitar player with an amp that kept squealing feedback.

THE FIRST CHURCH on Nicole's list was San Francesco a Ripa. It stood across the river in Trastevere, on a noisy intersection that didn't grow much quieter once Sam closed the vestibule door. Even after he dipped a hand into the holy water font he could still hear the harsh cries of the workers on the streets, the thunks and rumblings of passing cars and trucks, the wailing sirens of passing ambulances – *NEE-eu, NEE-eu, NEE-eu* – on their way to the hospital on Tiber Island.

The church itself was ornate, contained, with a dozen or so pews flanking the nave's center aisle, and seemed to be a museum of shrines and paintings. In the left transept was the Bernini sculpture Nicole had mentioned, the funerary monument *Beata Ludovica Albertoni*. On a wrinkled white bed atop a rug of mottled jasper lay the figure of a woman, eyes shut, head and neck stretched back. Her mouth was open in what was likely her final breath as her hand reached up to touch her breast. Light from a window to the left of the figure cast a glow upon her, particularly on her forehead and the gentle features of her face, the graceful curve of the pillow on which her head lay, the top of her outstretched hand.

As Sam stepped closer he felt he was coming upon a moment so personal and private he had no business being there. He had no right to witness this, and yet he could not take his eyes away. He stared at the woman's comely face, her strong nose, full lips, the sunlight on her perfect chin. He couldn't help but cross himself and kneel, mutter a prayer for her dear departed soul, pay his respects as would any decent person viewing the body. He tried not to think of Nicole lying in her coffin, but then of course he did.

Then he stepped back and reminded himself that he was looking at a slab of carved and polished stone. Still, the piece's realism unsettled him. It seemed nearly beyond belief that the figure lying before him wasn't made of flesh, that her robe wasn't cloth, that marble could be transformed into something so fluid, so lifelike.

Reminders of death filled the church. Even as Sam genuflected before the main altar, he noticed a jawless skull lying at the feet of a statue of a nun. A pair of side altars displayed the entombed bodies of saints, looking like skinny, overdressed mannequins stuffed sideways into glass boxes. Skeletons with pitch-black bones and outspread gold wings sprang from the walls, dangling their bony legs over the portraits on whose frames they squatted.

Outside, the rattle of trucks on the sampietrini and the roaring buzz of the many motorcycles speeding along the streets reminded Sam of life. He rolled his head and neck to ease some of the tension in his shoulders, then walked up the narrow length of Via di San Francesco a Ripa until he came to the pasticceria Nicole had mentioned in her notebook.

There he asked for what Nicole had recorded she'd eaten – a chocolate-covered sweet from the shop's glass display case, along with a cappuccino. Sam knew that since it was nearly noon it wasn't appropriate to order a cappuccino – Italians considered it a breakfast drink, a type of coffee with which to begin the day – but nonetheless he stood at the pasticceria's counter, going through the motions, eating what his daughter had eaten.

LATER THAT EVENING, as Sam sat drinking wine in a Centro Storico trattoria that pushed its many tables together as closely as possible, leaving only narrow lanes for the patrons and waiters to move about, a woman wearing a red notch-collar coat paused by his table and asked if the empty chair across from him was taken.

"It's you again, isn't it?" she said. "Forgive me, but didn't we meet this afternoon outside Santa Maria in Trastevere?" Already the busy waiter who'd ushered the woman in from the line waiting by the door was motioning for her to sit.

"Yes, of course," Sam said, rising from his chair.

"How delightful to see you again," the woman said and smiled.

As she folded her coat over the back of her chair and sat down, Sam grabbed a clean glass from a nearby table and offered her wine from his carafe. The woman had pale blue eyes and a choppy auburn bob that fell just below chin level. She wore a turquoise necklace over a black sweater and had a thin nose and a clear unlined face. Ever since Kelly had left him, Sam came to understand that much of a meal's pleasure lay in its sharing. And to share a meal with such an attractive woman, well, Sam nearly felt a tinge of glee.

"It's delightful to see you too," Sam said, not knowing what else to say. The waiter brought the woman cutlery and a napkin and plate along with another glass. Sam reached across the table and poured some of his mineral water into the woman's empty glass.

"Frizzante," she said and smiled. Her name was Ericka. "The way I like it." Sam watched the carbonated bubbles embrace the sides of her glass, then rush to the surface and pop. "I still say you should have come inside and visited that church." She seemed eager to talk. "If only to see the mosaics."

"Yes, of course," Sam said. At the time of her invitation he didn't want to admit that he feared the church was full of more images of death, and he was exhausted by death.

THEY'D MET EARLIER that afternoon in the piazza outside Santa Maria in Trastevere. After Sam left the pasticceria he wandered about Trastevere, allowing himself to become lost in the rione's winding, narrow streets. He passed by a couple of artists' studios and then his path opened and he came upon a narrow church, Sant'Egidio, where a man walking from the opposite direction hailed Sam and said, You must be new, the car to take the volunteers will arrive in a few minutes. Sam went along with the misunderstanding. After a short drive with three others, Sam found himself in Ostiense near Rome's Piramide Cestia, in an indoor market run by the Community of Sant'Egidio. The market offered a range of used and vintage items, with the proceeds going to charity. Sam was directed to a table where volunteers were sorting freshly laundered clothing. A dark-eyed woman in a gray top and skirt who watched Sam for a while struggle with his task came over and helped him learn the not-so-easy art of folding long-sleeved shirts.

The woman taught him to begin by smoothing the fabric out with his hands and then buttoning the shirt all the way up, then carefully flipping the shirt over, face-down, taking each sleeve and folding it over and then crossing the sleeve this way, then that way, taking care to keep the side seams straight, then taking hold of the other sleeve, like this, just so, then folding the shirt again carefully in thirds – and after ten minutes or so the woman took both of Sam's hands into hers and told him she'd keep him in her prayers.

Sam worried that his sadness was so obvious even a stranger could sense it. The woman held him then with her eyes for what seemed like a long time as the room in which everyone was working grew still and silent. It was like one of those moments in a movie when the camera freezes everyone's actions and all you can hear is the thump of your heart and the intake of your breath. Then it was noisy again and the woman smiled and Sam smiled, and Sam told her he'd keep her in his thoughts and prayers too.

After another hour the van returned the volunteers to Trastevere, where Sam sat on the steps of the large fountain in the piazza outside Santa Maria in Trastevere. He chose a small patch of fading sun and watched a woman on the other side of the square beg for coins. In her arms the woman held a baby. When no one was nearby, the woman stood impassively, ignoring the child until someone approached. Then she chucked the babe's chin as her face grew alive with desperation. She'd begin a low chant that rose gradually in pitch as she thrust toward the tourist an open hand. Though the woman's head was covered by a headscarf, the child's was bare. Sam wanted to tell her to cover the baby's head lest it become sick, since the late afternoon air held a wet chill.

"I was watching that Gypsy beggar," Sam told Ericka.

"Romani," Ericka said. "Or Roma. And sometimes Rroma, with a double 'r'." She sipped her wine, then looked at the carafe of wine and nodded her approval. "Confusing, isn't it, all these shifts in language, in perception?" She smiled softly as she shrugged.

"Let me get pen and paper," Sam said and smiled. "I think I'd better write this down."

Ericka laughed, hearty and clear, the laugh of a woman who seemed at ease with herself. Her laugh was an honest laugh that made Sam relax and want to laugh too. "Good God," she said, "you've known me for only a few minutes and already you've exposed me. I bet you can guess what I am."

"A lovely woman I met earlier today outside a church."

That made her smile again. "Try a university professor."

Sam realized his comment about pen and paper had offended her, so in apology he made a joke at his own expense. "And you've exposed me. I believe the last time I cracked open a book was seventh grade." He was lying, of course. His apartment in San Francisco was full of books. Detective and spy novels mainly, books heavy with plot, red herrings, timely discoveries, fortunate coincidences, sudden confessions. Books that didn't force you to think too deeply about characters' interior lives and their unspoken desires, their fears and hidden yearnings. There were enough unspoken desires, enough yearnings and fears in actual life not to want to spend your time at night when you can't sleep reading about even more of them. Sam preferred books with resolution. He liked questions answered, mysteries solved. Books like these offered him the promise that someday his life's own issues might be resolved. He also owned nearly every book written about dogs. James Herriot's collection of dog stories ranked among his favorites and was one he frequently re-read.

After the waiter brought them the antipasto Sam had ordered, Sam pushed the platter toward Ericka so that it rested equally on the table between them. "You saw her," Sam said, "you even gave her money. So tell me what you thought. Was the baby hers?"

"Whose?" Ericka asked.

"The beggar's. The Romani's. I believe in Italian the word is *zingara*." He thought of the New Year's Eve party card, Capodanno Gitano, he'd found in his hotel room. "I believe in Spanish she'd be *una gitana*. A man, *un gitano*."

"What I find more interesting is the relationship between the viewer and the viewed." Ericka tilted her head playfully and raised her eyebrows. "A sympathetic person might see the pair as they appear, as a poor mother with her baby. Someone more cynical might think she'd borrowed the child and was using it as a prop."

By now the waiter had returned and, without being asked, refilled their carafe with vino della casa. After several minutes he brought out their primi. Sam had ordered cacio e pepe while Ericka opted for spaghetti alle vongole.

"Like the beggars with their dogs," Sam said after a while. After Ericka nodded, he lay his fork across the edge of his plate. "Walking around, I noticed that I tend to rush past most beggars, but the ones with dogs, particularly the ones with puppies squirming on a blanket, they catch my eye every time."

"So you're a sucker for puppies."

"I'm an unrepentant dog lover. Actually I love all animals, but dogs – they're truly special creatures. I own a pet shop."

"Do you have a dog?"

Sam shook his head. "No, not at the moment. There's been too much else going on." He tried not to think about Nicole. "In my life I've had several dogs, and recently I had the honor of living with two particularly fine ones."

"What breed?"

"A little of this, a dash of that. Bella was a pit mix, and maybe also part boxer. Little Sophie was mostly terrier and likely a bit of everything else. Both were animals their owners gave up on. Blame the economy. Would you believe people simply abandoned them in my shop?" Sam paused to smile. "Well, they could see I had more than enough dog food." He sipped his wine. "They just left the pups there, as if my store was an orphanage. I found poor Bella sleeping beneath a shelf one night when I was closing up. I'd guess she was nearly three and about half of what her weight should have been. Little Sophie was maybe nine, ten weeks old huddled in a torn blanket someone had stuffed in a corner."

"Do you sell dogs?"

"No, no, no," Sam said, "certainly not. No reliable pet store does. I sell pet supplies, mainly. Food, leashes, harnesses. Quality products, the kinds you can't get in the big-box stores."

"You've changed the subject. So you're a cynic. You saw the baby as a prop."

"Not really," Sam answered. "I think I'm more of a realist. I saw the baby simply as a baby, and the woman as a less than responsible adult who's soon going to have a sick child on her hands."

"And the beggars with the puppies. Do the dogs convince you to drop money into their owners' cups?"

Sam smiled broadly. "Every single one. Caring for a dog shows that a person has compassion and more than likely is empathetic. I also toss the pups a little biscuit from my pocket after I came across a shop near the Spanish Steps that sells dog treats."

Later Sam insisted on walking Ericka back to her hotel. As they parted on the sidewalk outside the hotel's entranceway, they made plans to see each other the following day. It only made sense, Ericka said, since they were each in Rome without other company. Perhaps they could get tickets to the Borghese Gallery. She'd call them in the morning. They could have dinner together again, Ericka suggested. As Sam departed she gave him a modest hug and, to his surprise, brushed her cheek against his.

THE FOLLOWING DAY Sam continued his way down Nicole's checklist. There was so much traffic circling Bernini's Triton Fountain that Sam could hardly see the powerful figure – half man, half fish – blowing a jet of water through a raised conch. The figure knelt on a pair of scallop shells held up, impossibly, by the tails of four dolphins. For some peculiar reason the dolphins were pestered by bees. Sam couldn't understand Bernini's obsession with bees. In Nicole's notebook there was nothing about Bernini and bees.

Sam did enjoy the human scale of the nearby Fountain of the Bees, essentially another scallop shell decorated with a trio of the insects. Three bees seemed just about right to Sam. Perhaps bees meant that the water within these fountains was sweet. He wondered what Nicole had thought, perhaps even as she'd stood on the same square of sidewalk where he now stood. How did she feel? Was she sad? Happy? Or was she feeling that panic, that unceasing hurt? Did she dip a hand into the fountain's water, as Sam did now? Did she raise a drop of the sweet water to her lips?

He walked down Via del Tritone to Sant'Andrea delle Fratte, where he studied Bernini's two statues of angels. Sam crossed himself as he knelt beside the marble plinth bearing the colossal *Angel with a Crown of Thorns*, then prayed for his daughter's soul and added a prayer for the kind woman who'd taught him how to fold shirts. Sam was very much taken with the angel towering above him, its terrible height, its anguished face, its splendid feathered wings spread back and to the sides, the horrible crown of thorns in its hands. He imagined the angel dropping down from the heavens and offering him the crown – an instrument of unspeakable torture, something that could only cause excruciating pain.

Had there been a priest nearby Sam would have considered going to Confession. Already as he knelt beneath the angel, Sam was mumbling the Act of Contrition. He wanted to confess his sins the old way he'd been taught, kneeling inside a darkened box, individual soul to representative of God, separated by a thin wall and lattice screen. He wanted to admit each embarrassing thing he'd ever done, even the idea that he was now looking forward to his evening with Ericka. He'd also confess his truly great sin, the one for which he knew he could never be forgiven, the sin of a father not being present, missing what was there to be seen, a father who somehow let his daughter die.

Rome's churches were getting to him, he realized. They were awakening the dormant Catholicism instilled in him when he was a boy, back when he'd walk each morning past the house where the great Joe DiMaggio had lived, happily carrying Zia Lena's Marian missal, back in the days when his life was simple, monochromatic.

NICOLE HAD MADE a note about a turtle fountain in the Ghetto that she thought her father would enjoy, particularly since it was said that Bernini designed not the fountain but the turtles. Sam knew Nicole remembered how much he enjoyed selling turtles – baby red-eared sliders, each about the size of a silver dollar – back before their sale was banned. He headed across town, past the tourists and vendors massed about the Trevi, down and then across busy Via del Corso, through the winding lanes of the Centro Storico and past the cat sanctuary at Largo di Torre Argentina, toward the historical Jewish Quarter, where at once he became lost in its maze of narrow streets.

After stumbling about repeatedly, he finally came across the intimate Piazza Mattei and the fountain. Four figures were placing turtles – loggerheads, Sam figured, by the shape of their shells – back into a large bowl that rested high above their heads. Water spouted from the gaping mouths of dolphins and spilled at the boys' feet. Unlike Triton's dolphins, these were mercifully free of bees.

The turtles were perfect, Sam thought. Detailed, precise, each hovering over the lip of the fountain's bowl, as each thin boy raised a hand either to push the sea turtle back into the water or to protect them, catch them, as they were falling. Sam loved the image, the dual possibilities. He imagined one of the turtles slipping past the boy's hand, its fragile shell cracking, surely incurring a wound from which there'd be no recovery. Then he looked back at the boy's outstretched hand, how it was positioned to prevent that from happening, and he thought again about his careless relationship with Nicole.

THE TELEPHONE MESSAGE waiting for him at the front desk of his hotel was to meet Ericka at the Borghese Gallery, so Sam rushed through a shower and change of clothes, then hurried out of his hotel.

Once outside, he wasn't entirely sure how it happened. He was walking along the street near the vendors who sold magazines – later Sam would recall being distracted by the shiny, fetching faces of the doe-eyed models on the fashion magazine covers – when a crowd of children rushed toward him on the sidewalk, on his right. As he looked at the children someone jostled him, hard, as if by intention, on his left, which caused Sam to turn toward whomever it was who'd knocked against him. It was then that Sam glanced up and saw the flower seller in her usual spot, twenty or so feet down and across the road. She was offering her clutch of roses to a tourist as the gang of children swarmed him, as Sam felt their small hands patting him down as if they were blind and had to feel their way past him and then in a flash, before anything more could register in his mind, before he could think and react, the children vanished, the soles of their shoes slapping the sidewalk behind him as they ran. Sam stood by himself near the magazines, staring at the seductive faces of the models on the racks, still thinking of the Romani woman's dark bouquet of roses. The falling turtles, their broken shells. Nicole and Kelly. The imposing angel descending from heaven, bearing down upon him with a crown of thorns.

Then the realization of what had just happened seared hotly through him. His back popped suddenly with sweat. He dropped his hand against the now-empty right front pocket of his jeans and felt the hollow sense of having committed an irretrievable error as he ran both his hands over his front and back pockets and then the pockets of his jacket and then the front and back pockets of his jeans once again, as he understood that now both his wallet and his passport had been taken. Only later would he be able to sequence the events, comprehend the distractions, recognize the detailed trap, view himself as others had viewed him. Prey, able to be spun about, confused, diverted, exploited, plucked.

He returned to his hotel room and looked at the metal safe on the top shelf of his wardrobe. Its door hung open – a silent mouth paused dumbly between words. The numbers on its front plate waited abjectly for his fingers to punch in his personal code. Sam gazed about his room numbly. He looked at the print on the wall of the dead pheasants, the hunter's knife. Then at the Capodanno Gitano postcard and the long-haired brunette. Sam stared at her big eyes, the gold flower in her hair, her smug smile, at once inviting and altogether false. He stared at the skeleton gleefully playing the xylophone on the flattened teeth lining the bottom of the open mouth of the dead, laughing clown.

No, ERICKA INSISTED over the telephone after she learned what had happened, as Sam tried to beg the evening invitation off. You can't cancel, you absolutely need to meet me for dinner tonight. She'd made reservations and was so looking forward to it. Please, might it be her treat? Forget about not having met me at the Borghese Gallery. Of course I couldn't help but wonder what had happened to you, but the important thing is that you're safe. After all, what was taken was only money, mere paper.

Certainly it was more than that, Sam thought. More than having to contact his credit card company about the stolen cards and arrange for replacements, more than requesting an emergency passport from the Embassy. It had to do with being duped. The entire episode made Sam feel old. Even though the water trickling from the hand-held shower head was no longer warm, Sam crouched in the tub and soaped himself, then rinsed off with increasingly colder water. At the sink, staring at his sad face in the small mirror, he slowly shaved for the second time that day.

Ericka wore another beaded necklace – one that matched her dark red shawl – along with black hosiery and a blue dress that mirrored Van Gogh's *The Starry Night*. Again she'd made up her eyes and had on only a touch of lipstick. A white-jacketed waiter with a black bow tie pulled out her chair as they sat at their reserved table at the smart restaurant just a short block down from the Pantheon. To remind its patrons of its exclusivity, several framed photographs of smiling international politicians shaking hands with the restaurant's owner and chef hung on the wall facing the doorway.

"It's been quite a while since I've been out on a date," Sam told Ericka after the waiter cleared their appetizer plates and poured more wine – a garnet-red Barbaresco – into their glasses. Sam deferred the ordering to Ericka, and like a couple familiar with each other they casually reached their forks across the table and tasted the other's food. Ericka told him about a walking tour she'd taken that afternoon in the Vatican Gardens. How the sounds of the city had fallen away, how along with the many lovely shrines and fountains inside the grounds there was a cloistered convent of nuns who kept a garden where they grew their own vegetables, how some trees were filled with broken branches and tumbles of sticks, huge nests nearly the size of small cars, made by flocks of green parrots who screeched merrily as they glided through the air.

Monk parakeets, Sam told Ericka. Lovely birds. Illegal to sell where he lived, since farmers claimed that they'd eventually escape their cages and form wild flocks that would threaten their crops. Ericka remarked on the appropriateness of both nuns and monks nesting communally inside the Vatican's walls, and then she and Sam laughed loudly enough that a few of the other patrons in the restaurant turned to look at them.

After dinner they strolled back to her hotel on Corso Vittorio, and then at the doorway Ericka suggested they share another drink up in her room.

"It's early," she said. "And haven't you had quite a day."

They had no choice but to stand close together, face to face, as they rode the narrow elevator, its buttons and side railings gilded in gold. Sam could smell her perfume, something light, pleasant, vaguely floral. Ericka was smiling, happy after their excellent meal and their bottle of equally excellent wine. Sam felt something resembling happiness too. It gnawed like some unfamiliar yet not entirely unwanted creature at the edge of his feelings. He looked into Ericka's eyes and for no apparent reason nodded his head, as if in agreement with something yet unsaid, then tried his best to forget about his day, about the turtles and Nicole and the stolen wallet and passport.

LATER, AFTER THEY separated, as they lay together, spent, Ericka turned toward Sam and said, "You know, we live on opposite sides of the country."

Her room was far more spacious than his, with a full desk and comfortable armchair and a wing chair beside a small table near a window. Wisely, she'd chosen a room facing the hotel's courtyard – a camera silenziosa – so she wouldn't hear the near-constant traffic down below on the street. She'd also draped a flowered cloth over the TV so that its screen didn't stare out into the room like a blank eye. Her laptop lay on her desk alongside scattered papers and books and a fountain pen. Dangling from the back of the armchair was the soft black fabric of her brassiere, tossed there as they'd made their way into bed.

"There's something special about this," Ericka was saying, "about the fact that after a few more weeks here in Rome we'll never see each other again." She was sitting up, holding the bed sheet against her breasts. "So, indulge me. Tell me a story you've never told anyone else before. Something about yourself, something true, ideally something romantic."

Sam didn't have the courage to say he felt defeated, that he was considering leaving Rome as soon as he could secure a new passport. "I'll bore you to tears."

"No you won't. Come on, we're having the perfect evening." She turned and set her wine glass on the night table, twisting the bare length of her slender back, the bones of her spine, her soft skin.

"I once met a charming, intelligent woman in a courtyard outside a church with lovely mosaics who asked me to tell her a story."

"No metafictions," Ericka said. "I want a real story. Perhaps a guilty secret, or even better, something tender and sweet."

Sam knew he wasn't in the mood to dredge up something tender and sweet. Had he ever even had such an experience? He stared across the room at her laptop, the same type as Nicole's, that likely now sat on some cop's desk in Jake's district. Sam poured himself more wine. "Once there was a girl," he began, "who had a boyfriend, a bad boyfriend. Who took pictures of her. A video. A video of a sexual nature."

"Go on," Ericka said after Sam paused. "Use the storyteller's two favorite words. I'll give you a hint. The next two words in your story are *and then*."

"And then," Sam said, "and then the girl went along with it, for God only knows what reason, and of course she must have been certain that it would be kept private."

"And then – "

"And then after the girl discovered that the boy had lied, after she saw it was now public, she grew careless. She drank. She took a few pills." He drained his glass. "I imagine she felt trapped. Frightened. Ashamed. As well as angry, since her privacy had been violated, since her trust in the boy had been betrayed."

"And you were once this boyfriend?"

"Good Lord, no," Sam said. "I was someone else. Someone who was there" – he closed his eyes, putting himself into his story – "that night, the night it happened. I was there with her when she discovered it and I held her in my arms and took her drink from her hands and hid her pills and told her I loved her and that whatever she'd done didn't matter."

"Was this the woman you later married?"

"No, this was the girl I saved. Because at the moment that she needed someone I was there." Sam's lips tightened as he held back his tears, nodding as if he could make it so.

"Come here," Ericka said.

Sam couldn't move. "I mean," he said, "she was young, and young people do foolish things. They make mistakes. So there's your story."

"Please come here," Ericka said again.

AFTER SHE FELL asleep, after Ericka promised Sam she'd tell him her story the following night, Sam slipped out of bed and went to her desk and opened her laptop, wanting to check his email, to see if there was any word from Jake.

The investigation was now closing, Jake wrote, the COD listed as accidental. In the meantime they were doing what they could to have the video deleted from the sites where it had spread. Sam should enjoy his time in Italy and not worry about anything.

Beneath Jake's message was an email sent to Jake by the subordinate charged with tracking down the sites. The email reported that so far a couple of the videos had been removed. Below the text were several links – underlined and in different colored ink – which Sam scrolled past, and then for no good reason other than curiosity or stupidity he hovered the cursor over one of them and clicked. A site made up of boxes depicting stills of women frozen in various sexual positions and acts appeared on the screen.

Then Ericka was behind him. "What are you doing on my computer? What? You're looking at porn?"

One of the videos began playing, a young woman – clearly not Nicole – breasts swaying slightly as she smiled, lying down on a bench while someone approached her, a man, or were there several men now in the shadows, watching the pair. A hand was roughly shoving Sam's shoulder. The woman was turning toward the camera, mouth slightly open, her face melting in a dreamy smile. Ericka's other hand was lunging over Sam's other shoulder toward the laptop in an attempt to close it.

"Wait," Sam said, "let me explain. You don't understand."

"Get out," Ericka said, turning sharply toward the door.

THE NEXT MORNING, after stopping at a bank for an emergency cash advance and deciding to put off the tedious process of obtaining a replacement passport, Sam walked about Rome's back streets, going over in his mind the sequence of events that had occurred the day before. He went back and forth over the idea of contacting Ericka, begging her pardon, telling her about Jake's email, about Nicole. Sam felt the need to put what he'd done into context. Then he considered the issue from her point of view. Even trying to offer a rationale risked making matters worse. After all, he hadn't asked for her permission to use her laptop. And what sort of man gets out of bed after being intimate with a woman and clicks on a pornographic site? No, Sam decided, what the poor professor from New York had endured was bad enough. What he'd done, he'd done.

And what Nicole had done she'd done.

Sam walked past a trattoria not far from the Trevi, a simple place on a relatively tourist-free side street littered with cigarette butts and discarded gelato cups. Outside the restaurant's door a modest chalkboard announced the day's fare. It being a Thursday, the specialty of the day was gnocchi. After Sam took a seat and was served, he broke a wedge of bread from the basket brought to his table by a young woman with a single long earring and crossed himself. The bowl of gnocchi all'Amatriciana was so good – the gnocchi themselves so tender and pillowy they melted in Sam's mouth, the tomato and guanciale and pecorino sauce so perfectly spiced – that Sam was tempted to order a glass of Chianti, when from the table nearest the kitchen Sam heard sudden shouting. Seated at the table was a young man dressed in a Renaissance costume arguing with a male waiter who seemed to ignore the other's concerns. Sam did his best to try to understand.

Don't you realize who I am? the man in costume was shouting. I am Michelangelo Merisi da Caravaggio, and I insist that you tell me whether these carciofi were cooked in butter or oil. If you wish to know the difference, the waiter replied loudly as he turned away from Caravaggio and addressed his words to the patrons in the trattoria, pick up your plate and use your nose to smell them. No, tell me, Caravaggio responded. I will not, the waiter replied. I insist, Caravaggio demanded as he then tipped his plate of artichokes onto the floor and with a mighty roar swung the dish at the waiter's face. The waiter brought his hands up to his cheeks and fell to the floor with a pained grunt.

From where Sam was sitting he could see that the plate failed to even graze the waiter's chin, and yet the man writhed now near the table legs, moaning and caressing his head as if it were a broken jar. Yes, certainly, Sam thought, the event was being staged. Now the restaurant's other customers were standing, shouting, in an uproar as the waiter attempted to stand, then slipped on the fallen artichokes and fell again. Caravaggio fled into the kitchen as a few patrons rushed to the poor waiter's aid.

Grateful for the distraction, Sam tossed several euros on his table and slipped past the waiter and his helpers and followed the costumed performer through the kitchen doorway. There, leaning against the oven, stood Caravaggio, laughing with the beautiful young waitress who'd brought Sam bread and served his bowl of gnocchi.

"Bravo!" Sam said. "Bravo! Bravisssimo!"

Caravaggio looked surprised, then smiled and gave Sam a nod.

"You really shouldn't be back here," the waitress said. Her jet-black hair was pulled back tightly into a high ponytail. Her single long earring dangled from her right ear like a golden braid. Her complexion was rich and glowing – her attitude, even though she was correcting Sam, utterly nonchalant. Now that Sam looked at her more closely he saw that she had that effortlessly alluring quality common to so many Italian women.

"You believed it?" Caravaggio said, clearly eager for a review. "You saw it all? And it was believable?" They talked in a mix of Italian and English.

"Absolutely," Sam said. "It was marvelous. You were perfect. Though from the angle where I was sitting – "

"Yes, yes," Caravaggio interrupted. "If you are observant, from the one table against the wall you can detect the falseness."

"Only because I watched closely. But the others" – Sam spread out his arms – "your performance was so convincing, so true, several customers took out their cell phones to snap photos or to call the police."

"Convincing and true." The artist nodded. "The highest compliments."

"You should both leave now," the waitress said. She looked about, as if searching the wall of the kitchen for a clock, as if telling the two men their time was up.

"They don't allow me to throw the plate," Agostino explained as he and Sam made their way out the kitchen's back door. The performance artist had ceased carrying around his sword, reserving it only for his occasional trips to the Piazza Navona, where Caravaggio was said to have displayed it and subsequently been arrested. In its place Agostino kept hidden within the folds of his costume a dagger with a rounded pommel and curved iron quillons, one as close as he could find to the cheat's dagger portrayed in *The Cardsharps*. "Today was our fifth performance. Rosangela's uncle, who owns the restaurant, agreed to allow me to do seven. His fear was that if I threw the plate it would shatter and injure the patrons."

"Too dangerous," Sam said. He was happy now, pleased he understood. "So he lets you use his restaurant as a stage."

"Only during the time of lunch," Agostino said, "and only seven times. Understand, my request is less than usual, to use his place of business for something other than eating. Still, I am an old friend of the family. Childhood playmates with Rosangela, his niece, who works there, part-time cook and waitress." Agostino nodded, proud of the association.

Sam nodded in return.

"The girl with the long gold earring," Agostino continued. "Isn't she something fierce? My God! Such a beauty. God truly had to rest the day after he created her! If only there were two of me, one would fall at her feet and stay there for eternity. She wears the earring every day, always in her right ear. It's her trademark, yes? Many who frequent the restaurant come only because of her. Good for business, you understand? And on occasion she agrees to sit for me. When I do my best to paint."

"You paint?" Sam said, surprised.

"How could I be what I pretend and not?" Agostino's face registered offense, and then his expression softened. "Still, I have only a small talent. Like a child on all fours, still learning to crawl. I studied when I was younger, then for a few years put away my brushes, but now my work emerges from the soil, like the insects that sleep in the dirt for years, dormant, then crawl out and open their wings and fly."

"Cicadas," Sam said.

"Yes, yes, cicadas. Emerging from the earth. Raw, rough. Still, I say to myself, it is the doing of the thing rather than the results from it. The attempt. The climb up the hill. Once you stop you die, you understand? I focus now on the portrait. Caravaggio was a master of the portrait. The dramatic tableau, as well. The play between light and shadow. The capture of the exact moment of recognition, of realization."

Sam was nodding.

"But Rosangela, I tell you, in my mind I've painted her a thousand times. In her physical presence so far only five. She still attends Mass each morning accompanied by her two aunts and receives the sacrament. She does not pose for me with even a bare shoulder."

"Which makes her all the more desirable."

"Yes, precisely." Agostino smiled. "You are a wise man."

The men walked in silence.

"So you know women who pose," Sam said after a while.

"Of course." Agostino laughed. "What painter doesn't?"

"Women who pose" – Sam hesitated – "without their clothes."

Agostino's laughter continued. "Why? Tell me. You are a man who likes to look at women without their clothes?"

"No," Sam said. "No."

"Then you're one of the rare ones," Agostino said. "Most men, and even many women, like to look at women without their clothes. It's human nature. Rome's most popular model even lives with me. Rosangela's cousin, Valentina. Another of God's magnificent creations. Rosangela's darker twin."

Then Sam told Agostino about Nicole and the video. Agostino offered Sam his condolences. For several minutes the pair walked in respectful silence.

"Since you appreciated my performance," Agostino said after a while, "if you'd like you can come with me to meet my Valentina."

As the men continued to make their way across the river and through the twisting streets, they talked about their backgrounds and hopes and dreams – Sam about San Francisco and how his trip to Rome was a quest to come to a deeper understanding of his daughter's life, and Agostino about Valentina and her love for Italian singers from 1950's America – Tony Bennett, Frank Sinatra, Perry Como, Dean Martin, Julius de Rosa – and then Agostino discussed his views and goals as an artist.

When Sam pointed out that there were fewer than a dozen people in the trattoria to witness Agostino's play, Agostino replied that a real artist shouldn't be overly concerned with their art's perception. Did a painting stored in a dark attic, unseen, for over a century, suddenly transform itself into something more when it was brought out into the light? No, Agostino said, the piece was a work of art all along. A work's true essence isn't dependent on its being judged or perceived. Consider that there are countless things in the universe that aren't known to us, and yet they exist as certainly as every statue and painting in every church in Rome. True art imposes a sense of order upon what would otherwise be chaos. The artistic act releases energy that flies out into the universe's vast swirling stew and works against the natural forces of entropy. How that energy is judged or measured or even perceived by others is secondary. The performance with the artichokes and surly waiter would have been as successful in my mind, Agostino said, even if there was no one in the restaurant to witness it. The same is true of my paintings, raw as they may be. The pair neared Agostino's garage.

"I've been in this neighborhood before," Sam said as he looked around. "I helped a group sort used clothing. A very patient woman taught me the proper way to fold a shirt."

"The Croatian nun," Agostino said. "I know her. Dubravka."

Agostino called out a hello as they swung open the garage's side door. Brick walls. Half apartment, with an unmade bed and two crammed wardrobes, a bookcase and various shelves, a long wooden table on which sat a burner for cooking, several plates and mugs, a well-used Moka pot. The garage's other half was a studio. Heavy sheets of draping hung over an area in which were a couch and chairs and several mirrors and oil lanterns. The great master used lanterns and mirrors to shape and bend the flow of light, Agostino explained. From behind a dark curtain Louis Prima's "Just a Gigolo" bounced from a boombox. Several canvases – the upper torsos of two women, one naked, the other clothed – leaned against a far wall along with paintings of Trastevere's winding cobblestone streets and alleyways.

"Valentina," Agostino called as they entered. "Come meet my new friend. He saw my performance and comes all the way to Rome from San Francisco."

"San Francisco?" Valentina said as she stepped into the studio area from behind one of the drapes. "San Francisco! 'I left my heart.' Have you told him I adore Tony Bennett?"

VALENTINA WAS A tad taller than either Sam or Agostino and dark, swarthy, with a tattoo of a strand of barbed wire circling the muscled bicep of her left arm. She wore tight jeans and a colorful blouse that had a repeating pattern of circles and zigzags. Around her left wrist were at least a half-dozen beaded bracelets. Sam considered she was likely from Italy's South.

Not even Valentina knew that at birth she'd been named Malina, that her Romani family had lived in Serbia, and that all four of her grandparents as well as thirteen additional members of her family were interned in the Sajmište concentration camp located at a former Belgrade fairground site near the town of Zemun, where they were made to dig graves for the slaughtered Jews before they were also killed. They were seventeen out of the approximate five hundred thousand Romani women, men, and children massacred during the Holocaust. Malina's relatives who weren't captured fled south and then west, across the Adriatic, with a few managing to reach Rome's outskirts. When Malina was nearly three her dying mother left her in a basket in the alley behind Rosangela's uncle's restaurant, where Malina's mother could smell the dark, tempting aromas of sauce and roasting meat and felt assured that at the least her daughter would be fed one good meal. Told not to move, the child was taken in by Rosangela's two barren aunts, who heard the girl crying. The aunts came to believe that the child was an assignment given to them from the Almighty. "Do you know him?" Valentina asked. "Tony Bennett. Have you met him? Do you see him out on the street?"

Sam told Valentina no, that San Francisco was a big town.

"All in good time," Valentina said. Her lips were full and lush and invited the eye to gaze at them. "Sometimes the stranger you walk past on Monday by Saturday becomes your best friend. You know that his name, *Benedetto*, means *the blessed one*. His family is from Reggio Calabria." She stood and disappeared behind the curtain. Moments later Louis Prima and Keely Smith stopped singing, replaced by Tony Bennett's "Stranger in Paradise."

"He sings to the center of each note," Valentina said as she returned. "A true master of bel canto. And like Agostino he, too, is a painter."

Agostino smiled broadly. Sam saw at once that Agostino was quite proud of her. "She plays his records so often, one after the other, sometimes I think I'll go mad."

"You have already gone mad," Valentina said. She turned to Sam for agreement. "Look at the way he continues to dress when he goes out on the street."

"I thought you supported me," Agostino said with a laugh.

"Sure," Valentina said, bringing one hand up to her neck and then flipping back her long dark hair, "for a week, for a month." Again she looked at Sam. "Be careful," she said, laughing, turning back to Agostino, "or one day you'll lose me."

"She likes to joke that her bags are always packed," Agostino said to Sam.

"They are," Valentina said. "Just understand that I belong to no one but myself."

LATER, AFTER AGOSTINO brought out a jug of wine and the three settled back in their chairs and drank, Sam asked Valentina the question that had been bothering him since his conversation with Jake back on Russian Hill. Why would a woman consent to pose?

Valentina smiled. "If you ask a thousand women, you'll get a thousand answers."

"I'm looking for only one," Sam said.

"Sadly," Valentina said, "since your daughter has passed, you'll never know."

The three sipped their wine in silence.

"As for most women," Valentina said after a while, "let's start with the reason that's most obvious. Because she can. Because it's within her power to do so. Because for many it makes her feel alive. Because every woman experiences what it's like to be looked at, which is both blessing and curse. To be both a person and an object. Still, there's a pleasure that can't be described as you look on your own image and see that nearly everything in the glass is right. Or, even better, when an artist desires to make a work of art from your likeness."

"The woman makes of herself an object," Agostino said.

"No," Valentina said. "It's others and their lust who make women into objects." She nodded to stress her point, and then her face grew sad. "It's only when violence enters does an act become wrong. Only when an action is against the woman's will. In your daughter's situation, the sin was when the video was revealed without her consent."

Sam nodded. "And in response," he heard himself saying, "she grew careless with drugs and drinking. Or in response it's possible she took her own life."

"Don't think that," Valentina said. "You already told us she left no note. Certainly if she took her life it was an occasion to express her anger and name names."

"All she left was her journal, full of notes about Rome, where she went, what she ate, her admiration for Bernini." Sam paused. He felt he wanted to change the subject. "So I've been checking out Bernini's works. I think the piece I find the most moving is the woman in that noisy church by the river. You know the one I mean. San Francesco a Ripa."

"*Blessed Ludovica Albertoni*," Agostino said. "Absolutely captivating."

"A masterpiece," Valentina agreed. "Have you seen his *Saint Teresa*?"

"Not yet," Sam said. "Every time I've gone to the church it was closed."

"We'll see if it's open tomorrow," Valentina said, "and if it's closed we'll go the next day and then the next, but I'll let you see it alone." She touched one of Sam's hands. Her touch was warm, the tone of her voice soothing. "Believe me, my new American friend, who is so fortunate that he walks the same streets as the great Anthony Dominick Benedetto, believe me, your daughter did nothing wrong. If anything, she was brave and daring. Foolish, perhaps, for trusting someone so deceitful, but such is life. The way we learn. Tell me that when you were younger you never did anything foolish."

Sam shrugged. "I should have been there for her."

"No," Valentina said sharply. "I'm sure your presence when she discovered the video would only have made things worse." Her hand still held Sam's hand, then gave it a firm squeeze and released it. "Come, let's all go out together, eat, drink more wine. Tell us a few happy stories about your daughter. Tell us all about San Francisco. Share with us some good memories. And tomorrow I'll walk with you to the church."

SANTA MARIA DELLA Vittoria was yet another of those baroque masterpieces that Sam both admired and at the same time made him feel a bit weary. Though clearly dazzling, even resplendent, the sheer amount of gilded snow-white statuary protruding from the ceiling and walls made Sam think not of God but, strangely, of bakeries, of rosettes of thick frosting mortared elaborately on cakes. As Sam walked toward the main altar, which was a volcanic eruption of gold – immensely long, sharply pointed rays of shining grace emanated from an oval painting of the Virgin – he considered that while some liked cake with plenty of sweet frosting he generally pushed the frosting aside with his fork, then smashed it so that its form was broken, to give the impression it had been eaten. If the cake was not too sugary he'd eat a bite or two, but if not, well, give him something simple, something unadorned, like Zia Lena's almond biscotti or sesame seed cookies.

By the main altar were two dozen or so students with open notebooks – several red Moleskines like Nicole's, long ribbon placeholders dangling from their books' open pages. Other students stood around with raised cameras and cell phones taking photos, nearly all of them talking as if they were at a party, trying to be heard over the tour guide's droning voice. The guide was a small, smug man – unlikeable, Sam judged – with hair the slick color of black Kiwi shoe polish combed stiffly back and off his face. The heels of the boots the man wore to make himself appear taller thumped an irregular drumbeat as he strutted back and forth, waving his arms as he spoke.

Then all at once as if by signal the students grew silent and began filing out of the church. Sam watched the man link arms with one of the students, a thin girl, far too young for him – barely fifteen, Sam guessed – who seemed reticent to be touched and who initially pulled away from him, but then after he grasped her elbow a second time and had her stand still as his other hand reached up and parted her long, fair hair she gazed down at the floor and nodded as he whispered into her ear. Then the girl took a step closer to him, as if she had no other choice, exiting the church obediently at his side.

ALONE NOW IN Santa Maria della Vittoria, Sam approached Bernini's *The Ecstasy of Saint Teresa*. The figure of an angel holding a sharp golden arrow stood over the swooning saint, pulling down the cloth covering her breasts. She lay back on a bed as if resting, head tilted slightly toward the viewer. On the wall behind the pair was another splash of gold icepicks, likely meant to represent the rays of God's redeeming grace. Certainly everything about the composition emphasized the woman's lack of power, Sam thought. Was she surrendering willingly? Her head was fallen back, her neck lay fully exposed. Her mouth was open, slightly enough so that she appeared radiant. Sam couldn't decide what she was feeling. Anguish and pain? Delight and pleasure? Orgasm and ecstasy? For several moments Sam found the piece utterly lovely.

Then Sam noticed that on both sides of the figures, in flanking boxes, were carvings of eight men, four to a loge, watching what was happening before them. It was apparent that these voyeurs were powerful, influential, that they'd paid for the best seats. Sam recognized that Bernini had designed the entire piece as a drama, a tableau being played out upon a stage. So it was a performance, Sam thought. Perhaps it was meant only for the eight men, though several weren't even looking at the woman and the angel. Their heads were turned to one another as they talked idly to one another.

Sam wanted to break one of the gold icepicks off the wall and blind each man's eyes. He wanted to obliterate their stone faces. What right did they have to see this?

Sam stared at the floor, then up again at the statues washed softly in the late morning sunlight. He thought about his need to file for an emergency passport. He thought about the men in Jake's office, possibly gathered around a desk watching the video of his daughter. He thought about Nicole, quite likely standing where he was now standing only weeks before. He tried to look at the statuary the way she might have seen it. He tried to push the dark images in his mind away and turn what he was seeing back into something beautiful.

The church doors swung open, and another tour group tramped noisily into the nave. Sam remembered that one of his reasons for coming to Rome was to make new memories. He thought about the four sea turtles in the fountain in the Ghetto, the ones Nicole sensed he would enjoy, though he kept imagining them slipping through the outstretched hands of their caretakers, their fragile carapaces falling, shattering on the cobblestones. Though Sam willed his mind to focus on Saint Teresa's soft face, he couldn't help but picture his daughter's face. He thought of the smiling dancer on the Capodanno Gitano postcard. To ease the panic, he thought – the panic he now felt – the ever-increasing hurt of life. The images before him merged with Nicole's ashen face as she lay on a slab in the morgue, unseeing him as he identified her, and that melted again into Bernini's *Saint Teresa*. Sam stared at the smug angel and then at the sharp tip of his pointed arrow as others began jostling around him, all of them talking at once, now even more hurrying toward the spot where Sam was standing, weeping openly now, sobbing, as the others rushed toward him, jockeying with one another for room, raising their clicking cameras and cell phones, all doing their best to capture the image of the innocent young woman during her most intimate moment.

Sveti Jure

Biokovo, June 1983-2003

The sun didn't dance or spin in the sky, and the woman with the twisted legs, whose sons carried her and her wheelchair up and down Mount Križevac while reciting the rosary and performing the Stations of the Cross on thirty consecutive days, was still unable to move her lower limbs on the thirty-first. Regardless, the woman continued to pray. Each day Dubravka made the climb with her and her two sons after attending Mass at Saint James Church. And each day Dubravka searched for Anđela but was unable to find her.

Sipping a tumbler of slivovitz in a bar in town where several Međugorje pilgrims gathered each evening – some describing conversations with one or more of the visionaries, others relating stories they'd heard about the latest miracles and cures – Dubravka overheard talk about a cloistered convent on Sveti Jure, a peak in the Biokovo mountain range, running along the Adriatic and the Dalmatian Coast about a hundred or so kilometers to the west. Two women from Switzerland had stayed for several days there. Guests. Given a bed along with their meals. Simple fare, they said. Bread, a few vegetables, soup, served by nuns with white veils. The convent had pairs of heavy inner and outer doors, a dining hall and parlor library, a small church walled off by a brass grill so that the sisters could attend Mass. Bells ringing mid-day calling the congregation to prayer, vespers sung by nuns with black veils each evening. A place for silence and meditation. A community of religious women run entirely by women, the Poor Sisters of Biokovo.

Dubravka made her way there. As she approached the convent's imposing outer gate she decided to use the same strategy that earned her employment at Ukusno's. After one of the sisters unlocked the convent's heavy external door, which led to a second smaller locked inner gate, Dubravka asked if she might enter and be allowed a place to sleep and something to eat in exchange for work. I'm willing to do anything you need, she said.

So you haven't come here for lodging? the sister at the gate said. She wore a long black habit cinched at the waist with a knotted cloth cord, a white coif and guimpe, the simplest of black wimples. A plain dark cross hung from a leather string around her neck. She stared at Dubravka through wire-rimmed glasses.

No, Dubravka said. I believe I've come here to stay. When she saw the expression on the woman's face, Dubravka added, That is, if you'll have me. The words seemed right to Dubravka, and at that moment she dropped to her knees before the gatekeeper and touched the hem of the woman's tunic.

THE REST FELL fairly quickly into place. Dubravka speaking with the Reverend Mother and a group of six other elderly nuns over a period of several days relating the details of her life story, from her childhood in Dubrovnik to the fever that may or may not have killed her, her mother's departure and the pot of her father's favorite soup, her love of Saint Blaise and her long relationship with Father Josip, her work at Zagorac's, her father's accusations and beatings. Mostar and Ukusno's. Her prayers at the Koski Mehmed Pasha Mosque. Her leap off the Old Bridge. Her month in Međugorje, each day climbing Mount Križevac where she prayed the Stations of the Cross and recited the rosary with the two sons and crippled mother. She left out confessing her anger at Marija and her lingering feelings for Stanislav.

Dubravka's hair was cut short and all of her belongings were taken from her, though after a fuss they allowed her to keep Anđela's rosary. Dubravka explained that the rosary wasn't hers, that it belonged to a woman who lived in Rome and one day she'd have to return it. The Mother Superior shook her head at that. When they insisted she give it up, Dubravka said she'd have no other alternative but to leave. They did take the letters Father Josip had sent her in Mostar as well as Giorgio's business card and Anđela's handkerchief.

When you enter here you leave the world behind, they explained. After a trial period of several months, Dubravka was accepted by the community as a servant nun.

KITCHEN SISTERS, HER group was sometimes called. Largely uneducated and poor, the servant nuns slept in a large dormitory and performed the work necessary to meet the demands of the convent and its guests. They did the community's domestic jobs – washing, cleaning, baking, cooking, attending to the guests, caring for the choir sisters whenever one of them fell ill, fixing whatever broke down and required repair. The kitchen sisters worked alongside a trio of lay servants – widows from a town in the lower valley – who were free to roam outside the convent's double doors as they tended to the convent's vegetable garden as well as a small flock of sheep and a half dozen or so cows, along with several hens and a rooster that incessantly crowed.

To distinguish them from the others, the kitchen sisters were given white veils. After serving their years as postulants and later as novitiates, a vote was taken by the choir sisters regarding their acceptability. If the women passed, they were allowed to take their temporary vows. Six years later, again if they passed, they were allowed to take their solemn vows. Poverty, chastity, obedience. Even after they took their solemn vows they were made to sleep in the dormitory and wear veils of a different color. They ate their meals in the refectory after the guests and choir sisters had eaten. They ate what remained, which usually sufficed. They were to speak only when spoken to by one of the guests or choir sisters, which was seldom. Their lives in the convent consisted largely of work and prayer and silence.

The choir sisters wore black veils and had their own individual cells. Carpets on the floor. A wooden desk and chair beside their bed. Items provided by their wealthy families. Several of the choir nuns were painters. A few, writers of inspirational verse. Two threw clay and made pots, which were glazed and fired in the kiln donated to the convent by the family of one of the potters. Their works along with skeins of yarn from the sheep, milk from the cows, and eggs from the chickens were sold in the villages down in the valley to help offset the community's expenses. The choir nuns came to the convent with significant financial donations – *spiritual dowries*, they were called – given to the community by their families. Their families also donated a small annual stipend. The choir sisters were bound by the duties of the Divine Office, which involved the recitation of prayers at fixed hours of the day and night.

They took the three solemn vows along with a fourth – the vow of lifetime enclosure.

Dubravka spent the next twenty years of her life in the convent nestled in a green pocket on Sveti Jure, though *spent* is likely not the most apt verb. To spend, from the Latin *expendere*, meaning to weigh or pay out. Dubravka didn't feel she was paying or weighing something out, though she clearly earned her keep – scrubbing the convent's stone floors, churning butter, carding wool with a pair of paddles, roasting vegetables and baking bread in the kitchen – in what she came to see was not only a thriving female religious community but also a refuge for unmarried women, widows, battered women, even a few former prostitutes. The convent was an escape from the duties of family, the shackles of marriage and motherhood. The convent was an expression of female autonomy. The women who lived within its walls, purposefully separated in nearly every way from the rest of society, even separated by metal grills and screens whenever they met with their confessors or, in the case of the choir sisters on their name day, a member or two of their family, shared a common belief that their enclosure was a path toward spiritual growth. They believed that their meditations and prayers benefited the larger world. Combined with the prayers from the other communities around the world like theirs, they believed in a small way they were redeeming the world.

The convent was also a form of a family since all of the women, regardless of their status, considered one another sisters who answered to their mother, the Reverend Mother Superior. She assigned a confessor, who was called Father, to each sister. Dubravka's was a kind, elderly priest from the port town of Makarska, to whom Dubravka confided everything, and in turn he occasionally confided in her. The pair often talked about the sea. The priest from Makarska loved the sea. He helped Dubravka improve her abilities to read and write, slipping books and sheaves of paper beneath the bottom of the grill that separated them during their meetings, and he permitted her to send and receive letters from Father Josip in Dubrovnik, all of which of course were first reviewed by the Reverend Mother.

Perhaps it would be more accurate to say that Dubravka hid in the convent. To hide, from the Old English *hydan*. To conceal, preserve, hoard. To cover, wrap, encase. Dubravka encased herself within the convent's thick stone walls. As she worked each day in the kitchen, one without the benefit of a perpetually playing radio, she came to realize that the convent didn't so much lock the women inside its walls as it locked out the frightful world and its unspeakable violence and unimaginable horrors, as her country once again went to war with itself, intentionally destroying much of what it had built – damaging the Church of Saint Blaise, the Stradun, Zagorac's, Ukusno's, the Koski Mehmed Pasha Mosque, most of Mostar, and completely demolishing the ancient stones that formed the elegant span of the Stari Most, all while murdering countless women and men under the deplorable ideology euphemistically called *ethnic cleansing*.

IN ADDITION TO her prayers, Dubravka thought of her past life and imagined scenarios of what might have been going through her mother's mind that last night as she prepared to leave.

In one scenario Dubravka's father was right and her mother had entangled her life with a Serb's and the two were secret lovers. Because it would be far too cruel if Dubravka's imagination named him Stanislav, she thought of him simply as Slobadan. The name *Slobadan* meant *free*. Of course, leaving her husband would mean sure freedom for her mother, Dubravka thought. In this scenario, the woman, overwhelmed by grief over her daughter's fever and death, turned to her forbidden lover for solace and comfort, and he convinced her to run away with him. Perhaps they now lived in Belgrade or traveled further north, up into Hungary or the vast plains of Ukraine. Perhaps they made their way across the sea to Italy. Though not before her mother made the pot of soup.

The pot of soup presented an interesting problem to Dubravka.

Were the aunts right? Did her mother prepare the pot of soup out of spite? Was it a taunting symbol of her simultaneous presence and absence? A way of giving the man a final reminder of something he'd cherished and come to take for granted but now would no longer have? Dubravka didn't know. But what she did know is that her mother would not have left had there been even the slightest chance her daughter was still living.

She imagined other scenarios, ones involving her mother not running away at all. As she made the pot of soup, someone evil came to the door. He enticed her to leave the house and go with him, then took her somewhere where she was killed. Then he did what murderers in Dubrovnik normally did – he took the body out to sea where it was dropped overboard after being weighed down with rocks. Dubravka imagined a diver – a spearfisher doing his best to hold his breath – suddenly coming upon her mother's bones.

This scenario was too horrible to accept.

Over time as Dubravka matured and came to know and understand the others living in the convent, listening at night in the dormitory to their whispered stories, particularly the tales told by the women who had chosen the monastic life for personal rather than religious reasons, Dubravka wondered if perhaps in her mother's situation no man was involved at all. Dubravka reminded herself that a woman's story didn't require the presence of a man. Perhaps her mother was simply one of the many women who found the rigid constraints of marriage and mother-hood so unbearable that, rather than slice her wrists or drink herself to a slow death, she determined that her best alternative was to run away.

Eventually this became the most plausible theory. Her daughter's tragic death, confirmed by the priest who gave the body the Last Rites, offered her mother the opportunity to escape. Though she likely draped a black shawl on the door and pulled the shutters on the windows tightly closed, the child's death gave the woman a clear opening. Dubravka saw her father's house now as a walled prison where the woman was some-times beaten by a drunken husband and regularly forced into unwanted sex. Her mother must have wanted to escape the house for a long time. Perhaps the pot of zagorska juha wasn't her way of telling her husband goodbye. Does every action a woman commits in her life need to be seen in the context of a man? No, Dubravka decided. Maybe her mother made the pot of soup only for herself, as a way for her to think. Maybe it was a way simply to keep her hands busy as her mind decided what to do next, just as Dubravka was now deciding what to do with the remainder of her life as she stole gulps of wine from the various bottles she'd hidden in the cupboards, as she worked each day silently in the convent's kitchen.

AND WITH THIS realization Dubravka came to think that perhaps she had never really been given a sign or calling from God.

Not Marija's theft of her night with Stanislav or the unmovable locks on the net sheds. Not her survival of her leap off the Stari Most or even the miracle of the handkerchief. No, Dubravka came to think that if God had actually sent her a sign it was likely the moljac, the poor hummingbird hawk-moth trapped inside the rectory's dusty parlor, vainly thumping itself against the impenetrable glass of the room's grimy windows, trying its best to get out.

By now Dubravka had exchanged several letters with Father Josip – one of which bore the terrible news about Marija and Stanislav's disease – and then after the blockade and the siege and bombings of Dubrovnik, which Dubravka learned about from the lay servants, the flow of letters stopped. Dubravka grieved then, understanding what the absence of word from her beloved priest clearly meant.

There were moments when one of the lay servants came into the kitchen, stomping the snow off her boots, and Dubravka could smell the wet, fresh air emanating from her clothing. It was like an exotic perfume. There were moments when the kitchen's inner back door was left open and Dubravka could stand at its threshold and gaze up at the sky. There were moments when Dubravka was talking with her confessor about the port of Makarska and she would imagine she could smell fish and the sea. She would have recurring dreams about walking along the Stradun at dawn on Saint Blaise's feast day, at the moment when the city's many churches began ringing their bells. She would dream about Father Josip coming up from behind her while she knelt in a pew, staring up at Sveti Vlaho's gold statue, and the priest would tap her shoulder and smile and call her *little chicken*. She would dream about making her ablutions at the domed fountain in the courtyard of Mostar's Koski Mehmed Pasha Mosque. It would be morning, and she would hear birdsong.

One night Dubravka dreamed that she and Marija were making madjarica, an intricately layered chocolate and buttercream cake, even though she and Marija had never made madjarica. Music played from above, though in the dream Dubravka strained to hear it. Why couldn't she hear the music? Dubravka wondered in the dream. The two girls drew the cake out from the refrigerator where it lay beside a tray of brown eggs and cut two identical rectangular pieces and set them side by side on plates. As Marija ate a bite of her cake, she was engulfed by a swirl of smoke and disappeared. Dubravka sat upright in bed, gasping for breath, feeling as if her heart would burst through her chest. As she tried to calm herself, she felt absolutely certain that Marija had just died.

Eventually Dubravka realized that once again she seemed between things, locked inside a walled convent set on the side of an immense mountain, beneath the range's tallest peak that overlooked the valley below and, just to the south and west, the inviting, ever-pounding sea.

SHE LEFT THE convent at the age of thirty-eight, free to do so because as a servant sister she'd never taken the vow of enclosure.

Dubravka was given a simple black skirt to wear, a modest blouse she had to pin because it was missing several buttons, a woolen shawl, and a black cloth to cover her head, that she chose not to wear. She had had enough of veils. She ran a hand through her short hair and decided she'd let it grow out. From this day forward she'd face the world bare-headed. She left the convent with only Anđela's rosary and a sheaf of the letters Father Josip had sent to the convent, bound by a string Dubravka had pulled from a burlap sack. The choir sister who opened the twin gates didn't return the letters Father Josip had sent to Dubravka while she was living in Mostar, nor did she give her Anđela's handkerchief or her brother's business card. When Dubravka asked about these belongings she was given a strange look. Why, the nun said, of course all of the worldly things she'd brought with her to the convent were tossed into a fire and burned.

Dubravka stayed for a few nights at the house of one of the widowed lay servants down in the valley below that stretched itself out toward the blue sea. The Adriatic was a wonder to behold. Dubravka spent hours staring at the sea, watching each wave as it neared and then broke upon the shore, only then to begin its retreat, then again make its return as yet another wave toppled over it. She listened to the sea as if it were speaking God's word, as if it could reveal God's plan. Then she remembered she needed to return Anđela's rosary.

Not having any money, Dubravka had to barter for her passage, offering physical work in exchange for her way across the Adriatic, the marvelous blue sea that Anđela had reminded her has always connected Croatia and Italy. Once on shore, at the fortified town of Termoli, Dubravka traveled down through the rugged terrain to Campobasso, where she again heard Anđela's dialect spoken on the streets. Dubravka then made her way across Italy's spine, the Apennines, then through the rolling hillsides that led to Rome's scrambled outskirts. She pieced together what she could recall from her conversations with Anđela. A marriage to a Roman family that owned a pensione. A younger brother. The Field of Flowers. Once in Rome proper, Dubravka talked to shopkeeper after shopkeeper. Eventually she was led to the Centro Storico and the Campo de' Fiori, where she took a deep breath as she stood in the shadow of Giordano Bruno's statue.

Sant'Agnese in Agone

Rome, March 2005

As she headed up Via del Teatro Valle to Sant'Eustachio il Caffè for a mid-morning gran caffè, likely the best cup of coffee in all of Rome, Ericka was still angry. Not only was she not making progress on her book, she hadn't yet decided if she could do anything about what she'd learned about the recently hired poet. And if that were not enough now there was last night's creep who'd fabricated a story about losing his passport and credit cards, who'd let her take him out to an expensive dinner, drink two bottles of excellent wine, then come up to her room where she'd allowed him to be intimate with her – *twice!* Ericka thought bitterly, *twice!* – and then no sooner did he wait for her to fall asleep than he snuck over to her laptop to look at porn.

She berated herself for not being a better judge of character. She should have seen what kind of man he was the afternoon they'd met, as soon as he refused her invitation to come inside the church and look at the mosaics. Any sensible man would have agreed. At the time she guessed him Greek or Spanish. She liked his size, his rugged, somewhat careless look, his thick dark hair. She liked his hands, which seemed not unused to work. Best, he seemed troubled. These days only the truly naive were untroubled. She found him an ideal candidate. Alone, deep chocolate eyes, pleasant enough mouth. Older than Ericka would have preferred but certainly handsome enough. He looked like a man, and in her experience, particularly in her years working in academia, not many males did.

She spotted him that night wandering near the Pantheon's ribbed columns, head down, hands in his pockets, kicking a discarded gelato cup. He walked up a narrow street and paused, doubling back to join several tourists bunched outside a trattoria. Rustic spot, she thought. Like him. She waited several minutes, then joined the queue.

Ericka was usually good at reading people, and an expert at reading men. Men were relatively simple texts, the sort that didn't require extensive interpretation. Normally they allowed their intentions to lie just beneath the surface, like schooling koi. Even pretend to toss them a crumb and they thrashed about with obvious intent. She thought this one had depth, which she read as genuine sadness, some freshly bleeding wound. Ericka was attracted to wounded men. Wounded men were her weakness.

She wanted his story, his true story, and sensed it would take several nights before he'd give it up. But in the end, she imagined, it would be worth it.

Ericka had strict rules about men and sex. After her divorce she vowed she'd never sleep with anyone who might want their relationship to become permanent. She also ruled out the city where she lived, New York, and of course the university where she worked, where couplings between colleagues were as common as graduate seminars. She vowed to limit herself to occasional out-of-town sex. Twice or maybe three times a year out-on-the-road-away-from-home-at-a-conference sex. Further, she was a disciple of restraint – no one could suggest she was a tramp – allowing herself, at most, a single conquest per trip, like someone in a gelateria who deliberately selects only one flavor. And like Scheherazade in reverse she'd insist that the chosen one tell her a story, preferably something he seldom revealed, something true, ideally romantic.

Few of the men she was intimate with ever disappointed her. Most told her stories that sequenced predictably, though there were occasional rewarding moments when their tales took a surprising turn. She was amazed at how easily men opened up after sex, like littleneck clams dropped into a pan of bubbling white wine. Some needed to back their way into their tales – semis beeping slowly in reverse toward a loading dock. Others were like plumbers twisting the rust-frozen handle of a faucet. This one offered her more or less an outline, a brief summary she suspected wasn't entirely factual. But all eventually ended up spouting like fountains, giving her the impression they'd been waiting their entire lives for the chance to speak. It was as if beneath each of their narratives there was a tightly wound spring simply waiting to be tripped. All she had to do was turn the crank to hear their music. Sometimes Ericka thought she should shelve her academic projects and write a book about the men, something she could publish under a pseudonym. She'd title it *Love On the Road: Amazing True Stories from*

Men Who've Just Been Laid. She toyed with the idea of ending the book with her own story and giving the collection an epigraph from Saint Augustine. "Lord, grant me chastity and continence, but not yet."

SHE WAS PRONE to ritual. Whenever Ericka was on the road she did her best to decontaminate her hotel room. The first thing to go would be the bedcover, which she'd stash on the floor of the wardrobe or closet. Not even a microbiologist specializing in exotic diseases would be able to identify all that lay festering on the average hotel bedcover. Whenever possible she'd ask that the TV set in her room be removed, and in the cases where it could not she covered its screen with a flowered cloth she carried in her luggage expressly for that purpose. She tossed everything the hotel laid out on the tables and desk into a drawer, particularly the TV's remote control – a virtual petri dish teeming with continents of germs.

That morning it dawned on her to disinfect her laptop since Sam had pawed it the previous evening, and then Ericka realized that she needed to scrub the machine's hard drive of the viruses, spyware, and trojan horses it might have picked up from the porn site he'd visited. She promptly clicked on the machine's protective software. As the program began searching for contaminants, the laptop's yawning screen tempted her to peek in on her email, even though she'd set it on automatic out-of-office response, just to see what the others – her so-called colleagues at the university – were up to.

That was a mistake.

Ericka was fond of watching a show on cable about a crafty bunch of monkeys in East Africa – *Monkey Gangs*, the program was called – that portrayed two troops of vervets doing their best not only to wage a turf war but at the same time raid the resources of a residential housing complex lying on the border of their territories. Cute little things, vervets, the sort of creature you'd like for a pet for maybe two minutes, until the beast bit off the tips of your fingers and lunged for your face. The show's narrator gave each monkey a name matching some aspect of their appearance or behavior, like Snow White's seven dwarfs. As one might expect, each little beast did its best to screech, claw, and bite, or beg, grovel, and groom its way to the top of the group's pyramid of power.

Ericka found it fascinating to watch what the monkeys were willing to do to advance themselves. Some bared their fangs and made threatening gestures to everyone beneath them. Others leaned over and offered the leader their backside whenever he walked past. Of course at the university she never talked about the show and didn't even admit to her colleagues that she owned a TV. Within the culture of her department, watching television was tantamount to saying that one enjoyed country music or ate frozen pizza. Nonetheless, Ericka found *Monkey Gangs* a strikingly accurate portrayal of her department's social dynamics. As she watched the show and sipped her nightly glass or two of chilled white wine, she could easily imagine her fellow faculty members chattering away as they groomed the hairy back and chest of their department chair, Angelo, of tasty lice and nits.

Much to her dismay, there in her email's inbox in the annoying Book Antiqua Bold Italic font Angelo was fond of using – *Book Antiqua is a relative of Palatino font*, the quote he included in the signature block of each of his emails informed the recipient, *named for Giambattista Palatino, the famous sixteenth-century Italian master of calligraphy, who created a font that mirrored the graceful writing formed by a broadnib pen* – was a notice about an upcoming department meeting in which, at the request of the Advisory Committee, the early tenure and promotion of the new poet, Jason Lee LaRue, would be discussed and, Angelo added with an optimistic parenthetical note he trusted no one would object to, be put up for a vote on approval. LaRue was Angelo's nephew. After LaRue applied for the position he emerged as one of the top three candidates by the hiring committee, which Angelo both headed and named. In Ericka's opinion the nephew was given the job over two more highly qualified candidates, both females. And now his path to tenure was being fast-tracked. Worse, the discussion and vote were to be held in Ericka's absence.

A deliberate move, she understood at once. Take advantage of the fact that a potential dissenting voice was abroad on research leave – Venice, for a week of acclimation, Florence, to teach a two-week mini-course at their extension campus, then Rome for a few months of research on Rome's churches. Certainly it was reasonable for her to be suspicious. Academia bred suspicion since advancement in each department was based on forged connections and the unforgiving rules of the zero-sum game.

As the antivirus software ground its way through her laptop, Ericka decided to go out into the day and think. She grabbed her red wool coat and matching scarf, then checked her purse for her wallet and room key. Though she was not tall she was fit – slender was an apt way to describe her, she thought, though of course she always felt she could stand to lose ten pounds – with gray-blue eyes and a thin, straight nose and auburn hair cut into a choppy bob. Since she'd purposely avoided the sun when she was a girl, her skin was clear and relatively unwrinkled, making her look younger than she was.

Once her heels hit the sidewalk and she took a deep breath of the crisp March air, she thought she'd treat herself to a cup of gran caffè at the nearby Sant'Eustachio il Caffè, which, along with Tazzo d'Oro near the Pantheon, served the Eternal City's finest cup of coffee.

It wasn't so much that Jason Lee LaRue was a bad poet. He was a curiously chilly poet who ran so far from sentimentality that his work had the warmth of a hardware store catalogue. To mask his lack of emotion, he wrote about food. Food was a hot subject. Everyone with a pulse loved food. There were even TV channels dedicated entirely to food, displaying its various methods of preparation in such vivid, lingering detail that viewers might think they were looking at the gustatory equivalent of what Sam was caught peering at the night before.

Each of the poems in Jason's first collection, *Gumbo LaRue*, was titled after some ingredient that might be found in gumbo. Ericka couldn't keep all the details straight, which Angelo routinely listed in Book Antiqua on the department bulletin board, but one or more of the *gumbo poems*, as the department came to call them, was mentioned in the back of the annual *Pushcart* series, and another – it might have been "Filé" or "Okra" or "Andouille Sausage" – had recently been reprinted in *Best American*.

"J. L. LaRue cooks up a delightfully spicy treat in this distinctive debut collection," began nearly all of the book's reviews, most of them written by LaRue's friends or at least by a poet whom LaRue had invited to campus to give a reading after Angelo appointed his nephew chair of the Visiting Scholars and Writers Committee.

Ericka understood it all too well, the workings of what LaRue and his friends jokingly referred to as *po-biz*. It was a mirror image of her Rome project. To become a successful poet in North America involved positioning oneself in some seat of power, be it the editor of a literary magazine or the director of a reading series or summer writers conference. One then solicited and published the work of other editors of literary magazines, or one invited other directors of readings series or summer conferences to campus for a reading, and the rest fell into place, tit for tat, *quid pro quo*. One made friends and made use of those friends. One admired the work of others and received admiration for one's work in return. The final step involved putting the friends' books on the lists of required books for all of your courses so that each of your diligent undergrads toted home a dozen or so collections written by your buddies, fellow teaching poets who, in turn, placed your book on their required books lists.

None of that was necessarily bad, Ericka thought, though she couldn't help but notice that the process all too often failed to include women. Just like in *Monkey Gangs*, female poets comprised a sub-group of their own, though they weren't as powerful or organized, and anyone objectively observing either scene would note that females controlled considerably less territory than the males.

It was much the same through the rest of the department, as it was in politics. It was only human nature – monkey gang nature – to want to work with friends and make use of connections and affiliations to advance one's place in the world. Certainly that was true here in Italy, true for each of the Italians and new immigrants she passed each day in the streets. That was why Ericka asked the men with whom she temporarily shared her bed to tell her a story, because their stories individualized them, made them more a full human, less a hungry beast, and on very rare occasions perhaps even something close to the divine.

Ericka considered that the word *nepotism*, the granting of favor to someone known rather than to one who had earned the favor through merit or achievement, came from the Latin *nepos*, which was derived from the Italian word *nipote*, which meant *nephew*. The practice could be traced back to the fifteenth century and the reign of Sixtus IV and was continued by his successors. Gradually it became known as *nepotismo*, the papal practice of bestowing privileges on relatives and friends. Angelo's maneuvers behind the hiring of his nephew over the applications of more qualified candidates was the germ of Ericka's Rome project, which she disguised as a work that would focus on the life and death of Borromini and the narratives of several of Rome's most popular churches.

As for her work on Rome's churches and Borromini, Ericka considered it was – what would be the most diplomatic way to put it? – it was still germinating. Yes, *germinating* might be the best way for her to look at it, she thought. Indeed, the seed was in the soil. What soil exactly Ericka didn't quite yet know since, if truth be told, even though a fair portion of the sand had trickled through the narrow waist of her research leave's hourglass, she hadn't yet written a single word.

AFTER PAYING FOR and receiving the receipt for her gran caffè from the gentleman staffing the coffee bar's antique register, Ericka overheard three young men talking. Obvious performers, one was dressed formally in a suit while the two others wore black hooded robes and had painted their faces to resemble skulls.

"Look at this crowd," the first skull said in Italian. "We should have gone across – "

"I agree," said the other skull.

"No," the man in the suit said, "have patience. The coffee here, it's a kiss from God."

There was more that passed between them that Ericka couldn't understand. All the while the three along with Ericka pressed their way from the cash register toward the bar, the stubs of their receipts in hand, with the goal being to place their receipt along with maybe a small coin on the bar's marble counter as they caught the eye of one of the waiters, who issued orders to the busy baristas doing their delicious tricks behind the silver screens of their humming, hissing, magical espresso machines.

"I still don't understand what he thinks he's accomplishing," the first skull said.

"I read it's very big in Japan now," said the second skull. "On all of the streets."

"Cosplay," the man in the suit said. "Costume play. I watched a few of the videos. A pastime for young girls who dye their hair pink or blue."

The first skull nodded. "They dress like French maids or characters from comics."

"Manga," the second skull said. "*Ranma ½. Sailor Moon. Dragon Ball.*. But crazy Agostino – "

"He's only making an ass of himself," the man in the suit said, "thinking that somehow it's art."

"I'm told he wants not just to play the part but to become it," said the first skull.

"Yes," agreed the second skull. "Like the men in Latin America and the Philippines who dress as Jesus and his tormentors during Holy Week."

"I still say there's nothing at all artistic about what he's doing."

"Sometimes the guy playing Jesus is actually crucified. I mean, they end up really killing him. I guess pretending you're the son of God is no joke."

"Speaking of which, il Papa's at the Gemelli again. This time he's really sick."

The man in the suit remained silent.

"No, no, the old Polack's a pillar of marble. I saw pictures of him yesterday, standing at his hospital window, blessing the lambs flocked below."

"Something for the newspapers. A show."

"As if all of life isn't," the man in the suit said and smiled. "And speaking of shows, did I mention I've been spending a few hours each day with Valentina?"

"No. Gennaro, tell me you didn't. Though if I'm being honest I'd rather have her cousin. The unattainable one. The waitress. Rosangela."

The second skull clasped his hands in prayer. "My preference would be them both."

The suited man laughed. "Good luck with that. But for me, I'm content to take what's in my reach. Every day the coglione leaves her alone. Now in addition to his Caravaggio stunts he's back to painting again for real and then out on the street trying to peddle his work to passing tourists. Valentina showed me some of his cityscapes and portraits. Several were of her, in various poses. I came away quite impressed."

The skulls gave out a hearty laugh. "With Agostino's work or Valentina?"

"I think you know which one," Gennaro said with a wink.

Then they received their cups of coffee, which they swirled three times and drank in silence. Ericka pressed her receipt on the counter along with a twenty-cent coin. The man in the suit nodded at Ericka as the trio turned to leave, and the skulls gave her a smile and said something she couldn't hear as the waiter scooped her coin below the counter and tore the edge of her receipt and brought her a saucer and small spoon followed by a cup of gran caffè. As Gennaro and the two hooded figures of death walked out, an elderly woman standing outside in the square glanced up at the sky and made the sign of the Cross.

Ericka sipped her perfect coffee and thought about the dying pope and God, about Christ and the Virgin Mary. She thought of the magnificent mosaic in the apse of Santa Maria in Trastevere, Rome's oldest church, how it depicted both Mary and Christ seated on twin thrones, flanked by saints. Mother and Son, woman and man, equals. While kneeling before Santa Maria in Trastevere's altar, Ericka realized that she continued to believe in much of the Roman Catholic religion in which she'd been raised largely because of the Virgin Mary. Like watching TV, this was something Ericka admitted to no one. She was like the apostle Peter in that respect. If questioned, she'd deny involvement. She knew that most of her peers at the university thought Catholics were a joke, that Catholicism was antiquated, backward, historically monstrous, most definitely politically incorrect, at best an Old World superstition, something that deserved to be trashed. She knew that the apostle Peter was named from the word that meant *rock*, which many interpreted to mean a solid base upon which to build something, though the word *petra* also meant *tripping stone*, the pebble in the path that catches your foot and causes you to stumble. That was why Christ had named Peter the first pope, because Peter was so perfectly imperfect.

Other than his stance on contraception, homosexuality, and a woman's right to choose, Ericka admired the dying pope. She was what some called a cafeteria Catholic – a person who pushes her tray down the long line of doctrine and selects only what suits her palate. And why shouldn't Catholics do that, as long as they believed in the Apostles' Creed? Wasn't the Apostles' Creed the faith's essence? Ericka considered that even if one didn't believe in the Holy Trinity and the Virgin's sanctity, the taste of coffee as fine as the cup she was sipping might convince even the fiercest atheist of God's existence.

Ericka tried to savor the moment – the rich smell of coffee here in the marvelously crowded bar, the warm busy hum of the others happily gathered around her, the taste of the soft sweet delicious espresso she was drinking. She tried not to worry about Sam and Angelo and Jason Lee LaRue and all that she hadn't yet written about Borromini. She tried not to think about how the others in her department considered her a terminal associate and, as a result, how poorly in comparison she was both treated and paid. She tried not to imagine digital worms burrowing holes in her laptop's hard drive, and then she decided that just to hedge her bets she should light a candle in the next church she visited and recite a decade of the rosary. Indeed, Ericka carried a rosary, one with blue glass beads, in the pocket of her coat. A childhood gift, given to her by her mother on the morning of her First Holy Communion, the blue rosary was another of Ericka's many secrets.

"WE'RE A DEPARTMENT of writers," Angelo was fond of reminding the vervet troop each Friday afternoon at their weekly faculty meeting. The professors sat in a basement room ceilinged with an intricate maze of exposed, bandaged pipes. This wasn't to say, Angelo would add, that good teaching wasn't their calling, but what he and the Salary Committee as well as the dean ultimately valued was research – their published writing.

But who in the world truly cared if, indeed, everyone in the department was productively scribbling away? Who among the monkey gang, of which Ericka was a decidedly minor member, had actual readers? With the exception of the lone aging novelist who cranked out romances – *Happily Ever Afters* he called them – that received featured reviews penned by friends who worked for *The New York Times*, only a handful of the academics or poets or short story writers or essayists had any readers beyond their cohorts and friends.

Ericka envied the poets' level of organization, and under normal circumstances she might have liked LaRue – he was polite to her whenever they passed in the hallway, and he often gave her a flirtatious smile in the department mailroom – but he violated one of the basic rules of teaching. He played favorites. While he tended to bully his workshops' young men, often giving them unflattering nicknames as he julienned their raw attempts at verse, he fully embraced the young women, parceling out his attention commensurate with the return of their admiration and favors.

For several months before her Rome research leave, the aggrieved were making pilgrimages to her office. Why they chose her to be their sounding board Ericka wasn't entirely sure. Was it because the department had failed to hire any female poets? Or was there something in her field, nonfiction and narratology, that invited them to come to her and tell her their stories? "Do you have a minute?" was how the girls usually began. "I don't mean to bother you." Though of course the students wanted more than a minute, and they clearly intended her to be bothered. "But before I say anything, you have to promise, I mean really promise, not to tell."

Ericka always responded that she had no desire to talk about her colleagues. She'd add quickly that as a faculty member she had certain obligations, things she was required to report, such as word that a student was in danger of hurting themselves or others. She told the young women that if they had an issue about a class they should take it up with the instructor. They'd stare at her as if she'd said something incredibly dumb, then add that they thought she was different, that she was one of the few faculty who actually *cared* about students, that all she'd have to do was *listen*, that they needed someone who would *just listen.*

The students then described what went on after LaRue closed his office door. How he'd have them sit on a chair beside his desk, how he told them how much he admired their work, how he had a good friend, a distinguished editor, who, he was reasonably certain, would be interested in publishing their poems. But first the poems could benefit from a bit of polishing. Then as the pair bent over the poem on which LaRue's pen was already beginning to cross out and add words, he'd suddenly drop the pen and touch her hair – move a lock that had fallen out of place – or brush his knuckles against the girl's cheek, or make his fingers open like the legs of a spider and fall on her hand or her arm.

He told some students that in order to be a real poet she'd need to open up, get over her false concepts about art, her bourgeois sense of morality. She should move beyond the prescribed limits, knock down the barriers and walls. He'd talk about breakthroughs, poems that took risks, risks with a capital "R," poems that dared to do the unthinkable. For example, it might be in the student's best interests if she wrote a poem describing, say, how she felt when she touched herself. Or made love. Indeed, maybe she should go home and pleasure herself and then write a poem about it. She wouldn't even have to hand it in. She could call him when it was finished and read it to him over the phone. He'd give her his home number. Of course none of these assignments would go before the rest of the class.

As for the editing, it would have to be after hours, either here in his office or, even better, at his apartment, which was more conducive to conversation and wasn't that long of a walk from campus. They could set up an evening or two when they could meet.

After the first four or five complaints, Ericka could recite the progression by heart. Excessive praise, promise of publication, physical touch followed by an assignment of some sexual nature to be given to him either over the phone or through meetings at night in his apartment. There, he would motion for them to sit on a black leather sofa as he brought out a pair of heavy, cut-lead crystal tumblers and talked about the history of French poets who'd drink absinthe as he poured the students a glass of a liquor from a green bottle, something that tasted of anise and turned whitish after he added ice. The girls seldom mentioned what happened next. *And then, did he* was all the prompting they needed before they nodded, saying that everything that occurred afterward was all their fault.

Of course by the time they met with Ericka the editor's assistant had returned their poems with a barely legible *Thank you for thinking of us* on the bottom of the rejection slip. And by then LaRue's interests had wandered elsewhere. Sure, they were welcome to drop by his place, but more often than not he'd stand inside his slightly open apartment door and explain that they'd caught him at a bad time. Now, the girls said, they didn't know what to think. They felt lost and used. They didn't know where else to turn.

Would you be willing to talk with Angelo about this? Ericka would ask.

No, they'd respond. Besides, he'd never forgive me. They meant LaRue. And at least now we're friends.

And this is happening to other girls in your class? And you don't mind that?

Poets are free spirits, they'd answer.

And if one of these other girls complained? Would you –

Listen, I already know I'm not the only one. And I know that someday he's going to help me. He promised. I mean, isn't that how things are done in the real world? Isn't a whole lot of it who you know and who you're friends with?

Then the not-so-conventionally-pretty girls came to Ericka's office. I'm paying as much tuition as everybody else, they'd say, so why does she – and here they'd mention the name of a fellow student in workshop – why does she get to meet with him in his office and they have these super-long conferences when he goes over all of her work? You should see the amount of criticism she gets. He moves her lines around, makes notes all over her pages, and at the end it's every bit as much his poem as hers. And what do I get? They slap a nearly empty piece of paper on Ericka's desk. I get a single sentence on the bottom of the page. *Nice try!* Or this. *Nearly hits the mark!* Or this. *Some fine potential here!*

Can't we talk with Angelo about this? Ericka would ask. Somewhere along the line a student needs to talk with an administrator. Send an email. File something in writing.

Good luck with that, the students would respond, but count me out. Ever read any war novels? In my class on the Vietnam war novel, the soldier walking point always gets shot. Always. He's like the girl at the beginning of the horror flick who leaves the others to check out the noise she hears down in the basement. Tell me if she ever appears again.

Or perhaps you could talk about this with the dean? Ericka would say.

And slit my own throat in the process? I need him for a letter of recommendation. Don't you realize who he is? He had a poem in *Best American!*

THE DEAN OF the college was an imposing man, a former middle linebacker at one of the Ivies, perpetually tan, the sort who hung the jackets of his three-thousand-dollar suits on a beech-wood coat hanger near his office door and folded the French cuffs of his white shirts above the thick hair that matted his wrists and the backs of his hands. An active man, during meetings he seldom sat behind his desk, preferring to stroll about, often gazing out his ninth-floor windows as if he ruled all that was below. A titled professor in the biological sciences, he kept a life-sized painted polystyrene model of an Eastern American toad on his desk where one would normally expect to see his nameplate. Below the creature, whose bulging silver-and-black eyes stared unblinking at whoever sat in one of the low chairs before the man's desk, was a prominent gold plaque bearing the toad's scientific name.

BUFO AMERICANUS

The dean drew considerable pleasure from the creature, often absently stroking its back, running the pads of his fingers over the creature's cranial crest and the various bumps on its back and its bulging twin parotoid glands, nearly as if the thing were a dog. He delighted in asking prospective job candidates if they could identify it. It was rumored that no nervous candidate who mistakenly said it was a frog was ever offered a job. On the wall behind the dean's desk hung a triptych of sepia splotches and dots, an abstract piece that made sense only after one was told its title, *Metamorphosis*, and viewed the panels as the transformation of countless eggs lying within twirling shoelace strands to a small cluster of tadpoles to a still smaller knot of manic toadlets, each writhing frantically toward the security of a lily pad. The story among the faculty was that the piece portrayed the journey from graduate school to a job carrying a chance at tenure.

Ericka sat in one of the low chairs, and after exchanging polite greetings with the dean and complimenting the color of his tie said, "Let's say, and we're talking theoretically here, some of our undergrads are coming to a professor and voicing concerns – "

"Female students, I presume."

Ericka nodded.

"Complaints by female students coming to a female professor."

"Theoretically, yes."

"And have the students talked first with the instructor, then with the department chair, and then if they find they're still not satisfied have they raised their concerns with one of the associate deans or with the Office of Women's Affairs? Certainly the professor hearing the allegations knows enough to inform the students of outlined procedures."

"Yes," Ericka said, "of course. But in the event that the students decline to go through the prescribed channels." She paused. "In the event they insist on confidentiality."

"But, at least in the beginning, we can assure them of confidentiality."

"Yes, we both know that. But imagine if they might not trust – "

"Then we have nothing to be concerned with. Theoretically. And we *are* speaking theoretically, aren't we? We're not discussing specifics. As we both know, one refers student complainants to the appropriate offices. Otherwise, the complaints do not exist."

"But the students – "

"The students need to understand that they need to follow appropriate procedures, procedures that are there to protect both their rights as individuals as well as the rights of their instructors and the university's professoriate."

Ericka again nodded.

"Of course you certainly must have considered the possibility that perhaps due to your field, the making and structure of stories – narratology, personal essays, am I correct? – that theoretically, say, if you are in fact the instructor hearing allegations, the students might be bringing you tales, inventions, something they think might please you?" The dean rocked back on his heels and smiled. "Clever Hans, if you catch my drift. Or house cats, craving approval, bringing their owners the bodies of dead birds and mice."

The dean's eyes held Ericka in her little seat as he slapped his meaty hands together, breaking huddle, like the defensive captain he once was. "I appreciate your coming up here to talk with me, Ericka, but please understand that more often than we'd like to admit our students, particularly those in your discipline, do as they're taught, fabricate fictions, imagine scenarios that in the end turn out to be nothing more than hurtful lies, particularly young females who might be smitten by an instructor – "

Ericka did her best not to wince or object.

" – or who may be upset because they received perhaps a negative comment about their work or a lower-than-anticipated grade."

She took a deep breath. "But if there's validity to their concerns – "

"Then it's their responsibility to provide documentation." He stepped closer as he pressed his outstretched fingers on the dark polished wood of his desk. "Evidence." He nodded for emphasis, then repeated the word as if it were the solution to every problem. "Documentation. Something in writing. And then the offices charged with investigating allegations of this kind would be able to carry out their responsibilities with due and proper diligence and respect for the rights of all parties concerned."

Ericka stared up at the third panel of the triptych, at the desperate mass of toadlets swimming helter-skelter toward the lily pad.

"Of course we continue to speak theoretically," the dean said. He walked toward his office door, indicating that their conversation was over. As Ericka stood and turned to leave, the dean touched the small of her back. "Again," the man said with a smile, "as always, I appreciate your coming up here to see me."

PART OF WHAT attracted Ericka to Borromini was that he took his own life. He was said to have been a despondent loner, and he suffered a long series of bad breaks. Commissions he was promised were taken from him by others. Changes were made to his designs that marred their integrity and beauty. And throughout nearly all of his career he had to shadow Gian Lorenzo Bernini, who at the time was clearly favored by the popes.

Born Francesco Castelli, the architect took on the name Borromini out of respect for Carlo Borromeo, Archbishop of Milan, who was canonized by the Church shortly after his death. A leader in the Catholic Counter-Reformation, Borromeo wrote and published the *Catechismus Romanus*, which taught the rudiments of the faith. When both famine and an epidemic of the bubonic plague struck Milan in 1576, rather than flee to the countryside like the other wealthy Milanese Borromeo remained in the city, using his own money to care for the sick and starving. He walked Milan's streets barefoot, crucifix in hand, wearing a noose around his neck – a sign he was willing to offer his own life for his flock. His emblem was the Latin word *humilitas*. Humility.

Borromini was called to Rome by the master marble cutter Carlo Maderno. Through Maderno's influence, Borromini worked on Saint Peter's Basilica and the Palazzo Barberini, eventually climbing his way up the rungs of patronage to Pope Innocent X. Thus began Borromini's long feud with Bernini, whom the pope routinely favored but, like a fickle lover, on occasion ignored. The rest of the two architects' stories, as well as the competition and disdain that existed between them, was as intertwined as spaghetti on a plate. Whereas the melancholic Borromini preferred dressing in simple working-man's clothing, Bernini clad himself in the latest fashions. Both men worked on the magnificent twisting baldacchino over Saint Peter's altar, though Bernini was often given complete credit despite the fact that the concept as well as the enchanting childbirth sequence in the plinths were Borromini's creations. Both architects designed churches on Rome's Quirinale Hill, though Bernini's was usually considered the more fair. Even two of the statutes in Bernini's Fountain of the Four Rivers were said to be a deliberate slur against Saint Agnes in Agony, the nearby church Borromini largely designed. Indeed, the very idea of a fountain in the center of the Piazza Navona bearing an obelisk and depicting four rivers around its base was Borromini's, who was initially promised the commission. Bernini stole Borromini's plans and made a silver model of the design which, with a friend's help, was intentionally placed in the pope's path where it would be seen before any of the other models were seen, before the pope could even consider Borromini's model, which was humbly fashioned from wax and clay.

The end of the two men's lives could hardly have been more different. Whereas Bernini was buried with flourish and honor in one of Rome's four major basilicas, Santa Maria Maggiore, Borromini was denied burial in San Carlo alle Quatro Fontane, the first church he designed, because he was a suicide. To this day Borromini's remains lay, marked only by his name, alongside the grave of his patron Carlo Maderno near an altar dedicated to Mary Magdalene in San Giovanni Battista dei Fiorentini, a modest church with a narrow, almond-shaped dome at the north end of Via Giulia. San Giovanni is best known for being one of only two churches in Rome where the faithful can bring their animals to Mass. Dogs, mainly, scratching their fleas, free to roam about the nave, free to find Borromini's cool marble gravestone a comfortable spot to lie and rest.

ERICKA DECIDED TO start with the two churches on Quirinale Hill – Borromini's San Carlo alle Quatro Fontane, named for Saint Carlo Borromeo and commissioned by a discalced order of Trinitarians from Spain, and Bernini's Sant'Andrea al Quirinale, commissioned by Cardinal Camillo Pamphili, nephew of Pope Innocent X. Both churches had to be designed for tight, narrow spaces. One can walk from one church to the other in less than two minutes.

Because of its small size, San Carlo is often referred to as San Carlino and stands at a busy intersection marked by fountains on each of its four corners. The fountains themselves are a filthy mess, smeared black by the belching exhaust of countless cars and trucks. The church was Borromini's first commission and had to be built around the fountain, which was already in place. In size, the church of San Carlino is so small that it could fit, amazingly, inside one of the columns that support Saint Peter's dome.

After entering and crossing herself with holy water, Ericka stared at the dusty marble floor and then sat in one of the plain wooden pews. She bowed her head, closed her eyes. She'd resisted looking around as she entered, preferring instead to form an initial impression of the church from a fixed position. She knew Borromini was known for his use of geometry, that his designs were built around sets of triangles and ovals, rectangles and squares, and so she tried to push the theoretical aside and simply rely on her senses.

She was less than impressed. The interior of the church seemed drab, its dominant color a shade somewhere between gray and white, as if it were a drawing in a coloring book waiting for a child's crayons. She tried not to be distracted by the incessant noise of the traffic clattering by just outside the church's door.

The walls of the church undulated in rhythmic design, a series of dizzying waves, lifting her eyes from one surface to the next, up into the honeycombed coffers lining the oval dome, which seemed to hover over the church, as if unconnected. The eye then fell back down to the walls, which alternated between the concave and convex, and which seemed to have no actual corners. Indeed, from the outline of the entablature it seemed that Borromini designed the church with few right angles, more concerned with creating an uncluttered fluid open space, a sort of diamond with soothing, rounded edges. Ericka knew the Trinitarians who'd commissioned the church were a discalced order, which meant they walked barefoot and wore the poorest clothes, and had asked Borromini to design their church with the simplest and most modest materials. She pictured Saint Carlo Borromeo, the barefoot archbishop, tending to Milan's sick and dying, with the rope of his inevitable death dangling around his neck, and all at once like in the ending of one of the short stories that Ericka routinely taught – one of the brilliant pieces from James Joyce's *Dubliners* – the woman felt more than her mind understood and she experienced a sort of epiphany, and the humble church took on a sudden purity and elegance. Ericka felt a sweet regard for the dead man about whom she was now certain she could write.

In contrast, Sant'Andrea al Quirinale was a bejeweled theater, splendid beyond compare, stunning, breathtaking, a graceful showpiece, undeniably opulent, with magnificent marbles of so many rich colors Ericka could hardly keep count, topped by an elliptical golden dome made of hexagonal coffers filled with different types of flowers and the inevitable cherubs and putti peeking their playful little heads down upon the faithful. Entering the church gave Ericka the immediate impression of commanding width and space, nearly as if the chapels rounding the exterior walls were lifting her up. Inlaid mosaics on the church's floor mirrored the dome above and were set off by gold stanchions linked by red velvet ropes. The church was quite properly set back from the street and sidewalk, adjacent to a peaceful park, filled with gentle shafts of light softly filtering their way through the clear windows edging its ribbed dome.

One church was like a dazzling confection, shining in the window of Rome's finest pasticceria, the other a simple Communion wafer, perfectly formed, unleavened.

ERICKA WANDERED ABOUT in the general direction of the Tiber, thinking a walk might clear her head, and perhaps a nice lunch and glass of wine would be even better. She crossed bustling Via del Corso and headed up a side street to Via di Ripetta, where she stopped at a restaurant and ordered ravioli of pear served with a light melon-colored sauce made of blood oranges and Parmesan cheese. The drizzled line of balsamic dotting the side of her plate reminded her of the first panel of the dean's triptych. She ignored an older man's flirtations and drank a glass of crisp Greco di Tufo from Campania.

Walking north toward the Piazza del Popolo, she stopped before a storefront window crammed eerily with dozens of disjointed doll heads. All female. Every head a girl's. Some of the dolls held their eyes open, as if staring through their stiff lashes at passersby on the street, while others kept their eyes shut, embarrassed by the gaping holes beneath the stubs of their necks. Others had only empty holes where their eyes should have been. Several doll heads were cracked or broken and lay upside down or sideways. All were missing their hair. Ericka saw that the shop was a hospital, an establishment that specialized in the repair of damaged toys, as the sign above the door read *Ospedale delle Bambole*.

On a shelf above the jumble of heads stood several ceramic owls, each whole and intact, gazing out at the street or down at the broken remains of the girls who lay in the discarded heap below.

THE STORY ERICKA had promised to tell Sam the next night, had there been a second night, was her favorite. Of course the story was about her first love, since the best love stories focus on love when it's new. Ericka had read that the most serious threat to a marriage was renewed contact with a first lover. In her case it was a boy named Robbie, whom she'd met in college while dating her husband, Darryl, now her ex.

Robbie was a bad boy, a marginal student who seldom went to class, preferring instead to hang around the edges of campus, listen to music, and get high. He came from a working-class family, and in order to afford getting high he sold drugs. Weed, mainly, along with occasional chunks of gummy hash. Nothing you snorted or shot up with a needle. Just simple cannabis. Robbie purchased his cannabis by the kilo and processed it in his basement apartment with great care, breaking open each bundle and fastidiously removing the twigs and stems, then sifting the remains with a colander to filter out the seeds. He weighed out one-ounce baggies on the silver tray of a scale he stole from a university science lab, then sold his clean, honest lids to various friends and acquaintances at a price just high enough for him to be able to buy another kilo and have enough marijuana left over for his own use.

Darryl was conscientious, pre-law, a rigid straight arrow, conservative in an intelligent, über-articulate, William F. Buckley sort of way. Ericka admired him for his manners and for the fact that they often disagreed – entirely civilly, of course – on nearly every issue they discussed. Tracy and Hepburn, their friends called them, though Ericka had to explain the allusion to Darryl, who thought film a waste of time. He was a perfectly fine boyfriend who, Ericka's friends assured her, was an enviable catch, and in bed he was adequate. By the time Ericka met Robbie, she and Darryl were engaged.

The next part of the story was painful for Ericka to think about. Of course she found Robbie attractive and so she flirted with him, and he flirted back, and of course he was everything Darryl wasn't. Robbie was dark and daring, with an imaginative wit, though after he got high he grew increasingly quiet and introspective. He seldom argued. He loved film, particularly foreign film, French New Wave and Truffaut's *The 400 Blows*. He had a white dog, a deaf rescue boxer named Porkchop, whom he trained through a series of hand signals. Sometimes when she dropped by his apartment Ericka would find Robbie cradling the dog in his arms or talking to him with his hands or sometimes sitting by himself pressing his knees to his forehead, rocking back and forth. Once, Ericka found him actually crying. Weeping might be a better way to describe it, Ericka would tell the men she shared this story with, since Robbie didn't seem to cry normal tears but instead would rattle out a staccato of sobs, chest heaving. Soon she and Robbie found themselves entwined in the less-than-clean sheets on his bed, and at this point Ericka would pause and sigh, to imply what she still didn't want to admit, that their sex was the best she'd ever experienced. The first orgasms she'd ever had with someone occurred when she was with Robbie. Heavy emphasis on the plural. Orgasms so shattering she could replace the lone "s" in the word *orgasm* with a triple "z". It was then, during their afternoons of sex, that she could see the young man's bare back, which was striped by a crisscross of old marks or scars, a few the width of a belt. She'd leave these details out of her story because even thinking about Robbie's back made her want to cry, something she certainly wasn't willing to do in front of one of her on-the-road fucks.

What she'd tell the men was that Robbie touched her body with an attitude bordered on worship, with a tenderness edged with wonder that she'd never before, or since, felt. Then the touch would slowly shift toward a strength Ericka could describe only as a gentle firmness, like one color of the spectrum sliding imperceptibly into the next, and then with iron-hard confidence he would *take her*.

Of course even though Robbie fell in love with her, and she with him, Ericka married Darryl. What sensible young woman wouldn't? Outside of a bad Hollywood film, who would marry the boyfriend so void of ambition that he didn't even sell drugs for a profit? Sure, he'd trained a deaf boxer and bore on his back the marks of beatings he never discussed, but what did people think, she was a character in a cheesy romance? Ericka had goals. There were ladders in the world to climb, and she was going to climb them. On the afternoon she told Robbie about her decision to marry Darryl he said without hesitation that she was making a mistake, that he was certain she loved him more. Of course she could do whatever she wanted and he wouldn't interfere, though he was certain they'd see each other again.

He asked Ericka to pick a date, and when she refused he picked one for her, the night of her thirtieth birthday. On that night, he said, regardless of wherever she'd be living, he'd be waiting for her a block or so away, and all she'd have to do is walk out of her house if she wanted to see him again. And if she did, she could tell him then and there whether he was right or wrong about which of her two college boyfriends she truly loved.

Then Ericka and Darryl married and went on to graduate school, and after several years the young assistant professor in English Studies and the corporate lawyer befriending his way up through the ranks of his monkey gang woke up one morning on the opposite sides of bed and realized they had little in common. Fortunately, there were no children.

On the evening of her thirtieth birthday, Ericka was still living in the modest townhouse she'd shared with Darryl before their divorce. To celebrate she'd invited a dozen or so colleagues from her department. Angelo brought several bottles of Italian wine along with a tray of homemade pizzoccheri. The conversation that night centered around literary theory – the works of Vladimir Propp, Mikhail Bakhtin, Mieke Bal, and Gérard Genette as well as, of course, Todorov and Barthes.

In some versions of the story, Ericka said that she fled her party and found Robbie standing half a dozen houses away, smiling as he leaned against a tree with another deaf white boxer. He introduced the dog to Ericka in sign, and she and Robbie smiled at each other for several moments before they embraced. Then they shared the night – oh, what a night! – together. Ericka suggested to the men that she and Robbie reunited for a few months before breaking up again. Sometimes they made plans to live together, but on the eve of the move Robbie was killed in a tragic accident, usually one involving traffic. A long-haul trucker drifting off to sleep at the wheel. A doe and a pair of fawns dashing out from the darkness of a thick woods and then freezing in Robbie's headlights. Sometimes Ericka and Robbie were still working things out, living separately but hoping they still might get back together.

In an essay she worked on for a while but later abandoned, Ericka toyed with the concepts of fact and truth. Because in fact she didn't walk out of her house that evening, choosing instead to pour herself endless glasses of Barbaresco until her guests trickled out her front door and she stood alone in her house's stillness. She told herself that it would have been rude to leave her own party. Still, she knew that she'd stayed home because she feared that if she were to go out and look for Robbie she wouldn't find him. She knew she'd walk the streets, searching for him, till dawn. She'd rather never see him again than learn that he'd forgotten about her and his promise, that he'd allowed his life to move beyond hers, that he was happily living somewhere else, blissfully content with a wife and a couple of adorable kids and a dog that could hear him when he called its name.

Ericka needed the fiction – that part of story lying closest to truth – that Robbie was still out there, only a few houses away, and that he'd waited for her all night long and left only as the sun rose up from behind the roofs of the houses in the perfectly upper-middle-class neighborhood in which she'd lived, while the white dog on the end of his dark leather leash grew restless, and the morning birds tore the night's silent hem with their song.

THE GIRL WITH the thick black hair playing the organetto by the Ganges side of the fountain in the Piazza Navona glanced up and smiled as Ericka approached, then swung her long, wild curls back in that easy, fetching way that long-haired girls swing back their hair – a casual flick of her head over her shoulder. The gesture made Ericka think how much more lovely beauty was when it was unaware. The young woman's instrument had mother-of-pearl buttons and multicolored diamond designs marking its bellows. Though Ericka didn't recognize the song, she knew that most in the crowd around the girl found it familiar and that it greatly pleased them. She reminded Ericka of the pretties who sat at their desks in her classes, attentive, pens poised to write down the session's central points. Ericka dropped two euros into the girl's open cap, which lay on the ground alongside a few bright yellow clusters of mimosa.

The day was the Festa delle Donne, International Women's Day, and all across the city, on nearly every corner, vendors were selling bright yellow sprigs of mimosa. "Auguri alla signora!" each vendor cried as she passed. Ericka came to the piazza to visit Sant'Agnese in Agone, another church designed by Borromini. Ericka knew that the word *agone* had its roots in the Greek word *agon*, meaning *contest* or *competition*, a reference to Greece's Olympic games. At the center of every story lay agon, the struggle between a drama's central figure, its protagonist –

originally the leader of the chorus, now understood to be the first or principle actor – and antagonist – the first player's opposition. In fact, the long U-shaped piazza where Ericka now strolled took its name from such contests and was situated on the interior area of the ancient Stadium of Domitian, where since 86 CE athletic competitions were staged. Even the piazza's name, *Navona*, was a medieval combination and corruption of the words *in agon*.

As Ericka walked around the fountain, she studied the two figures legend claimed were Bernini's attempts to insult Borromini. The river-god Nile draped his head beneath a cloth, as if he couldn't bear the sight of Borromini's church, while the Rio de la Plata held out a hand, as if to protect himself from a building that, no doubt, was so poorly constructed it was certain to topple at any moment and crush him. Of course truth undid both stories since the fountain had been erected before the church.

The concave façade of Saint Agnes in Agony displayed Borromini's penchant for ripples and curves. Once inside, Ericka found herself enclosed in an exceedingly bright open octagon – Greek cross design – framed by a crypt and seven chapels filled with bas-relief sculptures, topped by a majestic dome rising above a circle of clerestory windows toward a tall lantern. The soft afternoon light poured generously from the lantern and the windows. On the wall opposite the doorway were two tables on which lay flyers announcing upcoming concerts to be held in the church's sacristy along with a scattering of holy cards and donation boxes for foreign missions and the survivors of the South-Asian tsunami of ten weeks ago. Ericka slid several euros into the boxes as she stared at the tragic photos of some of the tsunami's victims. In one photo, several bloated bodies floated facedown on a patch of calm gray-blue water. In another, a tumble of the dead, their skin darkened by the sun, lay knotted inside the yawning orange mouth of an excavator's bucket, waiting to be dropped into a nearby shallow mass grave.

As for the church, it seemed to Ericka both intimate and expansive. Its circular structure immediately enclosed her, and its concave altars drew her into their more defined spaces. Eight ribbed marble columns, ranging in color from caramel to maroon, separated the altars, which were off-white and framed by shorter green marble columns topped by gold pediments. The vertical lines of the many columns pulled the eye upward into a field of sharper color, rich variations of browns and golds.

Ericka crossed herself and knelt in a pew opposite a woman reciting the rosary. She stared at the dark wooden beads dangling from the woman's hands as she listened to the woman's whispers, prayers in a language foreign to Ericka's ears. Slavic, Ericka guessed. The beads of the woman's rosary ticked softly as they swayed against the back of the pew in front of the woman as she prayed. As Ericka took out the blue glass beads of her rosary and made the sign of the Cross, the woman turned toward her and gazed at her blue rosary and then at Ericka, and then their eyes met. Ericka flushed, held by the woman's dark eyes. The pair knelt together for the next half hour, fingers moving from one bead and knot to the next. Their whispered prayers took on the same cadence. After the woman completed her rosary and crossed herself and stood, she turned fully toward Ericka and smiled and then whispered something Ericka didn't quite hear.

SAINT AGNES'S CHAPEL was to Ericka's right, at three o'clock if the church were a timepiece, having been moved from the church's center closer to the spot where the saint had actually been killed. Borromini had erected the church on the site of an ancient brothel adjacent to the Stadium of Domitian. The church even shared a few of the brothel's original walls.

Born into a noble Roman family, Agnes was barely twelve and apparently so lovely that a powerful Roman prefect chose her to be married to his son. Having already joined the cult of Christianity and taken a vow to live the life of a virgin – both decisions made with her parents' consent – the girl refused the proposal. The Roman family then denounced her and had her sentenced to death. Since Roman law at the time didn't permit the execution of virgins, the prefect ordered that Agnes be taken to the Stadium of Domitian brothel where she would be presented to a group of Roman soldiers before being killed. Presented? Let's drop the euphemism. Where the barely twelve-year-old child would be gang-raped.

According to the stories related about Agnes's death, while the soldiers stripped the girl of her clothing her hair grew so long that it concealed her nudity, and each soldier who attempted to touch her was struck blind. In some versions of the story, the soldiers regained their sight after the child looked up to the heavens and prayed. In other versions the prefect's son fell dead but returned to life after Agnes prayed for him. In any event the young girl was tied to a stake where piles of wood were stacked around her feet, yet after the wood was set ablaze the flames parted, refusing to touch her flesh. After the girl loosened her bounds and stepped away, the soldiers drew out their swords and beheaded her.

Ericka knew that Agnes of Rome's story followed the basic narrative of other virgin martyrs. Lucia of Syracuse, Agatha of Sicily, Catherine of Alexandria, Juliana of Nicodemia, Euphemia of Chalcedon, Gundenis of Carthage, Cecelia of Rome, the Forty Virgin Martyrs of Thrace – the list goes on and on, into the hundreds, likely the thousands. Young women, nearly all in their teens, followers of Christ's teachings, threatened with marriage, unwanted sex. After their refusals, they were seized and raped and murdered. Little wonder as the stories of their lives were retold details of miraculous interventions crept into their narratives. Little wonder the fantastic replaced the horrors these brave young women endured.

Both Saint Augustine and Thomas Aquinas maintained that virgins who are raped retain their virginity, even if the consequence of rape results in birth. Aquinas wrote that in Heaven raped virgin martyrs are given a second golden crown of light – a second aureole – that bestows upon them a special share in the Almighty's divine powers.

THE MARBLE STATUE of Agnes in the church showed an older, obviously clothed, full-figured woman walking through the flames, which mercifully leaned away from her. The figure's arms were spread open as she gazed toward the sky. A wind blew back her cloak.

Ericka wished the figure were more faithful to the stories. The girl should be much younger, covered only by her hair, and obviously frightened, but Ericka realized that the statue had been commissioned and designed by men, and what did men know of the terror of a twelve-year-old girl about to be killed? What did men know of young women who desired to be the agents of their own bodies? Indeed, the lazy sculptor who'd created the piece copied for his design the bottom half of – what else? – one of Bernini's angels, one of the several standing on the Ponte Sant'Angelo, the pedestrian bridge spanning the Tiber, linking the city to the Castel Sant'Angelo. Ericka walked closer toward the statue, asking the saint for forgiveness. She knew that other images of Saint Agnes depicted her as a girl holding a lamb, the symbol of purity. Like all children raised Roman Catholic, Ericka was taught that Agnes was the patron saint of chastity. Later, as Ericka wrote about Agnes, Ericka learned that Agnes was also the patron saint of survivors of rape and sexual abuse.

Directly opposite the statue, at nine o'clock on the timepiece, was the chapel of Saint Sebastian. The martyred soldier stood in his typical pose, tied to the trunk of a tree, arrows piercing his shoulder, neck, chest, legs. His helmet, shield, and breastplate lay at his feet. Unlike other images of the saint, this Sebastian wasn't depicted as weak. This Sebastian had keen eyes and a strong chin that jutted out at the viewer, as if in defiance of the pain he was enduring. His legs were thickly muscled, his broad chest clearly defined. Ericka noted that he was staring directly across the church at the young virgin walking boldly through the flames. She wondered if the pair had been positioned opposite each other intentionally.

While Sebastian was a highly regarded captain in Diocletian's army, he was also a convert to Christianity who regularly used his position of power to help others imprisoned by Diocletian to escape persecution and death. Shot with so many arrows legend claimed his body resembled a sea urchin's, he was left for dead but then nursed back to health by Saint Irene of Rome, who, like Mary Magdalene had with Christ, came to claim his corpse only to find him still alive. Once Sebastian regained his strength he presented himself again to the emperor, who ordered his men to bludgeon the Christian to death. Because of this, Sebastian is known as the saint who was martyred twice.

Even though Sebastian died three years before Agnes was born, Ericka wondered what might have occurred had he been in command of the soldiers charged with taking Agnes to the brothel. No doubt Sebastian would have defended her and fought valiantly.

Ericka felt torn. Part of her identified with the brave young woman who stepped through fire while another part of her embraced the tenacity of the soldier tied to a tree and pierced with scores of arrows. A sudden pop of light flashed over the statue's determined face. Ericka looked around for the photographer as the church door behind her swung open and the outside world rushed back into the church. She heard the jumbled noise from the piazza and for a half-moment pictured her desk in her hotel room and thought that just to be safe she should run the antivirus program on her laptop a second time, and that prompted her to remember Angelo's email and the meeting scheduled to discuss and no doubt approve the advancement of his nephew's bid for early tenure and promotion, and that led her to think of the university's power pyramid and the hopeful toadlets madly wriggling their little tails toward the lily pad, which led to thoughts of the vervets and the rule of the monkey gang and the two token female candidates who deserved but weren't offered LaRue's position, and then Ericka pictured the magnificent fountain and the figures of its four river gods along with the sweet, clear face of the young woman who sat at its edge as she keyed the notes and softly pumped the bellows of her organetto. As Ericka stared at Sebastian, she knew what she should do.

"ARE YOU ABLE to speak and write in English?" Ericka asked the young organetto player. "I can pay you well for a couple of hours of your time. More than you'd earn here in a day."

Ericka learned that the dark-eyed girl's name was Chiara, and yes, she was able to speak English and could write in English but of course she would require assistance, since in English so many of its vowels remained hidden, silent, like children crouching inside the closed doors of wardrobes playing a mean game, unlike Italian, where nearly every child romped out in the open air, happily shouting its own name.

Chiara was from Ferentino, a mountain town southeast of Rome, where her father and three brothers worked in a factory. She lived with her two aunts in Ostiense. Each aunt was known for the delicacy of her embroidery, though the older aunt, Teresina, was losing her sight. It was as if a white flower was blooming in the center of her vision, Chiara told Ericka as the pair purchased stationery and a pen from a bookstore on Corso del Rinascimento. The two women walked along an alleyway past its gelato and pizza shops to the Piazza della Rotonda, where they sat beneath a wide umbrella at a table in a café overlooking the steps of the Pantheon. While white-coated waiters carried trays bearing ruby-red glasses of wine to the café's patrons, Ericka considered how she might begin her dictation.

Water splashed from the mouths of the figures in the fountain in the center of the square. A blinkered horse and carriage stood before the Pantheon's steps, awaiting the next riders. A bearded monk in a hooded robe sauntered by, wearing leather sandals and white socks, munching on a panino he'd purchased from the nearby salumeria.

The rubber wheels of a stuffed suitcase pulled by an impressively overweight North American then clattered loudly by on the sampietrini just a few feet away from where Ericka and Chiara were sitting. The clearly confused man called to them for directions to Campo de' Fiori. Before Chiara could help him, a pair of women walking arm in arm by the fountain answered him. One woman was slim, slight, Asian – the other was Italian and obviously pregnant, her dark hair pulled back by two colorful combs in the shape of chameleons, their long red tongues tasting the air. The thin woman was happily telling the pregnant woman that she'd received permission to remain for the remainder of the school year in Rome, where she could study the methods developed in Maria Montessori's original Casa dei Bambini, as the fat man repeated in a woeful voice that he was hopelessly lost and needed help. Then the pregnant woman pointed south and angled her hand west, and the teacher repeated the instructions so the man was sure to understand.

Ericka asked Chiara to identify herself as a student in the university's overseas study program in Florence, whose travel away from the States had given her the courage to write to the dean with her concerns. She hoped the administrator would respect her request for anonymity. All she wanted, really, was to bring an unfortunate situation to light. The girl's letter then chronicled the sequence of events involving LaRue that had been related to Ericka. She made certain Chiara included the details of the special assignment of a personal nature, the subsequent visit to his apartment near campus, and the fancy lead-crystal glasses and talk of poets and their fondness for absinthe along with the liquor that tasted of licorice, that turned milky after the professor added a cube or two of ice.

The letter ran a couple of tissue-thin pages and contained a sufficient number of colloquialisms to mimic the writing of an undergraduate. Ericka had Chiara end the letter with the admission that the writer was sad and confused and felt bad about what she'd done, or what had been done to her. She really wasn't sure about the difference. Yet she knew this was also happening to others. Being so far away now, in this beautiful Italian city, she wrote, sort of gives me the courage to speak out. And though it's probably partly my fault I think this sort of thing shouldn't happen in a university, should it? I mean what my professor did, what happened to me.

As she wrote each phrase that Ericka dictated, the soft pink tip of Chiara's tongue stuck out of the right side of her mouth, then quickly licked her bottom lip and then her top lip, always in the same order, before retreating back into her mouth. As Chiara bent over the paper carefully writing each word, Ericka thought the habit was delightful and at the same time sad since the girl was precisely the sort who, if she found her way into one of LaRue's poetry workshops, regardless of her talent would be invited to his office. The girl was like a perfectly ripe fruit, a firm and juicy peach or apricot, at the very peak of her succulence. Ericka then noticed that the girl's foot beneath their table was tapping time.

"I'm glad you're a musician," Ericka told Chiara after the girl addressed the envelope and licked it closed, as Ericka handed her an extravagant amount of money, which at first Chiara refused, saying it was too much, then happily stuffed into a zippered pocket inside her jacket. "Stay away from writing," Ericka added, "and writing teachers, if you can."

The young woman smiled. "There is no need of worry for that," she said, shaking her head. She looked down at her hands and the pen and extra sheets of paper on the table, then gave out a nervous laugh. "Writing. I am never any good at it. In all my years of schooling, I don't like writing."

"Give it time," Ericka said, patting Chiara's shoulder. "I was only joking."

Now that she had the letter, was it morally right to send it?

Ericka knew her Augustine, his arguments against lying in *De Mendacio*, his clear insistence that it was immoral to lie in any circumstance, even to save an innocent life. She found herself walking past the Pantheon and the church of Santa Maria sopra Minerva and Bernini's quaint little elephant gracing the front of the Piazza della Minerva's extravagant hotel, past Gammarelli's, beneath the Madonna's overhanging shrine, down Via dei Cestari, its shop windows bright with variously colored chasubles, glistening gold monstrances, and silver chalices, where two boys – identical twins – smartly played Vivaldi doubles on their violins. She walked across the furious traffic on Corso Vittorio to the Area Sacra di Largo Argentina, where a dozen or more cats roamed the tall grasses edging the ancient temples' ruins, and where open tins of sardines and cat food lay on a marble slab beneath a sign made barely readable by the recent rains. Ericka was aware of the eighth commandment, which forbade the bearing of false witness. Yet was the witness false? She was certain the narrative in the letter she now possessed was true.

She continued walking, deeper into Rome's Ghetto, and soon found herself in a small piazza beside a fountain in which four naked young men – ephebes – balanced themselves against its pedestal while resting one foot on the head of a dolphin. With their opposite hand they helped four turtles above their heads slide back into the pond of a large bowl. Water gushed from each dolphin's mouth. Ericka found the composition both arresting and lovely. Yes, the letter's story was true, she'd argue to Saint Augustine were he to appear suddenly beside her as she gazed at the fountain, though she knew immediately that he'd counter by saying that since the young organetto player was not one of the lascivious poet's students her testimony was false. And therefore her testimony was immoral. A clear lie.

Antique Jewish symbols – several stone menorahs and Stars of David – studded a wall as Ericka walked down a narrow street toward the Tiber. To her left towered the Tempio Maggiore, Rome's magnificent and imposing Great Synagogue. Soon Ericka was crossing the Ponte Fabricio – the bridge from Rome to Tiber Island – and as she stood in the little piazza between the Fatebenefratelli Hospital and the iron gates outside San Bartolomeo all'Isola she recalled reading the headlines about the Roman doctor Vittorio Sacerdoti, who, not quite a year before, on the sixtieth anniversary of Rome's liberation, admitted that he'd hidden as many Jews inside the Fatebenefratelli Hospital's wards as he could. When the Nazis occupying Rome discovered the Jews and tried to take them away, Sacerdoti claimed they were his patients and that they suffered from a contagious disease – *K Syndrome* – Sacerdoti called it, naming it for the infamous Nazi commander Field Marshal Albert Kesselring. The Roman doctor instructed the Jews to hold their chests and cough loudly whenever the Nazi soldiers neared. "They fled like rabbits," the doctor remembered. Forty-five lives were saved.

A sudden breeze from the south tumbled a waxed gelato cup in the church's courtyard. Ericka could hear the *NEE-eu, NEE-eu, NEE-eu* of an ambulance. The sound grew increasingly louder as it approached. A cloud of starlings broke from the nearby trees on the Trastevere side of the Tiber and wheeled, darkening the sky. Ericka looked beyond the screeching birds and then down at the river's muddy, churning waters, listening to its constant rushing thunder.

Yes, she thought, the brave Italian doctor had lied to the Nazis. Yes, the boys balancing themselves on the heads of dolphins were pushing the falling turtles back into the safety of the fountain's bowl. Yes, the muscular Sebastian was striding boldly toward Agnes as she did her best to escape the flames. Only the cowardly stood by while innocents were being mistreated. Only cowards made aware of injustices remained silent.

EARLY THE NEXT morning Ericka took a taxi to the Stazione Termini, where she caught an express to Florence, and where she stood with Chiara's letter before a red postal box, hesitating as she again considered Augustine's argument. After pausing at a food stand for a lampredotto, then at a café for a glass of wine, she returned to Rome.

She felt even more excited about Borromini and her project after visiting Sant'Ivo alla Sapienza. Like San Carlino, Sant'Ivo was a precious gem. One had to come in off the street and enter through the gates of a long courtyard, flanked by twin rows of columns supporting the balconies of the adjoining building, the Palazzo della Sapienza.

Typical of Borromini, the small white church was a wonderfully immaculate swirl built around a hexagonal star, a mix of concave and convex surfaces that delighted its visitors as its curves lifted one's gaze to the bright center of its white dome. Perfect in its simplicity, its interior seemed to Ericka among the least ornate and embellished churches she'd seen in the Eternal City. The immediate impression Sant'Ivo gives the viewer is one of height, along with light – the purest of light – since nearly everything in the church is white. The church itself is so contained that it seemed to Ericka smaller than the main altars of several other churches she'd visited. After she walked back outside and stood out in the courtyard, she gazed up at Sant'Ivo's spire, at the lantern topping the church's dome, which spun itself into the sky like a corkscrew. She knew that some compared the lantern to a twist of whipped cream or the abdomen of a bee complete with its stinger, but to Ericka the swirling spire rising to a narrow point crowned by a cross seemed more like a winding staircase.

She paused in the center of the courtyard and took the whole space in, thinking that perhaps the true entrance to the church was the gateway by the sidewalk and street. She saw that the Sapienza courtyard was similar to a classic church's nave. Given this perspective, Sant'Ivo was perhaps less a church than it was a main altar.

She would research the idea, she thought, return to San Carlino and Sant'Agnese, do her best to put her impressions into words. She was certain that in the architecture of each of Rome's churches lay a narrative, a story she could tell. And inside each church and sacred site lay more narratives, revealed by their commissioned art, their paintings and statues, each of which held stories waiting patiently for the eye to discover.

Ericka stared again at Sant'Ivo's concave façade, then allowed her eyes to rise up the spire's staircase and gaze at the cross. It made a dark outline against the sky. A pair of gulls cried out to each other – *skwee skwee skwee* – as their wings sliced the air. Behind her she could hear the sounds of the rushing traffic out on the street, then someone shouting a girl's name, followed by the eager command "Andiamo!"

Ericka obeyed, walking out through the gate onto the sidewalk, smiling now at the cool, bright day.

THE EMAIL FROM Angelo arrived in her inbox a week later. Strangely the message bore no heading, as if Angelo – a man never known to be short of words – didn't quite know how to summarize what he had to announce. But there in his usual Book Antiqua Bold Italic font, above his usual signature block about Giambattista Palatino, the famous sixteenth-century Italian master of calligraphy, was a notice that the department meeting previously scheduled to discuss the early tenure and promotion of Jason Lee LaRue had been cancelled, at the request of the Office of the Dean.

Campo de' Fiori

Rome, 12 August 2003

Giorgio was a small man, dark, with a graying mustache and an exceptionally polite demeanor. He wore black cuffed pants held up by suspenders, shiny black shoes, and a starched white shirt buttoned up to the neck. Every inch the Roman proprietor.

Though he did his best not to show it, Giorgio was incredulous when he met Dubravka at his door. To hear the shabbily dressed woman inform him in Croatian that two decades ago in Međugorje she'd met his older sister, Anđela, and had come now to see her and return her rosary, when Anđela was twenty-one years in the grave. I'm sorry but you're mistaken, Giorgio told the confused woman in an even voice, but then out of manners and consideration of the expression on her face and her unfortunate clothing he invited her into the pensione's parlor, insisting she put her pack down and sit. Then he did his best to gather himself as he excused himself from the room.

On the wall over the parlor's wide sofa and end tables and chairs hung several old photographs of Giorgio's family in ornate silver frames. Dubravka tried to remember what Anđela had looked like. She recalled only the smell of church incense and the rouge on the woman's cheeks. Above the photos was a mahogany cross, and to one side an antique map of Rome, the Tiber winding its way up through the city like an engorged snake. Dubravka stared at the bump of land in the river's midsection where it bulged, marking Tiber Island. The room smelled of the polish used to shine and preserve fine wood. Also, a hint of dust. After several minutes Giorgio returned with a pair of glasses and a bottle of brandy. Here, he said, before you leave, let us drink.

Dubravka declined Giorgio's offer. Thank you, she said, no. But please, don't allow my abstinence to interfere with your pleasure.

After leaving the convent, Dubravka vowed abstinence. The decision had been anything but easy, though over time it became inevitable. What Dubravka told others was that she'd discussed the concern with her confessor, who'd also come to the conclusion to abstain from drink after reading a book and attending a series of meetings. What Dubravka didn't describe were the afternoons when she lost sense of time and burned the bread, the evening when she drank so much wine she vomited on the burners atop the main stove. The days when the convent was busy with visitors and she omitted some key ingredient in a dish, the morning in the convent's church when she stood up from the communion railing, with the Eucharist resting freshly upon her tongue, and lost consciousness, falling to the floor in a heap. Sometimes when God grows weary of whispering, Dubravka thought later on, God speaks with a firmer voice.

Two servant sisters had to help Dubravka stand, an effort she obstinately resisted, while the others in her community did their best to ignore her and return to their prayers. That was how the others treated her – they ignored her many failings and prayed. It was only after the sisters walked Dubravka back to the dormitory, where they stripped her of her veil and tunic and placed her beneath a spurting shower, its cold punch insistently pounding her head and back, that Dubravka shivered and cried out as she vomited the wine she'd drank that morning along with the remnants of the Host she'd just received.

That was the moment. The bottom. The white shreds of the Body of Christ lying for an instant before her in a pool of swirling water and wine-stained vomit, then rushing down the dark hole of the drain.

GIORGIO SET THE glasses and bottle of brandy on the coffee table that rested between them. Of course, he said. Forgive me. Your abstinence. I was not aware.

There's nothing to forgive, Dubravka said. Please. Drink. I insist.

He left his glass untouched as Dubravka asked again about Anđela. Giorgio offered no reply. Though Dubravka felt the obvious tension in the room, she continued nonetheless. I've come to return her rosary, Dubravka said evenly. The day we met in Međugorje she handed me her rosary and gave me a card with your name and the pensione's address. She wrote something on the back for you to read, but unfortunately I no longer have it.

No, Giorgio said firmly, then did his best to smile. I'm very sorry, but no. You are mistaken. My pensione has never had a business card. His eyes met Dubravka's, then looked past her and at the door. You're obviously confusing my sister with someone else, some other woman named Anđela. You'll agree it's a common name. My sister was never in Međugorje.

But we walked up the mountain together, Dubravka said. And she told me about you and your family and this place.

Impossible, Giorgio said. He shook his head and then added, I don't understand what mean trick you're trying to play.

For several moments Dubravka didn't know what to think. I'm playing no trick, she said. What would make you think I'm trying to trick you?

She was tempted to stand and pick up her pack and leave. Clearly she'd made an error, she thought, come to the wrong pensione owned by the wrong former Croat on Campo de' Fiori. Was it possible there was another? The man sitting in the chair across from her grew still, unmoving, like a statue. She watched his starched white shirt breathe patiently in and out.

I'm sorry to insist, Dubravka said, but then how else could it be that I'm here? How else do I know these things if what you say is true? Your sister took my arm. She told me she'd come to Međugorje for a vial of holy water for your dying wife.

Giorgio laughed in surprise. I've never taken a wife.

He shook his head again and stood, smoothing the front of his pants as he tried to decide what to think, what next to do. The vial of holy water had been a joke between them, something Anđela would say to deflect her true reason for wanting to go to Međugorje – to seek a cure for herself. Yes, of course, how generous of you, holy water for my wife, Giorgio would agree. Yes, my wife is in need of holy water, and then the brother and sister would laugh, pretending for a while that Anđela wasn't dying. She'd left Rome for Međugorje a year after the apparitions began – 1982, he remembered – but succumbed to her illness on the way there, in Campobasso, where the family had once lived, and where she was now buried. Giorgio himself picked out the stone.

I'll drink, Giorgio said as he walked from the room, but only if I don't drink alone. After a while he returned with a tray on which sat a demitasse of coffee and a small spoon and a bowl of sugar cubes. Forgive my delay, he said. The young woman who worked here left recently to marry. As Dubravka drank her coffee, Giorgio sipped his brandy.

The pair sat together silently. From the next room a grandfather clock loudly clicked.

Dubravka watched the man drink and then decided that after she finished her coffee she'd give him the rosary and leave. There was nothing else to do or say. She wouldn't argue or mention the miracle of the bloody handkerchief, a miracle that Dubravka still remembered and believed in. She knew it would only open herself to ridicule, like the story of her fever and how she'd died and come back to life. She wouldn't press the issue about her having met Anđela. An obviously pregnant cat then strolled into the room, after walking around a bit as if she owned the place, and curled beside Dubravka's feet.

A neighbor's, Giorgio said, gesturing toward the animal with his glass. I fear that if she has her kittens here I'll have to keep one. Unlike Croatia, here in Rome cats have certain birthrights.

Dubravka drew the dark beads of the rosary out from her pocket. Here, she said. Giorgio leaned forward and took the rosary from her hand. For a moment he let its length dangle in the air, then put down his glass and slowly dropped the beads into the cup of his open palm.

I can remember once buying a rosary something like this for Anđela, Giorgio said. He ran his fingers through the beads, then stopped cold. Again he rose, asking Dubravka to wait, and returned with a large magnifying glass and sat again as he studied the back of the silver crucifix for an engraving.

This can't be, Giorgio said. He glanced at Dubravka, then back at the rosary. No, this isn't possible. How did you come by this?

She was coughing blood into her handkerchief and she handed it to me, Dubravka said. On Mount Križevac, while we prayed the Stations of the Cross.

In Međugorje. While the two of you prayed.

Yes.

No, Giorgio said, as tears began to fill his eyes.

Dubravka bowed her head and crossed herself.

Anđela was buried with this rosary, Giorgio said, looking up now at Dubravka. I myself wrapped it between her fingers in her folded hands.

THE PAIR MOVED into a back room, as the pensione's guests passed in and out through the parlor. So what would someone have me do now? Giorgio asked. He studied Dubravka's face. Believe you? Believe this? He raised the rosary beads in his hand. Exhume the body?

If that's your desire, Dubravka said. But as for me, I think I should leave.

No, Giorgio said, that makes no sense. Digging up the coffin as well as your leaving. He shook his head. And, now that I think, there was a time when she wanted the pensione to have business cards. I believe she may even have gone to a printer and had designs made.

I can't help you anymore, Dubravka said. Do what you'd like. Believe what you want. I've told you everything I know.

ALL THAT COMES to my mind is the story of the mother in Molise, Giorgio said. The pair had sat for several minutes in silence in the back room, where there was a wooden table and chairs. In San Giuliana di Puglia, Giorgio continued. A woman's son and daughter were buried in layers of concrete after an earthquake. Perhaps you know that in the last century Italy has suffered a tragic series of tremors and quakes. Without thinking this woman rushed to where her children lay and pushed aside several heavy slabs and freed them. To move the blocks again the town's workers had to use a crane. He shook his head. Tell me, how was that possible?

You answered the question yourself, Dubravka said. You said she did it without thinking. She saw what needed to be done and believed she could do it, and then did it.

So the impossible –

Sometimes becomes possible. Without our needing to understand how.

She died of a disease of the lungs, Giorgio said after he stood and paced the room and stared out a back window before turning. But I imagine you saw that.

Dubravka nodded.

Of course she didn't think the trip to Međugorje would cure her, but then again, a true believer, she was fond of saying that one can never tell. What one's faith can do. How far faith can take one's body. He paused. Me, I'm more someone who depends on what he's told by doctors.

Doctors, Dubravka said.

Giorgio shrugged. When you think about it, they're the only strangers we willingly undress for. We let them poke us this way, that way. In their hands we are lumps of clay. We let them do anything they want to us. They give us a jar of pills and we thank them and put them in our mouths. And so when we visit a doctor and are given a death sentence, we do what we've always done, what we've been taught to do since we were children – we obey. They tell us we have a year remaining, we live for another year. They tell us six months, we hang on for six months.

He sipped his brandy. So what should I conclude? To be honest – Giorgio looked warmly now at Dubravka as he spoke – I'm afraid to speculate. The steps of my thoughts fill me with fear. Yes, without doubt, this is my sister's rosary – he rolled the beads in his hands – of that there is no question. How else could the back of the crucifix be engraved as I had it engraved? But since it was handed to you and you've prayed with it for twenty years, I can only conclude that Anđela intended the rosary now to be yours.

LATER, GIORGIO TOOK out an album and showed Dubravka pictures of Anđela and the others in their family. In the album were photos of Anđela and Giorgio's younger sister, Katya, who died when she was nearly three. Giorgio grew silent then, stroking his mustache as he poured himself another brandy. For several moments he counted on his fingers as the room in which the pair looked at the photographs slowly darkened. From where Dubravka sat she could look out a window and see a slice of the Roman sky. Fever, Giorgio said finally. We had a priest come out who gave her the Last Rites. We buried her the following morning. Had she lived – he hesitated – I'm guessing she'd be about your age.

Dubravka touched Giorgio's hands and said nothing.

Rest, Giorgio told Dubravka as he smiled. Soon we will eat. He stared again at the album, then closed the book and sighed. There's so much. Your coming here, my mind, it's become too full. I imagine that after your years in the convent you have a far better understanding of these things than I do. Though I don't know how it was possible, I can't not think that Anđela somehow sent you here. In any case, you're here and you're welcome to stay. Stay for as long as you'd like, for as long as you desire to remain in Rome.

A YEAR OR so later, after the morning of the South-Asian tsunami, before Allison cut her hair and gave Dubravka the expensive cranberry-colored jacket in exchange for her cloth coat and azure scarf, Allison asked Dubravka about prayer.

Allison had been reading articles about experiments conducted with cultures grown on agar-agar in petri dishes, as well as other experiments that placed identical plants side by side beneath identical artificial lights. Half of the cultures and plants were ignored, left to their own devices. The other half were targets of prayer. These were double-blind, sometimes triple-blind experiments. To the scientists' surprise, the cultures and plants that were the targets of thoughts and prayer visibly thrived while the ones that were ignored struggled.

Dubravka nodded. All that prayer is, really, is focused energy, she said. You do know that I prayed special for you. The day after the morning of the tsunami, when we first met on the Piazza Navona, and you were telling me about some film.

The Double Life, Allison said.

The double life, Dubravka repeated and smiled.

Do you know what happens after you pray for a person?

I know what happened to you. You walked from where we met to Sant'Ignazio.

You knew that then?

No, of course not. I'm not a psychic. You told me that later on. But at the time I knew that you weren't going to go back to your hotel room to watch more films.

Then Allison asked if carrying out the vows Dubravka had taken was hard.

The vow of poverty was easy, Dubravka answered, because I've never really had money. As for chastity, though I was once tempted, that type of love hasn't been part of my life. Obedience was challenging because I fear I'm headstrong – they had me scrubbing floors for nearly a full year – though eventually they put me to work in the kitchen and came to enjoy and rely upon my bread. After the first few years I grew used to them and came to rely on them as well. I fell into a routine of meditation and prayer. As for the convent's silence, I've never been much of a conversationalist. Besides, nearly all of us spoke with our eyes.

But the enclosure, Dubravka told Allison, toward the end the convent's enclosure became an everyday struggle. Once, one of the lay servants came into the kitchen and whispered that she'd passed a full half hour watching a kestrel fly over a field, hunting, hovering patiently, wings spread, holding its place in the air, until the bird swooped down and then rose up from the grass with its prey writhing in its claws. The thought of the sight made me nearly cry out with envy. I came to miss the most trivial things, things that survived only in my memory. The sound of dogs barking in the alley outside Zagorac's. The sea splashing against the walls of Dubrovnik's harbor. The morning calls to prayer from the two mosques. The laughter of children at play. Music. Sevdalinka. I missed the sight of others walking about, each soul in their separate world, bearing the cross of their own private burdens as they hurried along the Stradun. I missed the limitless sky. Leaves fluttering on trees. Birds flocking on a piazza. All of the things we on the outside of cloistered walls take for granted, that many of us ignore as we walk about obsessing about this and that, weaving our sticky spider webs of worry and self-doubt, thinking about anything other than what is there before us, before our eager senses.

La Scala Sancta

Rome, 2 April 2005

As Blake knelt on the hard wooden plank covering the first of the twenty-eight steps of the Scala Sancta – the marble staircase Christ was said to have climbed on his way to Pontius Pilate's praetorium, where he was condemned to be crucified – he thought his life had taken on its true meaning the day he learned about the cord of Saint Joseph.

A missionary priest came to talk to Blake's high-school football team one afternoon after practice. The visitor was a rugged man who began by describing how priests dress to say Mass. Blake already knew most of the details, having witnessed the procedure hundreds of times as an altar boy at his Chicago North Side parish. After the priest puts on the alb – the white robe worn over the cassock – he ties the alb at his waist with a cincture, a long rope-like cord with knotted, tasseled ends. The cincture, the visitor explained, was a symbol of the priest's vow of chastity. The cord of Saint Joseph was a type of cincture, the priest told the team as he handed each of the boys a thin, resilient length of cotton cord. Each cord was knotted in six places, and if the young men who sat on the wooden benches in the locker room before him chose to accept the challenge they were to tie a seventh knot into it as they wrapped it around their hips. The knots were there to remind the boys to remain chaste.

Wear it at belt level, the priest advised, and don't tie it too tightly. Each day as you dress, say the Glory Be seven times, touching each knot as you pray. Add a prayer to Saint Joseph, guardian of virgins. If at night lying in bed you find yourself thinking about touching yourself, press the knots on the cords instead. And if you're out on a date and are tempted to commit an impure act, move about until you can feel the knots press against your skin. Let the sensations be a reminder of Christ's suffering and your commitment to chastity.

The next day after practice, as the team took off their pads and headed for the showers, Blake saw that about half of the boys wore the cord. By week's end the number who hadn't cut the annoying thing off was down to a handful. Truth was, the knots did much more than press against your skin. The knots dug painfully into your flesh, particularly if you wore a pair of tight pants. The knots rubbed your skin raw during scrimmages and games after you tightened your hip pads. The last thing I need when I'm trying to block a charging linebacker is a reminder not to jerk off, the boys said. Several boys, Blake included, already had obvious bruises on their hips.

"*OH MY JESUS!*" Blake whispered, reciting the prayer prescribed for the first step. It was early morning, the second day of April, and only he and two others were beginning the climb up the Scala Sancta on their knees. "*By the anguish of heart thou didst experience on separating from thy most holy mother to go to thy death, have mercy on me!*"

TRADITIONAL STAIRCASES FOR those who didn't want to ascend the steps on their knees bookended the planked stairway, which was walled in by paintings depicting key moments in Christ's Passion. The Holy Stairs were further enclosed by a domed ceiling, so the penitent beginning the ascent had the impression of entering a rising tunnel. The concept underlying the shrine was to share Christ's suffering in some minor way – to trace the Savior's steps, humbly, with devotion and set prayers, on one's knees. It was said that Martin Luther ascended the steps on his knees, but when he neared the top he hesitated and questioned the act's meaning. Above the landing at the top of the staircase where Luther's faith was overtaken by doubt was a fresco of the Crucifixion and beneath it the Sancta Sanctorum, a richly designed chapel once used exclusively by the pope. The chapel was laden with relics and closed off to the public, though one could snatch a view of it by looking through a metal grate.

Blake had played offensive left guard and was a more than reliable starter. He understood blocking and pulling schemes and took pride in what most interior linemen eventually realized – the admiration and cheers of the crowd would never come their way. Theirs were galaxies away from star positions. The best thing an offensive lineman could do on the field was avoid notice, and so Blake did his very best not to be noticed. Commit a penalty or let your man slip your block and everyone saw your failure. Jog back to the huddle and listen to the quarterback chew your ass for your mistake.

In the huddle all Blake wanted to hear were the signals indicating the next play and the words *Nice block there, Blake. Good hole, Blake. Way to play, Blake. Way to play.* Blake knew his place and embraced it with great happiness. His job in life was to hear the words *Way to play.* He understood at an early age that on the chessboard of life he was hardly a piece standing tall in the first row, with the bishops and knights, the rooks and the king and the queen. He was simply one of the anonymous pawns whose duty was to protect and assist the more powerful players. He was there on his square to serve others.

He knew what his coaches meant when they shouted that only losers love the dirt. Winners stayed upright, on their feet, and once they fired off the line they pushed forward, elbows out, thumbs up, hands targeting the opponent's numbers, with force and drive. They kept their feet moving, always moving. Blake believed winners endured without complaint the purpling bruises – and, later, the sores and seeping blood – that came with wearing the cord of Saint Joseph.

Blake took pride in wearing the cord throughout the entire season, and it was only after he put on weight the following spring and had to move up a couple of pant sizes that he cut the cord off and burned it ceremoniously in his backyard. Blake set fire to his cord one evening while his parents were off drinking at a neighborhood barbeque. He recited prayers of thanks to Saint Joseph as he set the match to it. Then he went inside the house and undressed and showered and recited the Glory Be seven times as he knotted on a brand new cord he'd ordered from a religious supply store, a cord white as the flowers blooming on his mother's dogwood tree.

"*Oh my Jesus!*" Blake sighed as he lifted his knees onto the second step. "*By the confusion thou didst feel and that caused thee to sweat blood in the Garden of the Olives, have mercy on me!*"

BLAKE WAS A big man, *a man of size* he liked to call himself, with a head of curly red hair and a round, button-popping gut. During his seven years as a De La Salle Brother, or Christian Brother – an order dedicated to the education of boys from poor families – Blake worked mainly as a secretary. His primary task was to record which boys that day were absent. By late morning he had the tasty duty of checking on the cafeteria staff, who were preparing lunch. Afternoons often found him dozily monitoring the late-period study halls.

He lasted less than a single year as a teacher. He was assigned a homeroom of freshmen and charged with teaching them Religion, and he was also given two sections of first-level Remedial Math. The students in the all-boys school where Blake taught were the kind of boys Blake grew up with – city kids, used to being knocked around, sent by their parents to the Christian Brothers for discipline along with education. They were relatively poor boys, the blue-collar sons of factory workers, bricklayers, plumbers, fathers who didn't want to risk sending their sons to Chicago's public high schools where classrooms were more often than not governed by switchblade-wielding gangs. Blake taught the boys whose parents couldn't afford the prestigious, expensive college-prep high schools run by the Jesuits.

When Blake's superiors relieved him from his role as a teacher, they explained that he exercised a distinct absence of authority in the classroom. Teaching and imposing rules on others were clearly not in Blake's skill set, they said. The assistant principal, who doubled as the coach of the junior varsity football team, reminded Blake that respect was never voluntarily given – it was hard-earned and gained – and, when it wasn't gained, discipline had to be imposed. He told Blake that putting him in charge of a classroom was like loading a nail gun with Q-tips, like asking a guppy to patrol a tank of piranhas.

Above the side blackboard in each of the school's classrooms hung a rectangular wooden paddle, the kind popularized by college fraternities. The teachers called the paddle the *Board of Education*. Whenever a student misbehaved, all a teacher had to do was call out the boy's name and ask that he come to the front of the classroom, then tell the boy the three dreaded words, "Assume the position." Even the most naive freshman quickly learned to bend at the waist and grab hold of an ankle. With the other hand he was to cup his genitals. The teacher would then ask, "Are the family jewels secure?" The boy would be required to answer, "All secure, Brother. Feel free to swing away." The teacher would then dole out three solid smacks on the boy's buttocks, careful not to strike the boy's tailbone. The others in class learned to stay quiet during these teaching moments lest they be called to the front of the room and be told to assume the position too.

Blake never once made use of the Board of Education. He couldn't imagine hitting a student he was assigned to teach. He knew they got enough of that from their fathers back at home. One brother, whose classroom was across the hall from Blake's, compared the noise Blake's students made in class to feeding time at the Monkey House at Lincoln Park Zoo.

The tipping point came the afternoon Blake was asked to cover a senior Honors English class for a lay teacher who was out sick. The boys in class hooted like lemurs as Blake attempted to carry out the day's study plan, which was to write relevant details about a previously assigned reading on the blackboard. As a child Blake was diagnosed as dyslexic and as a result he was hardly confident about spelling, and the boys in the honors class were entirely without compassion. Their continual barrage flustered him so much that even though he knew they were making up names as he stood at the blackboard, white chalk in hand, he recorded all he was told. He was too embarrassed to do otherwise.

Blake was told that the story's main character was named Phil Hatio. His best friends were Hugh Jardon and Jack Mehoff, their girlfriends were Jenna Talia and Connie Lingus, and their neighbors were Harry Balz, Ben Dover, Eric Shun, and Mike Hunt.

"*OH MY JESUS!*" Blake murmured as he slowly brought each knee up and onto the hard plank covering the third step. "*By the intense grief that filled thy heart on seeing thyself betrayed by the perfidious Judas, have mercy on me!*"

AS FOR BLAKE's name, it was less a blessing than a curse. Yes, his first name was William, though at the time of his birth his parents had no knowledge of the English poet, or even English poetry, and the busy nurses and the attending doctor determining the child's Apgar scores said nothing about it. "Billy Blake," his father said, as the nurses flexed the chubby newborn's arms and legs and wiped the cottage-cheese-like vernix off the baby's pinkening body. "I like it. Rolls right off the tongue." The heel of one foot pinched sharply by one of the older nurses, the boy issued a loud, lusty cry. Blake's mother, doped silly from the procedure, had no option other than to wipe the drool from her mouth and agree.

Blake's parents were told that over time he'd outgrow his problems of reverse lettering, that dyslexia was a non-specific umbrella term, that the boy's actual problem was one of directional confusion, or that he lacked full phonological awareness, or perhaps he suffered from a deficiency of orthographic coding, or since he was a late talker his basic problem was really a delay in language acquisition. The snag might be caused by something in the Broca's area portion of his brain or within his superior temporal and inferior parietal cortex. They were also uncertain if his left insula was being adequately activated.

All the fancy terms rolled off Blake's father's understanding like rain on a pitched roof. "I'll activate the boy's left insular," the father said. "If you want the simple truth, the boy's lazy. Either that or he's flat-out dumb. Stupid as dog shit, and I won't charge a ding-dong dime for the diagnosis. And besides, just like his mother here, he's *fat*."

In the sixth grade, Blake's English teacher expected him to know more than he actually did about British literature, particularly the poetry written by his namesake. As a result the boy was required to memorize "The Chimney Sweeper." To pass the class, Blake was asked to recite the bleak tale of little Tom Dacre before the rest of the class.

While the other students tittered with glee, Blake tottered to the front of the classroom and began his recitation of the poem in an English accent, as he was instructed, an accent he copied from listening to the song "I'm Henry the Eighth, I Am" by the British rock group Herman's Hermits. Like the poem's persona, Blake could scarcely utter the poem's four repetitions of the word *'weep!* – short for *sweep!* – meant to reveal how the poem's speaker was so young he couldn't even correctly pronounce the word that indicated the occupation he'd been sold into by his father after his mother died – before the class burst out in laughter.

"'*So your chimneys I sweep, and in soot I sleep*,'" Blake recited as they laughed.

Blake was asked to recite the poem in each of his subsequent English classes. It became a sort of school tradition, trotting out the boy with the literary name. Blake agreeably played along although he understood that a dull, chubby kid named William Blake reciting a poem written by a dead British genius was a show, a sham, a palliative offered to his betters in exchange for their giving him passing grades in English, a nightmare subject he deeply feared and knew he'd never grasp.

"*OH MY JESUS!*" Blake gasped. "*By the confusion thou didst feel when led as a malefactor through the streets of Jerusalem, have mercy on me!*"

WORDS AND LETTERS and their proper arrangements were far from young Blake's forte. His fundamental problem was that each word he encountered on the page seemed to him a stranger. Whereas his teachers seemed able to impart to the other kids in class a set of rules, and Blake's classmates seemed able to make sense of these rules and apply them to new words in their rapidly expanding vocabularies, little that Blake understood about words seemed to apply to the next one. It was as if upon meeting a stranger the others knew enough to shake the person's hand and say, How do you do?, while Blake wondered if he should touch the new person's nose or offer a knee or elbow. One specialist called this disconnectivity.

As Blake knelt on the steps of the Scala Sancta, he thought back to the day his parents discovered he had a disability. *Dill*, Blake printed proudly when his father pressed a crayon in his hand and told him to write his name.

"No, dummy, that's a pickle," Blake's father said as he ripped the paper from the child's hands, then slapped the crayon away and ordered the boy to write properly. Blake filled a fresh piece of paper with a long row of lower-case "L"s. When ordered to print a "B" he printed yet another "D", and then after noticing the disappointment on his father's face he printed the "D" backward, then lying on its side, then hovering in the air like a spaceship. He knew that one of the possibilities had to be right. From that day on his parents called him by his last name, Blake, with a clearly pronounced emphasis on the "B".

"Buh, buh, buh," his mother repeated to the child. "Le, le, le," she said. "Buh, buh, buh, Blake. Say it, son. Buh, buh, buh." The boy's mother clutched his fingers that held the crayon, and together their hands wrote a capital "B". For a long time afterward, whenever someone asked his name, the boy gleefully answered, "Buh, buh, buh."

"See," Blake's mother said, "see." She pointed to the paper as if it held some hidden secret. If he didn't gaze immediately at the sheet, she slapped his hands or the top of his head until she seemed satisfied that he was looking. "The 'B' has two humps, two bumps, understand, just like these." She pulled her son's hands onto her breasts, which, to the boy, were immense and disconcerting. "Just like these two boobies. Can you say *boobies*? Boobies. Big old boobies? Buh, buh, boobies."

'Weep, 'weep, 'weep, Blake thought whenever the boobies lessons surfaced in his mind, like a barnacle-speckled whale breaching the water for air.

"*OH, MY JESUS!*" Others now on the stairs were ascending them much more quickly than he was, but Blake thought it best to take his time. "*By the sweetness thou didst show when brought before the tribunal and struck in the face, have mercy on me!*"

DURING HIS FIRST year of college, each freshman was required to pass a proficiency exam in composition – an essay of at least five hundred words based on an unannounced subject. The topic that semester involved the hypothetical situation of being stranded on a desert island. If you were stranded on a desert island and supplied with food and water for the rest of your life, and you could take along three objects that would fit inside your coffin, what three objects would you bring and why?

Blake wrote about the cord of Saint Joseph and added a book about tying knots, ideally a reasonably comprehensive text, one without an excess of print, one with loads of diagrams and illustrations showing how to tie every conceivable knot the world has ever known. Unfortunately he spent so much of his time describing the Saint Joseph cord and the ideal book of knots that the proctor called time and ordered everyone to turn in their blue composition books before Blake was able to get to his third item.

While waiting for the results of his exam outside his instructor's office – a teaching assistant with skin the pleasant color of root-beer soda, fond of keeping a sharp red pencil tucked above his right ear – Blake overheard the man relate to his officemate the hilarious news that a sophomore named Jay Joyce had failed the proficiency exam for the third consecutive semester.

"Too many *riverruns*, I'll bet," the other instructor in the office said as he laughed. "Too many *snotgreen, scrotumtightening seas.*"

"Nothing that inventive," Blake's instructor said. "I talked to the two readers who failed him. The unforgiving axe of faulty syntax did him in."

"Yes, yes, the comma splice. The sentence fragment. The dangling modifier. Our bread and butter. Where in the world would we be without them?" The officemate sucked his teeth, then asked, "Oh, did they happen to mention his three items? Did Jay Joyce take along the inner organs of beasts and fowls? Thick giblet soup? Grilled mutton kidneys? Plumtree's Potted Meat? Or was he perhaps too paralyzed to finish?"

Blake's instructor laughed. "You give the kid too much credit. They said he wanted the usual – a stack of Playboys, several cases of whiskey, and a picture of his family."

"I graded an exam by a Melville," the other instructor said.

"Herman?"

"Becca."

"Did she want a harpoon or s-s-stutter or prefer not to respond?"

"Good one. Now you're talking solid 'A'. No, sadly she chose a mirror along with a comb and scissors. I can understand the scissors and comb, but for the love of God she's on a desert island. Why waste one of your objects on a mirror?"

"Signal a passing whaler?" The instructor waved to Blake, who hovered in the hallway like a float in Macy's Thanksgiving Day parade. "Ahh, my Romantic visionary, who gazes at the world and sees angels dancing in the trees. Enter." The instructor motioned toward a whitish, gum-stained square on the office's linoleum floor.

"'To see a world in a grain of sand, and a heaven in a wild flower, hold infinity in the palm of your hand, and eternity in an hour,'" the instructor said to Blake. "My naive friend, even though you failed to finish the test and challenged us once again with dozens of your trademark Bizarro World spelling errors, the gods above gazed mercifully down upon you and, based on your essay's originality, granted you a C minus."

"This must be William Blake," the officemate said.

"The one and only." The instructor took the red pencil out from behind his ear, waved it at Blake like a magic wand, and smiled.

"OH MY JESUS!" Blake wheezed as he lifted his throbbing knees onto the sixth step. *"By the patience thou didst exhibit amid the outrages and mockeries, of which thou wert the object throughout the night preceding thy death, have mercy on me!"*

BLAKE WAS VISITING Rome because after seven years as a brother he left the Order for reasons he couldn't fully explain. He told his superiors that it wasn't that he wanted to break his vows of poverty, chastity, and obedience, or that after considerable soul-searching he'd come up with a better plan of how he might serve God. Leaving simply felt like the right next step. Besides, he added, they were already aware that he sucked at teaching.

Since he was still very much a practicing Roman Catholic, he thought a pilgrimage of sorts to Rome, caput mundi, made good sense. He knew that somewhere along the path of his life he'd lost track of something. Perhaps what was missing was like one of those sneaky letters that hides inside a word, nearly invisible, just waiting to be discovered, and then when you find it you say Oh! and suddenly the word takes on new sound and sense.

Blake also traveled to Rome because his stepsister, Ginny, who was pregnant and unmarried, was suffering from preeclampsia, experiencing difficulties so severe that she was confined completely to bed. There was a significant risk that she'd lose the child, and even the chance that she would die. When Blake learned of her condition he told her he'd cancel his plans, but she insisted that he go, regardless, and asked him to pray for her there.

Blake's mother died of a heart attack during his sophomore year in high school on a Saturday afternoon while he was playing in a football game. A year and a half later his father remarried – a broom straw of a woman who treated Blake as if he had a communicable disease but who had a kind daughter close to Blake's age. At first there were jokes about Blake and Ginny, how they'd make a handsome couple, how Blake never had even a single girlfriend while Ginny already had had scads of sweethearts, so in terms of experience the two levelled the other out.

"*OH MY JESUS!*" Blake was sweating now, doing his best to concentrate on his prayers, trying to ignore the increasing pain in his knees. "*By the cruel insult thou didst endure when dragged many times on the Sacred Stairs, have mercy on me!*"

PERHAPS THERE WAS a church or shrine in Rome that Blake could visit, Ginny suggested as he made his goodbyes, that might help her carry her child to term.

The first thing Blake did was visit Sant'Agostino on Via della Scrofa. Sant'Agostino was a stunning Renaissance basilica laid out in the shape of a Latin cross, filled with travertine plundered from the Colosseum. Blake knelt before the sculpture of the Madonna del Parto, Our Lady of Childbirth, seated on a throne like an ancient goddess in a templed niche over which hung a gold scallop shell. The Christ Child stood boldly on her lap, arms crossed, defiant, one stocky leg on the arm of her chair, the other on his mother's knee.

In a shop near the Pantheon Blake had purchased a silver ex-voto in the shape of a heart. The heart was topped by a flame, on which were embossed the letters "GR". The letters stood for *per grazia ricevuta* – for a grace received. Blake gave it to the church's sacristan along with a ten-euro note so that the ex-voto would be displayed. In a glass case near the statue of the Madonna were scores of ex-votos on display, and hanging on a nearby wall were several handwritten letters of thanks, each bearing the name of a child safely born after prayers were offered to the Madonna del Parto. The practice of hanging an object, in Rome most often a silver heart, came from the supplicant's desire for a saint's intercession on behalf of a special request. The practice made sense to Blake. Giving a gift to someone from whom you're petitioning a special favor was the way the world operated. On the ten-euro note he gave the sacristan, Blake printed a large "G", for Ginny.

As Blake knelt at the Madonna's feet and prayed for his stepsister and her unborn child, he did his best not to present his petition as an argument. Instead of begging for a specific outcome, that both Ginny and the child be saved, he asked for the Madonna's most holy presence and guidance. He asked the Child standing on her knee for his will to be done and for everyone to be given the grace to accept it, no matter what it might be.

Caravaggio's *The Madonna of Loreto* hung in a chapel to the right of the shrine. In the painting a young Virgin Mary stands barefoot inside a decrepit doorway, displaying the near-naked Christ Child to a pair of peasants on pilgrimage. Blake was mesmerized by the work. He was struck by the lovely angle of Mary's neck along with the work's stunning realism – the cracked plaster on the wall near the doorway where Mary and the Child stood, the peasants' shabby clothing, their dirty legs and fingernails, the soiled soles of their feet. The Child's right hand was slightly raised, as if giving the pilgrims his blessing. Both peasants held their hands upright in prayer. Blake's eyes kept returning to the figures' hands. He held his hands like the pilgrims in the painting as he said another prayer at this altar, again asking to be given the grace to accept whatever was God's will.

"*OH MY JESUS!*" Blake said beneath his breath. He wiped the sweat from his brow and rubbed his eyes. "*By the silence thou didst observe in the presence of those who bore false witness against thee, and of the iniquitous Pilate who unjustly condemned thee, have mercy on me!*"

ON THE MORNING of the day she died, Blake's mother made his ritual game-day breakfast of pancakes. Blake ate two at a time, the top pancake drenched with imitation maple syrup. His mother put four slices of banana in each pancake – one for each quarter that he'd play. It was her way of wishing him a good game. Their most meaningful communications were through food. Neither knew the meal would be their last conversation.

At home after the game, after Blake was told that his mother had died before the ambulance even reached the hospital's emergency room entranceway, Blake noticed that two bananas remained from the bunch his mother had purchased a few days before. The bananas lay in a blue ceramic bowl his mother always used for fruit. Blake let the bananas freckle and brown, and even after his father began griping about the many fruit flies hovering in the kitchen Blake did nothing about the bowl or its contents. Over time the bananas shriveled and blackened, sticking fast to the bottom and sides of the bowl. Blake stared at the dark mass until his eyes began to tear. Then he carefully wrapped the bowl in the sports section of that morning's *Chicago Tribune* and buried the bananas beneath several aluminum TV dinner trays crumpled in the kitchen's garbage can.

Blake never ate bananas again. Whenever he was offered a banana he told people that he was allergic to them, that if he took even one bite of a banana his throat would close tight and he'd be unable to breathe. Anaphylactic shock? they'd say. I know you can get that from peanuts, but bananas?

In my case, yes, Blake would respond.

"Oh my Jesus! By the humiliation to which thou didst subject thyself amidst the derision of Herod and his court, have mercy on me!"

HE WAS STAYING in a pensione that overlooked the Campo de' Fiori. The piazza featured rows of stands where vendors of all types peddled their wares alongside the famous monument of Giordano Bruno, a Dominican friar who was imprisoned in darkness for seven years by the Roman Catholic Church. After Bruno's continual refusal to renounce his beliefs, he was tortured and burned to death for heresy. The Church believed that Bruno's ideas were so dangerous that in order to silence him from responding to the crowds of hecklers as he was paraded through Rome's streets on his way to his execution, his jailers drove a long iron spike through his left cheek, pinning his tongue and emerging out of his right cheek. A second spike was then thrust vertically up through his mouth and palate. Stripped naked, mouth locked shut with a metal cross, Bruno was brought to the Campo de' Fiori, where for centuries Rome's public executions were held. There, Bruno was hung upside down and burned to death. After the fires cooled, his remains were dumped into the Tiber.

Bruno's heresy was that he believed the sun was merely one star among many other stars. All one had to do was gaze up at the night sky, Bruno maintained. He then wondered if the number of stars in the sky was infinite. If the number of stars was infinite, he reasoned, it seemed only logical to conclude that these infinite number of suns were shining their light on an infinite number of other worlds. Given the Almighty's abundant and infinite mercy and bounty, and given the Almighty's eternal and unending love, it therefore followed that it was likely that countless other beings with God-given souls were living and dying on these other worlds. Man alone was not the center, Bruno believed. The universe around our spinning little ball of water and rock was limitless. The infinite universe reflected God's infinite nature and glory. Blake learned all of this one afternoon while overhearing a conversation between a woman and a man talking near the base of the monument, which was positioned precisely so that Giordano Bruno's statue defiantly faced the Vatican that had so mercilessly tortured and killed him four centuries before.

His were absolutely incredible ideas, the woman said. Her face was gentle, relaxed, rested, as if she'd recently awoken from a long, satisfying sleep. She wore a copper-colored skirt and drew out from her pocket a piece of paper. From her conversation with the man, Blake learned that her name was Elena and her husband was named Ben and he was or at least at some point in the past had been some sort of big-shot banker. They'd recently returned to Rome after a few months of travel in Italy's South. Since the new year began, they'd thrown their lives' plans into the air like so much coriandoli and took themselves to wherever the roads stretching down to Sicily's southern shores led them. Evidently it all began on the day of the South-Asian tsunami. Elena was now thinking of returning to graduate school, and Ben was giving up a life in finance. Now that they were once again in Rome they felt they were back at the starting point. From their manner of speech and the way their eyes held the other's face – from the movements of their hands, nearly always reaching toward the other, always touching – Blake could see that the couple was very much in love.

Elena unfolded the piece of paper. It was a poem by Heather McHugh titled "What He Thought," the story of a group of poets visiting Italy, talking over dinner about poetry's true definition, whether poetry might be the flowers or the vegetables and fruits sold on the Campo de' Fiori or whether poetry was perhaps Bruno's statue itself. The poem described how, as Bruno was burned at the stake, his cries were silenced by an iron mask. Perhaps poetry was that silence, Elena read. Perhaps poetry was what Giordano Bruno had thought but was unable to say.

Blake wanted Elena to read the poem again. "The poem is an experience of its own," she told Ben as they walked away. Blake wanted to experience the poem again. He wanted to hold the poem's words in his mouth as he stood before Bruno's statue, just like the woman who'd recited it.

Blake was awed by the dark, hooded statue. He had tremendous admiration for martyrs, though the idea of being tortured and burned to death made him shudder. Blake knew that if he had been Giordano Bruno he'd have renounced his beliefs in a minute. He knew he would have told the Church officials anything they wanted to hear, long before they threw him into a dark prison cell or silenced him with a cross of iron spikes or set fire to the stacks of wood over which his upside-down naked body was hung.

"*OH MY JESUS!*" Blake struggled to raise his aching knees up and onto the next step. The other penitents who had begun the climb when Blake had started were now standing beneath the fresco of the Crucifixion, looking through the grill into the Sancta Sanctorum. "*By the shame thou didst feel on being stripped of thy garments and tied to the pillar to be scourged, have mercy on me!*"

BLAKE HAD BEEN given a small room in the pensione and shared a bathroom and sitting room and kitchen with the other house guests. The previous evening he'd met the pensione's housekeeper, Dubravka. A lovely woman. A native of war-torn Croatia. She lived upstairs in the attic and had a distinctively unfriendly long-haired cat who wandered the house freely and enjoyed settling comfortably into a ball of purring fur on Blake's narrow bed.

"Anđelina," he could hear Dubravka calling as she descended the stairs. Though the cat's name meant *Little Angel* in Croatian, the creature was anything but angelic and not only refused to come when its name was called but was fond of vigorously scratching and tearing the side of Blake's bedcover as if she were a dog digging a hole for a bone. Within moments the woman stood in the hallway outside Blake's room, and at the sight of her Blake felt something inside him stir. The feeling wasn't so much physical as something else, some other manner of yearning.

Dubravka was thin and a bit taller than average height, with dark hair and full lips that pulled his focus down from her large brown eyes. She used no makeup, and her hair was a tangle, a snarl, a sort of wild nest made by a bird. She wore dark stockings and a modest gray skirt, a faded blouse patterned with dots or possibly flowers – Blake couldn't really tell without staring – and an open brown sweater with unmatched buttons, frayed at the edges of its sleeves.

Blake walked toward the doorway and introduced himself, and the woman said her name though she didn't extend a hand in greeting. Anđelina nonchalantly turned toward the woman and hunched her back and then stretched her front paws forward and leaned back and gave the room a wide, sharp-toothed yawn, as if everything in the room, if not the entire world and all of God's grand creation, was infinitely boring.

The woman asked Blake if he would like a cup, since she was on her way to the kitchen to make a pot of tea. Blake guessed that she was only being polite and her request stemmed from a sense of duty. Not wanting to impose on her he declined, though he would have enjoyed a cup of tea. Even more he wanted to accompany her to the kitchen to study her, to talk with her, to understand what it was about her that he felt.

"*OH MY JESUS!*" Blake huffed and puffed. "*By the pain thou didst suffer on being scourged, when thy body was all covered with wounds and bruises, have mercy on me!*"

BACK WHEN BLAKE was a student at the university, he had a summer job as a janitor at a factory. He worked the late shift, three-thirty to midnight, mainly emptying out offices and scrubbing and waxing floors. For a while the other men on the crew – mostly African Americans – called him *Bigboy*, or when he was particularly slow *Lard Ass*. Then, after a week or two, after Blake didn't protest and came whenever he was called and did all that was asked of him, they changed his nickname to *Youngblood*.

The crew worked with impressive efficiency, breaking into groups, each assigned a specific task. While one group cleared rooms of moveable furniture, a second swept the floors and then a third scrubbed them, and after the floors dried the first crew coated the floors with wax. Blake worked with the first crew, and after the wax dried he operated the buffer. Handling the machine made Blake feel like a bronco buster at a rodeo until he understood that his job wasn't so much to fight the bronco as it was to let it glide. He took pride in shining the office floors and performed the task with great care.

There was always an hour or two after the crew completed their night's duties before they could punch out. Their task then was to hide and kill clock. The hour or so became joke-and-story time, and the men took Blake under their wing and began offering him advice.

The main advice Blake remembered was that when it came his time to slip through the gates of the promised land the last thing he should be was a jackrabbit. "You know," the men told him, "like a jackrabbit is in the hole one minute, out the hole the next. Uh uh. That's no way to be. Once you get to the land of milk and honey, and we do mean honey, you want to settle in and go slow."

"Slower than slow, you understand. You can call this stage *getting familiar*. Take your time to get familiar. Then after you're familiar. you can decide when to take charge."

"*Take charge* is right," the men said. "But first you've got to be relaxed. Start things out fast and tense up and before you know it, bang! Lights out. Sayonara time, baby."

"'Adios, amigo,' she'll be saying. 'Sweet thing,' she'll be saying, 'don't let the door hit your ass too hard on your way out.'"

"Shoot the fireworks off too early and that'll be your last Fourth of July."

"No woman likes a jackrabbit."

"Words to live by, Youngblood. You can take them to the bank."

Blake didn't understand a word the men said but thanked them profusely.

"*OH MY JESUS!*" The pain was considerable now. Biting. "*By the torture of the sharp thorns wherewith thy adorable head was pierced, have mercy on me!*"

BLAKE'S CALL TO a religious vocation came about in an unusual way. He didn't feel a sudden tap from Christ's hand on his shoulder or hear a sharp knock on his door. Christ didn't walk into Blake's bedroom and raise an arm and point at him. Instead, Blake came to believe, the instrument that God chose to communicate with him was water, the insistently pounding waves of Lake Michigan, endlessly surging against the huge limestone blocks that lined the breakwater of Chicago's Edgewater Beach. The way Jesus chose to call Blake was to douse him with water, in rapid succession with three sudden waves.

To escape the near-constant disapproval of his stepmother, each day after school Blake walked to Chicago's lakefront and sat at the edge of the rocks, watching the lake's steel-gray waves tumble toward him as he struggled with his assignments. He often felt as if he were sitting on the edge of the world, gazing out at eternity. One afternoon Blake was doing his best to make his way through the pages of *Lord of the Flies*, feeling considerable pity for the littluns, particularly the nameless one with the mulberry birthmark who was afraid that somewhere on the island there lurked an evil beast. Had he been on the island, Blake thought, he would have helped Piggy and Simon care for the young boys. He would have done what he could to ease the fears of the kid with the birthmark.

At that moment a mighty wave rose up from the great lake, splashing Blake and his belongings. As the water withdrew, the wave's force tore the novel from Blake's hands. The book disappeared into the water and after several moments surfaced, bobbing, then swirling, floating cover down, clearly out of reach, its pages spread open like twin wings. As Blake watched it disappear another larger, taller, even more powerful wave leapt up and over the rocks. Like a furious tongue the second wave drenched Blake and returned to the patch of stone beside him his newly sharpened yellow No. 2 Ticonderoga lead pencil along with his laminated bookmark. The bookmark was a holy card depicting Saint John Baptist de la Salle, the founder of the Christian Brothers and patron saint of teachers. Then a third, smaller wave leapt up and slapped Blake's face, as if reminding him to look around and pay attention.

His novel lost – the waves pulling the paperback out farther and farther toward the gray edge of the world until the pair of wings became a blurred white dot that he could no longer see – Blake never finished reading *Lord of the Flies*. He never learned about Ralph and Jack and what happened on the island to Piggy and Simon and the littluns and the fearful young boy with the mulberry birthmark.

But that his yellow pencil and the holy card of the French saint named for John the Baptist were splashed up and back to him were signs too obvious for Blake to ignore. He interpreted the events as otherworldly. A calling. Even a sort of second baptism, one delivered by none other than John the Baptist himself.

"*Oh my Jesus!*" Again Blake wiped the sweat from his forehead. "*By the patience thou didst exhibit when, clothed with purple rags and with a reed in thy hand, thou were derided and treated as a mocking, have mercy on me!*"

"Why don't you become a priest?" Blake's father asked. "I mean, if you're going to give up a normal life and go to the extreme of all the vows and whatever the hell else they make you do, why not go whole hog and get to wear a black suit and Roman collar and say Mass and hear confessions? I mean, why not be a man about it? Being a brother – what's that? How do you explain that to somebody? Those guys wear silly little bibs and long black dresses. To look at it from where I'm standing, it's like you're deciding to become a male nun."

As with many of his father's questions Blake had no clear response, or at least one he felt his father would understand. "It feels right," is all Blake could say.

"A goddamn brother," his father responded, shaking his head. "At the very least you could get in with that gang out in California, you know, the ones who make the wine."

"No," Blake said. "I want them to train me to be a teacher. To work with the poor."

"A high-school teacher," his father said, barely able to disguise his disgust. "When you could go to Napa Valley and learn how to make wine. Every now and then you could send me a case. I'm sure when nobody's looking, all the Christian Brothers out there send their families a case or two. At the very least I could hold up a bottle and tell people Hey, drink up, my son made this."

"*OH MY JESUS!*" Blake grimaced as he glanced about, as he realized he'd finally reached the halfway point up the stairs. "*By the affliction thou didst feel when thou didst hear the people cry out against thee and clamor for thy death, have mercy on me!*"

BLAKE'S DUTY AS the team's offensive left guard was to protect the players in the backfield. His job was to block defenders eager to tackle the quarterback and to open gaps in the line for the running back. Because most QBs are right-handed and able to see whatever approaches them on the right, the guard on the quarterback's left is called the backside or blindside guard. The role fell to the superior player. Blindside guard was a position Blake played with great pride.

His favorite moments were whenever the QB called a trap run right. In the play, the offensive linemen would alter their blocking assignments. The QB would hand off the ball to the running back, who'd begin his race to the right, at the same time a defensive lineman on the right side of the field would be allowed to run into the backfield. If the blocking scheme worked out to plan, the right guard would ignore the lineman and run upfield instead to block the middle linebacker while the center would fire off the line and take out the nose tackle. Blake's task was to ignore his man and pull – to move laterally as fast as he could to his right, cutting behind the center – and then with his right shoulder and forearm blindside the lineman the right guard had let slip into the backfield. Timed right, the ball carrier would trail Blake, often with a free hand on Blake's back, weaving his way through the hole punched out through the defense by the two guards and the center working in tandem.

A trap run that worked was a thing of true beauty. Blake relished the expression on the trapped lineman's face, how it would shift from the elation of being allowed to run freely into the opponent's backfield to the shock of being hit and flattened.

"*OH MY JESUS!*" Several more people had come to the Holy Stairs and were passing him politely on the left, as if Blake were an overloaded pick-up making its slow way up the right lane of a highway. "*By the humiliation to which thou were subject compared with Barabbas, and on seeing that criminal preferred to thine adorable person, have mercy on me!*"

IN THE PENSIONE'S sitting room was a modest television, which offered the viewer regular updates on Pope John Paul II's declining health. Though Blake didn't understand Italian, he was able to follow the reports well enough to realize that Rome was in the midst of its deathwatch. Already immense crowds were holding twenty-four-hour prayer vigils on Saint Peter's Square, gazing up at the lit windows of the pontiff's apartment as they knelt on the piazza below. The pope had been moved back to his Vatican apartment from the Gemelli, the hospital where the pope and his staff had a reserved suite of rooms.

Tired of listening to endless commentary and discussions of things he hardly understood, Blake would change the channel, switch past dubbed reruns of old U.S. TV shows or black-and-white Hollywood movies, switch past the barely clad dancing veline, the smiling baci baci girls tossing their insincere kisses at the viewer through the screen, the raucous variety shows with their canned laughter, more talk shows, impeccably dressed panelists talking rapid-fire as everyone gestured with their hands, until he found a news station following a story about a lost elderly man in Testaccio, a southern rione of Rome.

From what Blake could make out, the old man had been captured by a notorious gang of hoodlums. Apparently he'd been handcuffed to a prison wall and made to wear a cowbell around his neck. Wisely, to silence the bell's clapper and fool his captors, the clever fellow had stuffed one of his socks inside the bell. From the photo displayed on the report, the man was tall and thin, with an untamed tuft of gray hair, like a cockatoo, and a beard and upturned mustache that made him resemble Don Quixote. He was seen wandering the streets, broken handcuffs dangling from his wrists as well as his ankles, evidently scouring Testaccio for someone, a woman – his lover, witnesses who spoke to him reported – reciting lines of love poetry as he searched.

Blake understood enough to make out the newscaster's joke that the man was a modern-day Don Quixote seeking his Dulcinea. The image on the TV screen cut away to a picture of an anguished Peter O'Toole in *Man of La Mancha*, and then hovered lovingly over a series of photos of the exquisite Sophia Loren portraying the prostitute Aldonza, Don Quixote's Dulcinea in the film. The anchorman then said something funny, and there was loud laughter in the studio as "The Impossible Dream" began playing in English and Peter O'Toole's image singing the song filled the screen, quickly followed by a lingering snapshot of the lost handcuffed poet.

"OH MY JESUS!" Blake begged beneath his breath. *"By the resignation wherewith thou didst embrace the Cross and proceed with it upon the road to Calvary, have mercy on me!"*

"DUBRAVKA," BLAKE MUTTERED to himself. Like Dubrovnik, Blake thought, recalling the photos he'd seen of the magnificent city on the Adriatic's eastern coast. And so Blake thought of the housekeeper as a sort of lovely walled city standing beside a glistening seaside.

Sometimes Blake would stand at the bottom of the stairs that led to Dubravka's attic room and listen to her music. If she was downstairs and left her door open and he dared to climb the first two attic steps, Blake could see her record player, the old-fashioned kind that resembled a suitcase with a handle, along with a few albums that rested against the bench on which the machine sat. The cover of one album featured a man wearing a red fez and brown vest staring out at the distance against a blue background. Blake guessed this was the one Dubravka was fondest of playing. He'd often hear her, sometimes singing along, sometimes clapping her hands, sometimes moving about the room as if she were dancing. Sometimes when the music stopped he thought he could hear her crying, but when he looked at her unreadable face the following day he felt he must have been wrong.

The first song on the album began with a painfully somber violin and a man reciting a verse before he began to sing – a doleful song, Middle Eastern, aching with longing, until an accordion and other instruments jumped in and the tempo increased, and then the unhappy man sang more of his story. Then the tempo quickened again as the song became a whirlwind before dying back down to the singer's wavering voice, ending with the wistful violin.

The song made Blake both sad and want to clap his hands and dance and then be sad again. Since most evenings Dubravka liked to sit for a while in the kitchen, where she drank a cup of herb tea, he thought he'd talk to her about it though he never had the courage.

She seemed not to mind his company. On some nights she'd be absent – going to a meeting, she'd tell Blake, though she didn't specify what kind of meeting and he couldn't guess what organizations would need to meet at night. He imagined it had something to do with what he guessed were her other jobs, working for various charities, volunteering her time, soliciting funds for the needy, organizing and arranging things, though by what he could tell from her appearance she wasn't paid much. Even though the South-Asian tsunami had taken place over three months ago, Dubravka still went out into the streets each day seeking donations for its victims. She told Blake the real work there was only just beginning. She was in touch with a woman who'd traveled to Rome shortly after Christmas, a woman named Allison, who now served as a volunteer on behalf of tsunami relief in Indonesia. The woman was planning a brief return to Rome, Dubravka said.

Blake knew there would always be tragedies like the South-Asian tsunami, catastrophes so dire they killed over three hundred thousand people and left even more hundreds of thousands destitute and homeless. Was suffering the price humans paid for original sin? Blake believed in original sin, the concept that from the moment of our birth it's in our nature to be sinful. He knew that Saint Augustine had written about it. Concupiscence. A word Blake knew but could never spell. Blake thought that Dubravka's work, as well as her friend's work, would never come to an end.

During the nights that Dubravka didn't go to meetings, the pair sat at the pensione's kitchen table sharing a pot of tea. Blake found himself telling Dubravka how sad he was now that John Paul II was dying. Blake knew that as a young man Karol Józef Wojtyła refused to fire a rifle when required to undergo military training, and that he spoke at least a dozen languages. He wrote several books and had visited over a hundred foreign countries, kissing the ground each time his airplane dropped from the sky. Wojtyła helped free his native Poland from the rule of communism, which led to the downfall of communism across the world. He was the first pope to visit Rome's Tempio Maggiore as well as the Auschwitz-Birkenau Memorial and the state of Israel. He met and forgave the imprisoned assassin who, years before, had nearly killed him. And perhaps most importantly, Blake believed, John Paul II bestowed upon the papacy a genuine global dignity. Undeniably, Blake said, the pope was a major spiritual figure, on par with Mother Teresa and the Dalai Lama.

Dubravka neither agreed nor disagreed. Her attitude toward the dying pontiff seemed, at best, lukewarm. Blake wondered if she were truly Catholic since nearly every Roman Catholic he'd ever met adored Pope John Paul II, yet he knew that she carried a rosary and for years had been a nun.

Blake greatly enjoyed her company, even when she didn't speak, and he particularly liked gazing at her face, at the lines around her eyes and the folds near her lips. He liked her chin and cheekbones. He liked her hair, especially when she let it down. She looked like a young girl then, Blake thought. He would have liked to reach out and touch her hair, as he sometimes stroked Anđelina's fur, though whenever he did the cat always turned toward him, hissing, raising a paw – nails extended – to scratch him if he persisted.

At the cat sanctuary at Largo di Torre Argentina, across the street from the Via Florida pizzeria where one afternoon Blake happily ate his fill as he watched the women working there scissor variously sized rectangles from the tantalizing display of pizzas in the glass counter – pizza with bufala mozzarella and cherry tomatoes and basil, pizza with asiago and asparagus tips and speck, pizza with escarole and anchovies, sausage and rapini, ricotta and arugula, prosciutto on a bed of burrata, porcini, mortadella, guanciale, zucchini flowers, pecorino, Parma ham – Blake talked with Lucy, the Canadian Montessori teacher who had kindly given him directions to the Campo de' Fiori on the afternoon he'd arrived in Rome. This was after his Roman taxi driver dropped him off at the Piazza della Maddalena and then, after pocketing the money Blake handed him, insisted on still more, claiming that the two twenty-euro bills Blake had just paid him had been only tens.

Blake was surprised to see the dark-haired teacher working at the cat sanctuary, standing near the bottom of the metal staircase in jeans and knee-high rubber boots. He had to call out to her from above to get her attention. After she unlocked the street-level gate, the pair walked down to the grassy sanctuary below. Lucy explained that she was volunteering some of her time there to cover for the hours assigned to her pregnant friend Pina, the gattara, who was home resting in bed. Blake told Lucy about Ginny resting in bed at home too. Then he asked for advice on how he might befriend Dubravka's cat.

"Give the animal space," Lucy told him. "Let her come to you."

"And if she doesn't?" Blake asked.

"Then she doesn't," Lucy said. "With cats some things can't be forced."

Kneeling beside his bed at night reciting his prayers before going to sleep, Blake considered that the same advice also applied to Dubravka. The woman was every bit as much a mystery to him as the many languages he heard every day now out on the streets.

"*OH MY JESUS! By the sorrow thou didst feel on meeting thy most holy mother, and on witnessing the anguish of her heart, have mercy on me!*" Blake then thought of his own mother and felt vulnerable and alone as he covered his face with his hands.

"BACK IN THE States I work in a community food bank," Blake told Dubravka one night as they talked in the kitchen, after she described her work at Sant'Egidio. "Stocking shelves, mainly, sorting donations from grocery stores and community drop-off points." A wide box of assorted sweets he'd purchased earlier that day from a pasticceria lay open on the table between them.

The kitchen was a small, simple room, in the center of which was a plain wooden table and several unmatched wooden chairs. A large brown cross hung on the wall. Someone had pasted an Amnesty International decal on the door of one of the cupboards. In the decal's center was the gold outline of a lit candle inside a curl of barbed wire bent in the shape of a backward "S". Blake knew all about writing a backward "S".

"And this trip to Rome," Dubravka began. She'd pinned back her hair into a sort of knot behind her head. Blake knew there was a specific word for the style. It was one of those words with silent letters. He wanted to know the word. He wanted to ask Dubravka to pull the pins from her hair and let it fall freely down toward her shoulders.

"My mother's insurance policy," he answered, anticipating her question. "Several months before she died she took out life insurance in my name, and since I was still a minor, in high school, my father was named custodian but then forgot to tell me about it." Blake put a cookie in his mouth, chewed for several moments, swallowed. "And then when I was in college the account, I guess, slipped from his mind because he never told me about it, even though he was drawing funds from it. Skimming a bit of the fat off the top, he told me later, which seemed only reasonable, I suppose. You know, that the fat be skimmed. And of course when I decided to become a brother and made the vow of poverty – " He let his words trail off. "I found out about it only last year after I filed an income tax return and read the letters from the IRS. Of course all of this was after I left the Order."

"And how do you feel about that?" Dubravka asked.

"Leaving the Order?" Blake shrugged. "After a while, staying just didn't feel right."

"No, I mean how do you feel about your father hiding the truth from you and taking your money?"

Blake scratched his curly red hair, ate another cookie, and said nothing.

"Fathers," Dubravka said, shaking her head. She looked down at her folded hands, then back up at Blake. "So now you have a bit to live on."

"Yes, now I have a bit to live on." Blake plunged another cookie into his cup of tea. "Forgive me for dunking." He inhaled the tea-soaked sweet, sucked his thumb and fingers, then took a large cookie from the box and broke it in half. Powdered sugar rained down on the table. "And after I finally withdrew the funds and paid the back taxes and penalties, I gave my father half of what was left."

"Why would you do that?" Dubravka asked. She seemed displeased.

"Because he wanted it more than I did," Blake answered. "And because giving it to him made me feel" – he paused for several moments – "please forgive me for sounding prideful." He waved the other half of the cookie in the air. "Giving him half of the money made me feel superior. And now if Ginny survives – " Again he hesitated. "I think I told you that her baby doesn't have a father. Oh, of course, it does, of course there's a real father, but Ginny doesn't know which of the men it was. Anyway, if she can get through this, I plan to give her and her baby the other half."

"So you'll give it all away?"

Blake nodded.

"Then what will you live on?"

Blake raised a finger. "I need a minute to remember." He bowed his head, then looked out blankly into the room. "'When my mother died I was very young, and my father sold me while yet my tongue – '"

Dubravka looked confused.

"' – could scarcely cry 'weep! 'weep! 'weep! 'weep!' So your chimneys I sweep, and in soot I sleep.'" Pleased with himself, Blake nodded. "I think that was right. Just showing off." He smiled, then cleared his face. "No, what I really should recite comes from *Matthew*. 'Look at the birds of the air, for they neither sow nor reap nor gather into barns, yet the heavenly Father feeds them.'"

"*OH MY JESUS!*" Blake gasped for breath. "*By the excessive weariness that overcame thee while bearing the burden of the cross on thy shoulders, have mercy on me!*"

NEARLY EVERYWHERE BLAKE went in Rome he saw great overflowing displays of green carciofi. He fantasized that in an alternative Rome there would be a church named Santo Carciofo. He absolutely loved carciofi and could easily consume half a dozen. More, he thought. He could eat eight. He could eat ten. He could eat an even dozen. He could eat carciofi until he turned green like a carciofo and burst and died. He preferred carciofi alla Romana – artichokes rubbed with lemon and then cooked with olive oil or butter, herbs, and white wine – over carciofi alla giudia, which were smashed flat and dipped twice in frying oil, though he knew he would happily eat carciofi any way it was prepared. In one restaurant, the succulent heads were stuffed with bits of garlic and breadcrumbs. In another, the carciofi tasted of a hint of mint. A few restaurants served chopped carciofi hearts with pasta. Blake particularly relished eating the vegetable's long, tender stems.

If he were named the pope, Blake thought, he'd make a pair of crossed long-stemmed carciofi his symbol, like Peter with his crossed keys of Heaven, Barberini with his three bees, Pamphili with his dove and olive twig.

"*OH MY JESUS!*" The pain was now so severe Blake was tempted to try to stand and then walk or stumble back down the stairs. "*By the bitterness thou didst experience when the gall and vinegar touched thy lips, have mercy on me!*"

"STILL," BLAKE SAID as he sat talking with Dubravka in the kitchen, "sometimes I just want to throw my hands up in the air and give up. It's like I understand that there's a sense to things, a proper sequence, a right arrangement, and I know that means all of the other arrangements and sequences are wrong. And sometimes I just – I mean, it's hard for me to get things right, to put all the letters and numbers where they belong." He sipped his cup of tea. "That's why they took away my classes."

Dubravka nodded as she let out a sigh.

"I would stand at the blackboard in my Remedial Math class, the piece of chalk in my hand, and I'd know that the right number I was supposed to write was either seventeen or seventy-one, and then I'd wonder if it was really one over seven, one-seventh, and then I'd think of one knot on a string of seven knots, something that made it more than just a string of seven separate knots, something that made it whole, meaningful, like the cord, and then I knew that if I wrote down the wrong answer the whole world would crumble down around me."

"Like the cord?" Dubravka asked, confused.

"The Saint Joseph cord."

Dubravka's dark eyes held his. "And did it?" she said. "The whole world. When you stood at the blackboard. Did the whole world crumble around you?"

For several moments Blake considered the question. "The afternoon I tried to teach the Honors English class it did." He looked away from her in embarrassment. "I knew that everything the boys were telling me was dirty, and yet I still let my hand holding the chalk write every filthy name on the board."

"And so a bit of life collapsed around you that day." She felt the beginning tingle of the special prayer. "Look at me," she said, "right here," as Blake seemed to calm himself. From across the table Dubravka took his hands in hers. "That's what the world does to us, Blake. Do you understand? That's the world's nature. The blocks we place one on top of the other are always going to collapse and fall. The ground beneath our feet will always tremble and break. That's what the world is constantly doing – falling apart – in every single moment of time. We need to learn how best to accept that."

Now their eyes were locked and Dubravka was praying. On the wall behind Blake a clock ticked off one second after the next. They were still holding hands. After a while Dubravka said in a soft voice, "Did the world collapse on the other days?"

Blake shook his head no.

"So it doesn't happen every time."

"No," Blake said. "Not every time."

"Well, at least that's something," Dubravka said. "That's a start." She released Blake's hands and stood and pushed in her chair, then walked to the sink to rinse out her cup. "Understand, no matter what we do or how hard we try, the world is always crumbling around us. One tragedy only distracts us from the one that came the day before. Our choice is whether we choose to let ourselves grow numb and train ourselves to ignore the catastrophes or whether we see what we can do about them. Your coming here to Rome, your prayers for your stepsister and her unborn child, they show how much you're trying."

Blake nodded and stood and pushed in his chair. Had the kitchen been larger and had there been room he would have gone to the sink and washed and rinsed his cup too.

"You don't give me the impression that you're one to give up," Dubravka said. "And whether the right number is seventeen or seventy-one or one-seventh or simply seven hardly matters in the end. You know what really matters in the end."

Again Blake nodded.

Smiling now, Dubravka said, "Even during the little time you were a teacher, you probably taught your students more than you'll ever know."

"*OH MY JESUS!*" Blake's knees pulsed with needles of pain. "*By the agony thou didst endure when thy garments were roughly torn from thee, have mercy on me!*"

MUCH TO THE delight of the anchorman, the news the next day featured an update about the wandering handcuffed man they were now calling Testaccio's Don Quixote.

SUCCESSO! SUCCESSO! SUCCESSO!

scrolled across the bottom of the screen. There on the TV was the image of a young, raccoon-eyed girl in a bubble-gum pink sweatshirt patiently leading the old poet by the hand up the street.

An instrumental version of "The Impossible Dream" played as the girl brought the man to a pair waiting outside an apartment building – an ecstatic woman in slippers and a house dress, and a powerful man in jeans and a tight T-shirt, a weightlifter of sorts, Blake thought. The muscles of the man's arms bulged as if they'd been pumped full of something vibrant and alive. Garbage littered what passed for a lawn behind the pair. Spray-painted on the side of the building in fierce sky-blue letters were the words *Forza Lazio!* The camera lingered for several seconds on the trio's reunion as the anchorman rapidly related what had happened, hardly a word of which Blake could follow. All Blake could imagine was that the brave child had somehow rescued the man from his kidnappers. The camera then cut away to a picture of a school playground and then back to the young girl, the apparent savior, who was talking rapidly into a reporter's microphone, her painted eyes darting this way and that, and then all of a sudden the old man broke away from the pair and knelt at the girl's feet as if he were about to tie her shoelaces or propose. The girl looked up helplessly at the camera as she cradled her pink cell phone to her chest and shrugged. Then the screen played the clip of Peter O'Toole singing "Dulcinea," and the report ended with another sequence of shots of Sophia Loren, lingering on the iconic image of her dressed as Aldonza, the photo in which she leans from right to left toward the camera, her eyes heavy-lidded, an uncaring expression on her face, her breasts barely covered, the sleeves of her filthy blouse ripped.

"Oh my Jesus!" Blake felt distracted, dizzy. *"By the pain thou didst suffer when fastened with great nails to the cross of Calvary, have mercy on me!"*

"Meet me by the fountain," Dubravka said to Blake the following morning. Her raven hair hung freely down to her shoulders. "This afternoon. By the Fountain of the Four Rivers."

Blake loved Bernini's fountain. He saw that it was one thing and many things all at once. The statuary was made up of four characters sitting on rocks and shells while various creatures and plants poked out their heads from niches between them. The fountain's swirling, gurgling waters were dynamic, stirring, like something breathing and alive. Blake walked around the fountain several times until Dubravka had to take his hand and lead him away from it, as if he were a child.

Dubravka led Blake past the musicians and the living statues, past the mimes trapped inside invisible boxes and the mimes climbing invisible ropes, past the gray-haired Sicilian in the Sgt. Pepper jacket, his gloved hands transforming into dancing hobos as Tony Bennett's "Rags To Riches" played from the boombox at his feet, past the Asian watercolor artist who was painting a tourist's name alongside a sprig of cherry blossoms, past the vendors offering scarves and jewelry and plastic gizmos that slingshot whirling saucers into the air. Dubravka led Blake through the cluster of parked motorini and past the formless statue of Pasquino and its many taped slips of paper flapping in the breeze like silent tongues. She led Blake past the wide, sweeping stairway of the Cordonata

Capitolina and the stern, steep steps leading up to the Church of Santa Maria in Aracoeli. She led Blake beyond the garish Il Vittoriano and the endless traffic circling the Piazza Venezia and down Via dei Fori Imperiali and the majestic Colosseum, where Blake was certain he recognized Don Quixote's son dressed as a Roman gladiator standing in front of the ruin's walls, posing with several tourists for a photograph. Dubravka led Blake up Via Merulana, where she stopped at the doorway of the modest Church of the Figlie di Sant'Anna, the Daughters of Saint Anne.

Untouched by tourists, not included in any of the guidebooks, the small church sat empty, as if waiting for the faithful. Its ceiling featured a stained-glass window in the clear, simple shape of a cross. A fresco of Saint Anne, mother of the Virgin Mary, marked a chapel on the right. Nailed to the church's walls were well over a thousand ex-votos. Countless handwritten notes and photos of newborns along with an assortment of baby clothes – tiny shirts and cotton bibs, framed or enclosed in plastic – hung beneath rows of glittering silver hearts. Several items bore the names of children. Federica. Luca. Gabriele. Matteo. Gaia.

Grazie per Francesca, one note read.

Per ringraziamento Simone. Nato a Roma.

Per grazia ricevuta!

Opposite the shrine to Saint Anne was a grotto inside of which stood a statue of the Madonna. The Virgin was adorned with a halo of lights. Around the statue were more candles and ex-votos, more handwritten notes of gratitude, more baby clothes.

"Stop looking around," Dubravka said. "You're in a church now. Pray." She knelt before the shrine of Saint Anne and pulled her rosary from her pocket.

Blake knelt on both knees before the shrine of the Virgin, then put one hand down in front of him and then the other as he lowered his belly and chest and bowed and pressed his forehead in supplication and petition against the floor.

"OH MY JESUS!" Blake saw that he'd reached the first of the last seven steps. The step marked the beginning of the final quarter, the time when the game's outcome is decided, when the contest is won or lost.

"By the infinite charity that moved thee to forgive thine executioners and pray to the heavenly father for them, have mercy on me!"

LYING ON THE marble floor before the statue of the Virgin, Blake thought of late July two-a-day workouts, the laps, the drills, the endless push-ups and sit-ups. I am a mere pawn, he thought once again as he lifted his head to gaze at the Virgin's face.

Pawn, from the medieval term for foot soldier, related to the word *peon*, generally able to advance only one square forward at a time. Like the sacrificial lamb, the pawn is offered – its blood spilled – so that the pieces in the row behind them may move more freely.

Use me, Blake prayed to the Queen. As one of your pawns, I'm happy to sacrifice myself so that Ginny and her child might live.

"OH MY JESUS!" Blake dug down deep for a second wind and lugged his weight up to the sixth-from-last step. *"By the goodness with which thou didst give paradise to the penitent thief, and Mary unto John, as his mother, have mercy on me!"*

THERE WAS A mad rascal running around Rome with a sword, an actual sword, dressed like a character in a medieval drama, performing antics that at first glance appeared more or less innocent but were now attracting increasing attention by the police. Blake watched a report about the man on TV, which aired shaky clips and blurred photographs of the fellow in action, recorded by the growing numbers of his delighted fans. From what Blake could gather, the artist was becoming one of Rome's most popular curiosities. Each day he popped up somewhere, unexpected, in splendid costume, with one report comparing him to a Roman version of Nessie, the elusive Loch Ness monster.

And now as Blake strolled down Via Vittorio Veneto's row of plane trees, outside the stone steps leading up to the Church of Santa Maria della Concezione, he spotted two angry, huffing carabinieri chasing the poor fellow, who was kind enough to slow down every few steps to turn around and laugh so that the two policemen could catch up. The long blade of the fellow's weapon glinted in the afternoon sunlight like something holy. As Blake watched what was happening, he realized the man was purposefully allowing the carabinieri to get within range so that he could hurl stones at the cops from a pouch full of stones he wore slung across his chest.

Blake wasn't aware that this was to be one of Agostino's final performances. For that reason Agostino had left his dagger back at the garage with Valentina and boldly carried his double-edged schiavona, thinking that if he were to be captured and imprisoned for his antics he didn't want to end his months-long performance piece half dressed.

The two carabinieri were closing in on the artist, shouting what Blake could only guess was the Roman version of *Halt!*, when, like in a slapstick chase scene in a Keystone Kops movie, the four men more or less converged. The costumed actor darted behind Blake's back and then did a sort of sideways dance – now you see me, now you don't – popping out on one side of Blake, then disappearing, hiding behind Blake as if the big man were a wall, then peeking out the other side and tossing another stone while dancing back again behind Blake as the two indignant policemen neared.

At that moment some muscle memory took control over Blake's body, something he'd been taught and repeatedly practiced during his endless hours on the gridiron. "Pull trap right!" Blake barked as if he were the quarterback, "pull trap right on two," as he set his feet and charged the first policeman – the nose tackle – knocking the man cleanly back and down onto the sidewalk. Then Blake looked for the other carabinieri, who was smiling, smug, charging along on the right, imagining he had a clear shot at the performer. Blake blindsided the policeman, clipping him sharply with his right shoulder as he'd been taught. Agostino wisely ran directly behind Blake – a running back dutifully tailing his pulling guard. The performer then scampered up the street with an ecstatic laugh and then turned and tossed a few more stones.

Of course the carabinieri shouted accusations at Blake, and the smaller of the two took out his handcuffs and shook them in the air like maracas, but after a third policeman arrived on the scene and the trio talked and argued and then talked a bit more they ended up waving Blake away, concluding he was merely a clumsy oaf, yet another unaware North American tourist caught up in the middle of something he failed to understand. In truth the two carabinieri Blake had knocked down were too embarrassed to admit to their colleague what Blake had done to them.

"Scusa," Blake said repeatedly as if it were a magic word. He backed away slowly as the three men discussed his fate. "Scusa, scusa." Blake knew enough Italian to say that.

"*OH MY JESUS!*" Blake moaned. He recalled how he felt at the end of each practice, when the coach called for just one more lap around the field, with an extra lap for the player who finished last. Blake often finished last. "*By the burning thirst with which thou was tortured on the gibbet of the Cross, have mercy on me!*"

FOLLOWING THE INCIDENT with the policemen, Blake thought it best to hide, as if he were the one who was wanted. He walked past the iron gates in front of Santa Maria della Concezione and down the steps to the church's basement into the Capuchin Crypts. After paying the woman at the desk and entering the dusty-smelling hallway, Blake stared at the orgy of death on display there. In six small crypts along a hallway were the intentionally arranged and preserved bones of over four thousand once-living Capuchin monks. Blake was amazed that someone had literally used the bones of the dead to create a series of designed works of art that could be called nothing less than utterly grotesque.

There were archways formed of skulls, femurs, and fibulae, under which lay, in hooded monks' clothing, complete skeletons in repose. Three more skeletons dressed as monks stood before a towering triptych made of skulls. Pelvises and pelvic girdles along with even more skulls and bones formed various designs on the walls. Bones were arranged on the ceiling in merry rosettes and multi-pointed stars. There were triangles of jawbones, flowers made of sacral bones, a winged hourglass featuring shoulder blades. Lamps made of bones hung from the ceiling. A winged skull grinned from inside a circle of vertebrae.

In the final crypt, a skeleton held a scythe in one hand and a double-pan balance scale in the other. Blake understood the symbolism. All of it, everything in the church basement, was absolutely and entirely crystal clear. As if to drive home the point even further, on the long corridor's back wall was a clock made of vertebrae, foot bones, and fingers.

As Blake left the Crypts of the Capuchins, he read what was written in Italian, French, German, English, and Spanish above the doorway.

WHAT YOU ARE NOW, WE USED TO BE
WHAT WE ARE NOW, YOU WILL BE

"*OH MY JESUS!*" Well, Blake thought, he might not be able to finish the climb. He might die of a heart attack, like his mother, before reaching the top step. "*By the torment thou didst suffer on seeing thyself abandoned by all, have mercy on me!*"

IN A PORTION of the semester when Blake taught Religion to his high-school freshmen, he was urged to offer them hypothetical ethical situations as a way of promoting discussion. The main lesson Blake gave his class centered on a runaway train.

Say you're on a platform above a train's tracks, Blake told his students, and you see that a train is speeding toward a group of seven people. You realize that if the train continues on its path unheeded all seven will be killed. You also realize that if you push something heavy down onto the tracks the train will stop before hitting the people. There beside you stands a fat man. Do you push the fat man onto the tracks to save the seven below?

All of the students laughed because of Blake's weight. "Sorry, Brother," they called out. "You're dead meat." "Meet your maker." "Too bad there's no time for Last Rites." " You're about to get smashed flat as a pancake."

"But wouldn't that be murder?" Blake countered.

Some of the students paused and, after a bit of discussion, agreed.

"So you'd do nothing?" Blake said, reintroducing the dilemma. "You'd stand there and watch the runaway train kill seven people?"

About half of the class said they'd do nothing, citing that the situation wasn't their responsibility. To push the fat man down onto the tracks would be morally wrong, and nothing would justify doing it. Plus, later on they'd be jailed and tried for murder. The other half of the class said they'd willingly sacrifice the man, arguing that it was only logical that if seven lives could be saved one life might ethically be offered in exchange.

Blake then changed the situation's terms. "What if the fat man was evil? Let's say he was Adolf Hitler. What if he was the most sinful man who ever lived?"

"Kill him," all the boys shouted.

"What if he were good? A saint? The most holy man alive?"

"Tough toenails for the seven. Let them die."

"What if the runaway train would kill a dozen? Fifty? A hundred? A thousand? A hundred thousand? Do you still let the holiest man on Earth live?"

"If there were a hundred thousand people in danger," the students responded, "and the holiest man was truly holy, he should be happy to die, to sacrifice his life for so many."

"What if the fat man were a woman? Your mother? Would you push her?"

That silenced the boys, even the class clowns. Finally the class said no, they wouldn't push their own mothers down onto the tracks.

"Would you push your daughter?"

A clear, resounding "No."

"What about sons? What if you had many sons? A dozen? Would you push one?"

A divided response, depending on the number.

"What if you had only one son? Would you push him?"

"My only son?" The unanimous answer. "Of course not. No."

"What if you were God?" Brother Blake then said. "And your son was Jesus Christ, and the salvation of the world depended on his death?"

It was Blake's favorite lesson, and he was terribly sad when he was told that he would no longer be able to teach it.

"*OH MY JESUS!*" Blake murmured, as he surrendered to the idea that he'd die of a heart attack on the Holy Stairs. "*By the great love for me with which thy Divine Heart was inflamed on breathing forth thy last sigh, have mercy on me!*"

"I WAS THINKING the other day about that lesson you gave us," a student said one afternoon as the study-hall period which Blake monitored ended. "I know everybody laughed about it but what if you really were the man looking down from the platform at the runaway train? Say it happened in real life. What would you do? Would you jump?"

Above the blackboard behind the desk where Blake sat, a dusty crucifix hung on the wall, flanked by framed prints of Jesus and Mary. The two pictures were a classic pair, the Sacred Heart and the Immaculate Heart – a long-haired Jesus in a red tunic and blue robe pointing to his heart with his left hand, his right hand raised in blessing, and a veiled Mary as his mirror image in an identical red tunic and blue robe, her right hand pointing to her heart, her left hand raised in blessing. Christ's heart was circled by a crown of thorns. Mary's, by a wreath of mystic roses. Both hearts were topped by crosses. The crucifix and the two pictures were so familiar to the boys who napped or doodled in their notebooks during the nearly unendurably long fifty-five minutes of study hall that they no longer noticed them.

To the left of the monitor's desk, next to the classroom's door, a wooden plaque depicting the bust of Saint John Baptist de la Salle was nailed securely to the wall. Beside it, dangling from a knotted leather strap, hung the classroom's Board of Education.

"Would I jump?" Blake answered. "In a heartbeat."

"*OH MY JESUS!*" Blake was breathing so heavily now that others on the steps of the Scala Sancta looked his way, and one woman even scurried up the stairs to kneel beside him and ask if he was all right. Blake nodded as he raised his knees to the penultimate step. "*By the boundless kindness thou didst manifest in permitting thy side to be opened with a spear, have mercy on me!*"

HAD THE PROCTOR not called time and instructed the students taking the proficiency exam to put down their pens and pass up their blue examination booklets, Blake would have described the third item he'd take with him to the desert island where he'd spend the remaining days of his life. Of course it would be rope, as much rope as could fill every spare inch of his coffin.

Blake guessed that somewhere on the island there would be rocks, and by breaking the rocks and scraping them together over time he could fashion a sort of blade. He could use the blade to cut the rope into any lengths he desired. With the shorter pieces he could practice tying the knots in his comprehensive illustrated book of knots. He could learn how to tie every knot ever created by woman or man. And whenever he needed a new Saint Joseph cord, he could untangle the braids that made up the rope to make a new one. He would tie six knots into the braids and with the seventh knot secure it snugly around his hips.

Even now he sometimes wondered if he should exchange the simple cord he wore with a thicker one, one with larger knots, knots that would remind him more insistently of his need to suffer as atonement for his sins.

Blake was so used to the cord that he hardly felt it. He couldn't guess the number of times he'd replaced it, but he knew that there hadn't been a day since the visiting missionary priest came to talk to his football team that he hadn't worn it. The cord and its seven knots had become part of him, nearly like his own skin.

"*OH MY JESUS!*" Blake said out loud as he reached the top step. "*By the tender condescension with which thou didst permit thy most sacred body to be placed in the arms of thy mother and afterwards in the sepulcher, have mercy on me!*"

LATER THAT EVENING, after Dubravka slipped on her leather jacket, Blake led her out onto the street, to Corso Vittorio and the bridge stretching toward the Vatican. The pair joined the tens of thousands already gathered in Saint Peter's Square – some standing, many kneeling – in a candlelight prayer vigil for the dying pope. Though Dubravka had gathered some of her hair on top of her head, the rest hung loosely and blew freely about in the wind. Again Blake was tempted to touch her. But even before the announcement was made, that John Paul II had died at 21:37, Blake found himself weeping out of grief. And when he looked at Dubravka he saw tears making their way down her cheeks too.

"You're crying for him now, aren't you?" Blake said.

"My tears aren't for him," Dubravka answered. She brushed her cheeks and smiled softly, as if she were patiently instructing a child. "Don't you understand? His death isn't going to change anything. He'll be replaced by someone who thinks just the same. Already they're printing the signs that say *Santo Subito!* Sainthood Now! Soon they'll again fill the square, waving their signs, and all that John Paul has proclaimed must be forbidden will continue to be forbidden." She wiped away a few of her tears. "No, I cry for all those who died in part because they followed his teachings. The hundreds of thousands in Africa, as well as those elsewhere. My cousin, Marija. Likely Stanislav. For all I know, their child. And I cry with joy for all of them" – she gestured widely – "for all the souls gathered here, for their marvelous expression of faith."

She touched Blake's arm. "Can't you feel it? The presence of grace?" Her hands inscribed a dome. "It flows from the crowd like a perfume and fills the air."

Blake nodded, half understanding.

At that moment Dubravka felt a sudden sense of relief, as if a weight she'd been carrying was being lifted from her. Her world would soon be different, she saw. Given the pope's death, she would no longer feel compelled to judge him. And with that thought an even deeper sorrow filled her heart, and she felt a strong surge of prayer for the newly dead man. As she stared across the square at the lit windows of the papal apartment, she felt prayer for Father Josip and the priest from Makarska and all of the women in her convent, and then prayer for the new pope to come.

"Understand," Dubravka said after several moments, holding Blake's arm until he gazed into her eyes, "understand that when I examine my conscience I find I've made a vital distinction, one that allows me all these years to live. I've separated my religious beliefs and Catholic faith from the institution of the Church and the rule of the papacy. I feel this even more now that I'm living here in Italy." She nodded as her eyes held Blake's, to give what she was saying further emphasis. "My true faith lies in Christ's all-loving Mother, the Blessed Virgin, and the doctrine of the Trinity, and not in the words spoken by whatever old, imperfect man who happens to be sitting that day on Peter's throne."

Above them stretched Rome's endless sky. Blake looked out at the crowds and felt himself drawn to a group now gathering around the couple who'd read the poem by the statue of Giordano Bruno. Elena and Ben, Blake remembered. He pushed his way through the crowds towards them, unaware that he'd taken Dubravka's hand and was pulling her behind him. Coming toward them now was Lucy, the sweet Canadian teacher who kindly gave him directions to Campo de' Fiori after he was cheated by the taxi driver. She was with Pina, the pregnant gattara. Then a blonde woman with short, spiky hair, wearing a tattered cloth coat and an azure scarf, greeted Dubravka. Blake watched the two women smile with joy and embrace. The family from Testaccio that had been on the news – the ox-like son with his mother and poet father – now joined the group that was assembling, and then behind them came a sad-eyed man – a dark prizefighter past his prime – and a woman in a red notch-collar coat praying with a blue rosary. Then the performer with the antique sword, dressed now in sweater and jeans, and a dark beauty who strolled beside him.

Blake waved to Giorgio as he neared. Behind him were the two carabinieri Blake had knocked down to the sidewalk. Others, whom Blake felt he should recognize but didn't know. A young woman wearing a single long gold earring and two older women, likely her aunts. The grizzled old man who roasted marroni. The nun with the cross the color of bone. The vendor from Senegal who sold plastic toys that shot rainbow-tinted soap bubbles into the air. The sacristan with the still-bandaged head. The wild-haired organetto player who sat beneath the great fountain. The waiter who cut loaves of bread in a drawer like a carpenter. Marcel, the finger puppeteer. Ying Yue, the watercolor artist. The barista from Sant'Eustachio il Caffè. The twins who played Vivaldi doubles. The priest from Lugano. The man with the thick dreadlocks and rastacap. The beggar with the oversized shoe, who softly jingled the coins in his waxed gelato cup.

As Blake stood with the others, he stared up at the sky and its countless splash of stars. He wondered how many other worlds and how many other God-created beings were gazing out at the universe as he was. Surely, he thought, given God's infinite love, there must be thousands, millions. Blake wondered if any of these worlds had also just experienced tragedies like the South-Asian tsunami or the death of a major religious leader.

Vast, vast, infinitely vast! Blake thought, as he felt the universe around him throb tightly for a moment and then expand, as a gust of wind tumbled a scrap of paper high into the air, and at that moment the door of the basilica swung open and a group of bishops, each wearing a scarlet zucchetto, approached the microphone and read the official announcement. Everyone on Saint Peter's Square then gazed at the three lit windows of the pope's apartment where he'd died, and then everyone on the square knelt and prayed. After a while the great bell on the left side of Saint Peter's Basilica began to toll.

Still later, Blake and Dubravka returned to the pensione, where Andelina lay, a sleeping curl of fur on Blake's bedcover. Blake washed himself in the tiny bathroom and knelt beside his bed to recite his evening prayers.

He and Dubravka didn't share a cup of tea that evening. The sweets in the box Blake had purchased from a pasticceria a few days before remained untouched. In the midst of Blake's prayers Dubravka knocked on his closed door, interrupting him to say that he had a long-distance telephone call. The call was from Blake's stepmother, informing him that Ginny had safely, miraculously, delivered the baby. It was a girl, Blake's stepmother said, tears thickening her voice.

But all of this would happen later. For now the heavy red-haired man would raise himself up gradually from the floor of the top step of the Scala Sancta and slowly stand, feeling no pain in his back or his knees, only an unfamiliar lightness. As he gazed up at the fresco of the Crucifixion painted over the Sancta Sanctorum, a golden warmth spread over him as if he were standing beneath a sunlamp. He rubbed his eyes. I am loved, he felt. I am loved. Then that thought was joined by a surge of pride that he'd made it all the way up to the top of the Holy Stairs.

By the Fountain of the Four Rivers

Rome, April 2005

Of course the next pope would be Italian. That was the word on the square, in every bar and café, throughout all of Rome, what nearly everyone was thinking. If not Camillo Ruini, Vicar General of the Diocese of Rome as well as a familiar face in the Italian media, the chosen one was bound to be Angelo Bagnasco, Archbishop of Genoa. While perhaps not as powerful as Ruini, not nearly as well-connected, the pragmatic Bagnasco was certain to be a major contender. And of course the list of papabile would hardly be complete if it failed to include Carlo Maria Martini, Archbishop of Milan, though some argued he was too old – twenty months shy of eighty – and, even worse, rumor had it that he suffered from Parkinson's. In addition, the Jesuit Martini was an outspoken liberal. Both Ruini and Bagnasco were conservatives. Few talking over endless cups of espresso gave serious consideration to Joseph Aloisius Ratzinger, Archbishop of Munich, Prefect of the Congregation for the Doctrine of the Faith, Dean of the College of Cardinals, nicknamed *God's Rottweiler* for his unswervingly orthodox views. Nor did they consider the South American Jesuit Jorge Mario Bergoglio, Archbishop of Buenos Aires. No one suspected that in each of the four ballots taken by the papal conclave the German and the Argentinian would finish first and second. No, the word on Rome's streets was certain – the white smoke that would soon twist from the chimney atop the Sistine Chapel was sure to reveal the name of one of the three Italians. Order would be restored. Some gray Italian head would once again wear the papal crown.

Meanwhile the purveyors of souvenirs rushed to get their wares on the street and into the hands of the hundreds of thousands of pilgrims who traveled to Rome, like eager schools of sardines, for the pope's funeral. They packed Rome's hotels and pensioni until their walls fairly burst. They emptied the larders and licked clean the plates of each of Rome's trattorias and restaurants, then rushed to fill their bags with whatever mementos and trinkets bearing the likeness of John Paul II they could find. Commemorative medals, rosaries, crucifixes, scapulars, holy cards, plaques, rings, buttons, spoons, stamps, mugs, necklaces, pennants, books, T-shirts, bottle openers, plaster busts, and, later on, even an impressive variety of full-bodied figurines and bobbleheads. One vendor specialized in gold-plated coins bearing the pope's likeness beside the words *Santo Subito!*. Suppliers couldn't keep up with demand.

The cafés lining the Piazza Navona filled their tables to overflowing while the living statues working the square wasted no time establishing their territories. The Passed-Out Drunk in the Bronze Suit assumed his place beside his usual marble bench on the west side of the piazza, while the Clown in the Tuxedo with Top Hat and Flower froze his essence near the cart that sold ciambelle and Nutella. The Statue of Liberty stood as straight as a flagpole atop her box, having added a single teardrop oozing down one cheek. The mime dressed as Columbina continued her perpetual struggle inside her invisible box. Tutankhamun held his crook and flail with stoic dignity, and the Levitating Swami climbed up on his chair anchored by the rod hidden inside his long sleeve. Marcel, the beloved Sicilian puppeteer, donned a glove bearing the likeness of Charlie Chaplin, duck-walking about, jauntily swinging his cane. Behind him a Romani woman offered passing tourists her bunch of red roses. She pushed the bouquet into each pilgrim's chest as they passed, as she thrust forward an open palm and rasped out a sharp "Dai!" Vendors from North Africa set up their cardboard stands offering wallets, purses, bracelets, scarves, earrings. Jugglers deftly tossed their multicolored balls into the air. Arms raised in delight, a chubby child chased a runaway balloon. And there, near the north end of the great fountain, in sight of the river-god Nile if the statue had dropped his veil for a moment and looked, stood Agostino in his Caravaggio costume doing tricks with his double-edged schiavona.

His final performance. It was clear to Agostino that his piece had run its course. Quit just before the audience tires of you, he reasoned. That he'd broken things off with Valentina and asked her to move out had nothing to do with his decision, he told himself. Still, he knew he should have recognized the signs. Her months-long affair with Gennaro, now sole leader of the guerrilla theater group that continued to perform the stale but still popular piece about Bush and Berlusconi, shouldn't have been a complete surprise. After all, didn't even Christ's betrayal come at the hand of a friend?

Besides, Agostino thought as he twirled his sword in the air, his appearances as Caravaggio had been a success. Perhaps his best moments were the two involving the North American tourists – the fifth of the seven carciofi plays at Rosangela's uncle's restaurant, and the crazy afternoon he escaped the two carabinieri by the church with the basement stuffed with the bones of dead Capuchin monks. That such a large man walking along the sidewalk would be willing to help him was a clear and obvious gift from God as well as an exquisite piece of street theater. Agostino knew he owed the man both applause and gratitude.

Still, the Caravaggio appearances were becoming so common, so familiar, that they no longer had a fresh effect. People had come now to expect them. The image he'd created had grown predictable. Though, curiously, as if one thing's death led to another's emergence, his life as a painter had recently prospered. It was as if by imitating Caravaggio Agostino had received a glancing stroke, the merest drop, of the artist's genius.

Likely it had something to do with process. Since no preliminary sketches or drawings of any of Caravaggio's paintings had ever been found, it was believed that the master merely painted. Simply, boldly, painted – literally extending his hand and placing his brush freshly wet with paint on canvas, like a swimmer who approaches a body of water and dives right in. Agostino had always sketched beforehand, outlining, plotting, planning. Thinking. So he stopped thinking. He abandoned his mind and gave full power and control to his eye and hand. He simply, purely, painted.

During the many afternoons when Valentina and Gennaro were sweating up his bedsheets, then running up the water bill with their long showers, Agostino had taken to displaying his paintings on the piazzas near Viale Trastevere, gathering up his canvases whenever the carabinieri neared. His work was met with surprising interest. Wearing only a hint of his Caravaggio costume – his chocolate-colored vest and striped blouse – Agostino discovered that foreign tourists with fat wallets found his work worth stopping on the street to view, to consider, to then inquire about and begin to haggle a fair price. His paintings were rustic and authentic, the visitors to Rome told him. They captured their subjects' essence. They walked the tricky balance between street and high art.

And now that he was no longer living with her cousin, Agostino was spending increasing amounts of time with his new model, Rosangela of the single long gold earring. She still refused to bare even a shoulder when she posed, but she deeply empathized with his hurt and sadness over her cousin's cruel betrayal. At their last meeting she took both of his hands in hers and gave his cheek a soft, lingering kiss, her lips ever so close to his mouth. Then she took a step back and immediately invited him to accompany her and her aunts to the following Sunday's Mass.

Agostino turned his thoughts back to his reasons for being on the square today, to the imperative of channeling the true, native spirit of the master Caravaggio. Agostino inhaled. Exhaled. Swung his magnificent double-edged schiavona. Presented himself to all those with eyes.

He thought of his favorite painting, *The Calling of Saint Matthew*, how he'd used the youth seated closest to the viewer, the boy sitting on the bench, hand ready to strike down any intruder, as a model for his dress. That Christ and the apostle Peter were clothed as they'd been in life was central to the work's genius. Agostino knew the anachronism was deliberate as well as telling. Caravaggio was suggesting that all of time can be simultaneous, collapsed into a single moment, and that there are single moments that can radically alter the direction of a person's life. With his sword Agostino outlined an oval in the air. There is no past, no future, only now, this moment, Agostino thought. Only this moment, the one right here, here on the Piazza Navona, by the Fountain of the Four Rivers, where he stood, a man very much alive, happily in his prime, proudly Roman born, baptized Agostino, though at the same time he was also Michelangelo Merisi da Caravaggio.

Agostino watched the Croatian nun who never wore her true costume enter the square, her lips moving, mouth likely mumbling her usual prayers, though today she arrived without her wooden charity box. Perhaps out of respect for the dead pope. Or she might just be biding her time until the next cause arose, Agostino thought. The next catastrophe. Given the ways of the world, no doubt her hands would not be empty for long.

As she passed the tables near the gelateria, the gang of children who routinely begged in the square rushed her, arms raised as if they were members of a team that just scored a goal. The woman paused, smiling as the little band of zingari circled her, and after a while as the children spoke to her she responded with a nod. She disappeared through the gelateria's doorway and returned with a tray bearing a dozen or so small waxed cups, each holding a bright mound of some iced sweet pierced by a tiny plastic spoon. The guests in the pensione where she made breakfasts must be generous with their tips, Agostino thought. The woman handed the cups to the children, and as more gathered around her she raised both her hands as if to say there was no more.

There was never enough, Agostino thought. Only Christ, with the loaves and fishes. He left the thought unfinished as he inscribed a sideways figure eight in the air, then an ever-widening arc, thinking that around him in the air was a circle, the face of a clock.

Time is a circle, he shouted in English to the tourists around him. As it was in the beginning, is now, and ever shall be. You, who raise your cameras and cell phones to capture my likeness. You, who are too asleep in your bubbles to live in this moment of time. You come here to Rome, why? To eat our food? To see our ruins? To say you were there when they placed on display the painted carcass of the pope? Here, take a step closer and taste my blade as you smell the sour dregs of last night's wine on my breath. Dare to look into my eyes and glimpse my soul.

The late morning sun pierced the dirty gauze of the sky and began filling the square, as if some curtain had been parted, some cover lifted. Light shone brightly now on the Piazza Navona and the Fountain of the Four Rivers. The sun shone on the travertine figures of the Nile, the Danube, the Ganges, the Rio de la Plata. The sun shone on the obelisk topped by the dove bearing an olive twig in its beak. The sun shone on the many creatures in the fountain's churning waters. The sun shone on Chiara, who was wearing a bright new orange sweater purchased with the money given her by the rich North American woman who had her pen a letter, as she sat near the base of the fountain playing her organetto. Flicking her unruly black hair away from her face, she tapped a foot and smiled as she began a lively saltarello.

Acknowledgments

Michael Mirolla, Frank Lentricchia, Diane Prokop, Mary Brennan, Jeanine Hathaway, Heather McHugh, Marina Antic, Errol F. Richardson, Carla Francellini, Walter Wetherell, Olivia Kate Cerrone, Anna Ardizzone, Scott Morales, Paul Gutjhar, Andrea Ciccarelli, and Ed Comentale. Special thanks to Diane Kondrat, my first reader.

About The Author

Tony Ardizzone is the author of five novels and three collections of short stories. His work has appeared in a variety of literary journals and anthologies published in both North America as well as Italy and been the subject of discussion by literary critics from the United States, Canada, Italy, and Greece. His books have received the Flannery O'Connor Award for Short Fiction, the Milkweed Editions National Fiction Prize, the Chicago Foundation for Literature Award for Fiction, the Virginia Prize for Fiction, an Oregon Literary Fellowship, two individual artist fellowships from the National Endowment for the Arts, and other honors. Born and raised in Chicago, he currently lives in Portland, Oregon.

Books By Tony Ardizzone

In Bruno's Shadow
The Arab's Ox: Stories of Morocco
The Whale Chaser
In the Garden of Papa Santuzzu
Taking It Home: Stories from the Neighborhood
Heart of the Order
The Evening News: Stories
In the Name of the Father